HENRIETTA'S LEGACY

HENRIETTA'S LEGACY

A LIFETIME OF CONSEQUENCES

CAROLYN P. SCHRIBER

For more information about this title or to order other books, contact the
publisher:

Katzenhaus Books
https://www.katzenhausbooks.com

ISBN-13: 978-0-9993060-5-5 (print)
978-0-9993060-4-8 (digital)

Cover Design by Avalon Graphics

Printed in the United States of America

CONTENTS

FOREWORD

A NOTE FROM THE AUTHOR

Recently I noticed a statement at the beginning of another historical novel: "This book is a work of fiction. People, places, events, and situations are the product of the author's imagination. Any resemblance to actual persons, living or dead, or historical events is purely coincidental."

I cannot make such a disclaimer. As a historian by training and occupation, I have always predicated my historical novels on a solid basis of historical events and the actions of real people who influenced those events. My fictional characters represent the anonymous men and women who lived through those events and whose lives were inevitably altered by the decisions of those whose names found their way into the history books.

In the process of writing some seven novels about the Civil War in South Carolina, I have created a cast of fictional characters who tend to wander in and out of each other's stories. Some bear familiar names and are based upon actual people about whom I have been able to learn little except for their existence at the right time in the right place. They include Union Army nurses, several Confederate soldiers, the families waiting back home, and various politicians and public officials. Other families—the Duboises, the Grenvilles, the Beauchenes—are cut from whole cloth. They are, indeed, figments of my imagination, although I am sure that real people like them shared their experiences and emotions.

Several of these fictional characters have found their way into *Henrietta's Legacy*, and some of their experiences overlap with those of the Beauchene family. To tie their stories together, I have experimented with ways to link their texts. For example, in the first chapter of *Legacy*, Henrietta remembers what it was like to be a new widow in Charleston. The endnote number links the reader to the actual description of her experience, quoted from *Henrietta's Journal*.

If you are reading this book in a print format, you will find endnote numbers scattered throughout the text. The notes themselves are grouped by chapter and number at the back of the book. If you have the Kindle edition, the effects are more magical. Click on the endnote number and the related quote pops up on your screen. When you have finished reading it, click on the little "X" to be taken back to your place in the text. Ah, the fresh advantages of electronic publication! Of course, if you would rather not be bothered by either endnotes or pop-ups, you can ignore them entirely. The text of *Legacy* is complete in itself and can be read without the notes.

In either case, I welcome you to my fictional world of South Carolina during the Civil War. Happy reading!

—*Carolyn Schriber*

CONFRONTATION

September 16, 1858
Charleston, South Carolina

 wo shrieks broke into the peaceful morning—one, a hysterical but masculine voice; the other, angry and feline. Then came the crash of several heavy objects falling against one another, followed by the sharp shattering of china or glass as something fragile hit the floor. Henrietta pushed her chair away from her desk and gathered her skirts out of the way as Calico skidded around the corner—stomach low to the ground, tail a huge round brush, eyes dilated to solid black. The office cat headed straight for her basket under Henrietta's desk, her usual place of safety when she had aroused the ire of the men in the office.

"What have you done now, puss?" Henrietta always talked to the cat as if she expected an answer, and in this case, she knew the answer would follow the cat's flight.

"If you don't keep that wretched animal out of my office, I swear I will skin him and turn him into a hat. See what he's done!" A much rumpled and stained Antoine appeared in the doorway as expected, his hand held out to show the three bright red gashes that traced their way across the back of his hand as blood dripped from his wrist.

"She," Henrietta corrected. "Good heavens, don't you have a handkerchief to wrap around that hand before you get blood on everything?"

"That's your worry, is it? Something might make a mess in your tidy little office? No concern for your brother-in-law who is bleeding to death in the reception room?"

"Don't exaggerate. You will not bleed to death from a cat scratch. How did you make Calico that angry?"

"I was moving her off my chair so I could sit down, and the next thing I knew she snarled, hissed, and slashed at me." Antoine was trying—but failing—to look innocent as he examined the back of his hand.

Henrietta fished a kerchief out of her reticule and handed it to him. But as he moved closer, she gasped and waved the air in front of her. "You smell disgusting—I can't decide whether it's a garbage can, the gutter, the fish market, or the barroom floor. Perhaps a combination. Where did you spend the night?"

"Never the gutter, my dear. Maybe a touch of a fishing boat and a barroom floor or two although I can't remember them. It was a busy night. I was bargaining with a boatman who wanted to sell me a used vessel in need of refitting as a blockade runner."

"Oh, please, tell me you didn't buy a boat!"

"No, I didn't, but I'm still considering it. It has everything I need—fitted with a steam-powered paddle wheel, plenty of cargo room, slim enough to maneuver through our inland waterways."

"If it's so perfect, why is the fellow selling it?"

"Well, he runs a mail packet service. He was hoping to speed up his delivery times. But the ship doesn't have enough room to accommodate paying passengers, and the mail fees alone can't cover the cost of the coal to power the steam engine. He needs to use sails or rowers. But for a luxury import business or for a blockade runner, it is ideal."

"And you didn't buy it because—?"

"Because he wants too much for it. I kept trying to get him so drunk he'd make a mistake and offer to give me a cut rate, but it didn't work. The guy was an absolute fish!"

"And he was trying to get you drunk enough you'd buy the boat at his cost."

"Yes. We ended up drinking each other under the table. By the time we parted ways, it was too late to make my way home."

"I thought Father Beauchene gave you that set of rooms on the second floor of the West Wing because it has an outside entrance to let you come home late without bothering the rest of us."

"True enough, but you've never tried climbing that iron spiral staircase. Son-of-a-gun rattles. I'd try to sneak in, and by the time I reached the top, Father was waiting and tapping his pocket watch. So, when I'm out late, I come by the warehouse and sleep in my office."

"On the floor?"

"Where else? That braided rag rug is soft at three o'clock in the morning."

Henrietta shook her head in dismay. Trying to talk sense into Antoine became an elaborate game in which his sole goal was to mislead his opponent and change the subject.

"No wonder you are so disreputable. Go home right now and get cleaned up. You can't let our clients see you looking—and smelling—like the town drunk."

"Do we have someone special scheduled for today?"

"We do. Elizabeth Dubois is back in town, and she wants to discuss prospects for cotton growers in the coming years."

"Elizabeth who?"

"Oh, Antoine, you remember her—Georg DuBois' widow."

"Is she the one who was such a close friend of yours?"

"She still is, even if I haven't seen her in several years. She moved to their plantation on Edisto Island right after her husband died. I understood why—Charleston is an unforgiving place for a new widow. When Julien died, I thought I might go mad if I didn't get away from the nosy neighbors and gossipy old ladies who wanted to tell me how to live my life.[1] I think Elizabeth felt the same way, but she also needed to come home now and reconnect with her grandchildren before it's too late."

"So why is she worried?"

"She still owns one of the largest plantations on Edisto. She's left it in the hands of a trusted overseer, with help from Susan's husband. He's a Yankee, but I understand he's working hard to learn the cotton business. Now she's concerned about the rumors she's hearing of a coming war."

"As she should be. It is coming, Henrietta, sure as anything. We will have to prepare for it."

"And that's why I need you here this afternoon to talk to her. I can't answer her questions, and, to be honest, I don't have the faintest idea what will happen to our factoring business if the South secedes. Go home, take a bath, change clothes, and try to appear presentable. She'll be here after lunch. Oh, and go out the back door in case prospective clients are passing the front."

Muttering to himself, Antoine shrugged and headed for the warehouse. "Use a sticking plaster so your hand is not so bloody—bloody!" she called after him.

∽

HENRIETTA DREW A DEEP BREATH AND LEANED BACK IN HER chair. She noted that Calico was busy grooming her front paws. "Good cat," she commented. "Make sure you get the raw flesh off your lethal claws."

Taking a lesson from her furry companion, she stretched to relax her muscles, clenched from the first howl that warned of Antoine's presence. She glanced at the account books that had occupied her earlier; now they were nothing but a jumble of numbers in her memory. She shook her head in frustration. Why was she so tired, so worn by responsibilities? She could not remember the last time she had done something for fun. She was only forty-five, but her bones ached, worry lines creased her forehead, and her days overflowed with tasks still undone, demands unmet, and responsibilities ever increasing.

She loved her three well-educated and talented daughters, but they were in their twenties with no marriage prospects in sight, their hope chests doomed by the family's lack of social clout. Their ancestral home stood with its back gate pressed up against Broad Street, missing by just that much the crucial address of "South of Broad." The family fortune was solid but based on the financial *faux pas* of originating from commerce, not landed wealth or professional acumen. And her own British citizenship marked her daughters as being "not old blood."

She knew she owed everything she had to her father-in-law, who had accepted her, loved her, and made her his heir when his first-born son died. But now he relied on her, too. A series of strokes had left his mind as sharp as ever but his body crippled with paralyzed limbs and an inability to care for himself. He responded with frustration expressed in angry outbursts interspersed with periods of hopeless despair. The slaves she had once decried now cared for him with touching devotion, but he lashed out at them, making her feel even more guilty about their lack of freedom.

And there was the business. Henrietta had learned the mechanics of it well. She understood how to test the cotton crops that came in and classify them for prospective buyers. She could predict where the textile markets were heading and had learned to charm their clients, both sellers and buyers of the raw cotton they brokered. But the responsibility weighed upon her. Their clients depended on her judgments to make or break their profits. What would happen to the cotton industry if the markets crashed, if a violent storm destroyed the crops in the field, or a fire wiped out their warehouses? And what if the doomsayers were right? If the North shut off southern trade, what would happen to them, both the cotton factors like The Beauchene Company and the clients who trusted and depended upon them?

These were the thoughts that followed her around during the day, nudging at her elbow any time she smiled at a small success, reminding her that all could change in an instant. They came at night, too, populating her dreams with little black clouds that threatened to engulf her and her family.

Meanwhile, Antoine Beauchene, irresponsible fifty-year-old boy-child, the Beauchene second son, drifted through life on a fine alcohol-fueled cloud, worrying about nothing more important than his next meal or drink. He still surrounded himself with young women who loved to see him spend money upon them. Marriage did not appeal to him, nor did he build up his own nest egg or claim responsibility for the family business. He flitted in and out of their lives as the mood suited him, disappearing for days at a time without explanation and then returning in full expectation that the family would cater to his needs until his next great adventure.

Henrietta allowed these thoughts to distract her until

Joshua, the old black man who took care of the warehouse, tapped on her office door.

"You all right, Miss Henrietta? You be just sitting there staring off into space."

"Just thinking—life isn't fair, is it?"

"Sure, it ain't fair. Nobody's promised us fair. If it was fair, I wouldn't have to sweep up broken coffee cups every time Massa Antoine gets mad at the cat."

Henrietta allowed herself to giggle. "I'm sorry for the mess, Joshua. Do we have any cups left?"

"I think I can find one. Shall I brew you up a nice cup of tea? We have that new kind that the Middleton family imported from Japan."

"The pale green variety that's related to their camellia flowers? I think not. I need something stronger and more British this morning. Do we have any of that Earl Grey variety my father sent?"

"Yes, ma'am. I'll get it right away."

"Thank you, Joshua."

"Oh, and Massa Manwaring just came back from his trip to the Low Country. He's waiting to see you if you have time."

Henrietta always enjoyed her visits with David Manwaring. She had expected to hate him when Father Beauchene hired him to take over her late husband's accounts, but David had understood her need to keep her distance while she grieved. When she came back to work full time, he had made himself an indispensable part of their price-setting deliberations. His competence, his cool head in a crisis, and his mastery of the cotton business made him popular with clients and cotton buyers alike. Henrietta had soon learned to rely on his judgments.

"Send him in. Bring a pot of tea with two cups if you can find them."

A FAVORITE CLIENT RETURNS

*E*lizabeth DuBois arrived, as promised, soon after lunch. Arms outstretched and a huge smile on her face, she headed straight for Henrietta's office. The women embraced and then held onto each other at arms' length, each of them searching the other's expression to see the changes the years had brought.

"Henrietta, dear, you look as young as ever. Running the company must agree with you."

"Island life has lifted your mood, I see."

"Life on the plantation soothed me, but seeing my old friends again has restored my high spirits. When I left Charleston, I needed to get away. But I have unbreakable ties here."

"You do. We've held onto you in our hearts, willing you to return when you were ready."

"And here I am, eager to hear the latest news. But I must not distract you with that in the middle of your workday. I'm here on business. As I mentioned in my note, the rumors I hear worry me—the possibility of secession and even war with the rest of the country. I have paid little attention to political developments because I've been living day to day with the details of raising cotton. Now I question the implications of these new conflicts for the cotton business. The Beauchene Company has always guided our financial affairs, so I'm here to seek your advice."

"Much of the political maneuvering is beyond me, too, Elizabeth, but Antoine can put your fears to rest. He went to get lunch, but I'm expecting him any minute. Oh, here he is now."

The fine gentleman coming through the door bore no resemblance to the grubby drunk who had walked that same hallway just hours earlier. "Madam DuBois, welcome home. Charleston has missed you." With a deep bow, he raised her hand and placed a proper kiss on her glove.

"My goodness, Henrietta," she exclaimed, "You've turned him into a proper Southerner at last."

"No, but he can behave when required. Come, let's sit over by the windows where we can enjoy the view while we talk. Settle in, and I'll ask Joshua to bring tea."

"Still trouble between you two?" Elizabeth asked when Henrietta had disappeared.

"We tolerate one another," Antoine replied, "and we work well together. We don't like each other much, but our feelings don't affect the business. Never mind. We're here to discuss your concerns. What worries you?"

"I wish I knew. This war talk has surprised me. Charleston's fine old families learned their wartime lessons from the Revolution. They suffered serious deprivations under British occupation for many years. Even during the withdrawal, the English troops plundered whatever they could carry away—everything from foodstuffs to the silverware and paintings on the walls, and the slaves, too. I can't imagine that it was an experience anyone wants to repeat."

"That was eighty years ago. I'm not sure anyone remembers."

"Family legends preserve the stories. Your Aunt Maggie— the one whose soldier husband died at the Battle of Cowpens —didn't she ever describe those years?"

"Maybe when I was small, but I don't remember it. She criticized the present more often than the past."

"Well, memories fade. But what recent events caused the leaders of our fine state to consider seceding from the Union?"

"It's a possibility that's been under discussion for years in the halls of government. We are so different. The North and the South have conflicting ideas of what our country should be doing. We've held an uneasy balance between slave states and free states—twelve of each ever since 1820 and the Missouri Compromise. The North wants to extend its idealistic version of equality and prosperity to slaves, and the South demands the right of each state to decide questions of slavery according to its own particular needs."

"But why now? What disturbed that balance?"

Henrietta returned from the warehouse and joined the conversation. "I'd say it's the horrible troubles that broke out in Kansas."

"Yes, that's where it became an issue. Stephen Douglas negotiated a compromise in Congress to let Kansas and Nebraska decide for themselves whether to allow slavery. But his solution ignored the 1820 rule of using the parallel 36°30′ as the line between free and slave states in the Louisiana Purchase. That popular opinion should decide such matters infuriated the North and caused a major fracture in the Democratic party."

"I don't think there was much chance that Nebraska

might vote for slavery," Henrietta said. "Their climate is unsuitable for raising cotton. But Kansas is a different story. Kansas resembles Missouri, a slave state. Along the Missouri-Kansas line, cotton raisers poured over the border to sway the vote for slavery. I haven't followed the shenanigans over that incursion, but hard feelings on both sides multiplied."

"Let's name names, Henrietta. It was that damned fool anti-slavery advocate, John Brown, who killed people for being what the papers called border ruffians. Once bloodshed started, the extremists took over. Since 1854, there have been over two hundred deaths and millions of dollars in property damage in what people are calling bloody Kansas—which suggests a complete breakdown of normal political activity. That's where the trouble lies."

"So, what's the federal government doing?" Elizabeth asked. "Don't we have laws or provisions for controlling such outbreaks of violence?"

"Well, the Dred Scott case proved that the Supreme Court is no help."

"I don't know what that case was, either."

"Dred Scott was a runaway slave from Missouri who took shelter in Illinois, a free state, and lived there as a free man for years. Then he returned to Missouri where his former master reclaimed him. The court ruled that spending time in a free state could not convey emancipation because no one of African descent could become an American citizen. Scott was, therefore, still the property of his legal owner. They ruled that neither Congress nor a state can outlaw an institution if the ruling deprives slave owners of their property. The North found that unacceptable, and the troubles deepened."

"I can understand that, but how could an argument escalate to warfare? I assume the reasonable people we send to Congress could come together on a balanced solution that keeps everyone happy."

"Reasonable people in Congress? You jest! They're beating each other to a bloody pulp in the middle of the Senate floor."

"Don't exaggerate, Antoine. Things are violent enough as they are. But it's true, Elizabeth. A congressman from our own South Carolina took a cane to Senator Charles Sumner for a speech he made supporting abolition, and the poor man suffered serious injuries. But that's how it happens. Small arguments loom large in the newspapers, and hotheads on both sides are just waiting for a spark to set the whole country ablaze."

Elizabeth's eyes brimmed with tears "I can't bear that thought. My teenaged grandson, Johnny Grenville, will be just the right age to serve in a Southern army and go off to his death on a battlefield!" Shaking her head, she stood and made her way to the window. She stared at the wharf without seeing it as she fought to control her emotions.

While Henrietta and Antoine waited, helpless to assuage her fears, the office cat took matters into her own paws. Calico jumped to the windowsill and head-butted Elizabeth, asking for attention. Elizabeth scooped the cat into her arms and turned back to Henrietta.

"What a sweet little cat," she said. "Didn't you once have a big orange beast who ran things around here?"

"You're remembering Marmalade.[1] He suffered an unfortunate accident out on the docks, but he left us with several generations of orange kittens by which to remember him. This one may well be his great-grandkitten. I think of him every time I see her orange patches." Henrietta smiled with relief as the tension in the room drained away.

Elizabeth returned to her seat with a determined smile. The cat followed, pawed once at her skirt, and then leaped into her lap, made two complete circles and settled herself for a nap. Elizabeth's fingers curled into the soft fur for comfort as she redirected the conversation. "I've had enough of politics. I'm a cotton planter and you are my factors. What does this war talk mean for us?"

"First, let me make one more political statement. War is not imminent, just inevitable. I predict there will be little more escalation until after the 1860 presidential elections. If the new president is a moderate, we may see several more years of jockeying for compromise—which will, I'm sure, please both you and Henrietta. If we get a president with a burr under his saddle, war could break out soon after his inauguration. But in either case, we have time to plan and prepare."

"Let's talk short term. When I left Edisto, several of my neighboring planter friends were planning to turn their fields over to vegetable crops next year. If we go to war, they think the North will destroy our ability to grow cotton and will blockade the major ports, preventing us from importing foods to feed our citizens. My son-in-law, who is just learning the cotton business, shares the same opinion."

"That's looking too far ahead. Let's discuss this year. You increased your cotton acreage, didn't you? I think I remember—"

"Yes, your father recommended that, and with the help of a loan from the company, we bought a hundred acres, plowed it over the winter, added a good helping of low-country pluff mud and decaying sea oats, and planted our first crops last spring.[2] So far, the plants appear vigorous. But now I face paying back that short-term loan. What if we can't sell that extra cotton?"

"That's not a problem, I promise. This year's crop should be a record-breaker, and the markets are taking notice. London buyers are stockpiling as much cotton as they can. They are making high offers for whatever left-over product remains in our warehouses. The offering prices are soaring.

Even if a major hurricane hits, it will only cause a shortage of cotton, and that will increase demand and prices."

"Is that the ever-optimistic Antoine talking, or do the other factors agree with you?"

"Oh, they agree, across the board."

"And I, too, agree with him, Elizabeth. Last year, top quality long-staple cotton sold for $145.00 a bale. This year we are seeing offers of $175.00 a bale for last year's crop. And next year—even before the elections—dealers are predicting the price per bale will go as high as $235.00. Indications suggest that buyers may double their usual orders. I didn't have time to fill Antoine in on this, but David Manwaring, our North American buyer, returned before noon from his trip to our outlying clients. He reports bumper crops wherever he visited."

"I think we should tap on wood. Is the outlook that good?"

"Yes. The threat of war is always an economic stimulus, Elizabeth, and we're poised to profit from it. We'll buy your entire 1859 crop at top-dollar rates. Cotton prices will remain steady because the crop will come in before the election. This is not the time to turn your cotton fields into turnips!"

"Good. I'll tell Jonathan Grenville to put his vegetable seeds away for another year. But after that—"

"Two years gives us time to make plans to meet the other threats you're hearing. A blockade is unavoidable. That's a lesson the colonies learned the hard way during the Revolutionary War, and the North will try it against us, if it comes to that."

"But the South doesn't own a single ship, let alone a navy."

"We don't need a navy. Visualize our coastline. If the cotton-growing states join us in seceding from the Union, as they will, we'll have a coastline of 4000 miles, stretching from

Virginia, south around the Florida peninsula, into the Gulf of Mexico and the coast of Texas. And we're not describing a sharp line where the land stops and the ocean begins. Our coastline includes innumerable islands forming an inter-coastal waterway.

"Now, consider the existing U.S. Navy. It's powerful, and so are its ships. Most of them are huge, with deep draft to bear the weight of cannons on deck. They are still sailing vessels because steam conversion requires enormous amounts of wood or coal to power such large ships. Armed sailing ships do well in battle, but they are slow and not very maneuverable. Northern ships can't penetrate our inter-coastal waterways because too many shifting sandbars block their way. And the North has too few ships to cover 4000 miles of coastline."

Antoine stopped and looked around the room. "You know what, Henrietta? We need a map in here. We're bound to repeat this conversation several times."

"I'll see what I can find."

"We need lots of little vessels, shallow draft, speedy, steam-powered, and agile. We'll paint them gray to make them hard to spot and give them collapsible masts and exhaust funnels to create a low profile. Put those little buggers into the hands of privateers and let them outrun the U.S. Navy! If the North blockades Charleston Harbor, they must do so from far out to sea. Meanwhile, our little blockade runners can wriggle their way through the channels to Wilm-ington or Savannah to avoid the blockading vessel. They'll have enough power to head for Havana or Nassau with small loads of cotton which they can then transfer to European ships in international waters, safe from the blockade. And on the way home, they can bring us shipments of what we need most—guns, rum, and cigars."

"Oh, Antoine," Henrietta interrupted, "You've been

singing this song for the past twenty-five years. It's always the same pipe-dream—you as a modern-day pirate smuggling rum and cigars out of Cuba to sell to wealthy Americans.[3] The only thing missing in your sketch is a parrot and a peg-leg."

"Laugh if you must, Henrietta, but it will happen. It's the only way we can win the war against the North. Now if you'll excuse me, I need to see a man who's selling a boat." Remembering his entering act at the last moment, he whirled to execute a bow in Elizabeth's direction and then stomped off to the warehouse.

THE LOST YEARS

November 16, 1858
Charleston, South Carolina

*E*lizabeth cocked a curious eye at Henrietta, whose thoughts seemed to have wandered off. "I'm impressed by how much Antoine has changed," she said. "He understands the situation. I see why you wanted me to talk to him."

Henrietta drew a deep breath as she re-focused her attention. "Yes, he's good at understanding political shenanigans, perhaps because he uses the same tricks. He's a firm warmonger, too. He can't wait for the shooting to start. His only real concern is that he may already be too old to play in the war games—hence, his plans to become a blockade runner."

"And you don't agree?"

"I don't disagree with his interpretations, but I do not share his enthusiasms. War terrifies me and—" She stopped, blinking to quell the tears that threatened to overflow.

"What terrifies you? The Henrietta I used to know might be furious, but never afraid."

"I don't want to talk about my fears, Elizabeth. My struggles are personal, and the cause of my fear is private—something I can't share with anyone. Please, can we find something else to talk about?"

Taken aback by the depth of Henrietta's agitation, Elizabeth gave her a moment to recover. "Fine. Tell me about my god-daughters. I've missed your little girls."

"Little girls? They're all in their twenties now, but they haven't changed. You'll recognize them."

"Let's go by age. How's Elise? I remember her as being strong-willed and fearless, so much so you dared not trust her a foot away. She loved all animals and would throw her little arms around an alligator if you gave her the chance."

"She still would. Nothing stops her. At a private function with the governor's wife, the dressmaker's label on her ladyship's dress was showing. Elise tucked it back in for her."

"That sounds like my girl. My favorite memory of her, which I didn't witness myself but heard you describe, came from your trip to London. What was she? Four? Five? When you took her to see London Bridge, she insisted on skipping across it, singing *London Bridge is Falling Down* at the top of her lungs all the way."

"She was adorable."

"Didn't I hear she was engaged? To someone quite 'old blood' and prominent?"

"Yes, Thomas Middleton Heyward, Arthur Middleton's grandson. You remember Arthur—his law firm handled all our legal affairs, and yours, too, I believe."

"So, is she married now?"

"No. I have had my doubts from the start. Thomas is head-over-heels in love with her, but she smiles at him as if he were one of her pets. She spent the first year of their courtship away at college. Father Beauchene insisted she enroll in the South Carolina Feminine Collegiate Institute at

Barhamville, outside Columbia. But when she came home for her summer break, she announced she was not going back because their classical curriculum was dull and too heavy on philosophy, ancient history, and literature. She wanted to learn to run a business, grade cotton, and analyze market trends—the details of running the firm. Her chosen teacher was her grandfather, a move that pleased him to no end."

"How is your father-in-law?"

"He struggles. He had a series of small strokes. They did not affect his speech or his sharp intellect, but they paralyzed his right side, so he must remain in his bed or a wheeled chair. And because he hates anyone to see his weakness, he never leaves the house. When Elise came to him as his eager student, she gave him something to live for. The two of them are inseparable.

"She spends every afternoon in his office, absorbing his lessons. After dinner, she turns to the books he recommends. Then she comes to the warehouse the next morning and tries to apply what she is learning. The combination works for them but leaves little time for courtship. Poor Thomas has accepted her preoccupation for a long time, but by summer I suspect he will pressure her to set a wedding date."

"They haven't done so?"

"No, she refuses to discuss the issue. She's willing to let Thomas act as her escort at social events, and they spend most Saturday evenings talking. They remind me of an old married couple, used to having each other around but rather bored with the whole relationship. If someone mentions marriage, she changes the subject. When most young women her age are looking at wedding gowns and picking out china patterns, she is grading cotton samples. She even turned down a request to act as an attendant at a friend's wedding. She told the young woman she would be too busy to keep up with all the festivities, but I realized from her tone of voice she considered the whole topic to be distasteful."

"So, is our strong-willed little girl becoming a determined business woman?"

"She seems content to do so."

"She may make that choice. And with a war looming, I might agree with her. But whatever she decides, I'd trust her judgment, Henrietta. She's a wise young woman."

"Oh, I agree. We were talking one evening about the terrible assumptions Southern men make about the incompetence of women. Elise looked thoughtful and then made an astute observation. It's not that men think women are stupid, she suggested, but rather that women believe they are stupid. They don't try their hands at business because they don't trust their own capabilities. I learned that lesson from her father. When I proved my abilities, he backed off and became my strongest supporter. I'm hoping that Elise's relationship with Thomas will take the same approach."

"She couldn't have a better example to follow than the one you gave her. But what about Juliette? Is she still in school?"

"She's finished. While Elise hated the classical nature of the curriculum at Barhamville, Juliette relished it. She flew through the four-year program in just a little over three years and graduated in June with honors. Now she's looking for a teaching position here in Charleston."

"Is that her goal, or is she filling time?"

"Oh, she doesn't want to teach in someone else's school for long. Her plan is to start her own academy for children—both girls and boys—who love academics. She insists our schools are too simplified, and she also wants to start a school for slaves."

"But such an effort would be illegal, wouldn't it?"

"Her grandfather has gone to great lengths to make that

point, but she has a solid response. She says slave owners justify their possession on the grounds that slaves do not know enough to manage their own affairs. We criticize them because they can neither read nor write, and we warn that they would be targets for con men. But then we turn around and make it illegal to teach a slave to read or write so they can't escape their bonds. She wants to see a slow but steady training program that prepares our slaves for the inevitable day when they are free."

"Bless her heart. She's one of the do-gooders, but her fellow citizens will disappoint her."

"You are right, but she hopes for a future in which she can contribute her talents."

"No young man, either?"

"Not that I can identify. Oh, she seems to know every young fellow in town. A lot of visitation went on between the boys at South Carolina College and the girls at Barhamville. And now many of those young men are here in Charleston, clerking in someone's law office or training at the medical school at Roper Hospital or drilling at the South Carolina Military Academy. Sometimes I feel as if they are all congregating on our piazza—every one of them huge, boisterous, and hungry. They're always hungry! I've met a lot of young men, but no one that stands out. Do you think Juliette is holding auditions, and I haven't caught on yet?"

"She'll tell you when she finds someone special."

"Oh, I'm not in a hurry for that. She's so happy now, so full of life's possibilities, that I can't wish for anything more for her. But Rachel is a constant worry."

"Why? What's wrong?"

"Rachel's at loose ends, drifting along without purpose. She's neither a businesswoman nor an academic like her sisters. She only hoped to be a wife and mother. But then the ladies of the St. Cecilia Society took that dream away from her."

"That's something else I missed while I was off licking my own wounds. What happened?"

"She had a clear plan. Unlike her sisters, who detested debutantes and refused to attend a formal ball to introduce them to polite society, Rachel wanted to be a debutante. Her theory was a sophisticated eighteen-year-old rather than a silly, simpering sixteen-year-old would more attractive to the cadre of escorts who attend all the parties and balls. She threw herself in her preparations—even took the French class that's always offered, even though she has grown up speaking French with her grandfather.

"Then the day came for invitations to arrive, and Rachel's envelope from the committee was of the 'We-are-sorry-to-inform-you' variety. They laid out a series of flaws: her father had died before becoming a member of the Society; her mother was an English woman of undistinguished lineage; she had been born abroad; and most serious of all, she could not produce her birth certificate."

"Oh my, Mister Beauchene must have been livid. He has been a member of that society forever."

"I feared he would shout himself right into another stroke. But no matter how much arguing he did, the committee demanded proof that Rachel was the daughter of a fine old Charleston family. When she was born, I didn't apply for an English certificate because we were leaving for home soon after her birth, and I assumed we would handle it here. When Father Beauchene scheduled her christening, I assumed that the baptismal certificate giving her parentage would serve the same purposes as a birth certificate."

"It doesn't?"

"No. Rachel sulked for weeks, and I didn't blame her. The local reaction was horrid and cruel. For a few days she was the talk of the town, with everyone speculating about who her father was and what stains lay upon her own reputation. And then doors slammed shut. People didn't speak to us on the street. Rachel's friends stopped inviting her to join in their activities. Busybodies whispered behind their hymnals when she attended a church service. It was heart-breaking.

"Even after the initial cruelties died down, people ignored and ostracized her. The gossip snuffed out her enthusiasm and sparkle, and she hasn't recovered. After three years, most people have forgotten the incident, but she hasn't. She stays home most of the time these days. She's been a help with running the household, and she comes into the warehouse now and then to help with letter-writing or record keeping, but she doesn't have a life of her own. No one has invited her to a party since the letter arrived."

"Oh, Henrietta, I'm so sorry she had to suffer through this. I have an idea that might help. What if someone offered her a job—a real job with serious responsibilities—an offer that came from a prominent citizen who trusted her? Would she take it?"

"I don't know. Perhaps, if the suggestion didn't mention fixing things for her—"

"Give me a few days. I may come up with a tempting proposal."

BROWN'S RAID AT HARPER'S FERRY

Wednesday, October 26, 1859
Charleston, South Carolina

ather Beauchene's personal slave had delivered him to the dining room in his wheeled Merlin chair before the rest of the family assembled for dinner. The frown on his face warned he was just waiting for someone to show up and set him off on a rant. Antoine was the first to blunder into his father's sight.

"Good evening, Father. I hope you've had a pleasant day."

"Pleasant? Pleasant, you say? The world's nonsense makes that impossible."

"Has something displeased you?"

"Displeased me? You might say that. I take it you haven't read the latest news."

"No. Has the *Times* arrived from New York with more inflammatory rhetoric about the evils of slavery?"

"Joshua brought two copies of the paper to the warehouse, didn't he? I don't pay for an extra copy of the news just to decorate the reception table. You should read it."

"I didn't notice what he brought in. It's been a busy day. Cotton deliveries are coming in fast these days."

"That's fine, my boy. But you also need to keep abreast of what's happening in the world. If we go to war and the North blockades our ports, your cotton crops won't do us much good languishing in the warehouse, will they?"

"Have we gone to war?" Antoine smiled at his father.

"No! But we will if that damned fool John Brown gets his way. We should have shot him years ago!"

"That's a little strong, isn't it?"

"Don't be such a namby-pamby, Antoine. You want a life of drinking and gambling and a little whoring on the side. But you watch." Mr. Beauchene shook his finger at his son. "If you and the other self-indulgent young men of your generation don't step up soon to defend South Carolina and her way of life, you won't have a life at all."

By now, Antoine was on his feet, using his height to intimidate the old man sitting across the table. "Wait. How am I the bad guy here? One minute you were talking about *The New York Times* and the next, you're attacking me. I doubt that my paltry love life made the latest headlines."

Henrietta hesitated in the doorway, an arm outstretched to stop her daughters from walking straight into the middle of an argument. "Excuse me. Is this a private fight, or can we join you?"

Both men breathed a sigh of relief. Henrietta often played the role of peacemaker in family quarrels.

"Come sit down, my dears. We were just passing the time while waiting for you ladies to join us."

"Um-hum! I gather that something in the latest paper set this discussion off."

"You haven't read it, either?"

"No, father, I didn't have time. But I'm counting on you to fill us in on what we have missed."

"In a few minutes, perhaps." Mr. Beauchene glanced around the room, nodding at the slave girls who hovered at the buffet board, ready to serve dinner. "You may serve the soup, Emmy."

No one had much to say during the meal, but curiosity made them eager to get back to whatever news had so upset the family patriarch. When Mr. Beauchene snagged a last grape and pushed his cheese plate away, the others stopped eating and turned toward him.

"You will remember the talk about a rabid abolitionist named John Brown back in 1856. The people of Kansas and Missouri were arguing about whether Kansas would become a slave state or a free state. In May, some supporters of making Kansas a slave state attacked the free town of Lawrence and killed several abolitionists. A few days later this John Brown and five of his sons attacked three small cabins near Pottawatomie Creek. Five pro-slavery men died in that attack, which set the stage for skirmishes that continued all summer long, causing the loss of over two hundred lives. That was John Brown's doing, and they should have tried him and sentenced him to death."

"Agreed," said Antoine, and even Henrietta nodded.

"Instead, they allowed him to go free, and he has spent the last few years cooking up a grandiose plan to save the country. He raised money from northern abolitionists and recruited a band of twenty-two followers, including two of his sons. The reporter says he tried—and failed—to get both Harriet Tubman and Frederick Douglass to join them. Tubman pleaded illness, and Douglass laughed at the plans as a 'suicide mission.'

"His target was the U.S. Arsenal at Harper's Ferry, where armorers were manufacturing weapons, and newspapers reported that the warehouses already contained 100,000 guns to prepare for a war between North and South. Brown's hope was to capture those guns and put them into the hands of slaves. An armed slave revolt, led by a reasonable man, he suggested, might put an end to slavery without a bloody war between North and South.

"Brown rented a nearby farmhouse and used it as a training barracks for his followers. He offered to supply captured guns to any escaping slaves who joined the effort. The plan was to lead them into the South, frightening the slave owners into surrendering without a fight. Brown estimated that 500 slaves would come forward, but only five slaves joined his band. Last Sunday, the sixteenth, Brown's men captured the guards and held the arsenal for a day. They also cut telegraph wires and held a Baltimore and Ohio train to ransom for a while. But within a day, the U.S. Government sent in a small troop of Marines, led by Colonel Robert E. Lee. By the nineteenth, they reclaimed the arsenal. Ten of the raiders, including Brown's two sons, died. The Marines captured Brown himself and turned him over to the State of Virginia for trial. The *Times* predicts that a jury will find him guilty on multiple charges of treason and murder. And this time, they'll hang the son-of-a-b—"

"Father! There are young girls present."

"Sorry, but this fellow's idiocy angers me. He's a murderer. He deserves what he gets."

"I'm not sure I understand all this," Juliette interrupted. "What did Brown accomplish? If he's an abolitionist, why would he want to stir up a slave rebellion? Aren't abolitionists supposed to be peaceful people, like Quakers?"

"Most of them are. And maybe Brown believed he could control the armed slaves. He hoped that the sight of a black man holding a gun would be enough to scare the Southerners into submission. What I see, however, is clear evidence that our slaves accept their lot in life. They are not interested in rebellion. He offered them guns, and they said, 'No, thank you.'"

"So why are you upset?" Now it was Elise who joined the questioning.

"Because, my dearest, his raid will have a polarizing effect on American society."

"How so?"

"You can see it happening already in the letters to the editor. Many Northerners see Brown as a hero and a martyr. They are ready to forgive his misguided assumptions because his cause is righteous. That's a prescription for war."

"But if Southerners feel, as you seem to, that our slaves want to remain enslaved, won't they levy for a peaceful solution?"

"I doubt that, because they will feel insulted, and there's one thing you never want to do to a Southerner—make him look ridiculous."

"But I don't see how—"

"Brown planned to take on all the slave-holding states with a band of twenty-two untrained fighters and some renegade slaves. That's insulting."

"So you're saying that Brown's Raid has made war inevitable?"

"I do not want to see a war, but I fear we have just turned the last corner."

"Mother, could we change the subject?" Rachel asked. "I can't bear all this war talk."

"I agree," Juliette said. "War terrifies me."

"Girls, you may excuse yourselves if you have finished your dinners, but I think we grown-ups have a few more things to discuss here."

"Well, I'm staying," Elise announced. "A war will affect not only our family but the business, too, and I worry about how we'll respond."

"You're welcome to stay, my dear." Henrietta smiled at her eldest daughter, who was trying so hard to be an adult. "I know I've been waiting to hear Father's solutions."

"Harrumph! If North and South go to war, our business will suffer. Any schoolchild could look at the South and see that our greatest weaknesses come from having a one-crop economy. We do a great job of raising cotton, true. But we don't raise enough food to feed ourselves, nor have we bothered to create any manufacturing industries to supply our basic needs. We rely on free trade with other states and with the rest of the world. Shut down our trade, and the state will collapse."

"Right!" Antoine leaned forward, his elbows on the table. "And the North learned its lessons in the war with England. They saw that the Atlantic shipping trade was keeping their army supplied. England's blockade of America came close to shutting down the Revolution before it even got started. The same thing can happen to us unless we're prepared."

"Prepared in what way? We don't have a Navy, or even a shipping industry. We rely on northern ships to deliver our supplies."

"Which is why the Beauchene Company needs to invest in its own ships right now. We can't rely on anybody else bringing us what we need. We must rely on ourselves to get what we want."

"Brave talk, my boy, or rather, bravado! Doing it is not as easy."

"If you'd listened twenty years ago, Father, we'd have our own shipping line by now, and a port and warehouse already set up in the Caribbean."

"Ah, yes, I remember that wild-eyed proposal of yours. You wanted to be a modern pirate, swashbuckling your way between Cuba and Charleston with loads of cigars and rum. That will not help us now."

"If we gave you an eye patch and a parrot, would you settle down and concentrate on reasonable business methods of dealing with a blockade?"

"At least I have a plan."

"And this plan of yours involves—what?"

"I want to buy a small ship and convert it into a blockade runner, father. That's not piracy. It's a real solution. The U.S. Navy with its cumbersome sailing vessels cannot get close to our shores without going aground, and they'll find it difficult to blockade our ports from far off-shore. They don't know our tides, or our channels, or how to deal with pluff mud. And they cannot maneuver through our Sea Island passages.

"I want to convert a smallish ship to one with a shallow draft and a narrow bow, propelled by a steam engine, one that can navigate where the Navy ships can't go. The people who are already building blockade runners have figured out how to rig steam pipes and sailing masts so the crew can raise or lower them as needed to give the ships a low profile. They paint everything a dark gray to make the ships more invisible against the sea or clouds. And they plan for smaller loads, making up for volume by a speed that allows more frequent journeys."

"You seem to have done your homework on this one."

"I have, Father. All I need is the capital to purchase the ship, get it re-fitted and hire a crew. And if we can get that done before war begins, we can make runs to Cuba to pick up loads of—"

"—cigars and rum! I knew you'd come back to that crazy scheme."

"These aren't crazy schemes, Henrietta. I'm looking at luxury goods for which rich men will pay high prices. A few months of trafficking in high-cost items and we'll have paid off what the ship cost. Even after the war starts, we can smuggle our cotton out and deliver it to Havana or Nassau where a European ship can pick it up. Then the little runner can return home with loads of rum and maybe guns or other small items, making the trips profitable in both directions. We'll make a mockery of the North's blockade."

"You'll do all of that with your one small ship? Be realistic, Antoine. Your plan works only until you face your first hurricane or take a cannon ball from a passing warship. Then your sleek gray blockade runner sits on the bottom of the ocean—and maybe you along with it."

"That will not happen, Henrietta."

"So say you."

"That's enough, both of you. You sound like squabbling children. It's a moot question. You've forgotten the most powerful player in this contest. Cotton is King!"

"Cotton we can't sell because of a blockade?"

"Our buyers will insist on making the deliveries happen."

"You've lost me." Elise was shaking her head in puzzlement.

"Then pay attention, my dear. South Carolina raises the finest long-staple cotton in the world, and European manufacturers rely upon us to keep them supplied. The thread spinners in England, the tapestry makers in France, the artists who make Belgian lace—they all need us, as much if not more than we need them. They will not stand to have their cotton supplies cut off. We're already seeing an enormous demand for our raw cotton, with accompanying price increases. Continental industries expect a short war, so they are laying in supplies to carry them over. But if the war lasts more than a few months, they must replenish their supplies. They will not tolerate the North seizing a British ship because it is transporting Southern cotton.

"So, no, Antoine, I cannot approve of your little scheme. It will be unnecessary if we are patient. We'll let the British Navy do our blockade-fighting for us."

"I can't agree, father." Henrietta didn't like ending up on Antoine's side, but she couldn't support her father-in-law, either. "You are underestimating English ingenuity. While we've been busy with our little disputes on this side of the Atlantic, Queen Victoria has been expanding British trade routes. If the English textile industry cannot get Sea Island cotton from us, they'll go to India for tree cotton or Africa for the long fibers of their Egyptian cotton. And once they finish the Suez Canal, the continent may not bother with trans-Atlantic shipping at all."

"That's a long way off. I'm telling you, we have the most valuable commodity in the textile industry, and no cotton manufacturers will allow a regional war to cut off their supply of raw materials. Cotton is King, I tell you. Cotton is King!"

A JOB OFFER

*F*all days in Charleston can be beautiful, and this Sunday was no exception. Henrietta and her three daughters walked to church, not out of humility but to enjoy breathing the sea-fresh air and admire the deep shadows cast by a brilliant autumn sun through the leaves. The Huguenot Church was only a few blocks from the Beauchene family home. Henrietta never entered its sanctuary without feeling the loss of her husband. He had wanted the French community to have a church of its own. He loved the liturgy and hymns expressed in his mother language. Most of all, he admired the simplicity of the Huguenot beliefs and the sense of community that the church fostered. In comparison, he found the Anglican rituals of St. Philip's Church too rigid and cold for his tastes.

A small group of like-minded Frenchmen were still debating whether to build their own church when Julien died, but his dream lived on. As soon as the builders finished

the new St. Philip's Church, the French community turned its
architectural efforts toward building a church they could call
their own. They rejected the Anglican tradition of St. Philip's
and chose an architect who favored the more romantic
Gothic designs. The Gothic Revival styling of the new
Huguenot church displayed elaborate pinnacles topped by
iron crockets, and the simple pink-tinged stucco of its outer
walls stood in sharp contrast to the classical architecture of
many Charleston landmarks. At the consecration of the new
church in 1845, the Beauchene family had enrolled as
sustaining members in honor of Julien's dream.

This Sunday was special in several ways. Many Protestant
denominations, including the Huguenots, celebrated the
Sunday closest to October 31, the date of Luther's nailing his
theses to the church wall, as Reformation Day. This year, that
date was October 30, and the church was ready for a celebration. Their new pastor, the Reverend Charles W. Howard, had
settled into his duties and was ready for his inauguration as
the official shepherd of his flock. Reverend Howard had
asked the Board of Elders to mark both occasions with a
church gathering after worship.

The Huguenots had once held an informal meeting—
called a Collation—after every church service. They modeled
the practice after a custom in medieval French monasteries
where the monks gathered in the evenings to read and
discuss the lives of Christian saints. Founders of the
Charleston congregation had written the custom into their
by-laws, and, with only a handful of French families as
members, it was a pleasant way to emphasize a sense of
community, celebrate their fellowship, and practice hospital-
ity. Members gathered for a light meal after Collation Sunday
services. The food was always French, and the beverage of
choice was wine. But as the congregation grew, so, too, did
the Collation meal become more expensive. Within a few

years the custom fell by the wayside until the new pastor revived it.

For the first time in several years, the Beauchene girls were home together, and Henrietta hoped this day would remind her daughters of their heritage. The girls, however, had ideas of their own. Elise made her excuses after the benediction. "I can't bear thinking about my grandfather home alone for lunch while we are here, sipping wine and exchanging pleasantries with the neighbors," she told her mother. "I will slip away and join him. Perhaps if I tell him about the inauguration ceremony, it will lure him into attending services again."

"You know he won't come out, darling girl. He refuses to let any of his former acquaintances see him being carried in and out of events."

"Well, I can try. I can at least stir his curiosity about the new pastor." She threw her mother an ingratiating grin as she left.

Juliette flitted from one friend to another, looking for someone interested in her ideas for a new school. Only Rachel stayed at her mother's side, smiling at those who ventured a pleasantry or quick greeting but not starting a conversation. She nibbled at toasts spread with warm brie and sampled the tiny cheese and ham tarts, but her thoughts were far removed from the surrounding conversations, at least until the new pastor approached.

"Mrs. Beauchene! How lovely to see you and your daughters," he said before he realized that two of the three were missing. "Didn't I see—?"

"Elise? Yes, she was here for worship, but she went home to check on her grandfather."

"How is Mr. Beauchene?"

"You heard he has suffered paralysis after his latest stroke?"

"I understand, but I've been hoping he would find a way back into the church. Community prayer often heals."

"He's a prideful man, reverend. He won't let others see his weakness."

"Ah. I see. Too bad."

"I have a way to fix it."

Startled, Henrietta glanced at her youngest daughter, wondering if she had misheard her.

"Do you, Mademoiselle—Rachel, is it?"

"Yes, Reverend Howard. I walked around the churchyard this morning and noticed the loading dock behind the building. Where does that door lead?"

"I don't go back there often, but I'm sure the dock provided access to the builders. I'd guess the door leads to the kitchen. But why would you—?"

"Because it might give my grandfather access to the church. May we check it?"

"Yes. Let's go through the kitchen. Are you coming, Mrs. Beauchene?"

They pushed through the crowd, trying not to be obvious about disappearing. Rachel snatched at a pastry as they passed the buffet tables. Her whole demeanor had changed. She was grinning and her eyes sparkled. Henrietta watched her with a curious smile.

Reverend Howard opened the back door, and they stepped out onto the loading platform.

"See? The doorway is wide enough for his wheeled chair to pass through it. And compare the height of this platform to these carriages. Aren't they about the same level?"

"Yes, I imagine they built the dock to match the height of the wagons bringing supplies in."

"We could put grandfather into his chair at home and have our driver deliver him to the platform. If we send a carpenter over to build a ramp and handrail between the carriage and the platform, he could pull himself onto the dock. Then he could wheel through the doorway and into the sanctuary through the choir's entrance. Simple!"

"The lessons we learn from the young! That's quite an ingenious plan, my dear. Where did you learn to solve such problems?"

"Not in a classroom. Schools produce little parrots who repeat whatever the teacher says. I'd rather work through a problem and find my own solutions."

"Not a fan of schools, then? Have you finished your education?"

"Yes, thank goodness. Grandfather insisted that I graduate from Miss Kelly's School, but I refused to follow my sisters to Columbia for four more years of reading dull books written by dead old men."

"Rachel! That's disrespectful."

"But it's true, mother."

To head off what sounded like a continuing family argument, Reverend Howard pushed for more information. "So, what comes next? Marriage in the works, perhaps?"

"Heavens, no. I don't even have a fellow." She shrugged, wondering why the pastor was so interested in her life. "I stay at home. When I'm there, Mother and Elise are free to spend their days at the cotton warehouse, and Juliette can be out looking for a teaching position. Me? I'd rather spend my days supervising the slaves and figuring out ways to make their work easier."

"An organizer, too."

"Yes. We already have the most organized silverware drawer in town."

"Aha! An important accomplishment! I wonder—would you care to help me organize the mess around here? We need help with the silver."

Rachel laughed to disguise her confusion. "If you have a

real problem, I will stop by sometime and do a little sorting."

"No, no, I'm not explaining myself well. I wasn't asking you to volunteer your services. The thing is, I've been meaning to hire someone to run our church office so I can concentrate on the things I do well, such as counseling the bereaved, praying with the sick, and preaching rousing sermons. Our Board of Elders has agreed to support that effort, so I have a job to fill."

"There must be several women who—"

"The gossip-mongers, you mean? The women who spend their days keeping tabs on their neighbors? No. I want an energetic person in the office, someone in step with the younger generation, someone with new ideas."

"Are you asking me to—?"

"Organize our silverware drawer? No, there's more. Our membership files have disappeared. The calendar is a joke. Nobody knows who's responsible for what. If the congregation expects me to create social events, they don't happen. I need an office manager."

"I never considered seeking a real job. And, to be honest, I'm not the right person for you. I'm a pariah in town. People my age have made me an outcast ever since the St. Cecilia Society rejected my application to be a debutante. That decision wiped out my social life. And among those who are older than I, my ideas meet with more ridicule than enthusiasm."

"You underestimate yourself. I'm sure you'd do a better job at this than I'm doing. Let me tell you what happened last month. I didn't record a wedding date and then scheduled a funeral too close to the same time. The bridal party planned a church reception and promised to handle everything themselves so I wouldn't have to worry about it. They set up decorated tables and a refreshment buffet in the churchyard. After the ceremony, the guests assembled outside. When the newlyweds had signed their marriage certificate, they came out through the front portal. Their friends greeted them by throwing rice and ribbons, holding up signs that, I admit, bordered on suggestive, and shouting 'Have fun!' 'Congratulations!' and various other encouragements.

"Just at that moment, a casket appeared on a wagon draped in black and pulled by two black horses. The family followed, some in carriages, some on foot. Their arrival stunned both groups. The wedding party faced weeping and grieving relatives while the funeral attendees had to walk through a crowd of celebrating party-goers."

Rachel tried hard to be serious and then burst out with a fit of giggles. "I see what you mean. You need a calendar keeper, too."

"I do, and you're just the one to deal with it. Can you come to the office on Wednesday around ten? The Board of Elders will be here between nine and ten, and I'd like them to meet you."

Rachel grimaced and looked toward her mother for advice. Henrietta, however, refused to return her glance. She studied the floor as if counting the boards between her feet and the wall.

On the way home that afternoon, the only one talking was Juliette, who rattled on about parents she had met who were interested in her ideas for a better school. Rachel waited for her mother to denounce the whole idea of a job, but Henrietta did not want to say anything that might dissuade Rachel from taking advantage of this offer. Rachel broke first.

"Talk to me, mother. What do you advise? Should I jump at the chance to take on the responsibility, or will it mark me once again as the strange Beauchene girl who never follows the rules?"

"If by 'rules' you mean the restrictions on women holding property or earning money, you already know my opinion.

I've been a *feme sole* ever since Elise was a baby.[1] I have legal papers to show that my husband allowed me to work in the warehouse. Even your grandfather approved of my being a part of the family enterprise, and no one ever criticized me for it—at least, not to my face."

"But they didn't criticize you for having been born in England, either."

"Ha! You're wrong! Charleston's prominent women acknowledged me only when I was with your father. Alone, they shunned me as an interloper from that horrible little island of England. I tried to ignore it until they got over their jealousy, or curiosity, or whatever made them fear a foreigner. I understand what you've been going through, but I also believe it will pass."

"That hasn't happened so far. Won't the gossip start all over again if I accept a job in the church?"

"And what if it does? How will that be any worse?"

"Oh, it could be much worse. I won't be able to do the things Reverend Howard outlined if the congregation won't cooperate with my efforts. What if I plan an event like a children's Christmas pageant, and no one comes?"

"That won't happen. Not attending would be an attack on the pastor, and no one would do that. Don't imagine trouble for yourself before it happens."

"But this meeting on Wednesday. What does he want? Should I be preparing for it? Or what if he wanted to ask me about the rumors surrounding my birth and didn't want to mention them in front of you?"

"Rachel, you're doing it again—making things up so you can use them as an excuse not to do something you fear. Perhaps he also wants to show you around the office or give you more details about the duties involved. Whatever it is, you'll show up, listen, and then give him an answer—yes or no. I'll support your decision, whatever it is."

RACHEL'S NIGHTMARES

November 2, 1859
Charleston, South Carolina

*R*achel rejoiced when her mother quit mentioning the job offer, but the problem was never far from her own thoughts. Sometimes she tried to imagine how pleasant it would be to have a real job and a salary that would accompany it. More often, she made excuses.

No matter what her mother said, most girls Rachel's age did not seek paid employment after they graduated from Miss Kelly's School. The idea was embarrassing. People would think the family was having financial difficulties. The gossip about her suitability to join the highest level of society would start again. "That's why we wouldn't accept her as a debutante," people would say. "She was born in England. That makes her a foreigner," they'd sneer. "She ought to go home."

And the elders. What would they think of her? "She's too young," they'd protest. "We need someone who is an integral part of our congregation—someone everybody likes. We don't want a gossipy old lady in the office, but we need someone who knows what's going on among the upper crust. This girl has told you she is unpopular among the young people and their parents alike. People will ignore her."

Another would chime in, "And when we offer to pay her, we're joining the rest of society in treating her like a second-class citizen. She'll realize that. She may accept the job because she doesn't know how to say no. Hiring her would be an embarrassment. Pastor Howard suggested her because he's new here, too, and doesn't understand how our society works."

"I won't do it," Rachel promised herself. "In fact, I won't even go to the Wednesday morning meeting. I'll send Chrissy or Nate with a note saying I've decided not to consider their offer. Busy men have important matters to handle. I'm sure they'll be glad to bypass this one."

At other times, Rachel's imagination took over. She pictured herself at a desk somewhere, handling the organizational problems of the church with new solutions to old problems. The membership files were a mess? A card file, with two colors, one for the head of each family and the other for each family member, would help with membership. On each card, she could list any duties the person already assumes, like the elders, the organist, the ushers, or the ladies who arrange the flowers every week.

In a second file, she could use color cards to separate individual responsibilities—food for Collations, babysitters for the nursery, or Sunday School teachers. Then she would keep two lists for each responsibility—the person now doing the task and people willing to fill in during an emergency.

The church calendar is a joke? Why not use a school blackboard? White paint would create a permanent grid with seven columns for the days and six rows for the weeks. She could use chalk to fill in details, like church holidays and scheduled activities like the Board of Elders meeting or choir practice. Individual requests, like weddings or baptisms or funerals, could fit into the open days, and no one should enter events except the secretary, so there are no overlaps.

We don't have enough social events? She would start with Collations and events to celebrate something each season— an Easter egg hunt for spring, a Bastille Day picnic for summer, a Harvest festival in the fall, and a children's Christmas pageant. She could add more if people enjoyed them.

"These plans won't happen unless someone steps in to organize things. That's the talent Pastor Howard sees in me, and he is right. If that's my talent, it would be wrong not to use it."

By Tuesday evening, Rachel had decided. "I'll see Pastor Howard in the morning," she told her mother. "I'll listen to his proposal, put on the charm with the elders, and ask some intelligent questions. If I give the job a try, I can always quit if I don't like what I'm doing."

"That's wonderful. It's time you faced the real world."

"Well, if I can come home and sort silverware now and then—"

Rachel went off to bed, confident she had made the right decision. But after midnight, rapid-fire dreams interrupted her sleep. First, she was back in school and surrounded by friends. She heard Madame Fortier compliment her French pronunciation, and she smiled to imagine speaking collo-quial French with the leading figures in the Huguenot community.

Then the scene shifted as the girls in her pre-debutante training class gathered their books and left their final lessons. Their voices carried through the streets, sounding like the chirping of spring birds. They laughed, shouted to one another, and once even broke out into a chorus of *La Marseil-*

laise. The girls reminded Rachel of flowers as they danced through the streets on their way home. Their simple dresses displayed lovely pastel colors rather than the ginghams that schoolgirls wore. It was the day the St. Cecilia Society issued invitations to its annual debutante ball—the most important affair on Charleston's traditional social calendar.

In Rachel's dream, those little-girl dresses changed into more sophisticated gowns. Necklines plunged, bared shoulders appeared, and waistlines seemed to contract above full skirts over hoops and petticoats. The pastel shades were all that remained of the schoolgirl look. Then those colors faded until the gowns were white. And the girls spun on their toes, swaying and dipping to music only they could hear.

Rachel waited to see the transformation take place in her own gown. Instead, she gasped in horror as her dress disappeared, leaving her naked. "No! No!" Her screams woke Chrissy, the little slave girl who slept at the foot of her bed every night.

"Miss Rachel? What's wrong?" Rachel was too far immersed in her dream to answer. She clutched at the blankets and pulled them to her chin. "Where is my beautiful gown," she cried. "Where are my clothes? I can't let my friends see me naked."

She tried to wrap herself in the bed quilt, but in her dream, she held a large potted fern, its fronds not able to hide her nakedness. "Chrissy! Bring me my ball gown!"

"What ball gown, Miss Rachel? You don't have no ball gown."

"Yes, I do. Go ask mother where it is. I'll wait out here on the piazza, so the girls know I'm coming with them."

"Hurry, Rachel. We can't wait much longer," a shrill voice called. "And you can't go to the ball as a potted plant!"

Everyone laughed.

"I'm coming. Just a minute!"

But the young women in their white ball gowns were impatient to greet their beaus and admirers. Off they swirled, moving like a cloud away from the house. Rachel searched for help. Her mother stood on the far side of the piazza's glass doors, but when she tried to grasp the door handles, the doors turned to a solid wall. No one answered when she pounded on the boards. She rushed to the railing of the piazza, calling to her friends to come back. Then the railing gave way, and she was falling, falling—

Rachel awoke on the floor, disoriented and tangled in bedclothes. Chrissy was bending over her with a worried look. "Chrissy! I'm sorry. I didn't mean to wake you."

"Looks like you waked the whole house," the little slave girl answered as Henrietta and her other two daughters pushed their way into the bedroom. Their voices ran together, bringing back fragments of the dream. "What's going on? What happened in here? Rachel, what are you doing on the floor? Did you fall? Are you hurt?"

Rachel's heart was still pounding with fear, but now a red wave of anger washed over her. Why do my personal crises concern everyone else? Why can't the family leave me alone?

She struggled to her feet, dragging the blankets with her. "I'm fine. It was just a dream, and I fell out of bed. Go back to your rooms."

"Well, the next time you dream, make it a quiet one, please," Elise grumbled. She and Juliette wandered out, but Henrietta stayed behind. She perched on the edge of the bed and pulled Rachel down beside her. "Was it the same dream? The one about the debutantes?"

Rachel clamped her lips together in a tight grimace even as she nodded. She wished her mother would go away without delivering the usual lecture, but it was a vain hope.

"Darling girl, you must quit obsessing over that little incident. It happened three years ago. Everyone else has forgotten about it. Why can't you?"

Rachel wanted to point out it hadn't happened to everyone else, and it was no one else's business, but she couldn't insult her mother. Rachel shook her head.

"Why don't you describe the dream? You never have, you know."

"No."

"It might help."

"No."

"You're worrying about your interview tomorrow, aren't you?" Henrietta persisted. "No one will reject you. Remember, you didn't ask for a job. Pastor Howard asked you. You'll be doing him a favor if you accept."

"I understand that."

"Then why all this fuss?"

"You're the one who—never mind. I've calmed down now. I'm going back to sleep."

"All right. Think pleasant thoughts." Henrietta dropped a kiss on her cheek and tiptoed out of the room. She missed the glare of pure hatred that Rachel shot at her back.

Pleasant thoughts? Her anger still burned. The letter said Rachel could not be a debutante because she did not have a valid birth certificate. And why was that so important? Because each debutante needed to prove she was a Charleston citizen. Why did they not accept Henrietta's statement about Rachel's birth in England? Rachel kept demanding an answer to that question. And each time, Henrietta refused to explain. The Society rejection had hurt, yes, but her mother's refusal to talk about her birth made matters worse. That was the family secret no one would talk about—the secret her dream interpreted by blocking the doors to the house. Her mother knew. Her failure to reveal the secret caused the grief haunting the child she meant to shield.

THE EMOTIONAL UPHEAVAL HAD DRAINED RACHEL, AND SHE fell into an uninterrupted sleep. By morning, she awoke with a smile—eager for her interview. She headed off to her ten o'clock appointment, her head buzzing with ideas.

She waited in a corner pew until Pastor Howard opened the door and beckoned her to come across the hall to his office. He introduced the three gentlemen who were waiting there—T. P. O'Neale, the church organist; Daniel Ravenel, who served on the Board of Elders and as president of the church; and Charles Vedder, who sometimes preached at a Presbyterian church in Summerville but attended the Huguenot church because of its proximity to his home. Mr. O'Neale squinted at her with some measure of disapproval, but since she had heard he hated everyone, she didn't let it bother her. She smiled at Mr. Vedder, who had lost most of the hair on the top of his head and seemed to compensate by growing a healthy crop of chin whiskers. Mr. Ravenel, the one with the most authority, was also the one with the kindest expression, so she concentrated her charms on him.

Reverend Howard opened the discussion. "We have two items of business to discuss this morning, gentlemen. The first deals with a suggestion that Miss Beauchene has made concerning her grandfather's inability to attend church services. As I understand it, she wants to send their slaves to build a ramp behind the loading dock, so her grandfather can use his wheeled Merlin chair to enter the sanctuary through the kitchen. Is that right, Miss Beauchene?"

"Yes, sir. We've already adapted a carriage to raise and lower his chair to the ground. He can access buildings by using a ramp to get from one level to the other. If the slope is difficult, he may need a slave to help push; if it's a gentle slope, he can propel himself by turning small wheels at the ends of the chair's armrests."

"Does our loading dock meet his requirements?"

"Yes, sir, and the church has wide doorways. I have speculated that the doors may show the influence of ladies who wanted more room for their hoop skirts." She grinned at Mr. Ravenel, who was nodding.

"I remember those discussions well. Several of them took place around my dinner table. It sounds like we did something useful beyond catering to the changing styles of ladies' dresses."

"How much will this cost?" grumbled the organist.

"It won't cost the church anything. Our family is more than willing to supply the materials and labor."

"I don't think you should have to assume that expense," Mr. Vedder spoke up. "Once the ramp is in place, other church members will use it. Besides, I think we can prevail upon some of our members to donate materials. In fact, the gentleman who owns the lumber yard on Cumberland Street is behind in his pledge payments. I'm sure he would help. Give me a few days and I'll drop by with other offers."

"All right," muttered the organist, "but how do we know it will work as this young girl promises?"

"I can show you how it works, Mr. O'Neale. We've already built one such ramp over at the Beauchene Company warehouse so that grandfather can keep an eye on the business he founded. Let me know when you are free, and I'll have Samson bring my grandfather over to the office. While he's taking care of business, we'll have access to the carriage and chair, so you can try the system out for yourself."

"Oh, well—ahem—if you've already perfected the system, I don't need a private demonstration. Who designed this for you, and will he be able to adapt the design to our needs here?"

"I—"

"Let me answer that one, Miss Beauchene. It brings us to our second item of business—hiring a board secretary and office manager. Miss Beauchene told me about this ramp plan on Sunday, and I asked almost the same question: 'Who taught you how to do that?' When she said it was her own idea, I knew we needed her working that kind of magic for us."

"I agree," said Mr. Ravenel. "And I'm sure the board will approve." Vedder nodded his acceptance. "How does a salary of a dollar and a half per day sound, Miss Beauchene?"

"That's generous, sir, although if you hire me to get your financial and membership and scheduling operations organized, I will need some operating expenses. I can't keep records on the back of old envelopes."

"Consider yourself hired. And we'll provide an expense account. How soon can you start? Next week?"

"Yes, sir."

"We'll expect you by nine o'clock on Monday, then."

A CHRISTMAS PAGEANT

November 1859
Charleston, South Carolina

*H*enrietta expected the month of November to pass without a crisis. On the surface, everything was under control. After his resounding lecture on the invincibility of Cotton as King, old Mr. Beauchene settled into a period of optimism. He didn't fuss at the political news and ignored the rancor leading to the 1860 presidential elections. He dismissed the challenges of Lincoln, ridiculing him as a backwoods upstart with hands and feet too big for him to manage. "Nobody votes for somebody like that," he promised.

Antoine dropped the subject of his proposed blockade-runner. When Henrietta tried to mend a few fences by telling him she approved of challenging a blockade by using the swampy waterways of the Low Country, Antoine brushed her off. "It will not happen," he conceded. "I can't afford to buy the ship on my own, and the banks won't give me a loan because I have no collateral to put up against it. Those clauses that Julian and Father included in their wills make it impossible for me to get credit with anyone. They entail all my potential assets to your daughters.[1] I don't begrudge them their inheritance, mind you, but it leaves me stranded as the penurious younger brother for as long as I live."

Elise was spending more and more time at the family business as the cotton harvest continued at a record pace. The three-way discussion over the future of cotton sales had left her confused, but she understood enough to know this year's harvest—the one not yet threatened by a blockade—would determine the future for both the planters and their cotton factors. Most mornings found her with her head buried in the news of overseas markets, and her afternoons out in the warehouse going over their inventories. She was spending less and less time with Thomas, but he seemed willing to wait, at least until after the holidays.

And Rachel, the child whose well-being had worried Henrietta the most, was thriving in her new position of authority at the Huguenot church. She had begun construction on her grandfather's ramp, hoping to have it finished before Christmas. As promised, Elder Vedder found several parishioners willing to donate construction materials, and the Beauchene carpenters enjoyed work that took them into town for a while. Rachel could hear them singing to themselves as they sawed and hammered behind the church.

Rachel's other projects were also coming along. The blackboards that would serve as calendars were on order, and church members were cooperating by turning in their membership information. There seemed to be nothing she could not handle—until the morning Reverend Howard mentioned the date for the Children's Christmas Pageant.

"Pageant? You mean, the story of Christmas, like the ones

I can remember from when I was little?" Rachel looked up from her desk in terror at the idea.

"Yes. It'll be such a good way to kick off our holiday celebrations. I understand we haven't had a pageant in several years."

"Pageant? But I don't know how to go about something like that. When I said I could handle church records and scheduling events, I forgot you would also expect me to make those events happen."

"Oh, you can teach the little ones how to sing and dance around a stable," he suggested.

"Sing and dance? Oh, no! I—I—"

"It was a joke, my dear. Madame Dubois has offered to take charge of this year's pageant. You know her, don't you?"

"You mean Elizabeth Dubois? She's my godmother."

"Wonderful. Then you will work well together. She will handle the actors and the script. All you have to do is to schedule the date and arrange cookies and hot chocolate in the kitchen afterwards."

"Knowing Aunt Elizabeth, she'll wrangle me into doing more than that, but, yes, we'll work well together. I'll see her this afternoon."

Over a cup of tea, Rachel confessed the pageant terrified her. "I can remember one in which I played an angel," she said. "Were you there? It was a disaster. Our angel wings kept falling off, a shepherd tripped over his bathrobe and bloodied his nose when he fell, and Joseph wet his pants."

Elizabeth smiled. "That sounds about normal for a children's program, I think. No one expects perfection, and the parents are proud even when their children forget their lines. Don't worry about it, darling girl. We'll do the best we can and enjoy telling the horror stories afterwards."

"Reverend Howard wants us to set a date right away, but he didn't give me any guidance on when this should take place."

"I have been thinking about that, but I didn't want to set the date without checking with the church's event coordinator." Elizabeth smiled at her favorite goddaughter. "If you want me to make suggestions, I recommend a Friday night to make it a special affair but one not connected to a Sunday church service. Either the second or the ninth of December will work."

"They are both clear. Which would you prefer?"

"Well, Advent starts on the first of the month, so if we choose December second, the pageant will introduce our Advent celebrations."

"Can we organize it by then?"

"I've already marked November 12—that's this Saturday— for auditions for our young actors."

"I appreciate your help, Auntie Elizabeth."

"No problem. I enjoy the little ones when I can hand them back to their mothers if I've had enough of their silliness."

Rachel relaxed when she learned that the pageant was the same every year. "I thought I had to write the script, too."

"Ah, someone more talented than either of us did that a long time ago," Elizabeth replied. "Mr. Vedder has agreed to read the Christmas story straight from *The Gospel According to Luke*."

"Do the children understand biblical language?"

"Maybe not, but the words will imprint themselves on their little souls, even if they don't understand them. They'll grow up knowing the story better than any other, and they'll come to understand it, too. That's all part of the ritual of holding the same pageant every year. We'll throw in some familiar Christmas carols, like *Silent Night* and *Oh, Little Town of Bethlehem* to round out the program."

"Do the children know those words?"

"Maybe. Maybe not. But their parents do. We'll ask the audience to join in the singing and have the church choir members ready to lead the way. No one will notice if the angels mumble their words."

"It sounds like you have it under control."

"Don't worry about a thing. I have announced the auditions scheduled for next Saturday morning. We'll see how many children want to take part. I'll find roles for all who show up, and if we don't get enough volunteers, I'll have time to draft some unwilling or shy ones to join in."

"HOW DID THE TRYOUTS GO, AUNTIE ELIZABETH?" RACHEL asked the next Sunday.

"A success. Lots of little children—and older ones, too—came out to apply. We've filled all the important roles. Mary Carolina Huger will play the biblical Mary. She's a lovely fourteen-year-old with golden blond hair and a sweet voice so she can sing a lullaby on cue. The Manigault boy, Tolbert, will be Joseph. He's a strong, well-built lad who can carry Mary if he needs to. The innkeeper and his wife are minor characters, but Pastor Howard's children have volunteered for those roles. And I recruited three strong young men, including my grandson, Johnny Grenville, and two of his friends, Gus Smythe and John Calhoun Clemson, to play the Wise Men. The older boys will be shepherds, and the older girls will be angels. The littlest ones will be the sheep. We still need a few children to play animals, like the mule and a cow and the camels, but they'll turn up."

"Oh, my! How will we ever handle all those costumes?"

"Simplification, my dear. The children playing people will wear bathrobes. The Wise Men wear crowns, and the shepherds get crooks. Some of those items are in the church attic, I believe. The ones playing animals will wear signs around their necks. Think how cute a whole bevy of tiny tots wearing SHEEP signs will be."

"Are you sure about that? The sheep will be adorable. But you can't ask a school-age girl to wear a COW sign, or a growing boy to label himself a MULE."

"Oh, dear, I hadn't thought about the cow problem. Maybe we can eliminate that one."

"You know what? I'd prefer to use real animals."

"You can't be thinking of bringing animals into our sanctuary. We laid new carpeting last month."

"No, but we can move the pageant into the churchyard. The story takes place at night. We can build a temporary stable stall, and there's a convenient little hillock at one side, where we can have a pen for some sheep. I don't suppose we can find a camel, but the Wise Men can report they have parked their camels down the street."

"What do we tell the children who want to be a part of the pageant?"

"We'll turn them into a choir of angels. Little boys and girls can be angels, too, and wire haloes will do the trick for them. They can sing Christmas carols when they are appropriate, and since the audience will join in, no one will notice the children's mistakes."

"I don't know, Rachel. I don't relish trying to get animals to do whatever it is we'll need them to do. It's hard enough herding children!"

"I'll offer you a deal. You handle the children who have

speaking parts, and I'll manage the animals. Animals do nothing but stand around."

IT SHOULD HAVE BEEN EASY! RACHEL BUSTLED THROUGH THE days leading up to the pageant, twisting one arm after another to get parishioners to loan her an animal or two for the evening. She collected lanterns to provide light and used the scraps of lumber left over from the wheelchair ramp to build a stable and a sheep pen. The rumor that the pageant would use real animals spread through the French-speaking community. Soon everyone was talking about attending.

Rachel's luck held through the early evening. The cooperating parishioners had delivered their animals in the afternoon, and they were by now settled into their temporary pens. The weather turned out to be perfect—warm and dry, with a soft breeze that blew the animal odors away from the audience. Even Mr. O'Neale had gotten into the Christmas spirit. He played light-hearted Christmas songs on his portable melodeon as the audience assembled, and he gestured for them to sing along. Then the narrator, Reverend Vedder, called for silence and introduced the biblical narrative. The angel choir sang *Silent Night.*

It was time for Mary and Joseph to arrive with Mary riding on a real mule. Elizabeth Dubois signaled for them to enter. Nothing happened. Rachel hissed at the organist. "Play *Silent Night* again or something else appropriate while I go find the mule."

Mr. O'Neale snickered but complied. He made his way through *O Little Town of Bethlehem*, and then started over. The choir of angels looked confused. Some sang; some didn't. Rachel ducked behind some bushes concealing the waiting characters. She found Mary and Joseph looking at an animal splayed out on the ground.

"It's the mule, Miss Beauchene. He's dead." Tolbert Manigault looked up from where he had knelt to prod the animal.

"Are you sure? Maybe he's just taking a nap before his performance. Mules can be stubborn about following orders."

"No, ma'am. This mule's for sure dead. He was lying here when we arrived. We found him cold as anything, and it's not from the weather."

"Well, the audience is waiting, a dead mule or no dead mule. You and Mary can walk in and explain the long journey has tired her mount."

"I can hold Mary in my arms."

"Bless you, son. That would be perfect. Get going. The organist is about to explode."

Thus the pageant began. Mary and Joseph looked travel-worn, their bathrobe costumes in some disarray from their kneeling on the ground to inspect the mule.

"I bid you good evening, Master Innkeeper. My wife and I have traveled from afar to obey the decree to pay our taxes in Bethlehem."

"Walked the whole way from Nazareth, have you?"

"No, sir. We used to have a mule, but he died along the way. We seek shelter."

"I wish I could provide it, but all my rooms are full."

"Please. You can see that my wife is with child. She can't walk any further. The birth will happen soon."

"Well, since your mule is dead, there may be an extra space in the stable. You can have a stall there. That's the best I can do."

Even Rachel saw the humor and laughed along with the audience. "Great improvisation," she whispered to the waiting Wise Men. "Make up your lines as you go."

She meant it as friendly banter, but the children took her at her word. The shepherds informed everyone they had left their sheep back on the hill, "But," they promised, "They're still alive." And to prove that point, several sheep bleated. When it came time for their entrance, the Wise Men announced that they had come from afar, following a star until it came to rest. "We left our camels parked down the road a piece, next to that dead mule," one of them said. The audience burst into laughter.

Later, the Wise Men reported that King Herod had sent them to find the newborn child. "We have decided not to report the news of what has happened in Bethlehem because God told Melchior in a dream that Herod means to destroy the child."

When Joseph and Mary prepared to flee into Egypt for safety, the Wise Men warned, "You will need a new mule." The pageant ended with another burst of laughter and an invitation to all to come inside for hot chocolate and cookies.

The audience agreed it had been a wonderful pageant. The old man who had loaned the mule to Rachel apologized, admitting that he had sent her an animal that was sick and ready to die. "I'll bring a cart and some men in the morning. We'll get the mule hauled out of the churchyard before Sunday services, I promise, miss."

Only one woman protested that the program had been in poor taste. "The story of the Lord's birth is not an occasion for laughter," Belinda St. Croix declared as she left, radiating disapproval from every pore. Rachel heard the comment. Horrified and embarrassed, she felt tears gathering. She turned away and headed for the kitchen where she could pretend to be arranging more cookie platters. Instead, she found Reverend Howard hiding there, too.

"Oh, Pastor Howard, I'm so sorry about the jokes and the dead mule. I didn't want to be funny. I'm so embarrassed. If you want me to quit, I'll understand. I'm not cut out to be a social director."

"Quit? What are you saying, Rachel? That was the most entertaining pageant I've ever seen. People loved it, and the children will remember it all their lives. They'll want another dead mule next year."

"You're not angry?"

"No. I'm eager to see what you'll come up with next."

A CHRISTMAS TO REMEMBER

December 1859
Charleston, South Carolina

*A*s soon as Rachel's Christmas pageant was over, the Beauchene household went into full pre-Christmas preparation. Although none of them would have admitted it, the specter of war hanging over the country gave a special meaning to this holiday season. The world was still peaceful, the cotton harvest had been spectacular, and hurricane season had passed without a major storm. Family members had much to be thankful for this year. And when they coupled their gratitude with the fear that by the next year the country might be at war, the Beauchene family, like the rest of the citizens of Charleston, wanted this holiday to be one to remember.

Out in the slave yard, the men had already gathered a huge pile of grapevines and greenery out of which the slave women would make wreathes to decorate every window in the house. In the kitchen, mincemeat bubbled, a huge ham was soaking in a tub, and fruitcakes awaited their daily dribble of brandy to preserve their richness. Henrietta was checking off long lists of gifts for the family slaves—their yearly allotment of new clothes, grooming supplies for the adults and toys for the children—and the provisions supplied to each slave family to feed them through the coming months.

Much of the daily chatter in the household concerned plans for Slave Christmas, the four-day holiday period granted to all the slaves, this year starting on Wednesday the twenty-first. Suzanna, the oldest woman in the yard, told the story of Jesus's birth in the Gullah language the slaves used among themselves. Small children giggled as they thought about the special treats they would eat, the singing and dancing that would go on late into the nights, and the packages they would receive from their owners.

Family members also looked forward to the changes that four-day holiday brought to their routines. Meals were pickup affairs, nibbling at the cold dishes the cooks had prepared in advance. No formal dinners demanded their presence, so it was a time for the young people to meet with their friends. Neighbors used this time to visit among themselves. Those preparing small surprise gifts for family members slipped off to take care of wrapping presents. And everywhere in the house, Christmas decorations appeared— greenery, winter-blooming flowers, extra candles, treasured figurines, piles of fruits and nuts, candies, cookies, and pies. No matter where one turned, the house spoke of abundance, beauty, and love.

Now that the pageant was over, Rachel gave her full attention to her grandfather's wheelchair ramp. Because Christmas would fall on a Sunday this year, she was eager to present the ramp to him as her gift. She hovered over the workmen, reminding them they needed to finish the ramp before they could take off to enjoy their own Slave Christmas. The workers didn't need reminding, however; they, too, wanted the old man to move again. Someone designed a tiny incline to allow the wheelchair to glide over the threshold into the kitchen.

Henrietta also worried the project along. "You should do a practice run with your grandfather," she suggested. "It would be disastrous to have him arrive on Christmas morning and have something go wrong."

"Nothing will go wrong, mother. We measured and re-measured every step of the way. But you may be right about the practice run. If grandfather intends to give me an argument, I'd rather have him make a fuss before Christmas rather than that morning. I'll check the calendar and try to find an afternoon when the church will be empty—maybe Monday or Tuesday of Christmas Week."

Two weeks before Christmas, Elise looked up from her record-keeping at the warehouse to see her mother staring at her. "What is it, mother? Do you need me?"

"No, dear, I am just taking a breather from dealing with a difficult customer. I was wondering. Have you invited Thomas to have Christmas dinner with us, or will he be coming over at some other time?"

"Oh, I haven't planned to see him at all on Christmas Day."

"Why ever not? He's your fiancé. That makes him a member of the family."

"And his parents could say the same about me, I suppose. But how would we decide which family comes first? No, we talked about it, but we decided that we both would prefer to spend the day with our own nearest and dearest. This may be our last Christmas celebration as a family. By next year we may be at war instead of carving a ham and devouring fruitcake."

"Oh, I hope not. I see your point, however. So when will you see him to exchange gifts and plan your future Christmases together?"

"We talked about that, too. We decided not to give each other gifts this year. Thomas wants us to save our money for setting up our own household."

"Well, I suppose that's sensible, but it's not very romantic."

"It was as much my idea as his. And you know I've never been the romantic type. I'll leave that bit of role-playing to my sisters." She turned back to her account book, signaling she did not want this conversation to go any further. Henrietta took the hint.

Elise watched her mother's back as she walked away. Perky as she could be when talking to her daughters, she slumped a little when no one was watching. Her footsteps dragged, and her eyes looked downward. Poor, dear old thing, Elise thought. I wonder what goes through her mind in these moments when she thinks she's alone. It had been almost twenty years since Henrietta's husband died of a fall that fractured his skull. She had been alone ever since, never considering remarriage. She filled her waking hours with dual efforts to manage the family business and to raise her daughters to be well-rounded women. They were both noble goals, Elise admitted to herself, but not fulfilling for a woman who carried on alone.

Elise's engagement to Thomas Middleton Hayward was a part of her mother's master plan. The marriage would connect the Beauchene family to two prominent Charleston families. Grandchildren would cement the alliance. The children would receive fine-sounding middle names to make sure the social climbers knew what their heritage entailed. Henrietta's daughters had never experienced the frothy honor of becoming a St. Cecilia debutante, but her granddaughters would do so.

Elise sighed as her rumination about her mother's life forced her to confront her own doubts. She supposed that producing those grandchildren was the least she could do to repay her mother for her devotion. Marriage couldn't be all that bad, she reasoned. Many women took great pride in their roles as wives and mothers. Why did she regard it with such trepidation?

The answer to that unspoken question came sooner than Elise expected. Thomas had accepted his exclusion from the Beauchene family circle on Christmas Day, but he insisted that Elise plan to join him in making the rounds of New Year's celebrations.

"You've spent the entire fall cooped up in that dusty old warehouse," Thomas reminded her. "You need to take a break, have your maid set your hair in ringlets rather than that serviceable bun, and put on your swishiest, ruffled gown."

"Swishiest isn't a word," she reminded him, sounding like a schoolmarm.

"Well, it ought to be. I'll make that a part of my New Year's resolutions, along with finishing my law clerk's duties and becoming known as the best husband-to-be in Charleston. We'll start by doing the town on New Year's Eve, flitting from party to party and sampling the *hors d'oeuvres* to decide who has the best cook. And at midnight, we'll find a glass of champagne to toast our wedding date in the coming year." There it was again—that assumption, that demand they fulfill the promise of the glittering ring she wore on her love finger. The though sent shivers of dread along her spine.

To distract herself, Elise, too, had been keeping a close eye on the ramp construction. It was her idea to rearrange the church kitchen and meeting hall to leave a clear path to the sanctuary.

"If I know our grandfather, and I think I do," she warned Rachel, "he'll put up every argument he can think of to avoid dealing with something new. It's a good thing you are his favorite granddaughter. For you, he may make a stronger effort to cooperate."

"Well, you can help. We will do a practice run next Monday. Don't let him give you any lessons that afternoon. Tell him you have a date with Thomas. Make up an appointment."

On Monday morning, Rachel broached the news at breakfast. "I need you to do something for me this afternoon, grandfather."

"What could you need from me?" he grumbled.

"I can't explain. I need to show you. Nate and Joe will have the carriage waiting for us right after lunch. I promise you. You'll turn out to be the help I need. Please, grandfather, it's important."

"You know I don't like people seeing the slaves carrying me around."

"That won't happen. We'll use the carriage with the lifting platform for your wheelchair. You'll be sitting in comfort."

As their carriage approached the corner of Queen Street and Church Street, Father Beauchene gazed at the façade of the Huguenot Church. "Look at that," he exclaimed. "Five steps up to the entrance. What were we thinking? Why didn't we see that some people could not climb those stairs?"

Rachel suppressed her grin as Nate turned the carriage down Queen Street and then turned onto a well-worn path at the back of the building.

"What's back here?" Mr. Beauchene demanded. "This is just for deliveries."

"Yes, grandfather, and we are delivering you. Welcome to the Beauchene entrance to the Huguenot Parish Hall."

"What?"

"This is your Christmas present. I mentioned your difficulties in attending church services to Reverend Howard, and he realized that other parishioners, too, might face problems with those front steps. The Board of Elders solicited donations of lumber from the parish, and our own carpenters have been over here every day to build the ramp and clear your way into the sanctuary. This is a trial run."

"I'm speechless," he said. "Did you think of this yourself?"

"Yes, sir, and I designed the ramp, too. But now I need you to see if it works. We'll lower you to the ground, and then Nate and Joe will help you push and pull your way up the ramp using the handrail. Once you're inside the kitchen, you're on your own to wheel your chair through the meeting hall and the choir entrance at the back of the sanctuary."

"I don't know if I can—"

"That's why we're here. Let's do it, shall we?"

After one false start, the chair rolled to the top of the ramp, across the loading dock, and though the doorway into the kitchen.

"Are you sure the sanctuary doors are wide enough?"

"Yes, I'm sure. You taught me to measure things when I was little, remember?"

At the back door to the sanctuary, Mr. Beauchene hesitated again as he stared down the rows of box pews. "Where can I park the chair? Or do I stay back here?"

"Go down the outside right aisle, grandfather. When you get to the Beauchene pew, you'll see we've thought of everything."

"Oh, here we are—but what has happened to our pew? Its door is missing, and it's shorter than it used to be."

"Yes. But your chair will fill the open space."

With a little maneuvering, Mr. Beauchene wheeled his chair into position. He leaned back to stare at the pulpit and the altar in front of him and then to gaze up at the vaulted ceiling. "I had forgotten how beautiful it is," he said. A broad smile creased this face, and a tear glinted at the corner of his eye.

"Rachel, my dearest girl, how can I thank you? You've given me back my church."

"No, I've given myself the greater gift. Someone I love can once again attend the services he enjoys. And on Christmas morning, the entire parish will receive the gift of one of their founding members once again in his rightful place." She leaned over his chair to place a kiss on his cheek. "I hope you like the arrangement because there's something else you need to know."

"What's that?"

"We've set up the same arrangement at the warehouse. You'll be able to check on the family business any time you want to."

"No! How—"

"If you remember, there's already a loading ramp behind the warehouse to allow planters to move their cotton bales into the building. That's what first gave me the idea. We installed a handrail so you could pull yourself along."

"I am overwhelmed. But do you realize that you may have created a wheeled monster? Now I have my mobility back, there will be no stopping me. I'm already picturing myself careening down that ramp outside. The momentum should carry me all the way across Queen Street and right into the St. Philip's graveyard. I have a few acquaintances there I can visit. And it will strike terror into the hearts of those Episcopalians to see a Huguenot barreling down upon them."

A QUARREL AND A SECRET

December 1859–March 1860
Charleston, South Carolina

*E*lise tried to feel excitement about the New Year's parties their friends were planning, and she wanted to enjoy the evening. She knew the sausage curls that dangled behind her ears drew attention to her heart-shaped face. Her blue silk taffeta dress intensified the blue of her eyes, and Thomas's surprise gift of a delicate gold filigree necklace showed off her neck and shoulders to their best advantage. She smiled on cue, clung to Thomas's arm, and fluttered her eyelashes at the old men who commented on her charms. When someone asked about their wedding date, she steered the conversation away from an answer. "We haven't announced it yet," became her standard reply.

Their friends accepted that explanation, but Thomas had heard it once too often. He drew her out onto a handy piazza for a little privacy. Then his voice took on a harsher tone, fortified, perhaps, by one too many sips of champagne. He grasped her arms and forced her to face him.

"Answer me, Elise. How much longer are you intending to string me along?"

"I haven't been doing anything of the sort. I've just been busy. You know this is the most hectic period in the cotton business. The planters held on to their crops, hoping to see the prices increase, but they've been coming in fast in December. I already don't have enough hours in a day to keep up with our transactions."

"Well, I, for one, don't give a fig about the cotton crop. I care about getting my fiancée back."

"Which will happen later, but right now—"

"Don't say it. Don't tell me again that you don't have time for me."

"I don't mean it like that. It's just that I'm so conscious of my role in the family company. My sisters are not interested in the cotton business, so the future of the Beauchene Company will end up on my shoulders. That's a heavy responsibility, and if I go waltzing off right now to get married while there are crucial decisions pending, I might never regain control."

"What does it matter? After we're married, you won't control the business at all."

"What do you mean? Why would you assume that?"

"Because it's true, my dear. You know South Carolina laws concerning women. Married women do not—I repeat, do not —work outside the home."

"That's not so. My mother worked side by side with my father and grandfather for years. But that reminds me. The lawyers need to create the papers to make me a *feme sole* as they did for my mother. I assume your law offices can handle that."

"Can they handle that? Perhaps. But will they? Never. No Middleton or Hayward wife ever worked outside the home, and I have no intention of having mine be the first one to do so. You will be a *feme covert*—a protected woman. Your property will be mine, and I will care for you and your children."

"Oh, Thomas, quit pretending. You must have heard your grandfather talk about the Beauchene family entails. He was the one who drew up the wills that restrict the company's ownership to my mother and from her to her daughters."

"Your father's will may say that, but the Middleton Law Firm knew from the beginning that an individual's will may not supersede the law of the land. And South Carolina law states that when a woman marries, all of her real property belongs to her husband."

"Unless the engaged couple agrees to a marriage settlement before the ceremony takes place. You will sign a formal statement approving a third party to oversee my dowry and any inherited property. That individual will safeguard my inheritance from your meddling with my affairs or ruining my inheritance's value through bad judgment."

"I will do no such thing. And I resent the assumption I might use bad judgment or meddle in your affairs."

"I didn't say you would. It's a protection against future marital disagreements."

"Well, I won't sign that statement, and once the company is in my hands, I'll sell it. I have no interest in learning to deal in cotton even if it is a profitable venture."

"You can't do that!" Elise jerked her arms from his grasp and stared at him in horror. "You wouldn't. Not knowing how much I value the family business."

"Ah, that's where you are wrong. I will do that, because so long as you think you have your own little cotton factoring enterprise, you will put its interests above my own."

Elise took a step away but stumbled. Thomas caught her before she fell and then stared at her. Tears were streaming down her face.

"Are you all right, Elise?"

"Yes. No. I'm not all right. I'm angry and exhausted by the charade I've had to put on all evening. I've eaten too much and had too many glasses of champagne. Will you take me home, Thomas? Please? We need to talk about this marriage settlement, but not tonight."

In the carriage, Elise had nothing to say. Under the cover of darkness, she twisted her engagement ring and marveled at how easily it slipped off her finger. It was a beautiful piece —a centered opal in the depths of which colored shafts of light glittered and twisted. Surrounding the center were six smaller diamonds, the whole design resting on a silver band. It was lovely, but she had never felt it was hers. It was a Middleton family heirloom and another sign Thomas's family would own her.

She put the ring on again, then changed her mind. As their carriage pulled into the courtyard of the Beauchene house, Elise clutched the ring in her fist. She accepted Thomas's help to dismount from the carriage. Then she turned to him, took his hand, and placed the ring on his palm.

"You'll need this for the next girl whose life you try to change." She looked at him, no longer shedding tears or shouting at him. "I've enjoyed our friendship, but I cannot marry you, Thomas. We are too different in our values and our aspirations. I wish you well, but farewell."

And with that final comment, she swiveled on her heel and disappeared into the house, leaving Thomas to stare at the cold and lifeless bauble he now held in his hand.

ELISE WORRIED ABOUT TELLING HER MOTHER OF THE BROKEN engagement, but the others would not pay much attention to her love life. The Beauchene family had long valued privacy.

They kept secrets from each other and shared almost nothing of their friendships and social ties. Elise kept her left hand curled in her lap, palm up so as not to display the emptiness of her love finger. I'll wait until things have settled down after the holidays, she decided. But those days stretched into weeks as the doldrums of late winter dragged at everyone's energy levels.

February was notorious for being a foggy month in Charleston, and 1860 was no exception. Thick banks of fog rolled in off the Atlantic to mingle with the smoke of thousands of fireplaces struggling to warm drafty houses. The weak sun was no match for the resulting miasma. People stayed inside as much as they could, huddling by the fires and retiring early to the added warmth of their beds. The Charleston social whirlwind ground to a halt. Visits stopped. Those who had to be outside came inside plagued by coughs and runny noses. Old people succumbed to bouts of pneumonia, and babies cried with the croup.

In the Chalmers Street house, old Mr. Beauchene again fussed about his inability to be out and about. Once the novelty of his wheelchair ramps had worn off, the family insisted that he remain indoors until the weather cleared. Cotton shipments had slowed to a trickle, so Henrietta and Elise spent fewer hours in the warehouse. At the Huguenot Church, Rachel considered planning a spring event, but Valentine's Day was too cold and clammy and Easter came too early to stir up warm feelings. Even Antoine came home early and stayed in after dinner rather than seeking his usual companions in the local taverns.

It was not until the fogs lifted that people realized a blue sky was still a possibility. Shut-ins stretched and reached for the sun like flowers just emerging from winter hibernation. Even Elise felt a new bounce in her step. She had almost forgotten the whole New Year's episode until the day she wandered out to the warehouse to check on their cotton inventory.

The sounds of hammers and saws drew her to the back to investigate. She discovered her Uncle Antoine supervising a crew of black workmen as they built shelves and boxes too small to accommodate cotton bales.

"What's going on back here?" she asked. "Is grandfather planning another of his periodic office rotations?"

"No, no, this is just a slight remodeling of our storage facilities. But I enjoy seeing you back at work full time. I haven't wanted to embarrass you in front of the rest of the family, but I noticed you haven't been wearing your engagement ring. What's going on there, my dear? You haven't lost the ring, have you?"

"No. It's stashed away, I assume, in Mrs. Heyward's jewelry case. Nothing's going on, Uncle Antoine. One doesn't keep wearing an engagement ring when the engagement falls through."

"I see." His eyes narrowed. "I'm not surprised. You were never enthusiastic about the whole idea. Have you told your mother?"

"Mother? I didn't need to tell her. She noticed the missing ring right away."

"I should have known. Henrietta misses nothing. Did she lecture you?"

"No, and she doesn't know the details. I haven't told her, and she hasn't asked."

"How long do you plan to wait?"

"I don't know. Until it feels right, I suppose. I hope you're not getting any ideas about bringing it up at the dinner table."

"No. I don't want to hear the heartbreaking details. I'll keep your secret, if you'll keep mine."

"What? What kind of trouble have you been getting into?"

"Oh, I was thinking of our little carpentry project here. I'd rather not have it discussed at dinner, either."

"Because—"

"Because it's part of a bigger plan. I'm making room here in the back to store guns and—other things."

Now it was Elise's turn to raise an eyebrow at the family's black sheep. "You're not still thinking of getting into the smuggling business, are you?"

"I prefer to think of it as the import/export business."

"Oh, Uncle Antoine. You know mother and grandfather will never allow the Beauchene Company to get involved in blockade-running."

"They will give in once the war starts. I'm trying to get a head start."

"But you don't have a boat."

"A ship," he corrected. "No, I don't, but I have a friend—a business partner, so to speak—who has a remodeled vessel ready for a test run in May. I don't have a blockade-runner, and he doesn't know where to go and what to buy. We plan to pool our resources. We'll be taking his empty blockade-runner out to be sure she's seaworthy. And assuming she is, I'll help him fill her with luxury goods to bring home. We'll store them here until we can sell them, and then we'll split the profit. If I'm right, it won't take many trips to produce enough money to buy a new ship."

"Gracious! That sounds like quite a gamble."

"Maybe so, but worth it. I will not ask the family to approve the venture. I believe in the proverb about asking forgiveness rather than seeking permission."

"So that's our bargain? You don't mention my breaking Thomas's heart, and I don't mention your risking your life over a load of rum and cigars."

"And guns. Don't forget the guns. We'll need lots of those."

Elise shook her head at her uncle's naïveté. "You don't think—"

"That someone will catch us and accuse us of smuggling? That won't happen. We'll be careful. Just don't tell your mother! She's the only one I worry about."

DINNER TABLE DEBATES

April–May 1860
Charleston, South Carolina

*E*lise and Antoine need not have worried that their little secrets would end up as conversation topics around the family dinner table. The possibility of war between the North and the South filled the pages of newspapers all over the country. Father Beauchene, who had always advocated keeping up with the news, came to the table most nights fueled by righteous indignation or frustrated disappointment at the political antics of his countrymen.

"Have you seen the latest?" he would demand as his family settled into their places. The girls soon learned that the easiest way to deal with their opinionated grandfather was to ask him a question and then let him lecture.

One night in early April, Juliette raised a question about President Buchanan and where he stood on slavery. "We've avoided war so far under President Buchanan," she said. "Why isn't he running for a second term of office? He's a Democrat, but he sits on the fence about slavery. He tries to appease both sides which could win him support in both the North and the South. Wouldn't it be better to have him remain in office rather than have a new politician with strong one-sided political views?"

"Fence-sitting is not something politicians do well," her grandfather argued. "First, to answer your basic question, Buchanan is not running for re-election because, back in 1856, he promised not to do so. He made such a point of that promise he can't go back on it now. Besides, if you survey his political views, you'll see he is closer to being a Federalist than he is a Democrat. But the Federalist Party died out in 1816 when they lost several elections. They favored a strong national government and had little faith in the common sense of ordinary men. They were elitist, wanted to keep the right to vote in the hands of a favored few, and were not fans of democracy.

"When Buchanan was running for the presidency, he sided with the South over the question of how new states would come into the union. He favored popular sovereignty as do the Democrats. But try pinning him down beyond that and you'll see how he hedges his bets. He says he opposes slavery, but he believes the Constitution protects slave owner-ship. And on the question of secession, he says nothing gives a state the right to secede from the union. However, when asked about the federal government dealing with secession, he says the president has no right to stop a state from seced-ing. Do you see how that leaves him in the middle, able to agree with anyone who confronts him?"

"Yes, I see that, but he's just trying to keep the peace, isn't he? And avoiding war is a good thing. Wars send thousands of young men to their deaths. Wars destroy property and pit family members against one another. The Beauchene Company would suffer enormous losses if the North burns the cotton crop or stops us from shipping the crop to customers." Juliette's eyes filled with tears as she thought of what was at stake.

"Sometimes war is the only way to settle an argument. Would someone please pass the rice?"

"So, who will the Democrats support if Buchanan isn't running?" Rachel stepped into the discussion.

"Well, that's another part of the problem, ladies. The Democratic Party is splitting apart over that issue."

"How so?"

"The split is again North versus South. The Southern Democrats feel something close to what Juliette was advocating. They want more room to hedge their bets, so they've asked Buchanan to endorse a candidate. His choice is John C. Breckinridge, his own vice president."

Juliette smiled. "That's good, right?"

"No. The only states that support Breckinridge are South Carolina, Florida, and Mississippi. Three states can't win an election. And further, if he appears to be gaining support, someone will mention South Carolina has no popular vote. Our state legislature chooses electors to the Electoral College. Some argue a popular vote elects our legislators. But for most people, our system does not look very democratic."

"Which means Breckinridge is a lost cause?"

"Yes."

"All right, now I'm confused, too." Elise threw up her hands in mock surrender. "Have the Southern Democrats broken away from their own party?"

"Yes. The Northern Democrats are holding a convention this week—right here in Charleston—to choose another candidate."

"Why on earth would they choose to meet in a pro-slavery state?" Henrietta asked. She had not been following this discussion, but a party of Northerners meeting in Charleston was too ridiculous to ignore.

"I don't know," Father Beauchene said. "Perhaps they chose it before the slavery issue became so prominent. But it may not matter. From what I read in our local paper, they're deadlocked with six or eight possible candidates, none of whom has a prayer. They're talking about adjourning and meeting again next month in Baltimore."

"From what I've heard about Baltimore, that's an even worse choice. Maryland sits right on the border between North and South, and renegade bands of thugs outnumber the good citizens of Baltimore. If things come to blows, there's nowhere more likely for a fight to begin."[1]

"True, Henrietta, but at least it will move their fight away from our backyard."

MEANWHILE, ABRAHAM LINCOLN WAS HAVING AN EASIER TIME in the Republican Party. He had gained national prominence in his home state of Illinois when he ran for the Senate against the Democratic incumbent, Stephen A. Douglas. In a series of 1858 debates, Lincoln had taken a strong anti-slavery stance and cast Douglas and his party as supporting an evil cause.

Father Beauchene did not support Lincoln the candidate, but he admired Lincoln the man. When the Republicans opened their convention in May in Chicago, Beauchene followed the reports. Even before the newspapers could carry the story to Charleston, he had dredged up his favorite Lincoln quotes. That first night at dinner, he greeted his granddaughters with a line that Lincoln had made famous in 1858: "A house divided against itself cannot stand," he pronounced.

"You've not become a Republican, have you?" Henrietta rebuked him.

"No, my dear, but it has an eloquent ring to it, doesn't it? And the man is right. Our country cannot continue to prosper when we have such a fundamental split in our values."

"So, Lincoln is advocating war?" Elise grimaced as she asked the question.

"No, you can't label him from a single quote. He has denied he favors war. Again, girls, if you read the newspapers, you'd know more about this. On the day they hanged John Brown for his treason at Harper's Ferry, Lincoln took a stand. He praised the man for his dedication to the idea that all men should be free, but he also condemned violence. He announced that war was not the answer, declaring that the ballot box must rule on slavery."

"And you agree with him?"

"I do."

"But—"

"There are no 'buts,' Elise. Lincoln insists that electing a president who opposes slavery will not cause a war. He even denies that Southern states will secede from the Union if there is a Republican president. He has reminded everyone that, according to the Constitution, Congress is the only body with the right to make laws within territories. These debates, such as the ones over Kansas and other territories, are nothing but rhetoric. People can vote all they want about whether they prefer their new state to be pro-slavery or free. But the law says it lies in the hands of Congress. Lincoln's right again."

NO ONE DOUBTED ABRAHAM LINCOLN WOULD BE THE Republican candidate. He had already stated his preference for his vice president—Hannibal Hamlin, a staunch abolitionist—before the convention started. Their platform was clear. The Republicans were anti-slavery. They insisted on no further extension of the South's peculiar institution. But they would not interfere with slavery any place where it was already legal.

"I don't understand," Elise said. "Why isn't Lincoln worried the Southern states will carry through their threats to secede? He seems to ignore the South."

"As well he might," said Father Beauchene. "It doesn't matter what he says about the South. His name will not appear on the ballot in Southern states, so why should he waste his time? The states that control the Electoral College support him. He can win without caring what the South thinks of him."

"But if the Democrats bring forth a strong candidate—"

"Such as?"

"I don't know. Someone who supports popular sovereignty, like Stephen A. Douglas, I suppose."

"When the Democrats meet this week in Baltimore, that's what they will do. But how can you—or they—think Douglas will have a chance against Lincoln?"

"Well, there must be people in the North who believe new territories should be able to decide for themselves whether they want to condone slavery. Won't some of them turn to the support of Douglas? I remember, it hasn't been all that long ago that you yourself said people wouldn't vote for a man like Lincoln—something about his hands and feet being too big."

"I was wrong. The record of those 1858 Lincoln-Douglas debates proves it. Remember what Lincoln did to the more experienced and eloquent senator from Illinois."

"Which was?"

"He handled him like a suckling pig being prepared for a fancy dinner party. First, he eviscerated him and then roasted him to a crisp. He arranged him on a platter and stuck an apple in his mouth! The same thing will happen again in the coming election."

"What a horrible image." Elise leaned back in her chair and held up her hands in defeat.

Now it was Juliette's turn. "Wait, there's a fourth party, isn't there? This new Constitutional Union Party is also meeting in Baltimore right now. Couldn't their candidate throw a monkey wrench into this contest?"

"With John Bell as chief monkey-wrench thrower? Hah! Not likely. What do you know about him?"

"Not much, I guess. He's from Tennessee, isn't he? That puts him somewhere between the two sides."

"Not at all. He comes from the middle of the country, but he's not a believer in the middle ground. He argues for the sanctity of the Constitution and the need to defend the Union against all threats—"

"Hence, the name of his party."

"Yes, but he doesn't understand a thing about secession. His politics are out of date. His support comes from some old Whigs, who can't admit that time has passed them by, and from the remnants of the Know-Nothings. The less said about them the better! The Unionists seem to believe they can hold off the threat of secession by arguing that it is unnecessary."

"How so?"

"Well, they say the Constitution allows slavery, which puts an end to the discussion. No one believes them—not those who are ready to secede or those who fear that secession will tear the Union apart. You can't make the bogey-man disappear by wishing him away."

"I'll never understand Americans!" Henrietta shook her head in frustration. "To hear you tell it, the election is already a foregone conclusion, so why bother with the vote? Lincoln wins. The Southern states will secede. And before they count the ballots, we'll find ourselves at war with ourselves. You're hopeless, all of you!"

In this dinner table debate, Antoine might have stirred up even more disagreement, but he was missing. No one had noticed at first, but this was the fourth night he had missed dinner.

"Antoine would argue that the election is not all that certain," Father Beauchene pointed out. "He's holding out for a mash-up that will leave no one a clear victor."

"Speaking of Antoine, where is he?" Henrietta asked. "He hasn't been in the office all week. He's not out on some campaign trail, is he?"

There was no answer. Everyone at the table shrugged, except for Elise, who grimaced before she spoke. "He didn't tell you? He's gone off with a business partner—whose name I don't know, so don't ask—to try out a new blockade-runner design."

"Will he never give up that pipe dream!"

"No. He told me about their plan but made me promise not to tell you for fear you would try to stop him."

"And why did he tell you?"

"Because I caught him at the back of the warehouse where he was having the slaves build some wooden crates to hold—uh, to hold whatever the new ship would be carrying."

"Come on, Elise. You've let part of the secret out of the bag already. Where is he going?"

"They're trying for the Caribbean—Havana first, and then Nassau."

"To smuggle home his precious Cuban cigars and Jamaican rum?"

"And guns," Elise admitted.

"Guns? Oh, Heaven help us all! Doesn't he realize that there are high tariffs placed on luxury goods coming in from foreign sources?" Henrietta asked.

"He does," Father Beauchene said. "That's why it's called smuggling. But he would tell you that those tariffs are just another way the North exploits the South to their own profit. That makes disobeying the law a good thing in Antoine's eyes. But it could land him in prison. I don't know whether to hope he succeeds or to pray he fails."

LIKE MINDS

Tuesday, June 26, 1860
Charleston, South Carolina

*T*he Beauchene women reacted to the threat of war in different, but predictable, ways. Henrietta turned her back on further discussions about politics and concentrated on the economic impact of a potential war. She followed market trends, realizing that her father-in-law was correct in his assessment that foreign markets would drive cotton prices to historic highs. She also attempted to get to know the other cotton factors in Charleston. As she did so, she recognized a growing consensus. Fear of a Union blockade encouraged more interest in blockade running. Rumors that the North would try to get their hands on the South's cotton crop led to discussions of an embargo on sales and decentralizing the storage facilities of the current crop. Henrietta was already at war with the North in her own thinking.

Elizabeth Dubois often stopped by the warehouse to discuss similar problems with Henrietta. Her daughter, Susan

Dubois Grenville, worried about two of her children in such a conflict. Charlotte was just seventeen, but she and the young man who had served as her escort for her debutante ball were already discussing a quick marriage. Peter Rogers intended to join one of Charleston's first infantry units. If war came to a head, he predicted it could last a long time. Charlotte might have to wait years for him to come home. If the choice came down to a rushed wedding ceremony or a prolonged engagement, Charlotte and Peter were both in favor of acting now rather than waiting.

Charlotte's brother, Johnny, had caused major family arguments by refusing to consider going to Harvard in the fall. His northern-born father had always wanted his son to follow in his academic footsteps, but Johnny did not want to find himself in Massachusetts if war broke out at home. He and his best friends—the same young men who had played Wise Men in December—now agreed on their academic futures. They would enroll at South Carolina College in Columbia in the fall. There they would become members of an academic cadet corps, combining basic military training with their studies. If war erupted, they would report for duty as a unit. Listening to this litany of troubles had one beneficial effect on Henrietta. She gave silent thanks for her family of girls.

Elise worried about the cotton business, but her thoughts, too, often strayed to the young men of Charleston. Would Thomas turn to soldiering as a balm to his wounded ego, she wondered. She had trouble imagining him as a soldier, but she was sure he would not shirk his patriotic duties. Like many of the young women of Charleston, Elise realized an entire generation of potential husbands might disappear into the jaws of war, never to return. Her heart ached when she thought of that prediction, but she also felt relief. She would be one of many young Charleston women making her own way in the world rather than depending on a husband.

Juliette worried, too, but for different reasons. She had failed to find a teaching job in any of Charleston's private schools because the schools themselves did not know if they would open again when war became a reality. What was a trained teacher to do with her skills? For Juliette, the answer was clear. She had a backyard full of potential students. She turned to her grandfather once again to persuade him to permit her to teach their slaves the basics of reading and arithmetic.

"You admit that war is coming, grandfather, so you cannot deny it will affect our slaves. If the South wins the war, there may be even more stringent laws about teaching slaves to read. This may be their only chance to become literate. And if the North wins, they will be free without understanding how to survive on their own. Either way, the period between now and the war offers an opportunity for our slaves to learn to read. Please let me work with them here in our own enclave. No one will see us, and if war comes, no one will care what's going on in our slave yard."

The old man studied his granddaughter. "You care about this, don't you?"

"Yes, I do. I've known our slaves all my life. They are human beings, not some mandated three-fifths of a person. I know they are intelligent and capable. They have taught themselves to read. This is their chance to get formal training for their children. Please let me try this."

"All right. Do as you will. You may use the empty chambers off the warming kitchen on the ground floor. Start with the youngest children first and see how willing they are to sit still and learn their letters rather than playing in the yard. If that works, you can expand to the older ones."

Juliette prepared for a school opening in the fall. After

putting the slave women to work clearing out the storeroom whose windows would let in fresh air, she asked the carpenters to build benches for her students. But when they asked how many students there would be, she realized she wasn't sure. With a small notebook in hand, she hunted them down. She identified every child old enough to sit still but too small to have assigned duties within the household. Then she had to convince their mothers to let them learn to read.

"Don't that be illegal?" asked one woman. "I heard the law don't say we can't read; it say a white person can't teach us to read. I don't want my son to get in trouble."

"Don't worry. That law is about to disappear, along with several others. I'm just trying to give the black children in our family an early start."

Within a few days, Juliette had enrolled seventeen little scholars. Then she met with the children and their mothers to set the ground rules. School would start at 10:00, and she would ring a small bell on the back porch to let them know it was time. Students were to show up in clean clothes, with faces and hands washed. Shoes were optional. She would provide a healthy lunch for them, and the cooks would deliver it to the warming kitchen by noon. Classes would then resume until three o'clock when children would return to their quarters for a nap. Most mothers agreed to enforce the rules because they made their lives easier, too.

Next came a need for teaching tools. Several private schools in downtown Charleston offered discarded McGuffey's primers and first readers. Teachers showed her how the youngest children could trace letters in the dirt with a little stick or use beans for counting. Supplies of chalk and roofing slates came from construction sites. And in the evenings, Juliette prepared sets of flash cards with words on one side and pictures on the other.

WHILE ELISE THREW HERSELF INTO THE COTTON BUSINESS AND Juliette created a slave school, Rachel took a different path. What we need, she told herself, is something to take our minds off this horrible threat hanging over us. What we need is a party! She took the idea to Reverend Howard.

"It's been six months since our Christmas pageant. I think it is time to get the congregation together again for something fun. How about a Bastille Day picnic?"

"Splendid! Who better to offer the community a French celebration than our own French Huguenot Church? Start with that idea, my dear, and see what activities you can devise. I'll prowl around in the attic and see if there's anything up there you might use. That's where former pastors stored Christmas decorations. Maybe there are other items, too."

"Some French flags would be nice," she agreed. "And you might look for recreational equipment—balls, racquets, board games, things like that."

"I'll do my best," the pastor replied. "Oh, don't forget! We will need fireworks—lots of fireworks. In France, every Bastille Day celebration has fireworks going day and night."

A week later, Rachel wandered through the church grave-yard and the open lawn between the sanctuary and the Huguenot Parish Hall. She was trying to visualize the grounds as a picnic area. Were there enough clear patches of lawn to allow people to bring their own chairs and relax under the trees? Could picnic tables have close access to the kitchen? What if it rained? Was the area near the wheelchair ramp flat enough to allow games? And where inside the city could they have fireworks? These problems kept her from noticing a young man who approached her with some hesitation.

"Excuse me. Have you seen the church secretary anywhere? Reverend Howard sent me to find her."

"That would be me. Can I help you with something?"

"Oh, I thought—or rather, I was expecting someone, uh—"

"Older?"

"Well, yes, I imagined an elderly spinster with her hair in a bun and a high-necked woolen sweater around her shoulders."

Rachel laughed at the image. "A few more years in this job and that's what I'll be. I can feel myself aging every time someone hands me a problem."

"I hope not. You're so pretty," he blurted out and then blushed.

His innocence charmed Rachel. "Why don't we start over? Good morning. I'm Rachel Beauchene, social director for the Huguenot Church and girl factotum around here. Were you looking for me?"

"Oh, I think I've been looking for you all my life." The young fellow was still blushing but he could not take his eyes off this wonderful creature. "Forgive me for interrupting you. I'm Roger Izard St. Croix. My family attends services here, but I've been away at school. I'm a stranger in my hometown."

"Welcome home, then. Where do you attend school? If you've been in Columbia, you may have met my sister."

"No, I'm studying law at Dartmouth."

"In New Hampshire? That's quite a change from Charleston."

"Like black and white—and I'm not referring to the slavery issue."

"Are you finished with your studies now?"

"No, I have another year to go, but my mother wanted me to take a summer break before those grueling final courses. To be honest, though, I'm bored because I know no one in the neighborhood. Mother suggested I might offer my services to the church. And when I asked Reverend Howard if I could help him, he pointed me straight at you and said you could use assistance with a new project."

"He was more correct than he knew. I can keep you busy for several weeks."

"So, what is the project? I saw you walking around the grounds and poking at things. Are you planning some landscaping or a garden?"

"No, no! I'm planning an all-day Bastille Day celebration, one with games and a picnic."

"Is a picnic that complicated?"

"Oh, this one involves several activities beyond eating. That's what I was pondering when you spotted me. I've been looking for the most useable spaces."

"I am at your service. What activities are you planning?"

"Reverend Howard wants games, a picnic supper, and fireworks. 'Lots of fireworks,' he said. But this will be in July. It doesn't get dark until after nine o'clock. My biggest problem is finding enough entertainment to fill the day and last until dark. I can come up with various activities. The problem is putting together a schedule that will keep people here after supper while they wait for the sun to set. When you arrived, I had decided that I should start with the end and work backwards."

"Clever!" He grinned and pointed a finger at her in a mock salute. "But that means you're starting with the most difficult problem of all. As I remember, Charleston is famous for catching fire at the slightest provocation. How can you shoot fireworks in this crowded city without burning it to the ground in the process?"

"I don't know!" Rachel looked crestfallen.

"I have an idea," Roger said. "But it will take some negotiating. Are you up for it?"

"Tell me."

"Better yet. Give me until tomorrow to work out a few details, and then I'll show you."

"I'll try to control my curiosity."

"If I come by tomorrow after lunch, will you be ready to move on to a picnic menu and other details?"

"I should be, yes, and I'm eager to hear your suggestions. I don't wander out here in the churchyard all day, however. You'll find me at a desk in Reverend Howard's outer office."

"I'll see you then!" he grinned at her and gave her a mock salute as he walked off. She couldn't be sure, but she thought she saw him skip a little as he turned the corner.

WHATEVER WORKS

Wednesday, June 27, 1860
Charleston, South Carolina

True to his word, Roger showed up the very next day. He was whistling as he walked, and there was still a skip to his step.

"If you were a cat, you'd be wearing canary feathers." Rachel laughed at his eagerness. "What have you come up with?"

"Well, first, the news. The city fathers are not scheduling a display of fireworks this year for the Fourth of July celebration."

"No! I hadn't heard. Why? What made them decide—?"

"The same problems I mentioned to you yesterday—the dangers of fire and no safe place to set them off."

"Well, I guess that solves our problem. If fireworks are impossible, Reverend Howard will have to settle for a picnic with extra desserts."

"I'm not vetoing extra desserts, but we're not canceling

our own plans. The solution is easy. I'm just offering it to you rather than to them. Come with me."

He led her out to the front of the church and then turned her to look straight south down Church Street. "What do you see?"

"Buildings and water. Not a clear space anywhere."

"Except for the harbor," he pointed out. "And what do you see out there?"

"Boats? Sea birds? Waves?"

"And that ugly mound of concrete at the entrance to the harbor."

"The fort, you mean? It's not even finished. They've been working on it for years, but it's nowhere near complete, and there's no one out there. It's an eyesore."

"But it's a fireproof eyesore. Suppose we could get permission to use it for one evening and send local volunteer firefighters to handle our fireworks. The display would be visible not only from here, but over much of the city. We could call it a gift to Charleston from her residents in the French Quarter."

"Could we get permission?"

"I can arrange that. My father's law firm has been helping the Corps of Engineers get official ownership of the artificial island on which the structure rests. They owe him a favor or two."

"And what about the volunteer firemen? How do we to persuade them to fire the rockets?"

"Easy. Volunteer firemen are like schoolboys who love playing with matches. They also share a love of eating. Look. The German Fire Company is only a block from here. Invite them to the picnic. Offer them all the French food they can eat. They'll be fighting for the privilege of helping with the fireworks. Problem solved?"

"Yes, except for the overriding one concerning the timing.

We can't delay the picnic much beyond six-thirty. The children will be hungry, and their parents will be ready to relax. But we can't keep eating for several hours, either."

"That's easy enough. Once folks have eaten, they'll not want to move. They'll sit and gossip right where they are. And if they get restless, we can do a sing-along. People love that. There's a pianoforte in the hall, isn't there?"

"Yes. And if the church organist won't volunteer to play, we'll find someone else. My godmother's daughter, Susan Grenville, has a portable melodeon in her parlor, and she often entertains the family and guests."

"See? Once you look for solutions instead of worrying about the problems, there's always an answer."

"Maybe, but what about the children? They won't sit around and talk."

"Ah, for them we'll have little fireworks that don't need darkness. We'll hand out sparklers and *serpents* ..."

"Snakes? Not if I'm around!"

"Not live ones, silly girl. I was referring to those folded-up boxes that burn and leave behind long black trails of ash that look like snakes. Didn't you ever ...?"

"No. I grew up in a household of girls, and mother kept us busy with chores like reading books and darning socks. We didn't play outdoors much."

"Poor deprived little ladies! You have much to learn. I promise you, today's children will love their toy fireworks, and that'll keep them busy until dark."

"You have answers for everything," Rachel said. "So where do you see enough open space to hold games in the afternoon, as Reverend Howard has suggested? I can spot a few places for checkers or chess players, but there's not much room to move around among the trees and the new tombstones sprouting up in the church yard."

"What about the area behind the church where people leave their carriages on Sunday mornings?"

"I thought of that, but when I went out to look, the ground is rough—tree roots, holes, patches of thorny bushes, and ... well, lots of horse droppings, too."

"All right, then. There's always City Hall Park."

"Where?"

"That open green space behind City Hall. It stretches along Meeting Street between Chalmers and Broad. You must have walked through there."

"Oh, I know where you mean. It has an iron fence around it, so nobody ventures inside."

"Right! And it's time to put it to better use. The city council designated it as a park a long time ago, but then forgot about it. It's only a two-block walk away from the church. I'll bet we can get permission to use it for the day. The men of the parish can hold a *pétanque* tournament. It has room for two match fields and a children's area for *escargot* and *bilboquet*. We can mark the fields with chalk that will wash away with the first rain. If you announce contests among our parishioners, people will flock there to play or watch."

"Wait! Remember my deprived childhood. *Pétanque* is that game where men throw metal balls at a little wooden one, right? I watched them with my grandfather once. But the children's games you mentioned—*Escargot*? Snails? Why are children's games named for slimy things?"

"Because little boys love messes, and I imagine little girls do, too. *Escargot* is like hopscotch—ever play that?"

"Yes, sometimes."

"All right. *Escargot* is like hopscotch in the shape of a snail."

"A spiral?"

"Yes, and it gets harder as the child moves toward the center because the landing blocks get smaller. I was never good at it because my feet were too big."

"What was your favorite game . . . that other thing you mentioned . . . *bilbo*-something?"

"*Bilboquet*. In English, a ball and cup. A string attaches the ball to the cup. The child tries to throw the ball up and catch it in the cup one-handed. You never had one of those?"

"No, but it doesn't sound very challenging."

"Ah, try it. You'll soon learn how difficult it is. I saw a whole box of those in the church attic when Reverend Howard and I were exploring. We'll have contests, and you can try your hand."

Rachel laughed, but she continued to scribble in the small notebook she kept in her reticule. "You've been a wonderful help, Mr. St. Croix. I'll put these notes into a formal schedule and present it to the Board of Elders tomorrow morning at their weekly meeting. Once they approve it, we can move ahead to get permissions for these borrowed venues."

"When will you know?"

"Oh, right away. Some of them will fuss about never having done this before, but they'll approve it before the end of the meeting."

FOR THE NEXT TWO WEEKS, RACHEL AND ROGER SPENT ALMOST every day together, planning, experimenting with table arrangements, and bargaining with local officials. They visited City Hall, the local fire department, and the Army Corps of Engineers, and in those places, Roger took the lead in the discussions. He introduced himself as an assistant to

Reverend Howard for the summer and gave a nod to Rachel as the church secretary. The officials in charge directed their questions and comments to Roger. Rachel soon learned not to interrupt as the negotiations proceeded. She smiled and copied the details into her ever-present notebook.

At home, however, she vented her irritation. "Why do all Southern men seem to think women can't talk? I've never been so ignored in all my life."

"Why are you surprised? You live in South Carolina, where women don't count for much," Juliette said, looking up from the alphabet flash cards she was making. "And why should they pay attention to you? You can't vote, you don't pay taxes, you can't testify in court, you have no money, and you own no property."

"Right! And none of that is fair!"

"My goodness, Rachel! You sound just like Henrietta when she first arrived here from England." Old Mr. Beauchene shook his head and smiled at her silliness.

"Well, she was right. And look at her. She made sure those rules did not apply to her."

"That's because your grandfather declared me to be a *feme sole,*" Henrietta said. "It wasn't a popular move in the 1830s, but the finances worked for me. You could do the same, if you wished, but it wouldn't affect your dealings with City Hall or the Corps of Engineers. They'll still treat you as only a woman."

"See? There's that dangerous phrase—only a woman— even coming from you, mother. Why can't I walk into City Hall and ask for permission to use their park for a church event without having a man along to speak for me?"

"Spoken as your mother's daughter," Mr. Beauchene replied. If a knowing glance passed between her mother and her grandfather, Rachel did not notice it.

"The important questions have to do with your results," Juliette suggested. "Did you get the permissions you needed?"

"Well . . . yes, we did. They will allow us to use the park all day for free, so long as we don't leave trash lying about and if we remove our playing field chalk marks. The Corps of Engineers gave us permission to shoot off fireworks from inside that half-finished fortress in the harbor. They will even use their boat to transport the fellows managing the displays. And the German Fire Company promised to come to our picnic and help with the children's fireworks, too."

"See, Charleston's business methods work. Would it have gone better if you had been there alone instead of with Mr. St. Croix?"

"No, but—"

"Then you have no room to complain."

Mr. Beauchene nodded with approval at his middle granddaughter's school-teacher's lecture. "I'd be willing to bet when this little picnic is over, Mr. St. Croix will disappear into the background, letting you take full credit for pulling off the affair of the summer, even though you couldn't have done it without him. We raise good Southern boys like that, you see."

Rachel dropped the subject since the family did not share her indignation. She realized they were not the source of the problem. Even if the whole family agreed with her, patriarchal attitudes ruled South Carolina society. The unwritten laws defeated any woman's attempt to change them.

By the next morning, Rachel settled for organizing the dinner. Parishioners offered to provide foods for the picnic supper. Slave women would cook and clean up while their mistresses took full credit. And Rachel offered suggestions for what to bring.

"It will be like a potluck supper, with every family bringing more than enough food to feed themselves. I'll have a list of dishes at the back of the church this coming Sunday morning. The women can volunteer whatever their cooks do well. What do you think of this list?" she asked Roger. "We'll have *salade Niçoise*, olive tapenade, French baguettes, cold ham, assorted cheeses, sliced tomatoes, tiny sweet cornichons, quiche Lorraine, vegetable tarts, *gougères*, warm lentil salad, macarons with raspberry jam, madeleines, and assorted wines. Sound good?"

"Sounds wonderful, except for those items I've never heard of. I explained French games to you. Now it's your turn. What is *salade Niçoise?*"

"It's a lettuce-based salad with anchovies, tuna, boiled potatoes, and green beans. You might say it's a meal in a bowl."

"And *gougères?*"

"Little puff pastries flavored with your choice of grated cheese."

"Tapenade?"

"A spread containing chopped olives, capers, parsley, lemon juice, and seasonings. You can eat it plain or smear it on anything from bread to meats."

"And quiche Lorraine?"

"A custard-like egg and cheese tart baked in a pastry shell, flavored with bits of ham, or even a vegetable such as broccoli. My goodness, Roger, what do you eat in your house?"

"Pretty much nothing but beef, potatoes, and peas. My father is not one to experiment with food. If we get him to come to this picnic, which I doubt, he'll settle for a baguette filled with slices of ham." Then he laughed at the worried expression on Rachel's face. "My father's Irish, through and through. You're planning a party for a neighborhood of Frenchmen. They'll love every bite you serve."

"Even the Germans? You said we should invite the German volunteer firemen, but what if they don't like French food?"

"They're firemen. They'll eat anything. Don't worry. They'll love it."

BASTILLE DAY

July 16, 1860
Charleston, South Carolina

*T*he night before Bastille Day, Rachel had a nightmare about a dead mule ending up on the picnic table. But in the morning, with the sun warm and glinting off the iron tips of the church spires, her spirits soared. By afternoon, City Hall Park was swarming with teams of *pétanque* players drawing lots to discover their match-ups. Children ran and tumbled on the grass, not yet needing any adult guidance to keep themselves entertained. Back in the churchyard, old men claimed their seats at the chessboards, inviting young challengers to try their skills at outwitting years of experience. And in the meeting hall, excited slaves chattered among themselves as they delivered covered dishes and arranged them on the long buffet table. In the kitchen, fresh foods filled ice chests, while cooks preparing their dishes on site assembled their ingredients.

The women of the parish wandered up and down Chalmers Street, debating what to do first. They felt respon-

sible for keeping their cooks on task. They wanted to keep an
eye on the children whose giggles echoed from one end of
the street to the other. And many of them wanted to watch
the *pétanque* games, not so much because they enjoyed being
spectators but because they knew their husbands' good
moods would depend on the outcomes.

Making her way through the early crowds, Rachel smiled
with pleasure at how well everything had turned out. She
had recovered from her earlier fears of disaster and was now
enjoying the day. Roger checked and rechecked his mental
lists of potential trouble spots as he made his way through
the revelers. He and Rachel went in separate directions but
were never too far from one another. If trouble broke out
somewhere, both could step in with solutions.

As the heat took its toll and activity slowed to a more
languorous pace, the soft murmurings of summer gave way to
a rhythmic drumbeat and the steady sound of marching footsteps. From the dock end of Queen Street came a small
parade. Leading the way was the horse-drawn wagon of the
German Fire Company. Then came a squad of uniformed
firefighters carrying a banner proclaiming their name in
German: *Deutschen Feuer Compagnie*. Next, a row of drummers tapped out the cadence for all. In the following row,
four soldiers carrying Austrian Lorenz rifles performed a
series of precision moves. And bringing up the rear came a
band of musicians, most of whom carried brass wind instruments of various kinds. Not quite believing what she was
seeing, Rachel pushed her way to the front of the crowd and
gestured for Roger to join her.

"What's going on? Who are they?"

"Those are the firefighters who will shoot off your fireworks later. Smile and applaud them."

"But those outfits! They look like a band of invading

camel drivers left over from my Christmas pageant." Her voice wavered as she struggled not to cry.

"My dear girl. Those are their new dress uniforms, modeled after those of the famous French Zouaves, who are light infantrymen in Algeria. Elite troops all over Europe have adopted that costume of baggy red trousers over leather boots, topped with a short blue jacket and a red, tasseled fez. It's the latest thing."

"But they aren't infantrymen. They're firemen. Why are they putting on a military display of weapons in the middle of our Bastille Day? I wanted this to be a day to forget all the war talk, and they are beating drums and whirling their guns around."

"Ah, but they are proud soldiers with approval to form a company of the First South Carolina Infantry Regiment under the leadership of Peter Gulliard. They are only volunteering to fight fires until war breaks out and offers them real battles. And this is Bastille Day, Rachel. You need to remember the storming of the Bastille was the start of the French Revolution—a military attack directed against a tyrant's fortress. Guns and drums are appropriate. Besides, I approved it."

"Without asking me?"

"I didn't think I needed to. What they are doing is harmless. And look, they're getting ready to serenade us."

At that moment the band struck up the first chords of *La Marseillaise,* the French national anthem. Their audience stood at attention, and a few voices sang along. Members of the church choir moved to the front of the crowd, and, by the end of the refrain, everyone had joined the chorus:

Marchons! Marchons!
Qu'un sang impur
Abreuve nos sillons!

The people cheered and applauded. Then they took up the chant. "Again! Again, *Encore!*"

The band director looked at Roger for approval, and seeing his nod, gestured to the band to reorganize their music. Band members flipped pages of the small booklets attached to their horns and drained their mouthpieces. Drummers gave a flourish, and the music started again, this time with everyone singing along.

At last the musicians dropped their instruments to their sides, and the firemen on the water wagon worked their pump. They pointed the nozzle of their hose straight up into the air and let loose a spray of cool water. By the time the droplets came falling onto the crowd, they were nothing more than a refreshing mist, but the children raced toward the wagon to see it spout again. The accordions played a polka, and before long people were dancing in the streets.

"You see?" Roger whispered to Rachel, "Everyone's happy. You have nothing to worry about. Your party is a great success."

And so it appeared to be. Hungry folks moved toward the social hall where the buffet now displayed a dazzling array of French delicacies. Rachel and Roger separated again, Rachel to encourage people to enjoy second helpings while Roger supervised the wine-pouring to make sure no one over-indulged. Everything went as planned. Winners of the *pétanque* tournaments accepted their trophies while the sure-footed little fellow who had won the *escargot* contest received a small medal on a ribbon to wear around his neck. Mr. O'Neale proved to be an excellent pianist and soon had his audience singing again. Even the sparklers and *serpents* proved more popular than Rachel had expected.

Then as people drifted out to the streets to await the fireworks, Roger sought Rachel. She saw him coming and grinned at him. Then the smile died on her face as she recognized a woman walking beside him—the same woman who had called her Christmas pageant a disgrace and in poor taste.

"Mother, I'd like you to meet Mademoiselle Rachel Beauchene, the mastermind behind today's festivities."

Rachel spoke around the huge lump in her throat. "Madame St. Croix. How very nice to meet you."

"My pleasure," the woman replied, although her pleasure did not extend to her tone or her sour expression. Instead, she turned to her son. "Roger dear, I have a horrendous headache from all this noise. Would you gather the small carriage from the back and drive me home, please?"

"Now, mother? You'll miss the fireworks."

"Yes, now. I can't bear fireworks. They are so . . . so *bourgeoisie*." Her eyes sparked daggers at Rachel as she turned her back and headed for the door. Roger followed after her, not brave enough to meet Rachel's horrified glance.

The fireworks display delighted everyone, both the picnic attendees and the townspeople on their piazzas. When the last rocket exploded, and the sparkles gave way to real stars, the celebration closed. When the crowds left, Rachel sank into a lonely chair in the social hall, so tired and heartbroken she thought she could not move another step. A few moments later, Roger found her there, head on her arms as she sobbed. "Rachel, dear girl, please don't cry. All is well. You've done an amazing job, and everyone is talking about your talents."

"Your mother's not. To her I'm just the girl who makes messes around here. And why did you bother coming back, anyway? She needs you to soothe her headache."

"I came back to apologize for her and to ask you a question."

"You needn't apologize. I'm sure she wouldn't. Just go home, Roger."

"No, I won't. I've found a woman with whom I could spend the rest of my life. Now I can't bear the thought of losing you. I need you to give me—and my sometimes overbearing mother—a second chance."

"She won't change her opinions."

"Yes, she will. My parents and grandparents play host to an elegant Harvest Ball every year. It's a Drayton tradition, held at Magnolia Plantation. This year it happens early—on September first. They expect me to attend, but I have already told them I will not play the role of a dutiful son unless I can do so with the lovely young lady of my choice on my arm. You will be there as my guest. I'll pick you up in our carriage and dance attendance upon you every moment of the evening. You'll meet the movers and shakers of Charleston society, charm your way through the mandatory cotillions, and dine on the richest of delicacies. And then I'll return you to your castle, a Cinderella princess with her slippers intact because she will have already captured her prince charming. Please say you'll come."

"Your mother will never stand for it." Rachel gave a small laugh that had not a touch of humor in it.

"She needs to see you in that kind of setting to know you are everything I might ever deserve."

"And if she still sneers at me, as she did tonight?"

"Then I will still choose you over her. I've fallen in love with you, Rachel Beauchene. What more can I say?"

"Tonight? Nothing. Let's give this some time. I'll check with my family, and if we have no plans for that night, I will attend your Harvest Ball. But don't label me and don't ask more of me than I can give."

~

DESPITE HER RAGING EMOTIONS, RACHEL SLEPT WELL THAT

night, so well, in fact, that she did not hear the rest of the family leave for church. When she emerged from her room late in the day, her sisters were bubbling over to tell her how complimentary everyone had been. "They loved the band, and the fireworks over the water, and the games —everything."

"All of those were Roger's contributions. Most people enjoyed the day, then?"

"Most? All of them did," Henrietta said.

"Except for Roger's mother, who was as nasty as she was at Christmas. She even labeled our fireworks *bourgeoisie.* Roger had to take her home before they started."

"Some people enjoy being angry. I'm sorry she's disagreeable."

"Me, too. But that reminds me. Roger has asked me to be his guest at their annual Harvest Ball on September first. Is that all right?"

"The famous Harvest Ball? The one at Magnolia Plantation?" Elise's eyes were wide with surprise. "That's High Society stuff."

"I gathered it's important."

"Well, you'll need an elegant gown, but we have plenty of time to arrange that." Henrietta gave her youngest daughter a squeeze, but inside, she felt a shudder of trepidation when she pictured the snobbish and supercilious mavens of Charleston's upper crust snubbing this innocent girl.

It didn't take long for Henrietta's worries to manifest themselves. On Tuesday afternoon, Reverend Howard sent Rachel home from work early to relax. She was in her room, leafing through an issue of *Godey's Ladies' Book* when an unaccustomed racket from downstairs demanded her attention.

Someone pounded on the front door rather than using the knocker. When a servant opened it, an imperious voice demanded to see Miss Rachel Beauchene.

"I don't care if she's resting! I must see her at once. Summon her now!"

Rachel froze, recognizing the tone, if not the identity of the visitor. She was already on her feet, straightening her skirt and smoothing her unruly curls, before the young slave tapped on her door.

"Miss Rachel, there's a white lady downstairs in the parlor who insists on seeing you. What should I tell her?"

"Tell her I will be there in a few minutes."

Rachel forced herself to sit on the edge of her bed. Several deep breaths slowed her heartbeat, and she lifted her chin in defiance. "I shall not let her fluster me," she said out loud.

"Won't you have a seat, Mrs. St. Croix?" Rachel asked as she entered the parlor. "You must be hot and tired."

"I'm never tired, but I am in a hurry, and you have kept me waiting much too long."

"How can I help you?"

"Help me? I don't need your help. I want to tell you something you seem not to understand."

"And that would be —?"

"That you are to stay away from my son. You are not of his class. There are deplorable stains on your pedigree, about which everyone of importance in Charleston is aware. You are not a suitable companion for my son at a high society revelry."

"That's his decision."

"Roger is much too foolish and impressionable. He made an unforgivable social gaffe when he invited you to attend our family's society affair. I have decided he will not be present at that event, and neither will you."

"Again, I would prefer to hear this from him, not you."

"That will be impossible."

"Why?"

"Because his father and I put him on a train bound for New Hampshire this morning. We have decided it will be in his best interest to return to Dartmouth early to get a head start on his studies for the year. Our Roger is not the keenest of students. He needs a long time to learn his lessons."

"But it's the middle of summer!"

"You need not concern yourself. We have arranged housing and tutors to keep him focused on his lessons until classes begin. He also understands that he is not to return to Charleston."

"But the holidays—"

"—will offer extra reading time."

"Graduation?" Rachel shook her head. "He can't stay at Dartmouth forever."

"Upon the successful completion of his law degree, we have arranged for him to proceed to Annapolis, where he will embark on a crash course to earn his naval commission. The Navy will assign him to the office that directs courts martial and other disciplinary matters requiring legal disposition. He will not return to Charleston unless he agrees to certain requirements. We expect him to propose to a suitable girl of our choosing and consummate a marriage that will benefit our entire family."

"That's barbaric! How can you do that? Why would he agree?"

"He has agreed because he now understands that we will disown him and cut him off without a farthing unless he does as we say."

"Roger wouldn't—"

"He has. I'll see myself out. I will have no further reason to see you again." The woman's footsteps echoed across the floor Then the door slammed behind her.

Juliette soon popped into the parlor. "Who was that old harridan?" she asked. "Was she still trying to storm the Bastille?"

Rachel shook her head. Then, as if someone had pulled a plug and drained every bit of strength from her spine, she collapsed onto the floor, tears washing down her cheeks.

A HOUSE DIVIDED

From the first days of her arrival in Charleston, Henrietta had tried to understand her husband's country. She obeyed its laws and learned about its history. She honored its traditions and respected its cultural heritage. Above all, she delighted in its ability to open its shores to all comers and then transform them into American citizens.

By the late eighteenth century, The United States of America comprised a colorful mosaic of regions and peoples, all held together by a fragile cement of shared goals. There were dour New England Puritans, intent on building the perfect, God-like "City on a Hill" and wandering tribes of natives who had found successful ways of living on this untamed continent. Hard-headed Dutch businessmen had pulled off the deal of the millennium by trading pretty baubles to other native tribes for Long Island, where they still dominated New York, a city of international importance.

Peace-loving Quakers maintained their austere but comfortable lifestyle in Pennsylvania by encouraging the still rebellious Scotch-Irish to move further west. French planters pulled their land-holdings together to form Gallic enclaves from South Carolina to Louisiana, while the descendants of Spanish explorers moved westward to expand their territory. And in states like Virginia, aristocratic European families upheld their cultural standards even when their neighbors turned out to be the dregs of society sent off to settle in something resembling a penal colony like Georgia.

They shared common goals—political independence, freedom from oppression, and an equal opportunity for a fresh start for everyone. But what the early settlers of the new country did not expect was the disturbing reality that their new political unity would arise on the backs of the less fortunate. American institutions and their impressive new buildings grew from the labor of people earlier settlers thought of as heathenish Africans, lazy Irish, greasy Italians, slant-eyed Chinamen, and other good-for-nothings. The American ideal of equality was already crumbling.

By 1860, the mosaic was in great danger of coming apart. Individuals of all shapes and sizes complained when their fresh start in life did not bring them any more success than their old ways. The goals were still there, but they had taken on new definitions. The fragile bonds of unity cracked under the strains of regional differences and ideological arguments. Some still praised their independence from the bonds of continental Europe while others saw the federal government as a threat to local independence. Some deplored the practice of human slavery while others chafed at the debased subjection of states to congressional rulings. Abolitionists demanded instant equality, enforced by the federal government, for all peoples, despite their skin color or national origin. Proponents of States' Rights demanded a more local form of decision-making about such matters as the legality of slavery. The North emphasized the word "United" while the South stressed the "States."

Political discussions and the threat of war overtook every element of society as the election of 1860 approached. Henrietta spent more and more time contemplating the beliefs and motivations of her family. The mosaic pattern repeated itself in conversations at the Beauchene dinner table, for the family was more of a patchwork quilt than a carefully crafted design. At its base was Pierre Beauchene, seventy-five-year-old founder of the family business and fortune. When Henrietta arrived in Charleston in the 1830s, Father Beauchene was at the peak of his power. He was a dyed-in-the-wool (or a dyed-in-the-cotton) proponent of slavery. When she questioned his treatment of one of the household staff, he had a stock answer: "This is the way we do things in the South, girly. He's a slave. Get used to it!"

Now, Henrietta realized, Father Beauchene had mellowed. He had granted freedom to only one of their slaves, but overall, his treatment of those he enslaved had taken on a much more benevolent attitude.[1] She could see that fact reflected in the kindness and gentleness with which the slaves treated him now that his physical infirmities had made him more dependent upon their care. His politics, too, had changed. He often remarked that he liked that "Lincoln fellow."

"Lincoln's sensible," he said. "He sees both sides of an issue. And he's a good man. I'd like to get to know him. He'd be a good friend, I'll bet. I'd like to have dinner with him sometime. The conversation would go on for hours. The trouble is, he thinks everyone is as good and intelligent as he is, and that's where he makes a mistake. I like him, but he's wrong. If he's not careful, he will lead us straight into a war. That's why I wouldn't vote for him." Henrietta knew Mr. Beauchene's public support went to Breckenridge as an advocate of States' Rights and the *status quo*.

Henrietta looked at herself as an outlier in the family. She came to Charleston as the nineteen-year-old English bride of Pierre Beauchene's oldest son and heir. She had grown up in the rarified air of Oxford where her father was the Keeper of Medieval Manuscripts at the Bodleian Library. But all her British education and cultural exposure could not prepare her for the strange world of Charleston, South Carolina.

Henrietta hated slavery; the family provided her with personal slaves to do her every bidding. She believed in women's equality; Charleston law treated her as less than a person. As a woman, she could not vote, speak in public, work at a paying job, own property, or act without her husband's permission. She had always made friends with ease; here, the rules of high society shunned her for having been born elsewhere. Her political views—which she could never express—sided with the federalists, with the abolitionists, with those Northerners who upheld constitutional restrictions on all states. If she could have voted, she would have been a staunch Lincoln supporter, not because he was likable but because he was right.

She often wondered what her late husband would think of the current political upheavals. She'd never talked about such things with him, but she assumed that he would have assimilated the attitudes his father displayed during his children's formative years. That meant Julien would oppose any talk of freeing slaves or abolishing slavery. He would not have tolerated praise of that rabble-rouser, Abraham Lincoln. In that, she knew, he would follow his younger brother's fire-eating political views rather than those of his father.

Then there was Antoine. The thought of her brother-in-law made her cringe. And Antoine was often cringe-worthy. He was a womanizing wastrel, a drunkard, a reckless gambler, a ne'er-do-well. He was always the second son, the one who never measured up to his wonderful older brother. Antoine quit trying to succeed at an early age. He became a seeker of pleasure, acting on the spur of the moment without regard for the consequences. As a result, he remained a man-child, still living under his father's roof at fifty. Even when his brother died, and he became his father's only living son, Antoine did not grow into that role. He decided he would be a blockade-runner as soon as war broke out. And, in his view, war could not come soon enough. No presidential candidate could match the extremes of Antoine's viewpoint.

Antoine wanted secession. If he had his way, he would split the Union, form a separate country that promoted slavery, and declare an immediate war. Then, according to Antoine, when the Union tried to blockade the South, he could spring into action and break through the blockade with a specially designed ship. He would continue to sell cotton by trading it for a steady supply of Cuban cigars and Jamaican rum, which he would then sell to Southerners at a tremendous profit for his own pocket. His political hopes lay with the South Carolina legislature, whose representatives were in favor of secession and the complete legalization of slavery.

Rounding out the dinner table most evenings were Henrietta's three daughters. Not one, she realized, understood much about politics. "I should have raised them better," she scolded herself. "I should have lectured them on political ethics and seen to it they developed a social conscience. Instead, I have been so busy trying to hold Father Beauchene's company together that I have left their education to the lackadaisical efforts of Southern society. Their interests are introspective and personal. When we talk about the coming of war, all they want to know is how it will affect them."

Her musings and self-incrimination continued long after the family left the table. In the wee hours of the night, Henrietta's conscience still lectured her about her failures as a mother. "The dangers of war don't seem to bother Elise. She worries most about the business. I suppose, if Antoine gets his way about his blockade-runner, she will support the Southern efforts to keep the cotton trades going. But as far as I can tell, she hasn't thought what it will mean for the South to lose an entire generation of young men. She doesn't look to the future or her responsibilities to future generations. Pity.

"Juliette has the better social conscience about such matters. At least she is doing something about the plight of the slaves. If she can teach these little ones to read and write, she will have prepared them for the day when the country emancipates them. That's good, although she doesn't understand that politics will have a great role to play in the eventual outcome of any effort to abolish slavery. She worries about it, but her vision is narrow rather than broad.

"And there's Rachel, who may not even know there's an election campaign going on. For a while earlier in the summer, I thought she might show an interest, but since Bastille Day . . . well, better not to go there. The child has had unfortunate experiences. First, the St. Cecilia Society rejected her, and now a boy's parents quashed her first real romance, both because of a blemish on her pedigree. The blemish is real enough, but it would do no good to tell her what it is.

"She won't talk . . . hasn't done so since the day Mrs. St. Croix sailed out of our parlor, leaving the poor girl to dissolve in tears. She holds me responsible for knowing about this so-called blemish and refusing to tell her what it is. But I dare not reveal the truth. She is a fragile young thing, still unsure of her own abilities or her role in this world. The only place she feels safe is here at home, surrounded by family. Can I take that away from her, too? Never!"

Henrietta's worries were real enough, but the problems of the political and economic spheres continued to distract everyone from finding solutions to their personal concerns. At the Beauchene Company's warehouse, conflicting responses to the threat of war had everyone confused. When the cotton factors of Charleston looked at the business reports of the day, they were optimistic. From their point of view, even the talk of war helped business. As they neared the end of 1860, cotton prices had risen from an average of thirty-four cents a pound to forty-seven cents a pound. For a single bale of cotton weighing perhaps five hundred pounds, that was an increase of sixty-five dollars, equal to over a months' salary for the average city worker. The growing demand for cotton had raised the sales figures for 1860 to 15.6 million pounds. Those enormous increases could carry most factoring companies through several bad years.

The downside to the threat of war, however, was the possibility that the North might cut off all trade between the ports of South Carolina and their European markets. And if the war continued for more than a year or two, those high prices and high demands would force European textile markets to turn to other sources for their raw materials. What then for the fortunes of families like the Beauchenes? Could they circumvent a blockade? Antoine was sure that would work. Could a total embargo on trans-Atlantic shipments force England to enter the conflict and side with the South? Several of the Beauchene Company's competitors advocated that approach. Even the local paper jumped into the discussion by warning cotton growers not to ship their cotton to Charleston because it was too easy a target for Northern aggression. "Cutting off one's nose to spite one's face," Father Beauchene called that recommendation.

If Lincoln is right about a house divided not being able to stand, what hope is there for us, Henrietta wondered. Not only are North and South on opposite sides. The South contains internal divisions. If the enemy does not destroy us, we shall sink our own efforts.

ELECTION DAY JITTERS

Late October 1860
Charleston, South Carolina

*A*s the November election day approached, Father Beauchene grew quieter. Henrietta worried that his health was deteriorating. Sometimes he was tight-lipped over some foolish political statement that made the papers. On others, she could tell his worries were more personal and emotional. One night, he looked around the dinner table and sighed.

"Has anyone heard from Antoine?" he asked.

The girls met the question with shrugs and soft denials. They did not want to discuss it. Henrietta heard the plea in a father's voice, however, and reached over to touch his hand.

"You mustn't worry about him. You know Antoine. He thinks of no one and nothing other than his own personal interests. It would never occur to him to send one of us a reassurance he is doing well."

"But it's been—what?—a month, or more. I didn't worry

for the first couple of weeks, but he said it was just a shake-down cruise of local ports."

"Remember. He told Elise they might try for Havana and Nassau."

"Much longer voyages, with all that empty ocean, I know. But it's the middle of hurricane season. They could disappear in the middle of a storm. Davy Jones' locker may have claimed them, and we'd never know."

"There hasn't been a single Atlantic hurricane this year, father. The only severe storms have been a couple that developed in the Gulf of Mexico and headed for Louisiana."

"It doesn't take a landfall hurricane to sink a ship."

"No, but you need not worry. Like a bad penny, he'll turn up one of these days."

"Antoine's a mess. I'm aware of his faults. But he's my son, Henrietta. My only son, now. And I can't bear the thought of losing him."

Talking about the unknown accomplished nothing, the granddaughters knew, but they also understood that Father Beauchene needed to vent his concerns. The whole purpose of Antoine's trip, Elise reminded her grandfather after dinner, was to prove that the new blockade-runner could sail at will in the Caribbean without detection. He wouldn't reveal where they were.

"I hope you are right, dear."

THEN, JUST A FEW DAYS LATER, THE QUESTION RESOLVED ITSELF. Henrietta and Father Beauchene arrived at the warehouse at dawn, as was their custom on Mondays, to catch up on any new shipments or messages. As Nate maneuvered the carriage to the loading dock and its ramp, they discovered that this usually-deserted alley bustled with activity. A line of swarthy-skinned laborers, each with a wooden box on his shoulder, was winding its way from the wharf to the back door of the Beauchene warehouse. And there, leaning on the doorframe and chewing on a thin cigar, stood Antoine. His sunburn turned him almost as dark as the workers. He had a colorful cloth wrapped around his brow as if to keep the sweat out of his eyes. His shirt was a loose garment with billowing sleeves, and he had tucked his pants into boots that almost reached his knees.

"Good Lord," Henrietta said. "He has become a pirate!"

Father Beauchene struggled to position his wheeled chair so Nate could lower him to the ground. "Get me down from here!" he ordered Nate. "My son is home!"

Antoine came to the end of the ramp and helped propel the chair toward the warehouse door. He rested a hand on this father's shoulder and grinned down at him. "Had you about given me up for lost?"

"Several times over!"

"You needn't have worried. I'm invincible, you know!"

"No, you are not! Where have you been?"

"The Caribbean, sailing around with no one spotting us or detaining us. And we spent a good deal of time in Nassau, waiting to clinch a lucrative business deal."

"While I imagined you dead or rotting in a prison cell somewhere."

Antoine shook his head and laughed. "I have to admit, I think I remember spending a night or two in jail, but for nothing serious—just drunk."

"It's not funny."

"Well, it was."

"I hope it was worth it."

"See these fellows moving crates? They might as well be bringing chests of pure gold. You're seeing a small fortune."

"Of your precious cigars and liquor?"

"Some of that, sure. I wanted to bring home enough samples to win orders from every private club and every wealthy man's house in Charleston. But the real value lies in the chests of Lorenz rifles and their ammunition—just what our new government will need once the war starts."

"You're still convinced that it will come down to war?"

"It has to, father. That's the only solution. And I have the weapons our state will need to enforce its independence. This is the real reason we are so late in returning. Once we reached Nassau, we learned that a ship carrying Austrian weapons was inbound from the continent. We waited for it and were first in line to purchase a few weapons."

Henrietta had been walking behind the wheelchair, but she now stepped forward to catch Antoine's attention. "How did the ship perform, Antoine? Did it satisfy your requirements?"

"Oh, she's a beauty! She creeps her way through shallow channels you'd swear were impassable. She doesn't use much fuel, and there's more cargo room than you'd expect by looking at her from the outside."

"Did the ship meet the expectations of your business partner, too?"

"Well, yes, and no. A funny development there. Zack's been building boats ever since he was a tot running around in his father's shop. He knows what he's doing when he's drawing the design on paper. But put him in a real ship—on a body of real water—and he loses it."

"What? Frightened?"

"No, seasick. The minute the ship left the dock, he was hanging over the railing, throwing up everything but his socks. I've never seen someone turn green the way he does. The only way we could make progress was to feed him a few strong shots of whiskey and put him to bed before we untied from the dock. He'll never make a blockade runner."

"What will happen to the ship?"

"For the time being, he's willing to let me play with it a little. But then, I imagine he'll sell it. He can still build great ships, but he can't sail any of them."

"Are you going to buy it?"

"That'll depend on how much money this haul brings in, and how soon I can sell it off."

They had reached the warehouse door, and Antoine pulled it all the way to one side to let the wheelchair pass through. The squeaking of the door on its track elicited a response from somewhere deep in the building.

"Hola! Hola!"

Henrietta jumped and stared at Antoine.

"Hola! Hola! Lift a leg there, Johnny boy!"

"Who is that?"

"Ah! That's just Pedro."

"Pedro? Someone you brought back with you?"

"Well, you might say that."

A fluttering sound followed, along with a gust of air as something brushed past Henrietta's head and settled on Antoine's shoulder.

"Oh, Antoine, you didn't! You bought a parrot?"

"Ah! This big beauty is much more than a parrot." Antoine admonished her by shaking a finger in her face. Then he stroked the glossy feathers, pointing up their varied colors of green, yellow, and red. "Pedro is an old soul, imprisoned in the body of a bird and wise beyond our years—yours and mine. He insists on having his way, and he's ready for any activity a human can think up. You should have seen him the day when we sampled tropical fruit punches in an outdoor cafe. He insisted on eating the decorative fruits suspended in the glasses. Before long he was a drunken parrot. He whistled at the girls walking by, but he'd stagger and fall off my shoulder if they approached him."

"And just where will he be living?"

"Well, in the warehouse for now. He'll make a great watch-parrot. If I ever buy a ship, he'll come aboard with me, but until then he can keep guard over my inventory. Can you imagine a petty thief sticking a greedy paw into one of these cases and being attacked by Pedro?"

"I can also imagine that Calico Cat may have something to say about a loud angry bird moving into her territory."

"And Pedro will have an answer. I'm already teaching him to say, 'Damned Cat!' and he'll soon learn to mimic your sweet voice. It will drive the cat nuts—she'll come running for your lap and find only a parrot."

WITH ANTOINE HOME, POLITICAL ARGUMENTS ONCE AGAIN surged around the Beauchene dinner table. Father Beauchene grumbled that South Carolina's lack of a popular election disenfranchised its citizens. He admitted that he had voted for the state legislators who would cast the electoral votes, but their campaigns had come long before the 1860 election focused on slavery and the threat of secession.

"One man's vote on a single issue should not count as a vote for or against all other positions held by legislative candidates," he fussed. "What if I want to vote for Lincoln?"

"Everyone would know how you voted when you picked up your ballot. They'd run you out of town—maybe even out of the state," Antoine replied. "There's nothing wrong with our system. It's more efficient than requiring everybody to go to the polls again."

"The whole system seems wrong," Henrietta said. "You have four candidates, three of whom are against slavery but with different approaches to dealing with it. And a single candidate, whom the current president designated, represents the pro-slavery side. You talk about democracy, but more and more I suspect you don't have a clue about what the word means."

"What we have is better than having a hereditary monarchy," Antoine countered, throwing a defiant glance at Henrietta.

"You Americans made that decision eighty years ago. You still can't figure out the alternative to monarchy, thus revealing your political ignorance."

"Now, Henrietta, don't let the boy rile you. It's bad enough that this election will not yield a consensus—not with three Republicans running against each other. The decision about secession will overrule the election—no matter what the results are."

"The election is a formality? It won't decide anything?"

"We've already decided," Antoine announced. "We've been fighting the same issues for thirty years. Northern politicians refuse to grant states the right to secede. They've passed laws that keep Southern families from traveling in the North with their slaves. They've taxed our only commodity but refused to spend any of that revenue to the benefit of the South. And they have insulted us by insisting that slavery is not an economic necessity but only a great and mortal sin. If we now act to uphold our honor against the insults and accusations of the North, we have good reason to do so—election or no election."

Thus the discussions continued, often deteriorating into acrimonious accusations. On one occasion, Henrietta snarled at Antoine as they left the dining room. "It is nice to have you home again, brother-in-law. Without your nastiness, we had nothing to argue about."

"It will get worse. Just wait until Election Day."

UNIONS DISSOLVED

November 6–December 20, 1860
Charleston, South Carolina

*A*ntoine's prediction was accurate, as everyone knew it would be. On November sixth, no one voted in South Carolina, except for the state's already chosen electors, but that did not mean that Southerners were going about their normal business. Hundreds of people gathered outside the newspaper office and stared through the window to watch that new-fangled telegraph machine jump into action. Each time it did so, an ink-stained young clerk came to the door and read out the report: "583 votes for Lincoln in Nashville; 627 for Douglas, 2 for Bell, none for Breckinridge." And each time, the announcement elicited both groans and cheers.

Around the Beauchene dinner table that evening, Father Beauchene treated the family to one of his diatribes on the errors of the present age. On this momentous day, his wrath fell on that telegraph machine.

"Folks will regret the day that infernal gadget appeared.

What good is it? It reports the news of the moment, but five minutes later the information changes."

'Lincoln has a lead of five hundred votes.' People cheer.

'No, Douglas just passed him.' Those who cheered now moan while other groups take up the cheer.

'Now a report from Florida shows Breckinridge with a thousand votes.' The locals cheer.

'No, Texas just reported 1200 for Bell.' A small group at the back claps.

'Here's a report from New York. Lincoln has over 50% of the vote.' The Lincoln supporters smile.

"And on it goes. No report is reliable, and no one knows what any of it means. Emotions surge and fisticuffs break out among neighbors. All for nothing."

"But, Father, as soon as the tallies are in, we'll know the results."

"And you think it's a good thing? Mark my words. We'll come to regret that, too."

"Why? It's helpful to know the outcome right away."

"No, it's not. Without this kind of instant news, it took days—sometimes weeks—for election officials to announce the final decision. And by the time the word came out, all those overwrought emotions stirred up by the voting process had faded behind a slew of other problems—a flooded basement, a child with smallpox, a rebellious slave, some small wild animal taking bites out of the ripening tomato crop. By the time the newspaper printed the final tally, it didn't seem to matter much. The losers said, 'Wait till next time,' and the winners woke up to the realization that now they would have to deliver on all those campaign promises."

"Well, this time we Southerner losers will not say, 'Wait till next year.' We will act," Antoine said. "Lincoln may well win the election, but we won't let him keep us from seceding."

"That's what I'm talking about! You hotheads will act out of anger, and the rest of us will wake up to discover that losing an election means war. Samson, wheel me back to my office. I've had more than enough conversation for tonight."

THE GENERAL ASSEMBLY IN SOUTH CAROLINA AGREED WITH Antoine's interpretation. Within three days they declared their intention to secede from the Union because Lincoln's election was 'a hostile act' against the Southern states. They called for a convention to take up the question of secession and set December sixth as the day to elect delegates to that convention.

On December seventeenth, the delegates convened at the Baptist Church in Columbia and took just one vote—South Carolina would secede. The convention then moved to Charleston, explaining that there was a dangerous outbreak of smallpox in Columbia. Father Beauchene quipped that they preferred a city where they knew they would find better accommodations and food. Antoine wanted to hear the convention's decision, and he urged his father to accompany him.

"The meeting is in Institute Hall, with plenty of room for an audience. I can push your wheeled chair up Church Street and then over Queen to Meeting, and we'll be there. We might even get a front-row seat because of that chair."

"You know I hate being seen in this contraption, and I will

not use it to finagle a better view. No, you go, and then come home to tell us about it."

The convention made short work of creating an "Ordinance of Secession." When the *Charleston Mercury* published it on December twentieth, South Carolina became the first state to secede from the Union. They would explain their decision within a day or two.

That Thursday evening, Father Beauchene fidgeted as the family assembled for dinner. Samson, his faithful attendant, tried to get him to relax by bringing him a shot of his favorite whiskey, but it seemed to make him worse. His face flushed, his fingers rearranged the silverware, and he mumbled to himself. When Antoine arrived, Father did not even give him time to sit down.

"So, talk, boy! What did those fools we elected to decide our fate have to say for themselves today? Did they come up with any good reasons for their declaration of secession?"

"They called the new document 'The Declaration of the Immediate Causes Which Induce and Justify the Secession of South Carolina from the Federal Union.' Then they identified several examples. First, they defined 'hostility.' The refusal of Northern states to enforce the Fugitive Slave Acts proves their hostility.

"Constitutional claims came next. They argued that the North ignores the U.S. Constitution, Article 4, when they refuse to return runaway slaves to their rightful owner, thus refusing to recognize the rights of property guaranteed by the Constitution. Another clause says the U.S. Constitution guarantees the right of citizens to abolish a government that becomes destructive of the founders' goals."

"Harrumph. A fine mess that is. They are using the constitution of the government they wish to destroy to defend their right to do so? And how can they defend slavery by quoting a document that guarantees inalienable rights to all people, including their right to freedom and equality? That makes no sense."

"Maybe not, Father, but the gentlemen who are running this show seem to think the arguments are strong and justified."

"What strikes me as most odd in this whole situation is that those who wish to secede seem intent on recreating the same government they intend to destroy," Henrietta said.

"How so?"

"Well, in the American Revolution, your leaders did away with such ancient English customs as peerages, lords, and commoners, a hereditary monarchy, and a parliament that could only discuss, not solve, problems facing the country. Many of those changes were long overdue. And the new system you put into effect reflected an ancient model of a Republic, with lawmakers who represented the people and offered the wisdom of old age and experience rather than the single requirement of property ownership. Those were revolutionary changes. But this plan of secession offers nothing new. You call your new country the Confederate States of America. And what does Confederate mean?"

Antoine shrugged. "Beats me, but it sounds good."

"It means 'united,'" she said. "Didn't you learn anything in school? The gentlemen who are running this show intend to duplicate everything about the United States—House of Representatives, Senate, Supreme Court, Army and Navy, even the almighty U.S. dollar by substituting the word Confederate for United. It's a copycat government, not a revolutionary one."

"And what would you suggest?"

"How about a matriarchy?" Elise asked. "Put the women in charge, like ancient civilizations. The world would be a much more peaceful place. There could be a small force of women warriors in case of an emergency, but the women would make the laws and the men would do the physical labor. And that would do away with the need for slavery, too."

"I'll vote for you!" Juliette agreed.

"I don't think I'd better tell you about the final argument the Convention intends to put forth," Antoine said.

"Why not?"

"Because it uses religion. They intend to argue that the Bible supports slavery as the natural order of things. Therefore, good Christians support slavery, and those who argue against it reject the Bible and Christianity."

"Good heavens! How bizarre! They can't believe anyone will—"

"They do. What better argument can you make in politics than proving that your opponent is an atheist? That's why I was reluctant to mention it. Now you'll have us all worshipping fertility goddesses from the safety of your matriarchy."

"Enough banter, children! This is a serious matt—" Father Beauchene grimaced and raised a shaky hand to his head. "Oh, I have such a pain—" Then his chin fell forward to his chest, and he was silent.

Henrietta was the first on her feet. "Samson. Take him to his room at once and see if you can get him onto the bed. Antoine, go for a doctor. And girls, ask the servers to clear the table. Then stay out of the way unless we call for you." She rushed through the door and followed Samson with his unmoving passenger.

By the time Henrietta and Samson transferred Father Beauchene from his chair to the bed, his situation was clear. The left side of his face hung in an unnatural downward twist, his lower lip slack and drooling. The muscles on his left side were flaccid. Moving his body was like positioning a rag doll. The outward shape was there, but not the framework to hold it in place.

Dr. Eastgate confirmed Henrietta's worst fears. "Mr.

Beauchene has suffered a massive cerebral hemorrhage, signaled by the intense pain he suffered at the table. The bleeding has damaged his brain. He will not recover the movement he has lost, nor will he ever regain consciousness. Nothing will help him. Keep him warm and comfortable until he passes. I suspect that will not be long in coming."

Pierre Beauchene died in the early hours of December twenty-first. Because of the nearness of the holiday season, the family held only a brief visitation at the house, followed by his interment in the family plot on the day before Christmas. His business clients learned of his passing only after the event, so condolences continued to come into the business office for months afterward.

There was no Beauchene Christmas celebration, and no one noticed. The family mourned, each cherishing a separate set of memories that had defined the family patriarch for them. And each of them felt relief that Father Beauchene had not lingered to suffer the horrors about to engulf his beloved South.

On the third day of January, Williams Middleton, the family lawyer, made his way to the Chalmers Street house to read the will he had kept on file in his office. It contained only a few surprises:

I, Pierre Lefebvre Beauchene, of the City of Charleston and State of South Carolina, weak in body but of sound and disposing mind and memory, declare this to be my last Will and Testament in manner and form following,

I give my soul into the hands of Almighty God my Creator and my body for burial in a decent and Christian-like manner in the cemetery of the St.

Philip's Church in Charleston at the right hand of the body of my beloved wife, Elise Roget Beauchene.

I declare the following disposal of my worldly goods and responsibilities:

To my legal heirs, my son Antoine Georg Beauchene and my daughter-in-law Henrietta Ainesworth Beauchene, I leave the family home, Oak Hall, on Chalmers Street, this city, share and share alike. While the said inheritors may have full use of the property to whatever purposes they so choose, they may not sell said property or any portion thereof. At the death of one inheritor, the surviving inheritor may continue to hold the property with the heirs of the deceased. When both named inheritors have passed, the property will devolve to the children of my late son Julien Roget Beauchene and the said Henrietta Ainesworth Beauchene, to wit: Elise Antoinette Beauchene, Juliette Louise Beauchene, and Rachel Marie Beauchene, share and share alike.

Regarding our family business, The Beauchene Company, Factors of Fine Cotton, I reaffirm the joint ownership of the company by Henrietta Ainesworth Beauchene, who holds fifty-one percent of the stock, and Antoine Georg Beauchene, who owns forty-nine percent of the stock. However, by this, my last Will and Testament, I lift all restrictions placed by me or by my assigns upon the use or sale of such stocks by my son, Antoine Beauchene. By the terms of her husband's will, Henrietta Beauchene's shares in the company must remain entailed to her daughters.

To my son, Antoine Georg Beauchene, I bequeath all monies left in my public accounts after all my just debts, funeral expenses and charges of this my Testament have been in the first place paid and discharged. I also bequeath to him my personal effects, including the contents of my jewel case.

To my daughter-in-law, Henrietta Ainesworth Beauchene, I bequeath the attached key, which will unlock the contents of my safe box, including the monies, property deeds, and stock holdings in it.

I now nominate and appoint Williams Middleton of the City of Charleston Executor of this my last Will and Testament. I now revoke and make void all former wills by me made and declare this only to be my last Will and Testament, In Witness of which, I the said Testator, have set my hand and seal this seventeenth day of January AD one thousand eight hundred and fifty-nine.

[signed] Pierre Lefebvre Beauchene. [seal]

HIDDEN TREASURE

January 3, 1861
Charleston, South Carolina

When Williams Middleton had finished reading the will, he removed his spectacles and polished them on his cravat. He looked around the room and asked what he hoped would be a rhetorical question.

"Do any of you need a further explanation of the terms of the will?"

"What does this key open?" Henrietta asked.

"I presume it opens the safe box to which the will refers, but Mr. Beauchene did not elaborate."

"Well, I, for one, did not even realize he had a safe box," Antoine said. "Does anyone know what that is, or where it is?"

"I suspect he did not want you to know," the lawyer said. He glared at Antoine to tell him his question was out of line.

"But he left the contents to Henrietta, and she doesn't know where it is, either."

"If you don't know, Mrs. Beauchene, I suggest you ask his personal slave."

Henrietta sighed. Despite her grief, she felt a wave of resentment building. The man is dead, but he's still playing games with the family, she grumbled to herself.

After Mr. Middleton left, Henrietta sent for Samson. "Do you know anything about a safe box that belonged to Master Beauchene?"

"Yes'm, but I'm not supposed to tell anyone who doesn't have the key to the box."

Henrietta held the key up to his scrutiny. "This key?"

"Who gave you that?"

"His lawyer, when he read the will this morning."

"Then I can get the box for you, but it has to be in private. Come to Massa Beauchene's office after two o'clock this afternoon."

At two o'clock, Henrietta stood outside the office, fidgeting and still resentful. She had hated this room ever since she first arrived in Charleston. It was her father-in-law's inner sanctum. It smelled of tobacco, whiskey, and old leather chairs, dust, and books with crumbling bindings. No one entered without permission, and that permission came only when someone had broken one of the family rules. Her memories of the times he had reduced her to tears as she stood in front of his desk were still painful.[1] Even though she might claim this was her office now because she had inherited the house, her heart raced, and she felt familiar tendrils of fear close her throat and run down her spine.

"Miss Henrietta?" Samson opened the door from inside and held it for Henrietta to enter. "This is the safe box you sought." He gestured toward an ancient chest that reminded her of a pirate treasure. Despite the sadness she still felt, she smiled to realize that perhaps Antoine had learned his love of piracy at his father's knee.

"You should try the key to be sure it works, but you must not view the contents of the box until you are alone and after you have read this letter that goes along with it," Samson instructed her.

For a moment, her resentment surged again. This exercise in secrecy was unnecessary as far as she could see. And it felt more than a little insulting that a slave was giving the orders. Then her curiosity won out over her irritation, and she followed Samson's instructions. She inserted the key and heard a satisfying click as it unlocked the latch. She reached for the envelope Samson was holding.

"I'll leave you alone with the box, ma'am. But I'll be near. You can pull that bell cord to let me know when you have finished and locked the box. I'll hide the box again when you are through."

For several minutes, Henrietta stared at the wooden chest in front of her. What could be so important that it required this kind of skullduggery? How useful could it be if he had to keep it locked away in some secret hole? At last, she drew a deep breath and opened the envelope.

My Dear Henrietta,

In the accompanying chest, you will find the rest of your inheritance from your husband. When Julien was born, my wife and I took great care to make sure he would have everything he might need to live a life of comfort and safety. This chest became the repository for the wealth we could pass on to him. As our fortunes increased, we gathered gold coins from around the world, hoping that they would keep their value even if their countries suffered financial collapse. We purchased plots of land that lay in the potential path of Charleston's expansion, knowing the city must grow and every advance in its borders would increase the land's value. Through the years, whenever I saw that an investment was paying high dividends, I added to the stock holdings included here. And when my wife died after the birth of our second son, I deposited her rings and other precious gems here, so that her firstborn would have something by which to remember her.

We meant to endow Julien with the accumulations of his inheritance when he reached the age of forty. But, as you know, he did not live that long. When he died, I continued to build his inheritance for the benefit of his heirs. Now, with my passing (and if you are reading this, I must be dead), the entire inheritance will come to you. I hope you will treat it with reverence for the love it represents and use it to benefit your life and the lives of your daughters.

Yours,

Pierre Beauchene

She swallowed the sobs threatening to overwhelm her. This chest would have meant a great deal to Julien if he had lived. But how could she now take these implied riches for herself and her girls?

She lifted the heavy lid with care. On top was a stack of legal papers, tied together with a blue ribbon. She was much too overwrought to read them with any clear understanding, but she realized that most of them were property deeds. Some bore actual lot numbers along Meeting Street, while others described blocks of land bordering on what were now busy streets like Calhoun, King, and East Bay.

Gold coins glittered throughout the chest. Among them were the gemstones Father Beauchene mentioned. Some adorned rings or lockets; others were loose or broken away from their settings.

I seem to be rich, she thought, and then laughed at the irony because there might be no way to turn these prizes into ready cash on the cusp of war. The value of the items might be high in terms of dollars, but United States currency would soon have no value in a state that had seceded—a state that did not yet have a currency of its own. What could she do with these treasured bequests? Put them away again and pray that their secret hiding place could protect them from the damages of warfare? Hope that the family could survive the war and reclaim their possessions?

She wished that she had someone with whom to discuss her options. This was not information one shared with casual friends. Who could help? She couldn't trust Antoine, who would urge her to turn the contents over to him. The only other immediate family members were her daughters, and she dismissed them because they did not have enough life experience to offer financial advice. That left only the law firm that handled their affairs. She grimaced as she pictured Mr. Middleton looking down his aristocratic nose at her little collection. Henrietta had been staring at the chest for an hour when a knock at the door interrupted her chaotic thoughts.

"Miss Henrietta? Are you all right? Are you ready to have me put the safe box back in its hiding-hole?"

"Sorry! Come in, Samson. I let time get away from me. Where do you keep the box? I think you'd better show me. If something were to happen to you, no one else would know, and we'd never find it again."

"Yes'm, that's what Massa Beauchene said when he showed me, and it was a good thing, too." He closed the door against prying eyes and motioned her to approach the bookcases lining the walls. "See this shelf of law books? Try to take one down."

She grasped a book at the top of its spine and pulled forward. It didn't budge. She tried another with the same results.

"Are they fake books?"

"This shelf and the one below it. Now put your left hand on the outside edge of the bookcase—right here next to the shelf. Do you feel an indentation? Press it. Now try to remove that book again."

This time the entire row of books tipped forward at her touch. She gave them another tug, and the entire shelf folded downward, revealing a numbered dial set into the wall.

"It's a safe?"

"Yes'm. And now you need to know the combination to the lock. Here are the numbers: six-two-seven-one-eight-zero-four. Do you recognize them?"

She had written them down as he spoke. "Well, there's a pattern. The larger ones run up (six, seven, eight) and the small ones count down (two, one, zero)—no, wait! That's a date, isn't it? June twenty-seventh, 1804: Julien's birthday."

"Yes'm. Now you turn the dial for each number, back and forth, starting to the right."

With a click, the handle yielded to her touch, and the door to the safe opened. A hole awaited. Samson slid the safe box into place and closed the door. He nudged the row of fake books, and they clicked into place, leaving no sign that something lay behind them.

"It's been there all these years, and we never guessed."

"And now you know why Massa Beauchene was so careful about the people he allowed to come into this room. It's yours now, and your secret to keep."

"Did he ever—ever ask anyone to examine the contents of that chest—to tell him what the items were worth?"

"Not that I know of, ma'am."

"Thank you, Samson. I'll guard the room and its contents well." She remained in the office after Samson left, staring at this hidden safe. She, too, had secrets to keep. The journals she had filled during her marriage to Julian contained explosive information about the family, and she had kept them hidden, first in her room and then in a locked trunk in the attic. Elizabeth Dubois had urged her to destroy them, but she could not bring herself to do that. [2]

She re-read her journals when she needed a reminder of who she was and what her father had taught her to believe. She, knew, however, that they were never safe from prying eyes. I wish I could hide my journals in that safe, she thought, but I don't see enough room to hold them.

ANOTHER PLAN WAS TAKING SHAPE IN HENRIETTA'S MIND, BUT she did not act on it until she was sure of its viability. Two weeks later, she walked into the Middleton Law offices and asked to see the family lawyer.

"Mr. Williams Middleton is not in today, but he'll be back on Monday. Would that suit you?"

"Yes, that will do. Around ten, shall we say?"

At that meeting, she wasted no time in giving the lawyer her instructions. "I want you to locate four experts in their fields—a real estate broker, a banker, a jeweler, and an investment counselor. I want a separate meeting with each one, here in one of your private rooms so that no one outside of your staff will know those meetings are taking place. And I need the meetings to happen before mid-February. Can you arrange that?"

"It's an unusual request, but I assume you have your reasons."

"Father Beauchene entrusted me with a great deal of responsibility, most of which extends far beyond my ability or expertise. Now that I have inventoried the inheritance he left me, I need disinterested advice on several issues. I do not wish to advertise that I am in the market to buy or sell anything. This seems to be the most unobtrusive way to handle the matter, and I trust your judgment on the reliability of such experts."

"As you wish. I shall contact each person and arrange your meeting times. Please realize these experts will be busy men, and their time is valuable. Can you hold your calendar open for the next four weeks?"

"Yes. I understand."

"Good. Then I will have my personal secretary send you notes establishing your appointments as soon as I have set them."

It was an intelligent way to approach the question of what to do with a hidden treasure. No expert knew the others being consulted, nor were they aware of the inheritance. Henrietta brought to each meeting a list of the items she wanted an expert to examine.

When she met with the jeweler, she brought a small velvet bag containing the gemstones themselves. She spread them out in front of the gentleman and asked the pertinent questions. Which ones were the most valuable? Would some be easier to sell than others? And might others be more valuable in new pieces of jewelry?

His answer was brief and to the point. "For now," he advised, "leave these jewels in their current condition. The diamonds and the emeralds have the highest value, amounting to several thousand dollars in U.S. terms. They will increase in value. If you must evacuate the city because of encroaching war conditions, you can carry them with you. Hold them as a resource of the last resort."

The banker had similar advice about the gold coins. "Wealthy people hold onto gold in uncertain times. Gold does not deteriorate or lose its luster. The country of origin does not affect a coin's worth. We rate coins by weight, not the imprinted value." He had brought a small balance scale with him. He piled the coins onto one side and calculated their total weight in ounces. "The current value of raw gold is $20.67 per troy ounce, so you can see you have a considerable fortune here. You could have it melted down and cash it in, but I do not recommend that now. If we go to war, the price of gold may double or triple."

The stock broker was not so optimistic about the future. "Traders in industrial stocks are skittish creatures. Threaten their bottom lines and they'll fly into a panic. And panics are never good for the holders of a stock. If war comes, as it will, your holdings will fluctuate. If you need cash, I'd recommend selling the stocks off while business appears good. The railroad stock, for example, is doing well right now. But once a war begins and an army tears up just one mile of track, the railroad screeches to a halt. A train that cannot run becomes worthless, and so does its stock."

The last expert was the real estate dealer. "I know many of these properties," he said. "They are sitting as vacant lots, just waiting for development. But few developers would be so foolish as to start a new building program when war mongers threaten to bombard the city. You have two choices. You can hold on to the property for the long term, hoping that once the political situation settles down, there will be a new building boom. That could take many years. A young person with riches to spare can afford to take such a chance, but documents disappear in times of turmoil. You may have only one shot at getting your money out of these properties. If you need cash in the short term, I'd advise you to sell most of these properties to speculators right away. Most are valuable.

"These plots along the east banks of the Ashley River are the exception. On the west banks, tea and rice plantations do well, but here, on the edge of the city, the land appears to be inhospitable to useful plant life. Someone, however, marked these with a question mark and another symbol I do not recognize. Perhaps they have an unexploited value. At any rate, they won't bring much at present. I suggest you hold on to them for curiosity's sake."

Henrietta bit her lip to keep from shouting out. Thanks to the education her father had given her in England, she recognized that symbol on the map. It stood for phosphorus, a nonmetallic substance with the ability to glow without visible cause and to burst into flame at normal room temperatures. The phosphate rock from which it derived was much in demand. Its components could yield such disparate products as a fertilizer or an explosive. If there were phosphate deposits under those vacant lands, they might be worth a fortune after the war.

AS SLIPPERY AS AN EEL

Sunday, February 17, 1861
Charleston, South Carolina

*H*enrietta sat in her father-in-law's office with his safe-box open on the desk in front of her. Almost two months had passed since Mr. Beauchene's death, and her first reactions of near panic and confusion had turned into confidence. The advice she sought from financial experts had been helpful and encouraging. Thanks to those disinterested gentlemen, she now knew what she wanted to do with this treasure trove. She placed the stock certificates in one large envelope and the real estate holdings, except for those along the Ashley River, in another. She slipped Mrs. Beauchene's wedding rings into a small box and locked the chest containing the remaining gemstones, gold coins, and deeds. When she had hidden it behind the bookshelves, she asked a servant to summon her three daughters.

Elise, Juliette, and Rachel wore puzzled expressions as they tiptoed into the office. For them, this was one of the few times they had ever gained free access to their grandfather's lair, and they looked around with both curiosity and trepidation.

"Relax, dears. You're not in trouble and no one will jump out at you. I intend to use this office for business matters from now on, so it will remain private and locked when not in use. It will not, however, be the family's disciplinary center, as it was when your grandfather was here."

"We haven't made a giant *faux pas*?"

"No, I called you in because I wanted to inform you of some decisions I've made. After extended consultations with financial advisors, I have converted several stock options and real estate holdings your grandfather bequeathed. I have deposited the proceeds into an account at The Bank of South Carolina earmarked for use only to the benefit of the holdings of The Beauchene Company. Mr. Charles M. Furman, the bank's president, assures me that the bank is on solid financial footing with investments both here and abroad. The board of trustees has already voted and confirmed their full support of the laws and goals of the Confederate States of America. They expect the bank to continue operations even in wartime without interruptions. With luck, these additional funds will carry our firm through whatever vicissitudes the coming war will hurl at us."

"We won't go broke when war breaks out?"

"No. We'll be maintaining business as normal—or as close to it as possible—and our clients' affairs will be safe in our hands."

"I'm wondering about one matter, mother," Elise said. "If the company is stable now, why sell off properties before it becomes necessary?"

"Market fluctuations, dear heart. Don't you remember your grandfather's lessons? You sell when prices are high and hang on for dear life when the bottom falls out. The advisors

I've talked to think we are at the top of a cycle but that bottom is on its way."

"Is everything going onto an auction block?"

"No. I'm holding onto commodities whose values do not depend on the whims and vagaries of the marketplace. Never fear. There will be an inheritance waiting for all of you."

Rachel responded with an exaggerated sigh. Henrietta studied her youngest daughter. "Is there something you dislike about this, Rachel?"

"No, what you do is none of my business. I'm surprised you even wanted me here to learn about it." She shrugged and looked out the window while her sisters exchanged a head-shaking glance.

"The family business always includes you, Rachel."

"Unless it doesn't." She narrowed her eyes to glare at her mother. "May I leave now?"

"As you wish."

"She's still having a hard time dealing with everything that has happened," Elise murmured to her mother. "First, all that ugliness with the St. Croix family, and then grandfather's death. She'll come around."

"I hope so, but I'm not as certain as you are. Keep an eye on her, both of you. Now I need to discuss something with Antoine. Would you send him in if you see him?"

A FEW MINUTES LATER, ANTOINE TAPPED ON THE OPEN DOOR. "Are you holding today's session of the Inquisition? Is it safe to enter?"

"Oh, don't be silly, Antoine. Come in and sit down. I want you to know of any moves I make. We're in this together from now on, regardless of whether we like it."

"Except that you happen to be more powerful."

"Because I'm always here, not jaunting around the countryside. As I told you two days ago, I've sold off several properties and stock options that Father had hidden away in his safe-box. Other commodities I will hold as a hedge against the unknown. But I must tidy up a few loose ends. Here. This belongs to you."

As she spoke, she handed him the small velvet box. Inside, he found two tiny rings, one a simple band and one adorned with a cluster of diamonds. He glanced at Henrietta with a puzzled expression. "Where did these come from? Are you suggesting I need to find myself a wife?"

"Well, that's not a bad idea, but, no. Those are your mother's wedding and betrothal rings. I know you don't remember her, but you are the only one entitled to them. Do what you like with them. Maybe someday you'll find a woman willing to have you. If not, keep them or sell them. That's up to you."

Antoine was turning them over in the palm of his hand. "They are so tiny. She must have been a delicate creature."

"Yes, I thought so, too. And they are a way for you to get to know something about her."

"Thank you, Henrietta. I appreciate it."

"And now we have another item of business to take care of."

"We do? What else is going on? Have you found other secrets hidden away somewhere?"

"No."

Antoine was looking around the office with unconcealed interest. "Maybe not in here, but what about the attic? Father must have had a cache of currency somewhere. He always had cash in his pocket although he almost never visited a bank."

"He left you his bank accounts, his coffers, and the contents of his jewel case. If you have plundered all those sources, I doubt you'll find any more cash in the attic. From what I have seen of it, there's nothing much up there but old furniture and dust. Lots of dust."

"And what were you doing up there, if I may ask? Looking for something in particular?"

"If you must know, I was helping the servants store the baby furniture after Rachel was old enough not to need it. I knew there would be no further children in this house, and it was a sad occasion, not a greedy one." Henrietta's heart was pounding as she thought of what might happen if Antoine ever discovered her journals, hidden away in her trunk near the attic stairs.

"That was fifteen years ago. As far as I know, no one's been up there since. Look around this office, though, if you like. I see no safe place to hide a large amount of money. Do you?"

Antoine accepted her invitation. He lifted decorative objects to look under them, opened drawers, even moved the winter rug to examine the floorboards. Henrietta held her breath when he turned to the bookshelves, but after trailing his fingers across a few titles, he shrugged and sat down. He never was very interested in books, Henrietta remembered, but his actions had triggered another thought.

When she had moved into her father-in-law's office at the warehouse, she had recognized its similarities to the office at home. Even the bookshelves looked the same. Now she realized there could be more similarities than she had first thought. If there was another safe in the warehouse office, she might use it to hide her journals and other personal items to keep them out of Antoine's reach. She needed to distract him from the attic until she could find a more secure space for them.

"Have you thought any more about buying that blockade-running ship you and your friend have been testing?"

"No. I've sold the goods I brought back from the

Caribbean for five thousand dollars, but I must share the income with the owner of the ship. That's a factor I didn't consider."

"What does Joseph McNairy want for the blockade-runner itself?"

"Somewhere around twenty thousand dollars. It's a good price, but way beyond my shallow pockets."

"Well, as I told you, I will not allow Beauchene Company funds to finance a speculative item such as a boat. To do so would be a serious breach of our clients' confidence. However, my money has no such moral strictures."

Antoine's eyes widened as he studied his sister-in-law's expression. A small smile was developing at the corner of her mouth.

"Are you saying—?"

"I'm offering you a deal, Antoine. I have the money you need in my personal bank account—savings I've accumulated over the years. And now with the windfall from your father's bequest, I see an opportunity to get something I have long wanted."

"You? What do you want?"

"As you know, I have fifty-one shares in the family business, which I inherited from my husband. And, as you also know, I only hold them in trust for my three daughters. When I die, each girl will receive seventeen shares. That will allow them to keep control over the business if they work together. But according to the articles of incorporation drawn up by your father, no one can be a partner in the business or draw a yearly salary from its profits without owning at least twenty percent of the company."

She stopped and drew a deep breath, trying to decide if Antoine was following her explanation. So far, he looked puzzled.

"I need nine more shares, Antoine—shares you own but can now sell, thanks to your father lifting the restrictions he placed upon you. To assure each of my daughters a lifetime income, I want to purchase those nine shares from you, at twenty-five hundred dollars apiece. That's—"

"Twenty-two thousand, five hundred dollars." He whispered the amount.

"Yes. Enough to let you purchase the ship you want, hire a crew, and get on with your pirating."

"I would only own forty percent of the company."

"Yes, that's true, but it would be more than enough to support you. And face facts, Antoine. You're not interested in cotton bales. Luxury goods, associating with the upper crust of society, pulling in a fortune—those are your goals."

For a few minutes, silence reigned.

Antoine strolled to the window and stared out at the slave yard bustling with activity despite the thick fog. The heavy glass panes and draperies muffled the sounds from children and workshops. Memories of his father stirred when he noticed the pervasive odors long trapped in this room—the leather furniture and book bindings, smoke from the fireplace, the tang of whiskey and cigars. Antoine had never been nostalgic, but at this moment he stood poised between the quiet sameness of his childhood and the roiling adventures of his dreams. He teetered, leaning forward and then back, not ready to choose one over the other.

Henrietta watched him from beneath lowered eyelids. She, too, held onto the moment, knowing change was coming regardless of whether they were ready for it. But would their actions make matters better or worse? She couldn't be sure.

"What made you change your mind, Henrietta?" He asked without turning toward her, and she answered without looking up.

"Your father's death was the catalyst because it was the first time I realized what death means. When I was younger, I handled Julien's death the only way I could—by shutting down, feeling nothing, refusing to face what had happened, lapsing into a catatonic state. But this time, instead of my feelings shutting down, they became super-sensitive. I helped prepare father's body for burial. I felt the coldness of his skin, the stillness of that once-active mind, and the stiffness of *rigor mortis*. The hands that once trembled under the exertions of old age now lay composed but without purpose. I understood for the first time that our deepest desires and longings do not outlive us. They fade away because we are the only ones who give them any importance. The actions that matter are those we take on for the sake of others."

She took a deep breath and continued. "Your father kept that treasure chest hidden for fifty years. There were the riches he had accumulated—now meaningless baubles because he had not used them. I have taken steps to provide for my children and my clients. But as for the rest of my wealth, I want to use it to make others happy. Some of it is yours, Antoine. You've cherished a dream for twenty-five years. Let's bring it to fruition and see what it can accomplish."

"I don't deserve it," he said, looking at her for the first time. "I haven't earned your trust."

"Then it's about time you start. Take this chance and make a difference. Use it to serve the country you believe in. That's what will make your life worth living."

"All right. You have a deal. We'll draw up the paperwork in the morning. I've had a name picked out for the ship, you know. I will christen her the *Slippery Eel* because she can slip in and out of harbors and creek beds. When I take possession, will you be there to help me launch her with a bottle of champagne?"

"Only if you promise to move Pedro aboard the ship and keep him there. I want that parrot out of my warehouse before he drives my cat crazy."

FIRST SHOTS

December 20, 1860–April 12, 1861
Charleston, South Carolina

$\mathcal{U}$nprecedented confusion filled the months following Lincoln's election. South Carolina led the way, announcing its secession on December twentieth and four days later announcing their justifications. U.S. Army Major Robert Anderson transferred his garrison from Fort Moultrie on Sullivan's Island to the more easily defended Fort Sumter on the day after Christmas. Reactions in Charleston were mixed. Military leaders took the occupation of Sumter as an omen and made countermoves. They seized the now nearly abandoned Fort Moultrie, improved its sea-facing fortifications, and mounted new weaponry aimed at Fort Sumter. Elsewhere along the shores of Charleston Harbor, other fortified spots bristled with new ramparts and lethal-looking guns. Some citizens worried about what such preparations might bode for the future while others ignored them.

When Anderson took control of Fort Sumter, however,

some Southerners worried over predictions of unavoidable violence. Local groups seized U.S. arsenals and fortifications. Other states leaped to follow the example of South Carolina. Mississippi seceded on January ninth, followed by Florida on the tenth, Alabama on the eleventh, Georgia on the nineteenth, and Louisiana on the twenty-sixth. On February fourth, representatives of the first six seceded states met in Montgomery, Alabama, to form the Confederate States of America. On February ninth, they named Jefferson Davis as their new president.

Although no one had fired a shot, Davis held his inauguration on February twenty-second, ten days before Lincoln officially became President of the United States. Texas had left the Union on February first although its governor, Sam Houston, insisted that Texas should maintain its independence. Within weeks, rebels removed Houston from office and joined the Confederacy on March 1. The country waited uneasily as winter snows hampered the North, and Atlantic fogs threatened to swallow the Southern coastal states. Both Buchanan and Lincoln had refused to recognize the secessions as legitimate, but the South was beyond seeking their approval. Still no one wanted the stigma of having fired the first shot. Nor did either side want to alienate border states that were so far holding out against secession—states like Tennessee, Virginia, North Carolina, and Arkansas.

Around the Beauchene dinner table, only Rachel reacted. "How inconsiderate of the Northerners to turn our landmark into their own private fortification. Now we won't even be able to use it for our next Bastille Day fireworks display."

"Oh, Rachel! Don't you ever think of anything beyond your own inconvenience?" Elise shook her head in dismay and turned away, but Antoine had a stronger reaction.

"You'll see fireworks enough. I promise you that, my girl. But they won't be little sparkling bursts set off by volunteer firefighters. They'll be cannon balls and mortars, blowing up those concrete walls along with the men who think they can defend them. Those Yankees will be targets when we turn our fire power onto them from all sides."

"Won't they fire back?"

"The men who designed that fort meant it to defend the harbor entrance from foreign attacks. Its long-range guns point toward the Atlantic. There are several emplacements on the lower level—holding guns meant to take out any stray ships that penetrate the harbor. But none of those have the range to reach the city beyond the Battery."

"Then why did Anderson occupy it?"

"Good question. He evidently thought it would protect his men from hostile rebels. But he didn't consider the armaments or a way to resupply the troops once they settled in. That's what will bring this to a head. Anderson is running out of food and water. Without those essentials, he must surrender or go down in a massive killing attack."

"I don't want to hear about it," Henrietta declared, closing the discussion. The Beauchene family remained aloof from the political controversies, partially because they were still in mourning and partially because they worried more about other matters.

ANTOINE HAD WASTED NO TIME IN COMPLETING THE PURCHASE of his blockade-runner from Joseph McNairy. Now that Antoine owned the ship, he had a few adjustments to implement, and McNairy himself was happy to comply. The ship-builder knew a buyer saved him from further bouts of seasickness. He agreed to give the ship a new coat of dark gray paint to make it invisible on the water and hired an artist to design the lettering and an image of an eel for the bow.

There was a matter of a tattered sail, and Antoine wanted a smoother way to collapse the smokestacks when the ship was under sail. He planned his maiden voyage for mid-April, so the laborers were working against tight deadlines.

Henrietta, meanwhile, had completed her move into her father-in-law's old office. And just as she had suspected, she found another safe hidden behind the bookshelves. She had to guess at the combination, but it turned out to be easy. Father Beauchene had used the same secret combination—Julien's birthdate. Inside, she found another pirate's chest and in it, a hefty roll of U.S. Treasury bank notes. She smiled when she realized that Antoine's suspicions about a secret bankroll had been accurate. Since she did not need immediate cash, she left the roll undisturbed. Within a few days she added her own cluster of secrets to the chest—her journals, a memorandum on the value of the phosphate rock deposits under the Ashley river properties, and a confidential ledger that detailed her father-in-law's private loans to several of his friends and clients.

She spent most of her days juggling the business of the cotton factoring company and her private efforts to sell her unwanted real estate and stock options. More and more she relied on Elise to study the European markets and set price levels for their crops. The two younger girls were busy with their projects. Juliette's slave school had proven to be as popular with parents as it was with their children—so much so she was now holding evening classes to teach adult slaves to read and write. And Rachel continued to avoid the rest of her family by spending longer hours at the Huguenot church, bringing membership records up to date and delivering church bulletins at regular intervals. The vigorous and sometimes heated dinner-table debates were now only a fond memory because the family lacked a moderating voice of experience to guide the discussions.

THE FIRST HOSTILITIES BROKE OUT IN THE PRE-DAWN HOURS OF Friday, April 12, 1861. It had been a rainy night, and at 4:30 in the morning, the first shot sounded like thunder. But thunder does not keep repeating as these explosions did. All over Charleston, people awoke to the terrifying realization that war had come at last.

At the Chalmers Street house, Henrietta and her daughters stumbled downstairs in dressing gowns to find Antoine already up and monitoring the action from the piazza. His eyes followed the tracer shells as they arced beneath the low-hanging clouds.

"Do you still claim the Yankees can't hit the city from Fort Sumter?" asked Juliette.

"I do. In fact, Anderson's troops aren't doing much shooting at all. Their ammunition is in as short supply as their food ration, and they are limiting themselves to a warning shot or two per hour. They will have to surrender soon."

"Then why are our troops still bombarding them?"

"Because they can." Antoine's tone was bitter. "You're seeing another manifestation of war mentality. Once soldiers set off the first few shots, they don't stop. It's almost a reflex they can't control. There's another aspect. Have you noticed that some missiles flying over the fort are red and leave smoke trails? Our troops are heating the cannon balls until they are red-hot. Then they fire them into the fort hoping that they will land on something flammable and set the place ablaze. It works, too. The fort has masonry walls but wood furnishings and structures in the center. At least, they used to be wood. Now they're probably ashes."

"Why now? Has anyone said what started the fight?"

"No, but I can guess. Rumors have been flying for several

days that talks were ongoing between General Beauregard and Major Anderson. Beauregard didn't want to be the one to spark a war, and Anderson knew he had no hope of winning one. But they could not agree on the terms of surrender. Then Lincoln announced that he was sending ships to resupply Anderson's men and asked for their safe passage."

"Did the ships arrive?"

"Not that I've seen. But Anderson believed Lincoln would save him and refused to evacuate the fort. I suspect Beauregard had enough talk and opened fire out of frustration."

"None of it is logical, is it?"

"No. War flies in the face of logic."

Mrs. Jernigan, the Beauchenes' long-time housekeeper, appeared in the doorway carrying a covered sweetgrass basket. "If you are waiting for the sun to come up out here on this chilly piazza, I thought you might need some early breakfast to tide you over. I had cook stir up drop biscuits and sorghum, and she'll be along in a minute with a big pot of coffee."

"You are kind, Mrs. Jernigan," Henrietta said. "I'm sorry we have disturbed your sleep."

"Who can sleep with that infernal racket going on?" Mrs. Jernigan threw up her hands toward the harbor as if to chase the soldiers away. "We will have breakfast at the usual time. I'm not catering to those folks out there."

Antoine grinned. "I think she's got the right idea. Here, ladies, have a biscuit."

"Oh, how can you eat in the middle of a war?" Rachel's voice quivered on the edge of a tearful sob.

"The war may go on for years, dear girl. Are you planning on not eating until it's over?"

"No. Oh, you never understand!" She flounced away, letting the piazza door slam behind her.

"What gets into that girl?" Elise asked. "We can hardly

hold a decent conversation these days without her flying into a tizzy over something."

"She's young, she's had major disappointments, and she's afraid."

"Do you really think she's afraid, mother? Of what?"

"The unknown. Maybe we protected her too much when she was little—your grandfather and I both. We wanted to spare her, and instead, we did not teach her how to cope when things go wrong."

"You wanted to spare her? From what?"

"Let it drop, Elise. She's your sister and you must love her no matter how disagreeable she is. Those are the family rules. And this, too, shall pass."

"I hate that phrase!"

"Now you sound like Rachel, and for the same reasons. I brushed you off rather than answering your question. But I can't answer you because I don't know what demons are haunting her—just as I can't answer some of her questions about unfounded gossip among the neighbors."

Juliette threw her mother an appraising glance. "You keep posing these discussions as imponderable issues, don't you— whether we're talking about the war or about Rachel's latest tantrum?"

"And I refuse to believe there is such a thing as an imponderable question," Antoine said. "There are unknowns, for which finding answers is not only a possible but also a desirable goal. There are also questions that someone does not want to answer, questions that hide uncomfortable truths. The trick is to know the difference."

"You're over-simplifying, I think."

"Not at all. Take Lincoln's actions since his election. He couldn't change his story line about the impossibility of war as soon as he won, so he had to insist on it—or at least hope it was so. Once the first state seceded that interpretation no longer worked. Since then, we've all been assuming that no one knew what he would do. But I don't accept that. Lincoln's a shrewd politician. He knows exactly what he's doing. You watch his next moves. They'll come tomorrow or the day after."

"All right, Mr. Know-It-All, what are those moves going to be?"

"Like it or not, the Confederacy declared war the minute Beauregard fired on Fort Sumter. Now Lincoln has the excuse he wants. Since there will be a war, he needs an army—and a larger one than his little classes at West Point can produce. He will call for a volunteer force. The South already did that. Jefferson Davis asked for 100,000 volunteers, and he's getting them. Lincoln needs to meet that threat, but he won't want to give the rebel army too much credit. He'll call for volunteers, but his request will ask for fewer men—as if it won't take a huge United States Army to handle these upstart rebels."

"And then what happens? Do they set up a time and place to meet and hold a fight?" Henrietta hated this discussion, but she did not want Antoine to dictate the family's views.

"I suspect he'll continue with the same tactic he's used so far—holding back and hoping the Confederacy will make another preemptive move. He won't fight until he's forced into it, but that won't stop him from being provocative. I'm betting he will follow his call for volunteers with the threat of a blockade. That will have two effects. It will annoy the South, and it will worry the rest of the world. European countries do not want to see the Atlantic become a watery battlefield because those waters lap their shores as well as ours."

"Thus proving that you have amazing foresight, I suppose?"

"Maybe. Maybe not. But I'll tell you this. I will not wait for Lincoln to make his next move. I'm taking the *Slippery Eel* to sea tomorrow evening. The shooting display in Charleston

Harbor will be over by then. Anderson will be out of ammunition, so an outbound ship will not draw any fire."

"Where are you going, Uncle Antoine?"

"Well, I shouldn't say anything in front of your mother. She's always hated slavery, so she might be a Union spy."

"Oh, for mercy sakes, Antoine! Now you're the one being provocative."

"No, just stating the obvious. But considering our business interests, I don't mind disclosing my plans to you. I will sail north along the intercoastal waterways to Fort Fisher at Wilmington. Cape Fear provides a convenient last harbor before we head for Nassau."

"Not Havana for your usual supply of rum and cigars?"

"Nassau can provide those things, too, Henrietta, but it's also a prime location to find military equipment of all kinds. European countries won't ship guns directly to America, but they will use international waters to move their offerings closer to our shores. And the other advantage to Nassau, as I tried to convince my father years ago, is that we can develop our own trading outstation."[1]

"You promised not to involve the Beauchene Company, Antoine."

"And I will not do so. I've incorporated my trading company—ABC Provisions: Suppliers of Fine Luxury Goods."

"ABC?"

"The Antoine Beauchene Company. Or Artillery, Beverages, and Combustibles—take your pick. I'll be looking for an empty warehouse to purchase, or at least a part of a warehouse we can rent. I've hired a potential manager—a fellow recommended by your own David Manwaring—and he'll be sailing with me. We've loaded a small shipment of last year's cotton bales."

"Our cotton? How does that keep us uninvolved?"

"You will find a check and a receipt on your desk. I intend to sell or trade with ships coming into Nassau Harbor. Once we've offloaded the cotton, we'll stock up with the best bargains in weapons, rum, and cigars and sail directly back to Charleston—proving trade can continue through the Caribbean. Now, if you'll excuse me, I need to alert Pedro and the crew as to our new departure time."

Grinning, he flipped his family a mock salute and headed for the stables. Henrietta watched him go with mixed emotions. Because they had invested so much money in Antoine's little blockade runner, she could not wish it would come to harm. But she could not wish her treacherous brother-in-law great success.

"Are you planning to go to the warehouse this morning, mother?"

"No, Elise. I think those guns announce the general closing of businesses today. No one is thinking of anything else."

"Then I'm going back to bed, at least until the sun rises."

"Lucky you," Juliette said. "This fuss will have my little urchins awake and bouncing into the basement for their lessons any time now. I'd better get into a schoolmarm's dress and make a few more flash cards while I wait for them. Tell cook we said thanks for the early breakfast, mother."

The girls headed back to their rooms, leaving Henrietta alone on the piazza. Already the sound of cannon fire and the sight of smoke over the harbor seemed a normal part of her world. But what did it mean? And what would be her role in the coming conflict? She was a slave-owning Southern businesswoman with a strong abolitionist streak. The combination made her once again a stranger in this strange land.

THE THREAT OF BLOCKADE

Monday, April 15, 1861
Charleston, South Carolina

*A*ntoine's predictions had been accurate. Anderson surrendered Fort Sumter by Saturday afternoon. The first battle of the war left behind an enviable tally of zero battle casualties on both sides. A shell exploded as the Union soldiers left the fort, and two men injured in the incident died of their wounds, but those injuries did not occur until the battle was over. Ocean breezes soon cleared the smoke from the fort. Soldiers manning the coastal guns secured their weapons and went home. And on Sunday morning, dozens of pastors preached sermons of thanksgiving that all had survived. Monday morning brought business back to life.

Henrietta was meandering through the warehouse's lobby when the front door opened and two men entered. She recognized neither of them but put on her best *feme sole* expression and went to meet them.

"Mrs. Beauchene, I presume?"

"Yes. May I help you?"

"Is Mr. Antoine Beauchene anywhere about, please?"

"No, he's not. I can assist you or take a message."

"When do you expect him?"

"I don't know. Whom should I say—?"

"Oh, Excuse me! I'm George Trenholm. My brother Charles and I own your rival cotton factoring company. I assumed you recognized me."

Henrietta gave him a withering smile to suggest he wasn't as important as he thought he was. Then she stared back at him, waiting for him to state his business. She had offered to help him twice. That seemed enough—maybe once too often.

"Well," he began again, "Mr. Bunch and I are making the rounds to set up a meeting among Charleston's cotton factors. It seems prudent for us to present a united front if Lincoln and his henchmen blockade us. Do you think Antoine will be available later this afternoon? We plan to meet at the newspaper office around four o'clock."

"Mr. Beauchene is on an extended trip to the Caribbean. But I will represent our company."

"Oh, well—uh, we were hoping to have the owners present."

"I am the majority stockholder in the Beauchene Company."

"Oh? It was my understanding that the elder Mr. Beauchene left the company to his legal heirs."

"Yes, he did. I now hold sixty percent and my brother-in-law has forty percent. We share responsibilities, but final decisions are mine alone. If you want my cooperation, you'll quit looking shocked and realize businesswomen exist."

"Yes." He was backing his way toward the door as he spoke. The gentleman accompanying him blocked his path and whispered something in his ear. "Oh, one other matter. Mr. Bunch is the English consul in Charleston. He is trying to identify the British citizens in our fair city. It is my understanding you grew up in England. Are you still a British national?"

"That is correct, sir." She spoke to Mr. Bunch, ignoring Trenholm's nervous probing. "I was born, raised, and educated in Oxford, England, but received American citizenship when I married Julien Beauchene and came to Charleston with him."

"Is it also true you are of noble lineage—a member of our peerage, I believe?"

"Who told you that? Mr. Trenholm, who heard it from my irresponsible brother-in-law? No, sir. My father is Sir Ephraim Ainesworth, Keeper of Medieval Manuscripts at the Bodleian Library. He holds an honorary title of baronet as a privilege of his office, not his blood line. You'll understand the difference, I assume.[1]

"Yes, yes, but—you are Sir Ephraim's daughter? I know him—or used to know him when I was a student at St. John's College in Oxford. While my classmates were rowing on the Cherwell or gossiping over pints at the Eagle and Child, I was salivating over old books in Duke Humfrey's Reading Room, under the watchful eye of your father. What a small world we live in."

"We do." Henrietta arched her eyebrow at this rather hapless gentleman. "And why, may I ask, are you identifying British citizens? Are we suspected of being disloyal to whatever government happens to be in power this morning? Or are you going to send us home?"

"No, nothing of the sort. It is my sworn duty to see to the welfare of every British citizen who happens to find herself living in a war zone."

"Charleston is now a war zone? You are joking."

"There was a battle here this past weekend. Her Majesty Queen Victoria will want to be sure that all her people are safe."

"I'm sure she's worried sick about me!" Henrietta was reaching the end of her patience. "If that is all you need, gentlemen, I have work to do. Good day to you."

THE MEETING THAT AFTERNOON WAS INFORMATIVE, THANKS TO the telegraph wire in the newspaper office. Of primary interest to everyone gathered was a reported argument about the coming blockade. Lincoln's cabinet had met on Sunday, and their discussion was continuing. William Henry Seward, Lincoln's Secretary of State, urged Lincoln to take a strong position on all questions concerning the seceding states. When the question of a blockade arose, Seward had no doubts. It must be a full and open blockade, announced so the entire world understood the North meant to isolate and defeat the Confederate states.

Opposing him was Gideon Welles, a Navy man who resented Seward's meddling. He declared the government should leave such matters to those who had experience on the water. Welles wanted a *de facto* but undeclared blockade. If Lincoln announced he was blockading the Confederate states, Welles argued, the world would take it as an act of war against an equal opponent. It would, in fact, affirm the right of a state to leave the Union, an admission Lincoln had so far avoided.

"The Navy can blockade the major ports of the South," Welles declared. "We have men and ships available to do that without a problem. We can stop any ship that tries to deliver goods to Southern ports or carry their exports to customers in Europe. But we must act on individual cases. We can punish Southern ships and the sailors who ignore our maritime laws. Their actions are violations of United States laws, but we must not attack the whole Confederacy as if it is a country."

"I don't see how that makes a difference," Seward had protested.

"It matters to politicians. They will not interfere if we are enforcing our own laws on our own people. But if we admit the seceding states have formed a separate entity from the United States of America, European nations may recognize the Confederacy as an equal and belligerent country—and then support them in their rebellion against us."

George Trenholm took the lead as the cotton factors struggled to understand the technical details. "Don't worry about it," he advised. "Let the politicians wrestle over legal definitions. For us, what matters is the Northern attempt to blockade our ports. We can't let them do that here in South Carolina. Not only are we dependent upon our income from overseas cotton sales. Our survival depends on our ability to import manufactured goods and foodstuffs we cannot produce for ourselves. We have no Confederate Navy and no way to break such a blockade. For that we need the support of foreign governments. To be more specific, we need the help of the British Navy."

"It comes down to the argument between Seward and Welles, doesn't it? If Seward wins, the British Navy will support us."

"We hope so. If Seward gets his way, the English government can offer us military aid. Our problem is how to convince them to do so, which is why I've called this meeting."

"What's your plan, Trenholm?"

"As this newspaper suggested months ago, we need to prove British industries depend on Sea Island cotton. If we cut off their supply of long-staple fiber, they'll soon get the message."

"But that's slitting our own throats, isn't it?"

"It need not be. Here's the plan. We agree to tell our clients not to send us any more cotton, but we never admit we're declaring an embargo on cotton shipments to England. We look innocent and tell the British buyers we will provide all their needs just as soon as the United States lifts the blockade—or as soon as we can get the naval support to break that blockade. The British Navy will spring into action."

"No, they won't!" Henrietta spoke before she had time to consider her actions. She was on her feet, facing the group of men surrounding her. "You're underestimating British determination and resourcefulness. Englishmen don't like being told lies, and they don't like bullying. They'll turn elsewhere for their needed supplies. They can import cotton from Egypt or India instead of crossing the Atlantic for it."

As she stopped to catch her breath, she realized how quiet the room had become. The men stared back at her with expressions that suggested she had stepped in something noxious. In South Carolina, women did not speak at public gatherings, she remembered, but it was too late. She had already stepped over the line. These gentlemen would not hear what she said; they would only notice she had dared to speak at all.

"Please sit down, Mrs. Beauchene. Now, gentlemen, this office has printed cards for us to send to our clients. Here's what they say."

In the interest of public safety, we recommend you limit your cotton production for the coming growing season. In its place, we urge you to plant food crops to feed our soldiers and our citizens as we face the Specter of War. If you plant cotton, please store it on your own property. Our cotton warehouses will close to protect the supplies we have and will remain closed until there is no longer a danger of raids from marauding Northern armies. We will continue to support your agricultural efforts and look forward to the time when we can again engage in profitable cotton sales.

"You must sign each card and then deliver or mail them to each of your clients. There are two facts you need to remember. First, we are only ten days away from the traditional start of the cotton-planting season. We don't want our planters to get their valuable seed in the ground before they get this message. Like the cotton itself, the seeds can remain viable for several years. We don't want to waste them. So, take care of this mailing at once.

"Second, you need to understand that this plan will only work if every one of us is a willing participant. If some factors stop selling and others continue, it will defeat our purposes."

"So, what about the lady that complained?"

"As for holdouts, I will get word to the legitimate owners of any reluctant company. I promise you, we will get one hundred percent compliance."

Henrietta froze. She recognized the threat as bravado, but she also knew with people's livelihoods on the line there was little that an angry group would not do. As the men surged to the front of the room to get their cards, she gathered her things and hurried to the door, eager to get away while she could. With a dry mouth and thumping heart, she was running by the time she reached the street. Then she heard the footsteps pounding behind her.

"Mrs. Beauchene. Please wait. Don't worry. That talk back there was only bluster."

Henrietta clutched the handle of her parasol as she turned to confront her follower. Then, recognizing Mr. Bunch, she drew a shaky breath and slowed her steps until he could catch up with her.

"I'm not running away. Such bullying does not bother me, but I find I cannot trust myself to keep my mouth shut when others misbehave. It's safer for all concerned if I avoid such conflicts."

Bunch smiled. "I would think twice before riling you. However, I hope you'll let me escort you home so we can talk about what just happened."

"You intend to persuade me to change my mind?"

"I should be so talented. No, I have no intention of making you do something you don't want to do. I did, however, pick up your bundle of cards so that the hotheads will not have clear evidence of your non-compliance."

She was quiet for several minutes as they walked toward Church Street. She gave him a sideways glance. "You're an Englishman. Do you think I'm wrong?"

"You're not wrong. Queen Victoria will see through this ruse in no time, and chances are that the whole scheme will backfire on your colleagues. If I were you, I'd keep my head down and wait for events to play themselves out. As for the cards? You might do a little judicious editing before sending them out. Let your clients know this is the general plan but you are open to supporting their efforts whichever way they choose."

"You have a little devious streak yourself, don't you?"

"I have my moments. I suspect we both will meet many challenges before this conflict settles itself."

"Oh, yes. I've faced a dilemma ever since I arrived in Charleston. One side of me abhors slavery and wants to abolish it even if that means the North destroys the South. But I've lived as a slave-owner for twenty-nine years and understand what abolition would do to the Southern way of life. I don't want to see that happen, either. I'm neither a Yankee nor a Rebel. South Carolina is a sea of rabid believers in everything I distrust. And there's nothing I can do about it."

"That's where you are wrong. You are not alone, and this crazy world needs more people like you. There's work for you to do, if you will accept it."

DIPLOMACY OR ESPIONAGE?

April 17–20, 1861
Charleston, South Carolina

*L*ater that evening, Henrietta remembered Mr.
Bunch's final remark: "There's work for you to do, if
you will accept it." He hadn't elaborated on what
kind of work he had in mind before they parted ways. Was
the expression just an empty platitude, or would he seek her
out? And if he did so, what would he have in mind?

The answer was not long in arriving. Bunch returned to
the Beauchene warehouse on Wednesday morning, this time
alone rather than as a follower of the annoying Mr.
Trenholm.

"Do you have time to discuss a proposition I have in
mind?" he asked as Henrietta led him into her office.

"Provided it is a legitimate request."

"And do you object if I close your door?"

"I assume you need privacy. There's no one here but me—
and the cat." She nodded at the ball of fur asleep on the back
of her desk chair. "I'd worry if Antoine's parrot were still

around. He was too good at repeating what he heard. But he's off on the Caribbean trip, and Calico Cat has no interest in human affairs."

"You're laughing at me. I don't mean to seem cautious, but I'm here on a matter of international diplomacy. I don't know how much you understand about the position I hold here in Charleston."

"Nothing. I didn't even know you existed until two days ago."

"Well, then—as the director of the British Consulate in Charleston, I act on behalf of any British citizens living here. If the police charged you with a crime, for example, I would get you a lawyer and help him manage your case. I represent your native country by guarding your welfare and your physical safety and by protecting your business or financial interests. I am forbidden, however, to take any political action or to interfere with the natural functions of the country in which you now live."

"All that sounds fuzzy. What does it mean?"

"Well, let's go back to the scenario of your being charged with a crime. My job would be to see you got a fair trial, but I could not break you out of prison, whisk you away, or disrupt the court trying your case."

"When you attended the cotton factors' meeting the other day, were you violating your orders?"

"Not at all. You were there as was at least one other British citizen—one of Trenholm's functionaries. If decisions made at that meeting affected your legitimate business interests, I needed to know about them. But, you will remember, I did not speak at the meeting, nor did I take any part in the deliberations. Although I agreed with your stated assessment, I could not have expressed the same sentiment. I couldn't even tell them you were right."

"Hmmm. Must frustrate you."

"Very much so, now when this war is about to—"

"How do you handle it—the frustration and awareness of what's going on but not being able to interfere?"

"If I feel that an issue is important enough to warrant interference, I try to persuade one of my compatriots to do what I cannot do."

He stopped there and let the silence build as he looked at Henrietta.

"I don't handle innuendo well, Mr. Bunch. What are you asking?"

"I'm asking for your help."

"To do what?"

"Let's back up for the moment. Remember what Trenholm proposed? He encouraged you to withhold your cotton shipments until the English textile mills realize they need southern cotton. They might then put pressure on Her Majesty's government to send the British Navy to break the blockade. But it will be the cotton factors who create the embargo. Remember his comment about looking innocent? That's unfair, and someone needs to tell the decision-makers in London what's going on. I would do it if I could. Instead, I need to find someone who can do it for me."

"I know no one with influence in Her Majesty's government."

"Let me explain. I want you to write a letter to an imaginary friend. Let's call her Miss Phoebe Porterfield. She's an old school mate who now works as a primary school teacher. I'll give you an address and a message to include in the letter. After a little small talk, you can mention what's troubling you. Someone's pressuring you to exaggerate the seriousness of the blockade. I'll give you the exact wording to copy. You'll prepare the letter and mail it via our diplomatic pouch. That saves you money and gives us hope that no one will snoop into the contents."

"And what will this imaginary Phoebe do about the problem?"

"Someone will deliver the letter to my contact in London, and he will know what to do with it. The message will reach the proper authority, and the Admiralty Office will not let Trenholm's embargo mislead them."

"Now tell me again why I would want to do this?"

"Because you abhor slavery, and you want the North to win a moral victory. That victory must come before too many people die. The South's quick defeat will not destroy your business, your home, and your family. And the country of your birth will not interfere and prolong the war. You'll be helping to bring about a diplomatic solution to a serious threat."

"This is diplomacy, is it? I suspect we might call it espionage. How much danger will I face if I agree to be one of your spies?"

"If someone discovers the letter and traces it back to you, you can plead innocence. Someone must have pretended to be your old mate Phoebe. And you've done nothing but tell the truth. Keep remembering that. It's essential you pass on only information you know to be factual. If I were not the consul, I would do this myself. Since the law keeps me from political activity, I must rely on others whom I respect and trust."

"I'm flattered, but I hesitate to take part in the scheme. I suspect this won't be your last request. How often will you come back with a need for another letter?"

"I don't know, Mrs. Beauchene. We don't know how long this conflict will go on. I may well need you again. But you are not my only contact. There are many British citizens here in Charleston, and several of them help me with different matters. Today, I sent a gentleman to New York City to discover whether we can send our diplomatic pouches through their scheduled mail carriers. I won't trouble you except for matters concerning the blockade. Fair enough?"

Henrietta still hesitated. She stood and wandered around her small office, seeming to be deep in thought as she touched some of her favorite objects. For several moments she stared out the window and watched the activity on the dock. She avoided Mr. Bunch's glances although she sensed he was watching her every move. She caressed Calico's soft fur and smiled when the cat yawned at her.

"All right. I'll do it. I don't like being a spy, but this is the right thing to do. When will I get the information?"

"It's all enclosed here," he said, handing her an envelope. "You'll find the address, the stationery, the stamp you'll need for the Royal Mail, and the text I want you to include."

"You knew I would agree?"

"I hoped you would. You are a woman with strong moral convictions. And I need you."

HENRIETTA FINISHED THE LETTER THE SAME EVENING, BUT SHE hesitated once again over the notification cards furnished at the factors' meeting. She had tried changing the wording as Mr. Bunch had suggested, but did not like the way it looked. Nor did she like the implications of those changes. I can't play both sides anymore, she thought. I have compromised all my life, and I'm not proud of the results. If I am a spy for Her Majesty's government, I can't also do things that benefit the Confederate rebellion. It's time to take a stand against this evil institution of slavery.

Thursday morning, she sent Joshua to the Consulate on his way to get the daily papers. He carried a bundle of letters that included her letter to Phoebe along with short messages to her family in Oxford and a note to Mr. Bunch, asking him to inform her of any new business developments. Then she turned to her account books to distract herself from the nagging guilt because she had used a slave to run her errands. "This will not be easy," she told the cat.

It got no easier when Joshua returned with a scribbled note from Mr. Bunch:

Thank you for your efforts on our behalf. I promise you will not regret your decisions. Since you asked for information on changing events, I must tell you of new developments. Will you join me for dinner here at the Consulate tomorrow evening? Our chef is an Englishman who will remind you of your homeland while I fill you in on the latest news. Please come around seven o'clock. Robert Bunch

---

Henrietta worried over the invitation all day. She wanted to know more about what was going on in England. An authentic English meal after so many years of Southern stewed vegetables also tempted her. Nor did she like to admit that her heart beat a little faster when she thought of sharing an intimate dinner with this unusual gentleman. Such silliness, she scolded herself. I don't want him to think I will leap at his every summons. Dinner crosses the line between business and personal, and I should not accept. What would be a plausible excuse?

Still, she had not sent her refusal, and when Elise came into the office Friday morning to talk about the weekend, she said the unthinkable.

"I won't be home for dinner tonight, dear, so if you and your sisters want to plan something informal and silly, you go right ahead."

"You won't? I didn't know you had something scheduled."

"I'm having dinner with a friend."

"Oh, you and Auntie Elizabeth up to something, are you?"

"No, no. I'll be at the English Consulate if you need me."

"The Consulate? Whew! That's impressive. Whom do you know there?"

"The consul himself. He has information he wants to pass along because we cotton factors have trade agreements with England."

"Is that the pleasant fellow who travels in the governor's entourage? Mr. Brand or Branch or something?"

"His name is Robert Bunch, and he provides assistance to English citizens abroad if they need it."

"Have you been holding out on us, mother? Is he after your money, or does he have a wife and family in that fancy house?"

"I don't know. He didn't mention a family, and his invitation was to 'have dinner with me,' not 'have dinner with us.' This is a business dinner."

"Why don't I believe you? Could it be because you are blushing?"

"Don't be ridiculous, Elise."

"Oh, come on, mother. You're still a young woman, and a beautiful one at that. I know you loved my father, but there's no reason for you to remain single and celibate for over twenty years. You've handled your widowhood with great aplomb, but I think it's high time you had a new man in your life."

"You're making too much out of this simple meeting. So why don't you run along to your desk and get to work."

"Yes, ma'am. But I'll expect a full report when you get home!"

Henrietta's embarrassment lingered as she approached the consulate that evening, but the lovely dinner soon made her forget everything except how much she had missed the meals of her childhood. A starter of trout pâté on tiny toast points arrived with a glass of white wine. Then followed a roast joint of beef, a spectacular Yorkshire pudding, and her favorite vegetable, mushy peas—not the sickly yellowish variety that came in a tin can, but the vibrant green of peas just shucked from their pods and mashed with butter and lemon juice. A bottle of sparkling water accompanied the main course, but more alcohol arrived after their sticky pudding. Coffee came with a copita of aged sherry.

"I've made a glutton of myself," she said as she leaned back in her chair. "I had forgotten how glorious English cuisine can be. Foreigners make fun of our simple cooking, but each single bite of that meal contained pure flavor. Thank you for reminding me."

"I hoped you would enjoy it, my dear. I count myself fortunate to have an excellent chef on my staff. But now, are you ready for the latest news bulletins from the *Charleston Mercury*'s telegraph machine?"

"I am. After a meal like that, I can withstand even the bad news."

"Well, then. After your departure from the factors' meeting on Monday, word came down that Lincoln had issued a call for 75,000 volunteer militiamen to serve for a three-month enlistment. That told most observers two things: one, Lincoln believes there is a threat of widespread secession, and, two, he doesn't think it will take his standing army long to settle our hash."

"He didn't declare war?"

"No, but you don't call out 75,000 men with guns to play knucklebones. At least, some slave-states noticed and took his action as a warning. Virginia seceded and joined the Confederacy on Wednesday. Today, Lincoln announced his intention to blockade the southern Atlantic coast. He hasn't implemented the blockade yet, and he promised that international ships who blundered into the intended blockade area would receive a warning, with no other punishment unless they committed repeat violations. That was enough, however to convince Virginia's most famous West Point graduate and U.S. Marine officer, Robert E. Lee, to resign his commission and join the Confederate Army. Three additional states—Arkansas, North Carolina, and Tennessee—have called conventions to decide whether to secede. Their decisions will come down soon."

Henrietta's face was serious. "All the children are choosing up sides," she commented.

"You might say that, yes, and each step makes war more inevitable."

"And England?"

"Nothing official yet, but I understand that Her Majesty Queen Victoria has asked Parliament to meet and debate our country's role during the conflict. The Queen herself will address them in three weeks. We have to hope—you and I—that our messages reach her in time."

SECRET AGENTS

April–May 1861
Charleston, South Carolina

*A*fter that first week of overheated reactions to the firing upon Fort Sumter, life in Charleston resumed its usual languid pace. The harbor patrol reported there were no left-over shells or other hidden dangers in the water around Sumter. Dock workers came back to their jobs and soon had traffic moving in and out of the harbor. Stores and shops reopened. In private homes all over the city, slaves dust-pounded the heavy woolen rugs and draperies that helped keep the residents warm through the winter. Sheer muslin curtains and sea-grass floor mats would replace their woolen counterparts for the hot and sandy summer months. Flowers bloomed, and in the slave yards, vegetable plots were already thriving.

Local citizens returned to their usual routines. Women resumed their afternoon visits. Some gathered in tea shops to ponder what might happen next. Wealthy businessmen dropped by their banks to review their accounts. Elizabeth

Dubois came to the warehouse to see Henrietta and report that her grandson, Johnny Grenville, had not been a part of the actual battle.

"Susan sent her husband to check on the group of cadets that came down from South Carolina College in Columbia to get in on the fight," she said. "He found them on Sullivan's Island housed in a local inn. The commander at Fort Moultrie had issued them rifles but with strict orders that they were only to drill with them. They didn't even have ammunition. As the real soldiers were firing upon Sumter from Fort Moultrie, Johnny and his friends were marching up and down the main street and trying to get a glimpse of the firefight. And now they're on their way back to Columbia to finish their studies for the term."

"I'm sure you are sleeping better," Henrietta said. "Wars make me appreciate being the mother of girls."

"Well, I hope we've seen the beginning and the end of this war. Lincoln thought we Southerners would not fight. But now that we have sent his troops packing with their tails tucked in, he'll be reluctant to face a second embarrassment."

"I'm not sure you should count on that, Elizabeth. Lincoln called for an additional 75,000 volunteers for his army."

"Ah, but only for the next three months. And everyone knows it'll be too hot to fight around here during the summer. By fall, I expect the whole matter to lie behind us."

Similar discussions were taking place in the offices of other cotton factors. Charles Trenholm had admitted his plans for an embargo to counteract a Northern blockade had been premature. Shipping firms had encountered no efforts to hinder their movements, and the arguments for and against an official blockade put forth by Lincoln's cabinet continued without resolution. Even after Lincoln published another proclamation adding Virginia and North Carolina to the intended blockaded region, the North had no actual blockading vessels in the area. Most cotton factors now accepted Henrietta's analysis of England's position.

Those cotton factors who had sent out the cards Trenholm had provided now followed them with retractions and more reasonable recommendations. The cotton warehouses would remain open, and sales would continue. The factors advised planters to follow their usual practices of devoting some of their available land to food crops while devoting the majority to cotton acreage. Optimism prevailed.

Henrietta enjoyed two weeks without drama or crisis. Her daughters were all busy with their own activities. Beauchene clients were optimistic about their futures. Mr. Bunch dropped by the warehouse with news tidbits, but even he seemed unconcerned about the future. Best of all, Antoine was somewhere in the Caribbean, no doubt enjoying himself while not stirring up trouble at home. When he left on this trip, he had planned to be away for at least six weeks. That meant Henrietta might have the entire month of May to relax and enjoy Charleston's prettiest season.

WHEN HENRIETTA ARRIVED AT THE WAREHOUSE ON MONDAY, May tenth, however, she discovered Antoine lounging in the doorway.

"Antoine! You're home already?"

"It would appear."

"But you said at least six weeks. Has something happened? Did you run into trouble?"

"Nothing of the sort. In fact, I would classify the trip as a rousing success. But come. Open the door and let me in. I have stories to tell you."

"Pirates? Running afoul of revenuers? Blockaders?"

"You sound hopeful."

"No. But I'm more than a little surprised to see you. Tell me about your successes."

"Well, first, you realize that news spreads fast these days. A Nassau newspaper reported that the U.S. Navy has just assigned the steamer *Niagara* to cruise the Atlantic between Wilmington and Savannah to enforce the blockade of Charleston Harbor. It predicted the *Niagara* would arrive from Boston today and assume patrol duty along our coast tomorrow. I cut my revelries short and came home ahead of her arrival. No sense in allowing my little blockade-runner to be the first to blunder into the gun sights of that lumbering steam frigate. I wanted to tie the *Eel* up at a private dock on the Ashley River before the *Niagara* arrives in Charleston Harbor later this afternoon.

"I'll tell you this, Henrietta. The *Slippery Eel* is the finest little ship I've ever sailed. She slips and slides her way through the narrowest channels and dances right over sand-bars. With her masts up, she runs before the wind. And when we're under steam, she skims over the water. She covered the 500 miles between here and Nassau in less than forty-eight hours. I am forever grateful to you for helping to make her possible."

"That's all lovely. But is she going to pay her way?"

"She already has. We sailed into the harbor at Nassau on our second day out and tied up next to a bulky-looking vessel flying the Portuguese flag. Her captain was on deck to watch our arrival. He was studying the *Slippery Eel* with such curiosity I invited him aboard. He spoke good English and over a small spot of brandy he revealed that he was looking for a load of cotton."

"A Portuguese looking for cotton? Why? I understood that Portugal was trying to build up its own cotton production in West Africa."

"They are. What he wanted was a load of good quality

American cotton that his overseers could distribute to their plantations. He wanted some of our best cotton for comparison with their own production."

"Trying to discover what we do well, so they can do it better?"

"Yes, but I didn't see that effort as much of a threat to our own economic interests. It takes a long time to improve the quality of cotton seed. Anyhow, I made him an offer he liked. The price I quoted was higher than we would have asked at home, but he didn't know that. And the advantage he gained would balance the higher cost. With our two ships anchored next to one another, his crew could hoist the cargo from one ship to the other without paying cartage or warehousing fees."

"What sheer good luck."

"It was. I had an empty hold, cash in my pocket, and an open mind about how I intended to spend it. Suppliers were begging me to buy their goods, so I've brought home an assortment. I bought Jamaican rum, Cuban cigars, and military wares of all kinds—a supply of Enfield rifles, ammunition, canteens and mess kits, boots and ponchos, bayonets for various other rifles, knives, and even a few bugles for sounding commands."

"All of this destined for storage in the back of our warehouse, I presume?"

"Well, yes, maybe, but it won't be there long, I promise you. The Confederate Army needs this kind of equipment. I plan to pay a visit to General Beauregard tomorrow. We may pull off another lucky move by unloading the *Slippery Eel* straight into the Confederate stores."

"I hope you can do that. I have allowed you to use our warehouse for your cigars and rum, but I'm reluctant to store military goods. You promised your imports would not infringe upon the family firm's business reputation. I don't want the Beauchenes to look like gun dealers."

TWO DAYS LATER, IT WAS ROBERT BUNCH WHOSE ARRIVAL turned Henrietta's day upside down. She was in the warehouse with Antoine, assessing how much room they could make for his latest shipload of Jamaican rum. The bell that signaled someone's entrance jingled, followed by a shout.

"Henrietta! Where are you? I have news you will want to hear."

"Back here," she shouted as she recognized the voice. Then she realized that Antoine was staring at her with a calculating expression.

"Who is that? Someone I haven't heard about, eh?"

"Don't be annoying, Antoine. It's only a friend—he's the English consul for Charleston."

"With whom you happen to be on a first-name basis? Maybe I shouldn't have left you home alone, little lady."

Henrietta glared at him, hands on hips. "Don't you dare patronize me. I'll be on a first-name basis with whomever I choose. And you have no say in the matter of my friendships."

"As the only man in the family, I feel responsible for you. If you've become involved with someone, I have a right to know about it."

"You have no rights over me. Whatever gave you that idea?"

"Oh, settle down. I worry about you." Antoine caught her by the arm as she whirled away from him. She backed away, throwing up her arm to pull it loose, only to find he had grasped the other arm.

"Henrietta, my dear. Is this man bothering you?" Robert

Bunch hurried through the warehouse toward them. "Take your hands off her, sir."

"And who do you think you are, throwing around orders in my place of business?" Antoine's temper was turning his face a deep red, and Henrietta flashed back to a day twenty years ago when he had looked at her husband the same way, just moments before that temper led him to strike a fatal blow.

"Don't, Robert. Don't interfere. This is my ne'er-do-well brother-in-law, and he enjoys throwing his weight around. He's not as threatening as he likes to think he is."

"I won't allow someone to manhandle you, Henrietta."

"It's over." She jerked her arms from Antoine's grasp and then pushed Robert toward the front office. "I'm used to seeing you burst in here with news, but he isn't, and he misunderstood your motives. You, Mr. Bunch, might do well to remember this is a place of business before you walk in shouting for attention. And you, Antoine, can either cool down or get out of here until you can behave like a grown man instead of a bullying brat."

Both men took a step back from the dressing down she had given them. Bunch was the first to break.

"I'm sorry, Mrs. Beauchene. I forgot myself when I saw a stranger grab you. You might take that as a backhanded compliment. And Mr. Beauchene, I apologize for jumping to conclusions. I do not interfere in another family's dynamics. Can we start this encounter over?"

"I still don't know why you burst in here in the first place, sir." Antoine was not about to humble himself without some face-saving bluster.

"Hush, Antoine. I want to hear your news, Mr. Bunch, as will Antoine, too. Can we sit down in the reception area and talk without shouting?" It was more of a command than a question. When she spotted Joshua in the doorway looking frightened, she gestured to him to bring tea. Then she walked ahead, sure that both men would follow.

"Let me explain, Antoine. As the Charleston consul, Robert is privy to the latest news reports. He receives daily briefings from London and checks the telegraph in the newspaper office. He has helped me decide how to handle our company's reactions to political crises that have popped up during your absence. That's part of his job as Her Majesty's local representative."

"Today's news bulletin falls into that category, Mrs. Beauchene. I have learned that Queen Victoria will address Parliament this afternoon—just about now, given the time difference. She will declare that her government intends to— Here, I wrote it down to be sure I quoted her:

'The British government intends to remain neutral regarding the recent controversies and unpleasantness between our American cousins North and South.'"

"Neutral! That means—" Henrietta hesitated. "What does that mean?"

"First, Victoria recognizes what's happening over here but will not dignify the conflict by calling it a war before the two sides have themselves declared war. Second, England will not take one side against the other but intends to let the states fight it out among themselves. And third, in the eyes of the British government, both sides are equal in their roles as combatants. It is, in fact, recognition of the South as a separate entity."

"That's the most significant statement, is it not, Mr. Bunch?" Antoine's demeanor had changed from hot-headed anger to sober contemplation of the message rather than the messenger. "She has legitimized our actions in seceding. And that gives other nations permission to see us as an independent country rather than a rebellious minority."

"It does. I think it will carry enormous weight with France and with Brazil, both of whom have declared their independence from their former rulers. The significance will not escape them. In 1776, the colonies proved that they had a right to overthrow a tyrannical government. Following their example came the French Revolution and Brazil's break with Portugal. Both countries are proud of their hard-fought independence and will sympathize with Confederate efforts to separate from a government trying to destroy the basis of the Southern economic system."

"France and Brazil. Neither one of them has the strength or naval power to help us defeat the United States if it blockades us." Henrietta looked back and forth between the two men flanking her.

"True, Mrs. Beauchene, which takes us back to the second point I mentioned. If England brought the full force of the Admiralty against the United States Navy, she might well put a quick end to the war. There may be some residual bitterness in this decision. I recognize it because as an Englishman I feel it, and you may, too. We're pointing out to the United States that they wanted their independence. Now they have it, and they cannot expect England to come running to their aid. You were right all along, my dear. Those who thought they could force England to help the South misjudged the British character."

"I wish I were sure of that. We must wait and see."

"Harrumph." Antoine could not contain a final sneer. "I suppose we will, but in the interim I have real business to take care of. If you will excuse me."

As Antoine headed toward the back of the warehouse, Henrietta shook her head. "He doesn't like to lose an argument, even if his opponent has only changed the subject. Ignore his displeasure, Robert. Try to rise above his pettiness instead of meeting him tit for tat."

"I understand, my dear. Please don't let this confrontation change your mind about next week's dinner. My chef has been twittering for days about what tastes he can offer you from the homeland."

"I wouldn't want to miss that, but you must promise me we shall not spend the entire dinner discussing politics."

FALLOUT

Friday, May 19, 1861
Charleston, South Carolina

*D*espite her protests about further political discussions, Henrietta found that she could not control her own musings over news events. With a single sentence, Queen Victoria had taken the Union blockade of Confederate ports from possibility to reality. When she declared British neutrality, she implied she regarded both the United States and the Confederate States as belligerents. By doing so, the queen also recognized the Union blockade. It might inconvenience her countrymen. Her government might question its legitimacy. But by accepting it, she forced the United States to quit threatening and to act against an external enemy. The blockade became an integral part of the war effort from that day onward.

Lincoln no longer had a choice, Henrietta realized. Within days of the official British announcement, he issued a proclamation declaring a blockade of several ports on the Atlantic Coast. Charleston was the primary target, with

Savannah and Wilmington close behind. His plans and procedures followed the standards set by the Paris Declaration of 1856 although the United States had not been a signatory. The president had now given notice to the world of his intentions. His reasons were clear: Southern privateers threatened to assault Northern ships in international waters, while the Confederacy prevented the United States from collecting its legal revenues. He promised that all ships would have a grace period of fifteen days to clear the enemy ports. He guaranteed that ships caught violating the blockade for the first time would receive a warning. But if they became repeat offenders, the United States meant to imprison the violators and confiscate the ships and their cargoes. The blockade was an act of war, designed to break the economic backbone of the Confederacy.

With those thoughts swirling through her mind, Henrietta reported to the English Consulate for what had become a twice-monthly interlude. Robert met her at the door with a glass of dry sherry and ushered her into a dining room filled with soft classical music. Henrietta looked around, startled by the sound of the music. "What—I mean, who—?"

"The music? There's a small harmonium in the parlor. The musician is one of our compatriots—a young lad paying his way through the College of Charleston by providing musical interludes for special occasions."

"And our little dinner qualifies as a special occasion?"

"It does. I'm lucky enough to be entertaining the most charming woman in all of Charleston. I'm also issuing a rule of the evening. We shall not speak of the blockade."

Henrietta could feel a flush moving up from her neck to engulf her cheeks. This interesting man was standing much too close to her, and she couldn't force herself to stop looking into his beautiful brown eyes. But when he moved to touch her arm, she stepped back to avoid contact. She took a deep breath, attempted a quirky smile, and drew his attention back to their common interests.

"That suits me. I'm tired of thinking about ships and navies and gun-runners. But I was hoping to pump you for more information about Queen Victoria."

"Have you ever met her?"

"Heavens, no. I saw her once, though. It was before she married Albert, so she was just a slip of a girl. I was in London after visiting my parents, accompanied by two toddlers and their nurse. A London bobby told us about the queen's habit of slipping out of the palace to attend early church services at Westminster Abbey. We were in place, lurking at the east portal when her entourage arrived. We caught a brief glimpse as she stepped out of her carriage, lifted a hand to the crowd, and then disappeared through the doorway. All I could think of was how tiny she was to be holding such an enormous responsibility. She made me stiffen my spine."[1]

"She still has that effect on people, although she's grown matronly after bearing nine children."

"I can't imagine having nine children—even with all the help in the world."

"She and Albert have done a fine job with their offspring, although they are having a spot of trouble with the heir to the throne."

"Oh?"

"Bertie's a pleasant fellow, from all accounts, but he's eighteen and has little interest in academics or athletics. He's spotted on the social scene, however—loves smoking, drinking, and ogling the girls. And Victoria is not amused."

"I would think not."

"Well, I see him as quite a brave lad to risk her formidable displeasure. Ah, here's dinner."

Once again, the consul's personal chef had outdone

himself. The meal began with a creamy potato and leek soup with fresh dill fronds. A bottle of fine Chablis accompanied their entrees of pan-fried Dover sole in brown butter sauce and a medley of roasted asparagus and chanterelles. Dessert featured small wild strawberries in clotted cream. Over coffee, Henrietta sighed with contentment. She had eaten every morsel.

"I would call that meal a culinary ode to summer," she said when the chef himself came to the door to ask if all had been satisfactory. Then she frowned as she studied her dinner companion. "You've been rather quiet this evening. Are the events of the day still troubling you?"

"I apologize if I've been inattentive. Do you remember my mentioning another of our compatriots, a certain Robert Mure, an English-born Charleston businessman? He's been investigating the best way to transport our diplomatic pouch during a blo—sorry, during an act of war."

"Yes. I don't believe I've ever met him, however. Has he caused a problem?"

"That's the thing. I don't know. He was planning a visit to England, so I provided a British government passport and asked him to carry this week's diplomatic pouch when he traveled to New York. On every other occasion when he has handled our mail pouch, he has telegraphed to tell me the pouch was aboard its transport. But this time, I have heard nothing from him, and I worry that something may have gone wrong."

"Think about it for a moment, Robert. On those earlier occasions, he put the pouch aboard the ship and then went off to the telegraph office. But this time he boarded the ship along with the pouch, so he couldn't have sent the usual message. You would have more cause to suspect a problem if a sudden message arrived."

"Thank you, Henrietta. I'm sure you are right. I shall try to relax."

DESPITE THE COMFORT SHE OFFERED, ROBERT BUNCH discovered at the end of May that he had been right to worry about Mure's journey. He received a private letter from Lord Russell, Queen Victoria's foreign secretary:

I must inform you that our ambassador to the United States has sent me disturbing news that involves you. On May 19, 1861, just as Her Majesty was announcing our policy regarding the disturbances in America, federal officers arrested a British citizen by the name of Robert Mure. He was transporting a diplomatic pouch from Charleston, South Carolina. In it were several personal letters, a stack of pamphlets promoting the Confederacy, and two letters from your office to members of Parliament, encouraging their support for the Southern cause. As you must be aware, British officials serving abroad must not engage in such political activities. The United States declared Robert Mure a spy, and he now resides in Fort Lafayette Prison in New York Harbor. Because President Lincoln has suspended the law of *habeas corpus* for the duration of the War Between the States, no plans for a trial exist.

As for your activities, I have in hand a request from the United States government to withdraw you from your post and recall you to England at the first opportunity. I consider such action to be too Draconian. You may, however, take this letter as an official reprimand and a warning that Her Majesty's government will tolerate no further political actions on your part. You must limit all contact with citizens of the Confederate States of America to discourses required by your official defense of English citizens living in Charleston and its surrounds.

Bunch came to the Beauchene warehouse once more to inform Henrietta of these developments and to explain why he could no longer see her or entertain her for dinner.

"Your letter-writing days are over," he warned. "I don't think you are in any danger, my dear, so long as you remain here in South Carolina. Your activities supported the Confederate cause, so your local officials will have no reason to see you as a threat. I will continue to consider you a friend and remain at your service should you need my help, but our contacts from now on will have to be impersonal."

"I'm sorry for your troubles, but I understand the need for discretion. I shall retire to the sidelines of this horrible conflict and let others carry out what intrigues they will."

"I shall miss our evenings, Henrietta. You brought a breath of fresh air to that gloomy old consulate—and to my bachelor life. Would I be too presumptuous to say I hope the war will reach a quick and satisfactory conclusion so we can resume our friendship?"

"You are not presumptuous, Robert. We all hope for that speedy conclusion to the war. And I shall long for another lovely evening spent with fine food and drink, beautiful music, and your warm companionship."

She watched him leave the warehouse with a pang of regret for what might have been. Then she closed her office door against any casual visitors and gathered the copies she had kept of her secret correspondence with the anonymous

Phoebe. She sealed them into a large envelope and deposited them in the office safe. Once the war is over, she promised herself, I shall burn the evidence of my brief career as a spy.

THE EARLY SUMMER PASSED WITH ONLY SPORADIC SIGNS OF actual warfare. Most of the battles fought in May and June occurred either in western Virginia or in Missouri. Of those, most involved small units and only two resulted in a conclusive victory. In the deep South, where the cotton continued to grow undisturbed, war remained a rumor, not a reality. A few militiamen received assignments from the war office, but their tasks involved construction, fortification, or improvements to transportation. The volunteers of Charleston's German Fire Company traveled a hundred miles from home to build two forts to protect Port Royal Harbor, which lay between Charleston and Savannah. A few miles inland, other volunteers hurried to finish the rail link between Charleston and Savannah.

The USS *Niagara* persisted with its patrols of the southern coastline, and other ships joined the effort. Shipments of cotton out of Charleston, however, continued. Some 30,000 bales of cotton found their way out of the harbor every month, and three to five ships of foreign registry arrived at Charleston every week. Dozens of new blockade runners picked their way through the inland waterways and entered the Atlantic from unexpected locations. When Lincoln declared on July 7, 1861, that he had blockaded all southern harbors, Southerners paid little attention. They knew better.

Charles Trenholm, whose early plans to counter the blockade had failed to materialize, now called Charleston's cotton factors together again to discuss their options. But this time, Antoine Beauchene attended the meeting along with

Henrietta. When Trenholm mentioned Lincoln's declaration, Antoine laughed out loud.

"Don't be ridiculous, Charles. Lincoln enjoys hyperbole—a large blockading vessel patrolling the coastline looks and sounds impressive. But anybody with a tuppence worth of common sense knows a ship can't be everywhere at once. Blockade runners watch for the *Niagara* to pass and slip out of their hiding spots behind it. Even if the lookouts spot a blockade-runner, it takes a while for a ship the size of the *Niagara* to make a complete turnabout. And while it's jockeying around, the little smuggler is speeding toward Nassau. The U.S. blockade isn't working, and everybody knows it."

"I'm not so certain," Trenholm answered. "Only yesterday, the *Niagara* captured a small ship carrying cotton out of the Low Country."

"Fact or rumor? Look. I'll prove my point by risking my neck. Give me a load of your cotton and I'll take it to Nassau myself, provided I can keep a half-share of the profits. If I'm not back within two weeks with money in my pocket and a load of military supplies to boot, my firm will pay you the total price of the cotton you supply. Deal?"

"Deal!"

Henrietta fumed when she heard the bargain, but it was too late for her to protest. "Don't get caught, Antoine. We can't afford that kind of payment, nor can you afford to lose your ship."

POLITICAL MANEUVERS

Late Summer, 1861
Charleston, South Carolina

*T*wo weeks later, Antoine and his *Slippery Eel* eased into Charleston Harbor at midnight and tied up at the Trenholm wharf. When Charles Trenholm arrived at his warehouses, he found Antoine in what was becoming a familiar pose—leaning against the doorway while he smoked a thin Cuban cigar.

"Brought you some money, Charles," he said, pulling a roll of bills out of his pocket. "That's your half of what I got for the cotton I was carrying. Now I could use a little help from your workers to unload the cache of guns and ammo I've brought for our troops. I'll even share those profits with you."

"You won this time."

"Yes, like the times before. But on this trip, I also gained knowledge that may change the way we handle this blockade problem."

"I don't know whether people will care. Our soldiers have

been successful while you were away. We've had a real battle at Bull Run in Virginia, and the Confederate forces scored a major victory. General Beauregard led about 20,000 men against a much larger Union force, and we drove those fellows right back to Washington. Scared them with a rebel yell. They suffered over 3000 casualties, compared to our 1,750. It was a great victory all around, and most folks think the war will be over soon."

"Sounds more like an opening salvo. The victory is encouraging, but my news involves even larger numbers than the ones you are spewing."

"What did you learn?"

"I'd rather explain to everyone. Can you call another cotton factors' meeting like the last one we had?"

"How soon?"

"As soon as possible. Invite local officials, too—maybe even Governor Pickens. This is a critical issue."

"How about Friday? That'll be August first. We can start the month off right."

ANTOINE LOOKED OUT OVER THE GATHERING OF COTTON factors—men who had never experienced war, overfed businessmen accustomed to buying whatever luxuries they desired, Southerners with an overblown sense of self-confidence. He knew they would not like what he had to say, but the warning needed to get out.

"Gentlemen, I spent last week in Nassau. As some of you know, I won a bet I had with Charles Trenholm. But my trip was most important not for the business deals I concluded but for the talk I overheard around the docks. Every ship arriving from the United States or passing through the Port of New York observed the same phenomenon. The Northern

Army and Navy are both on the move. At least eight regiments of soldiers have marched into the area around Annapolis from as far away as western Pennsylvania. That's at least 8,000 men, with many more rumored to be on the way. And in Chesapeake Bay—from Annapolis to Hampton Roads—ships are assembling and taking on supplies. Observers have seen everything from little tugboats and whalers to three-mast schooners and naval warships. Estimates say there are close to sixty ships there now, with many others scheduled to arrive.

"The assembled wisdom is that the North is putting together the largest armada the modern world has seen. They are getting ready for a massive land and sea attack against us."

"For what purpose? What's their target?"

"I'm getting to that. As background information, you must understand the international rules of blockading. Neutral countries do not have to observe a blockade if it is not in place. Ships, like people, cannot always stay at sea. They must come back to land to refurbish and resupply their stores. A blockading ship needs quick and safe access to a harbor where it can load fuel, food, ammunition, new crewmen—whatever it needs. If, say, the *Niagara* suffers wind damage at sea, she must sail to New York or Boston for repairs. And while she is away, the blockade Lincoln bragged about does not exist unless a replacement ship is waiting to take over her duties or unless she has a safe place to duck in, get what she needs, and get back on station."

"Ah! I see. That's the goal, then! To attack and gain control of a safe harbor to protect the Northern blockaders."

"Well, they'd better not try to come here. They can't have Charleston Harbor."

"Or Savannah!"

"Or Wilmington!"

"Maybe that's why our German firefighters went to Port Royal to build fortifications."

Antoine listened to the comments with ill-concealed impatience. "Port Royal may well be their target, according to experts. Port Royal Sound is huge, well-protected on all sides, and accessible from Florida, Savannah, Charleston, and points north."

"But that's still far away from us, isn't it? It wouldn't hinder your trips."

"Oh, but it would. I can outrun the *Niagara*, but fifty, sixty, seventy ships out there on the water? I wouldn't have a chance. That's why I recommend that we try once again to plead with the British Navy to come to our aid."

"But they have declared neutrality."

"So far. But that can change. I didn't like your idea of an embargo. That would have been underhanded and childish. I would like to see a well-reasoned argument for their support put forth by respected negotiators talking to members of Parliament and top officials in the Admiralty Office."

"Whom do you recommend?"

"Well, none of us can do it. That's why I asked the governor to attend this meeting. Governor Pickens, as a politician, could you suggest suitable negotiators?"

Governor Pickens hoisted himself from his chair, perhaps giving himself time to consider his answer before launching into full speech mode.

"First, we'll need someone who has traveled in England and the Continent, someone who understands and respects the differences between American and British cultures. He needs to know the nuances of their vocabulary, have a taste for British cooking, and have impeccable manners toward British nobility.

"I would then look for a person who comes from a loyal Southern state, but not a coastal state. We want our representative to care about the whole country rather than representing his own local interests in avoiding the blockade.

"We would need someone with a deep love of the South, but with a clear-headed understanding of our vulnerabilities. I wouldn't want him to push the South as the best country in the world, but rather as a new country with great potential if it can learn from its allies.

"Next, we'll want someone with experience in government, and someone who understands international law. That would suggest a lawyer or a former governmental official—maybe a congressman who has served on several pertinent committees.

"Our choice will have to be a charmer, persuasive, and irresistible. We'll want everyone he meets to like him and want to please him. Not just a baby-kisser, mind you. We don't want him faking it. He must have great depth of personality and a reciprocal enjoyment of those he meets."

"Do we know anyone like that?"

"Does anyone like that exist?"

"Oh, and another thing. We need at least two people like that. Going straight to the British government is fine, but they have allies we will have to convince. I'm thinking of France in particular, but perhaps Belgium and Brazil, too. Our ambassadors will make their pitches and then come home, counting on their European contacts to discuss the matter among themselves and thus reinforce whatever strong points our people have scored.

"All that being said, I have in mind two former Congressmen—John Slidell of Louisiana and James Mason of Alabama. Both remained in service to the United States while it seemed possible to avoid conflict. Neither of them wanted to see secession. And now they are at loose ends— used to governing, aware of what's going on in the world, the fortunate possessors of wide experience. The final decisions on this must come not from my desk but from President Davis himself. If you approve, I will talk to the president and give him our recommendations."

THE SUMMER MONTHS SLIPPED BY. SHIPPING ON THE ATLANTIC slowed to almost nothing because this was the height of hurricane season. The storms began in July and threatened Florida and the East Coast several times in August and September. Reports of major ship damage filtered into the news, even when the storms themselves remained at sea. Wise shippers avoided the mid-Atlantic into October when weather patterns drove the storm activity northward.

Land battles continued in Missouri and western Virginia. Only one face-off occurred on the Atlantic coast where Confederate soldiers struggled to prevent Yankee ships from closing Hatteras Inlet along the northern shore of North Carolina. The Confederate losses there were an embarrassing warning of others to come in the area. But for South Carolina and the rest of the deep South, the biggest threats were rising temperatures, squadrons of biting insects, and attacks of torrential rain.

October brought welcome weather improvements along with a corresponding increase in political and military activity. For the Beauchenes, the changes began with a surprising visit.

"Governor Pickens is at the warehouse door, mother. What do we do?" Elise was wide-eyed, reacting with childlike panic. Henrietta, however, was well beyond caring much about the pretensions of those who demanded her attention.

"You had better open the door, Elise. He may want to buy or sell cotton."

"I doubt that! He has henchmen with him!"

"He goes everywhere with men in attendance, dear. Please remember this is a place of business. Let the gentlemen in and bring them to my office. I'll handle the visit."

By the time Governor Pickens and his two assistants reached her office, Henrietta appeared engrossed in her account books. At the tap on the doorway, she looked up and then stood in greeting.

"Governor Pickens. Welcome to the Beauchene Company, sir. How may I help you?"

"I need a personal favor, Mrs. Beauchene. May we talk in private while my men remain in your reception area?"

"Elise, please make these gentlemen comfortable and order them some tea. And do not disturb the governor and me for anything short of a fire."

"Yes, ma'am."

"Now then, you mentioned a personal favor. What could I do for you, Governor Pickens?"

"I need your expertise."

"Expertise from me?"

"Yes. Please. Let's sit down and pretend we are old friends exchanging confidences."

Henrietta cocked her eyebrow at him, as if expecting an unpleasant surprise, but she did as he asked. Then, noting that he was serious but hesitant to begin, she smiled. "What can I do for you, my old friend?"

"To be clear, I knew nothing of you until we met at that June meeting of cotton factors. However, our British consul, Robert Bunch, assures me you are a paragon of trustworthiness, an expert in matters of cotton cultivation, and well-versed in English culture. You have a rare combination of talents, he says. So—"

He took a deep breath and leaned forward across her desk. She responded by leaning backwards in her chair to preserve the distance between them. Whatever he wanted, she was not to be an easy sell.

"You remember that at that meeting, I discussed hiring two carefully picked men to serve as ambassadors of the Confederacy—John Slidell and James Mason. Both have resigned their seats as U.S. congressmen and will travel to England and the Continent on behalf of the Confederacy. They have arrived in Charleston to survey our problems here and to await transport to England when the Atlantic shipping lanes reopen in November."

"Through the blockade?"

"Yes. That's one problem we face. But they also need information about the unique qualities of Sea Island cotton. They are Southerners and familiar with cotton-raising but not with the special characteristics of the South Carolina crop. They need details about your normal trading relations with foreign textile companies. In addition, they have both asked for briefings on the pitfalls of dealing with English and French etiquette. I have found a Frenchman to coach Mr. Slidell before he assumes his role as the ambassador in Paris. But Mr. Mason needs expert guidance on the protocols of dealing with titled members of the English nobility and how one handles a queen who is 'not amused.'"

"Robert Bunch says I can do all that? He overestimates my abilities."

"He says you have been a major help to him."

"May I be frank? The small tasks I carried out for Mr. Bunch bordered on espionage, and I was never comfortable about that role. I cherish my privacy. When I am not dealing with my business, I prefer to stay at home with my family. I did not like meddling in political affairs, and I will not do so again."

"That's not what I'm asking. You know the cotton factoring business well. These gentlemen need a clear understanding of what you do. There's nothing political about that. As for the etiquette lessons, you need provide no advice other than what you would offer to a friend traveling to England for the first time. Mr. Mason wants to avoid embarrassment caused by an avoidable *faux pas*.

"But you also mentioned problems with running the blockade."

"Yes, I did. And Mr. Bunch has recommended that I discuss that issue with your brother-in-law, Antoine Beauchene, a skilled blockade-runner."

"He is, although—"

"You seem hesitant. May I ask why?"

"Antoine and I are not the best of friends, so I am not a good source of information."

"That keeps you from offering an overblown recommendation."

"All right. Antoine has been quite successful in running the blockade so far. He's skilled on the water, and he knows where to take evasive measures. You can also trust him. If he tells you he will do something, he will move heaven and earth to make it happen. I've never known him to lie, although he may not tell all he knows. His brand of honesty allows him to take your money, and he'll enjoy out-thinking you, but he will not cheat you to do so.

"My dislike of him is personal and buried deep in private family matters. He can be irresponsible, impulsive, and self-indulgent—a drinker, a womanizer, and a gambler. If none of that bothers you, then he may be the man you need."

"Sounds like an interesting fellow! Is he here so I can talk to him? I'd like to do that with you present, so you know what I'm asking him to do."

"I'll see if someone can find him." She reached up to a bell cord at the side of her desk, and a slave appeared.

"Is Massa Antoine here, Freddie?"

"Yes, ma'am. I saw him in the warehouse."

"Please ask him to come to my office. And thanks."

The speed with which Antoine appeared suggested he had been listening at the door. After the proper exchange of greetings, Governor Pickens explained his plans for the ambassadors.

"I'm putting together an impromptu committee to assure the success of Mason and Slidell. Your colleague Mr. Trenholm has housed them in a private residence in Charleston so they will appear to be casual visitors while they study the needs of South Carolina. Their political briefings and instructions come straight from President Davis's office. We have nothing to do with that although I know they will argue the blockade is illegal. They will also promote the value of a triple alliance with Britain, France, and the Confederacy, an agreement that would balance the United States' goals of naval and industrial expansion.

"I've asked Mrs. Beauchene to serve as a resource agent, providing the ambassadors with the practical knowledge they will need—such things as the special qualities of Low Country cotton, and the niceties of continental etiquette. Now, what I need from you is blockade-running help. I'm confident that Mason and Slidell will do a fine job for the Confederacy once they are on site. But first we must get them through the blockade and across the Atlantic. I hope I can prevail upon you to join our efforts."

"I'll do whatever I can, sir."

RUMORS ABOUND

October–November 1861
Charleston, South Carolina

*B*y mid-October the Charleston planners were ready to send their new ambassadors off to England. Thoughts turned to the best method to get them there. From the time they began this effort, Governor Pickens and his office staff had assumed Mason and Slidell would travel on a Southern-owned ship. A Confederate ship in a Confederate port faced no danger—unless she tried to leave. But even then, the South Carolina blockade was a joke. Once the *Niagara* passed Charleston on its regular patrolling run between Savannah and Wilmington, movements in and out of the harbor could resume without fear of interception.

In Pickens' view, the *Nashville*, at anchor in the Charleston Harbor, was the perfect transport choice. She had begun as a new side-wheel U.S. mail packet. In April, she had arrived in Charleston Harbor to deliver mail to the United States troops stationed at Fort Sumter. For her own protection when the first shots rang out against the fort, her captain anchored her where she lay. But once Anderson surrendered the fort, the Confederates captured the USMS *Nashville* and turned her into the CSS *Nashville*, refurbished and outfitted as a steamer passenger ship. The governor thought she would provide a comfortable passage for the ambassadors, but those more familiar with blockade-running disagreed.

Charles Trenholm and Antoine Beauchene argued that the *Nashville* was too obvious a choice. Anyone who saw it leaving Charleston would know it was carrying important passengers. Besides, it was slow and had a deep draught, which meant it could sail nowhere but a main channel or open water. When Pickens countered with the argument that the state could not afford to purchase a special blockade-running ship just to transfer two men, no matter how important their mission, Trenholm made a generous offer. He had discovered that he could charter the small steamer *Gordon* for $10,000. He offered to pay the fee, provided he could use the hold space to transport guns he hoped to buy on the way home.

Antoine jumped into the conversation. "I think the *Gordon* is a tremendous idea. She's fast and has a shallow draught. We can do a quick paint job on her, change her name to the *Theodora*, and send her off through a narrow channel. But I'd add one more element. Let me and my *Slippery Eel* go along on a more convenient route. We'll serve as a decoy and, I suspect, a more appealing one. Word has been getting out about the *Slippery Eel*'s ability to make a hash of the blockade. Every Northern ship now wants to capture her. She will draw any unwanted attention away from the *Theodora* long enough to let the real escape occur."

"That's taking a big risk, my boy."

"No, I don't take foolish risks. I'll travel empty when we set out. The Northern authorities cannot prosecute me for sailing if I'm not found to be transporting contraband. I'll pay for my adventure by loading up with goods in the Caribbean before I head home."

On Thursday evening, October tenth, the *Theodora* and the *Slippery Eel* made their way from private docks on the Ashley River into the navigable maze of the Low Country swamps. When they reached the open water of the Atlantic, they veered off in what appeared to be two different directions. It was a dark night, and they met not a single challenge. From then on, they had clear sailing through the Caribbean. At home, however, those waiting for word spent a restless night, knowing it would be many days before they would learn whether the two little blockade-runners had escaped detection.

TWO WEEKS LATER, THOSE INVOLVED IN THE EFFORT TO smuggle the ambassadors out of South Carolina met at the Trenholm warehouses to pool their knowledge of how the mission was proceeding. George Trenholm had received a brief message from his brother Charles:

> Happy to report we made the initial crossing without incident. However, when we reached Nassau, we discovered that the ship on which the ambassadors had intended to cross the Atlantic had given up on our arrival and had already left port. No other transport appeared to be available. However, we learned that a British mail packet, the *Trent*, would arrive in Cardenas, Cuba, in three weeks. Mr. Beauchene declared that to be an ideal solution. Ports on Cape Cupey, he said, did not attract the same amount of attention from U.S. patrols as did the harbor at

Havana. We dropped the two ambassadors off at Cardenas. When last seen, they were sitting on the veranda of their hotel with fruit punches in hand. I then returned to Nassau where I am trying to arrange the purchase of needed military supplies to fill our empty hold before heading home.

Henrietta nodded as George read the letter. "That's the story I received from Antoine, too. But once Mason and Slidell settled into their temporary quarters, Antoine sailed down the coast to visit old friends in Havana. His plans included loading up his usual cargo of rum and cigars before returning to Nassau. I have heard nothing further from him, but he seldom lets us know where he is or what he's doing."

"It's reassuring to know they had no trouble avoiding the blockade, although they may face more serious problems on the way back," Governor Pickens said. "I've received troubling intelligence from President Davis's office. That massive troop movement in the Chesapeake Bay area has increased in size, according to the spies we have watching them. Here's the telegraph summary I received from Davis."

---

12 U.S. Army regiments now assigned to this area; now boarding those 12,000 men onto refurbished transport vessels. Speculations that final numbers of men—including the naval troops—will be twice as high.

83 vessels of varying types moving through Chesapeake Bay to line up in several columns bow to stern in the anchorage at Hampton Roads.

Admiral Samuel E. DuPont aboard his flagship, the *Wabash*. Army contingents under the command of General Thomas William Sherman.

While destination is a closely guarded secret, the *New York Times* already reported they will head for Port Royal Sound, where they plan to construct a permanent naval facility to service and resupply ships of the South Atlantic Blockading Squadron.

The fleet ready to set sail as soon as current tropical storms move away from coast and out into Atlantic. Departure rumored to be Tuesday, October 29.[1]

The assembled group exchanged worried glances. Jacques Lévêque, who had helped John Slidell prepare for his assignment as the French ambassador, mumbled a fervent "*Sacré bleu!*" Henrietta's comments were of a more practical nature.

"Port Royal! That is the center of our Sea Island cotton plantations. What kind of defenses do we have in place?"

"Defenses? Not much of anything. Volunteer militias have been constructing two forts, one on either side of the entrance to Port Royal Sound. They have wood palisades and a few fixed-base cannons. As for men? A maximum of 200. Oh, and we have a fleet—a 'mosquito fleet'—with about as much chance as a real mosquito taking a nap on your arm." The governor was shaking his head as he spoke. "The best we can hope for is that the Yankee soldiers will get bogged down in the pluff mud. My only option is to call for a total evacuation of the area to save as many lives as possible. That may also curtail residual damage."

"And the cotton crop?"

"Lost." The governor grimaced. That was one curse of his office. He was the court of last resort when matters went wrong. Faithful voters expected him to provide magical solutions to hopeless problems.

"I figure we have about two weeks before those 12,000 soldiers pour off their transports and overrun that beautiful countryside. I suggest you use it well. Encourage your clients to get their cotton crop loaded onto wagons and on its way to your warehouses. It will be safer behind your locked doors than sitting in their shelters and barns. Maybe some of them can get a little more picking done. What gets left behind will fall into enemy hands. And that includes the valuable seed. Make sure your clients understand the need to get their seed to safety, too."

"Where will the evacuees go?" George Trenholm asked.

"Wherever they can. Some have second homes in Charleston or on inland plantations. Many already have family members with whom they stay during the winter. If your relatives are among those being evacuated, you must prepare for their imminent arrival. Many people will be on the road and looking for shelter.

"Even if our ambassadors reach England—even if they persuade Parliament to support the Confederacy—even if the British Navy agrees to challenge the blockade, it will be too late to prevent the inevitable damage the Low Country will suffer. Planters will lose their homes, the Yankees will destroy their cotton or ship it North, and their dreams will go up in flames.

"In time—ah, who knows what will happen down the road! We're facing an unimaginable disaster, and there are no guidelines for handling it. I will live to regret my decision to run for governor."

"No one will hold you responsible for this mess, sir."

"Perhaps not, but I accepted responsibility for the welfare of everyone in this state. And I can't think of a single thing to do to ward off this crisis."

"Perhaps the British government will act against the armada." George Trenholm was grasping for any argument that might make him feel less hopeless. He turned to Robert Bunch. "You're an Englishman and a representative of Her Majesty's government. Have you any real hope that England and other countries like France will come to our aid?"

Mr. Bunch looked from one face to another, stopping as he came to Henrietta. He could see her eyes were brimming, and he wished he didn't have to say what he was about to reveal.

"If I speak for my homeland, the answer is a definite 'No.' Even before our discussion became so grim, I hesitated to reveal what is happening in England. Friends in London have informed me of the details of a dispute that is preoccupying the queen. It's a minor problem, but it will have an enormous impact on America."

"What's going on?" Henrietta asked. "Whatever it is, it can't be worse than the prophecy of a looming disaster."

"The heir to the throne has a girlfriend."

"What? Who cares?"

"I know. I told you it was a minor issue, but little things can grow out of hand. Let me explain. Perhaps the story will at least provide a macabre touch of comic relief. The royal couple's eldest son and first in line for the throne is now nineteen and off at Cambridge, but it would be an exaggeration to say he is studying there. Bertie has always been a problem child and a major disappointment to his father. His teachers describe him as too thick-headed to succeed, a reluctant athlete, and a dismal failure in his military training. Young women, however, think he is a charmer, good-looking, fun-loving, a dare-devil, and rich to boot. He has a taste for tobacco, whiskey, and wild women, and the ladies are eager to accommodate him.

"Bertie has fallen in love with an older woman by the name of Nellie Clifden, and she has convinced him she reciprocates his feelings. He speaks of her as an actress which is an exaggerated claim. Her only stage is a bedroom, and she has devoted her entire working career to providing whatever passionate young men demand of her."

"She's a prostitute!"

"She is, and everyone knows it but poor Bertie. Queen Victoria and Prince Albert visited their son during his military service in August and met Nellie. Bertie was proud of her. His parents despised her. Albert has been suffering from several undefined ailments for the past year, and his spectacular fights with his son have aggravated his condition. The prince is by now weak and has been saying he believes his time has come."

"He's not that old!"

"No, he's only forty-one, but he's been suffering stomach troubles for some time, and he's now experiencing severe weakness of arms and legs. Still, his anger at Bertie's foolishness has him threatening to go up to Cambridge and beat sense into the boy. Albert's health worries Victoria, and she blames her son for his condition. The family is in total disarray, and the last thing on their minds is an upstart American 'ex-colony' making international trouble—again. Our ambassadors are in for a rude reception."

"The whole situation is ridiculous—two of our best-respected cotton factors off playing at being smugglers, a massive armada set to descend on an area whose most effective weapon is pluff mud, and a royal family torn to pieces by a prostitute."

"Don't shoot the messengers, Henrietta. We're only reporting what we see happening."

THE TRENT AFFAIR

Early November 1861
Charleston, South Carolina

*N*ovember ushered in a series of events so unprecedented that newspapers, telegraph offices, and the usual rumor mills gave up trying to sort out the stories. Unscheduled deliveries of cotton from planters and panicked inquiries from buyers whose purchases had not yet arrived bombarded Charleston's cotton factors. Blockade runners made risky voyages, and their families worried about their safety. The Trenholm Brothers Factoring Company rejoiced when brother Charles survived his latest run through the blockade and tied up his *Theodora* at her usual Ashley River dock.

"I have a cargo bay full of ammunitions," he informed his brothers. "We may not have much Low Country cotton, but I have guns, bullets, bayonets, and grenades to fill our empty warehouse. I'll be back in business with the local militias by the end of the week. Military goods come cheap in Nassau. It appears to be an even better source of international business dealings than our offices in Bermuda. And with only a few inept blockaders to guard against such imports, we'll soon be pulling in some eye-popping profits."

The Beauchenes were not feeling so optimistic. They had received no further communications from Antoine after his initial report. Henrietta reassured the girls that such negligence was nothing more serious than Antoine's usual self-centered preoccupation with the moment. She kept her concerns to herself, but she worried about the South Atlantic Blockading Squadron out there somewhere on the water and bearing down upon the shores of South Carolina. If Antoine did not soon reach the relative safety of home, he might sail straight into the clutches of this approaching enemy.

Reports of strong storms at sea during the first three days of the month played havoc with the emotions of Charleston's citizens. They did not want those strong winds to pummel their lovely city. No one could pray for flooding rains, house-damaging gusts, or sudden tidal surges. But the terrifying armada of Northern ships was in the storm's path. Would it be a sin to pray that this late-season hurricane would sink the entire fleet? Maybe so, but the alternative was unthinkable. One could not pray for the safe arrival of Northern ships when their avowed purpose was to destroy South Carolina.

On Monday morning, November fourth, Henrietta paused in her walk to the warehouse. She stood at the entrance to the wharf area and stared out to sea, past the deserted Fort Sumter to the wide entrance of the harbor. Beyond lay the open Atlantic. If she strained, she could catch glimpses of the tops of sails. The line of the horizon bristled with masts. Those ships out there were not proceeding in the bow-to-stern formations that the newspapers had described in October. They seemed to come from several directions, some fast, some in stuttering stops and starts. But the general trend was clear. They had survived the hurricane and were sailing south toward Port Royal Sound.

When she looked away from the horizon to stare at the sky, she gasped at the movement over her head. Huge white clouds looking like tattered remnants torn from sheets of canvas sailed above her. They, too, formed no set pattern, but their pathways headed toward the northeast. In her imagination she saw two unstoppable forces moving in opposite directions, each counteracting the movements of the other. Her eyes flashed from masts to clouds and back until she reeled from dizziness. The two forces now swirled in front of her, and she imagined them chasing one another. They formed a destructive funnel that dipped to the ground, swallowing up everything in its path.

Henrietta staggered to a bench on the wharf and covered her face to shut out the scenes of devastation the funnel left behind. This war might destroy everyone and everything she loved. And human intervention could not stop these forces.

"Are you all right, my dear?"

The familiar voice broke through her waking nightmare, and she lifted her tear-streaked face to see Robert Bunch staring at her in concern. He reached for her but stopped short of touching her.

"You're pale as a ghost. Are you ill?"

"No, no, I don't think so. I was watching the ships and the clouds moving in opposite directions, and a dizzy spell overtook me. It felt like a wave of seasickness. I'm recovered now, thank you."

"You still look shaken. Allow me, if you will, to accompany you to your office."

"You need not bother."

"You're no bother. I was coming to see you before I visited the Trenholms. The governor has asked us for another informational meeting a week from Wednesday. That will be the thirteenth. I'm hosting it at the consulate because it deals with 'matters most English.'"

Henrietta smiled at his phrasing and stood, accepting his escort.

"Real news or more speculation?"

"A little of both, I would imagine. I suspect he's hoping for something definitive by then, but we'll once again benefit from your input. Have you heard from Antoine?"

"Not a word. That's part of what is bothering me this morning. Even though I am not fond of my brother-in-law, I don't want him out there on the sea and separated from home by that huge Northern fleet."

"I understand. Perhaps the latest news will cast light on his whereabouts. I'll count on seeing you next week around four. And I will tell my chef you are coming. He'll want to bake you a crumpet or some Eccles cakes."

HENRIETTA ARRIVED AT THE CONSULATE ON THE THIRTEENTH looking somber and pale, but composed. The governor met her at the door and led her into the conference room.

"Has the wandering Antoine returned?" he asked, looking over his shoulder at her.

"No. He . . . he won't be returning."

"Not in prison, I hope," George Trenholm said.

"Worse. I'm sorry to cast a pall over this meeting, but you all need to hear this telegraphed message." She pulled a rumpled sheet of yellow flimsy from her reticule and read the sad words.

To Whom It May Concern:
    On October 28, 1861, near Nassau, agents of the

U.S. Customs Office stopped, boarded, and searched a vessel registered to ABC Purveyors of Fine Luxury Goods of Charleston, South Carolina, on suspicion of transporting goods banned by the current American blockade of the Confederate States.

In the vessel's hold, the agents found vast quantities of tobacco products, alcoholic beverages, and various weapons of war. The captain and crew could not, or would not, produce bills of lading or receipts to show they had paid excise taxes. The agents therefore declared the vessel, its crew, and cargo contraband of war.

Crew members allowed U.S. agents to bind their hands and take over the vessel. The captain—later identified as Antoine Beauchene of Charleston, South Carolina—leaped from the vessel's railing and disappeared into the murky waters of Nassau Harbor. Agents waited for him to surface, but he did not do so. They expanded the search to cover the harbor and nearby ships but found no sign of the captain.

The U.S. Government, therefore, has suspended further search activities and has a declared his death by drowning. The agents will transport the crew to the nearest federal facility to await trial and will turn over the confiscated goods to the U.S. Army for their use.

"Antoine was aware he was risking such a fate." Henrietta drew a deep breath before looking at her stunned audience. "In fact, he reminded me most blockade-runners do not evade capture for over four or five voyages. This was his sixth. I believe he would have enjoyed knowing he left this earth with a great nose-thumbing gesture at the blockaders. He would not want us to mourn him, but it might be well for us to remember our wartime victories sometimes come at great cost."

Governor Pickens' face reflected deep sorrow as he stood. "Please accept our sincere condolences to you and your family, Mrs. Beauchene. I have more bad news to convey although it will pale compared to the loss of Antoine Beauchene." He paused before assuming a more official tone.

"Last Thursday, our ambassadors, John Slidell and James Mason, boarded the *HMS Trent* to complete their Atlantic crossing. The next day, in international waters, the *USS San Jacinto* intercepted the *Trent*. Captain Charles Wilkes ordered U.S. agents to board the *Trent* and search its hold. Rather than subject the crew of the *Trent* to further harassment or guilt by complicity, Mason and Slidell stepped forward, admitted to being Confederate agents, and surrendered themselves. Captain Wilkes transported them to Boston and locked them up in Fort Warren Prison."

"Are you saying that the United States stopped and boarded an English ship in open waters? That violated international law. You understand that, I hope?" Robert Bunch's anger was palpable.

"I do, sir, but I believe our friends the ambassadors may not have realized the boarding was illegal. They acted to protect the *Trent* and its English crew, and by confessing their guilt they may well have done so. The Yankees allowed the *Trent* to proceed to its destination after they removed Mason and Slidell. But the ambassadors' admissions of guilt proved justification for the boarding. It also lessened the impact of Wilkes' outrageous violation of international law. I understand newspapers on both sides of the Atlantic are already fanning the flames of the controversy. We shall have to wait to see what develops."

∽

ROBERT BUNCH DID HIS BEST TO SWALLOW HIS ANGER AT THE insult the United States had just hurled at Her Majesty's government. Henrietta noted a muscle jumping in his cheek as he adjusted his reactions. "I suggest a round of sherry in tribute to Antoine's death and to our imprisoned colleagues." He lifted the bottle from the sideboard and poured the drinks with a flourish. "The events of the past few days may well turn out to be to our advantage."

"Difficult to see how," muttered Jacques Lévêque.

"The United States is antagonizing many diplomats, and they've also become a laughingstock. Let me give you an example. My dispatch case this morning brought an incredible story from the *London Times.* Back on October fifteenth, Commodore DuPont, who was busy organizing the fleet in Chesapeake Bay, received a telegraph message from the Navy Department in Washington, D.C. It reported that the *CSS Nashville* had set sail from Charleston and had run the blockade. It also stated that our two ambassadors, Slidell and Mason, were aboard."

"But we know that's not true."

"Yes. That's the point. DuPont didn't check the source of the report or its validity. He ordered one of his trusted underlings—a fellow named John B. Marchand, captain of the *USS James Adger*—to give pursuit and capture the ship and its passengers. Marchand knew his vessel was slower than the *Nashville*, so he took a shorter route. He planned to intercept the *Nashville* in the waters of the English Channel. His voyage was disastrous. The ship ran into violent storms, suffered wind damage, sprang an unrelated leak because of botched construction, and ran out of coal because someone had failed to load the full amount ordered. Marchand had to detour to a port in Ireland for fuel and landed in France rather than England. When he learned the *Nashville* had not arrived, he thought he had won the race.

"In fact, the *Nashville* had never left Charleston, and the two ambassadors were enjoying a tropical vacation while they waited for transport at Cardenas. Other articles suggest it embarrassed Captain Marchand to learn he missed the departure of the Southern Atlantic Fleet and damaged his ship while chasing a baseless rumor. Reporters chuckle over such stories and have little sympathy for the victim of a hoax."

"It makes the United States look foolish, but I don't see how it helps us."

"Well, there was a follow-up story in the *London Times*, reporting the actual arrest of Slidell and Mason. In that November seventh article, the paper denounced the United States for its reckless defiance of international law. The *Times* issued its own policy statement regarding the war. Let me quote them:

We believe the Secession of the South has destroyed the Federal Union. The contest is for empire on the side of the North, and for independence on that of the South, and in this respect, we recognize an exact analogy between the North and the English government and the South and the Thirteen Revolted Provinces. These are the general opinions of the English nation.

"If the English people side with us, Her Majesty the Queen may have to amend her stance on neutrality—in our favor."

"Yes, but will she?"

"We don't know. The royal family is still in an uproar over Bertie and his prostitute, so Victoria may not be paying much attention to events occurring beyond the palace. We must persevere until we can capture her attention."

As the small group broke up, Robert Bunch waylaid Henrietta. "Can you stay? You may need to talk about this terrible news."

"Perhaps so, Robert, but not tonight. I haven't told my daughters yet, and I must go home and do so. Poor dears. It will devastate them. They are all fond of their Uncle Antoine, for he has doted upon them ever since they were babies. This is family time. I would prefer to enjoy a visit and your company some time when I am calmer."

THE FATE OF THE LOW COUNTRY

November 13–14, 1861
Charleston, South Carolina

*H*enrietta often noticed that she and her daughter Elise were so attuned to one another they could finish each other's sentences. This evening was no exception. She met Elise as she climbed the stairs to the piazza of the family home.

"Thank goodness you are home. I have terrible news about—" They spoke in unison.

"You first."

"No, you first." They spoke at the same moment, and their messages crossed. Antoine's death and Cousin Richard's arrival blurred into a single statement.

"What?"

"Who?"

Henrietta held up her hands in surrender. "I'll shut up and listen. What did you say about somebody named Richard?"

"Cousin Richard Westhaven and his wife, Suzanne. They arrived about an hour ago, looking like gypsies and driving a wagon pulled by two mules. On it they had many odds and ends—their dog, smoked hams, bags of Carolina gold rice, bundles of greens, two trunks overstuffed with clothes, and boxes of who-knows-what. The two of them looked as if they hadn't slept in days. Mud covered their feet and brambles tangled their hair. I can't tell you how disheveled they looked."

"What had happened to them?"

"Soldiers drove them off their plantation on Edisto Island. Richard said some of those Yankees from the Northern fleet showed up at the door and told them the U.S. Army was taking over the entire island. They had two or three hours to get their things together, and they could only take what they could fit onto a single wagon pulled by two mules. They said their neighbors, too, are on the road, everybody looking for someplace that will take them in. And they're scared to death.

"So, Richard and Suzanne have come to the family home looking for shelter. They asked if they could have Aunt Maggie's old room in the East Wing, and I said they could. There was nothing else to do. I had the housemaids open the rooms over there to air them out. They put fresh sheets on the bed and located towels and a water pitcher. That's where Richard and Suzanne are now, cleaning up before you see them. I didn't know what else to do. I hope it's all right."

"It's fine. Your grandfather always said this house belonged not to him but to the family that had come before him. He made room for anyone who knocked at the door. But what a horrible thing to have happen to them. They've lived on that plantation for close to forty years—raised their family there, managed a whole village of slaves, produced exceptional cotton. How can anyone order them to go away?"

"Suzanne said the soldiers watching them pack pointed their rifles at them the whole time. I guess under those conditions you wouldn't ask questions."

"Whatever happened, we'll handle it. That's what families do, even if ours is . . . shrinking." Henrietta's voice cracked as tears threatened to flow.

"What's wrong, mother? What was that you said about Uncle Antoine? You didn't mean he was—uh, no. Did his mission fall through? Did the blockade trap him? What?"

"He is dead. All I know is what this telegraph message says. It arrived at the warehouse this afternoon." She handed the scrap of wrinkled paper to her eldest daughter and tried not to look at the stricken expression on her face as she read. Elise shook her head in denial.

"He can't be. I don't believe it. They have no proof. Uncle Antoine was—is—good at swimming long distances under water. I'll never believe he drowned."

"I've heard Nassau Harbor is full of shipwrecks and castoffs. He might have gotten himself snagged on something while he was down deep, and—"

"Don't say it. I won't listen. He's not dead! He's not!" Her voice rose until she was screaming. Everyone in the house could hear her. Curious black faces peered through the windows to see what the fuss was about and then disappeared as the slaves hurried away before someone blamed them for whatever was wrong. If the Westhavens heard the commotion, they stayed out of sight, but Juliette and Rachel came running downstairs from their rooms to see if they could help. Henrietta tried to comfort Elise as she passed the telegram to her other daughters. Soon all three were in tears.

"My dears, I know how distraught you must be, and I'm sorry to have been the one to convey the news. I'm sure you were fond of him."

"Fond!" Rachel whirled to face her mother. "Fond? Is that all you think we felt? You do not understand what Uncle Antoine meant to us."

"I know he was your only uncle, but—"

"Yes, and I also know you hated him."

"No, Rachel, I did not hate him. Hate is a destructive emotion, and I could not have worked with him all these years if I—"

"But you did. You hated him, and he knew it, too. He couldn't break through the barriers you set up around yourself, any more than we could. But he loved us, and we returned that love. When you were too busy to bother with us, he was the one who came home at lunchtime to play with us for a while. He became our father-figure—never the disciplinarian you were, or the family patriarch lording it over us like grandfather did.

"If you punished us by sending us to bed without supper, Uncle Antoine was the one who smuggled us something to eat—a piece of fruit, a chicken leg, a biscuit or two, whatever he could scrounge from the warming kitchen. When you were too busy to hear about our childish problems, he always listened with a patient ear. You criticized our outfits or hairdos or dirty faces, and he told us we were beautiful. If you ignored our little cuts and skinned knees, he bandaged them with love. You were our parent, but he was the one who enjoyed parenting."

"He could afford to do that," Henrietta replied. "because he wasn't responsible for turning you into productive adults."

"No. He turned us into adults who understand what love means. Somehow you did not include that lesson."

"Rachel, you are overwrought and lashing out at the nearest target. I understand that, but I need no lectures from you tonight."

"I don't care what you need. You still haven't told us why you hated Antoine."

"Once again, I did not hate him. We did not get along, I admit. Our animosities stemmed from events that happened before you were born, events whose details need not concern you. I witnessed him committing a multitude of despicable acts, including at least one that was a serious felony and for which he stood trial at an inquest. I witnessed his crime. But the law did not allow women to testify in court, and the judge exonerated him of all charges.[1] I tried to forgive him as my faith instructed, but I could never forget. You saw one side of the man. I had a more complete view, and I did not like what I saw."

"You're not any more perfect than he was. You're a hypocrite, and I won't listen to you condemn a man on the day we learn of his death." Rachel stormed from the piazza, slamming the door behind her and running up the stairs to her room. Another door slammed in her wake. Elise and Juliette struggled to pretend they had not heard every accusing word.

"Miss Henrietta?" Mrs. Jernigan, their longtime housekeeper, hesitated in the doorway. "The new guests sent word they will not be coming to dinner. Cook is now whipping up a pot of soup and some biscuit sandwiches to send to their room on a tray. I can have her do similar trays for each of you if you would prefer not to have a sit-down meal this evening."

Henrietta looked at her daughters for confirmation. They nodded. "That would be helpful, Mrs. Jernigan. Thank you."

"One more question, ma'am. I didn't mean to eavesdrop, but I heard you say Massa Antoine is dead. Shall I have the housemaids drape the house in mourning tonight, or can it wait until tomorrow?"

"We won't be making any show of mourning, Mrs. Jernigan. Antoine has suffered an accident and is missing. The police presume he is dead, but they have not found his body. His death will not be official until they do so or until seven years have passed."

"Seven years? Oh, my! I'd better see to supper, then." The housekeeper scurried off.

"Are you serious? Seven years? That's ridiculous!"

"That's the law, Elise. We can't read his will or place a marker in the churchyard until we verify the death by discovering his body or by the passing of time."

"And we don't mourn until then?"

"We do not make a public show of mourning. There's a difference. To mourn before the death is certain would suggest that we have lost hope or have failed to trust in God. What we do in private is a different matter. You may grieve for as long as you must."

THE NEXT DAY, AFTER THE INITIAL WAVES OF GRIEF AND GUILT had passed, Henrietta sat down with Richard to hear his story. She didn't know him well although he and his family had often spent Christmases in Charleston. Still, what she knew of him pleased her.

"We've heard stories about what happened in the Low Country, Richard, but I would value your input. I've always thought you were clear-headed and a careful observer of events."

"Maybe not too clear-eyed this time. We could not see what was happening for most of the month. It started with the procession of Yankee ships. On November fifth, they passed our beachfront on St. Helena Sound, and we held our breath for fear they might occupy it. But they kept moving south, headed for Port Royal Sound. On the seventh, we heard the guns. Sometimes they were so loud that the earth seemed to shake. Then around two o'clock they stopped, which was even more frightening because that meant the South had lost the battle. Our men didn't stand a prayer. General Beauregard had sent a hundred raw recruits to stop thirty thousand invaders. They had six or seven big guns on fixed mounts while the North had dozens of guns aboard fifteen ships, all with the ability to swivel at will."[2]

"Multiple casualties, I assume."

"Yes. Yankee guns blew the soldiers at Bay Point and Fort Walker apart. The only ones who survived were those who fled inland when the final order came to retreat."

"What about the civilians living on those islands?"

"They had orders to evacuate two days earlier, and the white folks did, except for one legendary old sot who stayed in Beaufort because he was too drunk to understand what was happening. The planters gathered their families and took whatever transportation they could find—boat or wagon, horseback or shoe leather—to head inland out of the line of fire. They had heard terrible rumors about what the enemy soldiers planned to do to anyone who stayed."

"The white folks, you said. What happened to the slaves? They bleed, too."

"They do. But there are so many of them. Those islands support little except cotton plantations. And a plantation has one white owner and his family—maybe half a dozen people —and two or three hundred slaves to do the work. No planter could hope to take his blacks with him as he fled. The slaves heard the Northern soldiers would send them to Cuba if they caught them, so most were just trying to hunker down and hide. But after a few days, they realized the Northerners had no interest in slaves. The soldiers went to work cleaning up the battleground and building a base camp that could house and support them all. They were building a good-sized city.

"Once the slaves discovered that no one cared about them, they took one of two paths. Some approached the solders and volunteered to work. As you might imagine, their strong backs were a welcome addition to the labor force. The house slaves realized that those rich planters' houses were now empty. They entered them to explore and plundered them. Wine cellars sometimes fueled their actions. They pulled up carpets and took down drapes to make new clothes for themselves. They made off with the stored foodstuffs and tore out the metal fixtures. For the first time they had access to real silverware and plates for their tables. They thought they were rich beyond measure. As far as I know, some of them are still partying.

"The most encouraging developments were on St. Helena Island, where most of the abandoned slaves went right on doing what they had done all their lives.[3] They ignored their white masters as much as possible, so their absence didn't make much difference. They've continued to pick cotton as if it were a normal season."

"My word! What will the slaves do with the cotton once they've finished the harvest?"

"I don't think they've considered that yet. They've never faced that problem. But don't get your hopes up about laying your hands on it. By the time the soldiers arrived at Edisto Island, they had stock answers to questions like yours. They told us to leave or risk imprisonment. They told the slaves to keep on working because Father Lincoln would send agents to buy their cotton."

"Cotton agents?"

"Yes. The North needs our cotton, and they consider it to be spoils of war. The most comfort I can offer you and your business is whatever you have stored in your warehouse will remain safe. You won't be getting any new deliveries, however. It will be easier for those agents to visit the plantations and load up whatever they can find. The poor slaves won't be able to stop them. Hoes are useless against rifles."

"But you—you and your fellow planters? What will happen to you? Do you expect to go back when the soldiers leave?"

"The Northern invaders are not going anywhere, Henrietta. That installation they are building at Hilton Head is permanent. No, the days of Low Country cotton plantations have passed. Small farmers will break up our holdings into manageable plots as they are already doing on St. Helena and turn to crops that meet their immediate needs."

"But still cotton?"

"Turnips, I suspect. What a bargain! You can eat the tops when they are green and save the bottoms for winter." His tone was bitter.

"But they must keep cultivating the cotton crops. Sea Island cotton grows nowhere else. It needs our unique climate." Henrietta concentrated on her hopes for continuity until Richard grasped her by the shoulders and shook her.

"Stop it, Henrietta. I understand how you feel, but it's over, my dear. Your world will never be the same. You need to think about this and make plans for the future—a future without Sea Island cotton."

"People will still need cloth."

"Yes, but others can meet that need. If the Beauchene Company wants to stay in business, you will need to think in terms of inland sources—cotton of lower grade but still useful."

"How do we do that?"

"I'll help, if you will let me. As an old man, Henrietta, I have few needs and much experience. Let me turn my knowledge into a tool to save the Beauchene Company. I need something to make me feel useful again. Together, I suspect we can put the pieces back together."

"I appreciate your offer, Richard, and I will welcome your advice. But I cannot think about the future yet. Give me some time to re-imagine the Beauchene Company without the Beauchenes."

BACK TO BUSINESS

December 1861
Charleston, South Carolina

*N*ight after night, Henrietta lay awake trying to sort through her options. When she came to South Carolina, she had expected to spend her life as a wife and mother. She knew nothing about cotton or the world of business until her father-in-law decreed that she should assume a role in the family company. Reassured the male members of the Beauchene family stood in ranks to conduct the actual business dealings, she had agreed to do her part. But now they were all gone—father-in-law, husband, brother-in-law—leaving no male heirs. Although Father Beauchene had tried to protect the legal claims of Henrietta and her daughters, the engrained Southern attitude toward women ruled against any easy acceptance of their rights to assume ownership of the business. The civil war that now engulfed the country only complicated the issues.

In the pre-dawn hours of one December night, Henrietta reached a shocking realization. As much as she deplored

Antoine's self-indulgent attitudes, as much as she resented his insulting treatment of women, as much as she hated him for his role in her husband's death, she missed him. Even though he held only forty percent of the company's stock, she had trusted him to support the best interests of the business and the family. He had grown up in the cotton business and understood the market. Now, she had no one to turn to, no one to offer a needed piece of advice, no one to blame if things went wrong. She had used him as a safety device; without him she was floundering.

Henrietta did not relish asking anyone for help, and Richard, kind though he seemed to be, was an unknown quantity. The girls were too inexperienced, and David Manwaring, although a reliable employee, was not familiar with the inner workings of the company. Instead, she turned to the one person she knew whose responsibility it was to advise—Robert Bunch. In fact, he had offered his help a few weeks earlier, but she had rejected his overtures out of hand. Now, however, she saw his advice as a lifeline. When the sun came up, she penned a note to the British Consulate.

As a British citizen by birth and an American by marriage, I find myself in a difficult position during this period of civil war and international disputes. My situation involves business-related currency issues, trust funds, and various inheritance matters. Is there someone available at the Consulate who could advise me on how to handle my financial affairs? I can meet today or tomorrow. Please reply through the servant who brings this message.

As soon as Nate had set out to deliver the sealed note,

Henrietta began second-guessing herself. What if the message went to an under-secretary who did not even recognize her name? Robert Bunch might be unwilling to meet with her. He might even mistake her plea as a flirtatious gesture.

Father Beauchene's private office had always been off-limits to the other members of the household, and, although she had now inherited it along with the rest of his family home, Henrietta spent almost no time there. Today, however, it offered shelter from the problems that pursued her. No servants would bother her, no visitors would gain admittance, and even her daughters would hesitate to knock. Henrietta wandered around the room, stopping to examine the leather-bound books on a shelf or to read the fading ink that identified the people in an old painting. Sometimes, her eyes hesitated on the false shelf that concealed a safe, but she had no interest in the bonds, the jewels, and the deeds that remained there. They were sacred—hers to guard, not to exploit.

WHEN NATE'S TENTATIVE TAP ON THE DOOR BROKE THROUGH her muddled thoughts, she rushed to take the folded note he offered. Then she settled into the creaky old leather desk chair and opened Robert's response.

My dear lady, advising our British citizens on matters both personal and financial is the purpose of this office. We stand ready to offer our help. Come to the consulate as soon as you can—before lunch so that my chef can once again work his soothing magic on your fraying nerves. I have cleared my desk and

cancelled all other appointments for the day. I await
your arrival.

Over a steaming bowl of smoky split pea soup topped
with fresh sprigs of dill and a generous dollop of *creme fraiche,*
Henrietta relaxed and outlined the details of her dilemma.

"As the majority stockholder of the Beauchene Company,
I have the power to buy and sell as I please. But I also have a
moral obligation—imposed in family wills—to preserve the
company's assets and pass them on to my daughters. I intend
to fulfill those promises. But the current war being waged
between the North and the South raises currency issues,
along with questions about the safety of bank accounts that
accept only U.S. treasury bills or Confederate dollars. My
dual citizenship—or triple citizenship, depending on the
outcome of the war—British by birth, American by marriage,
and Confederate by residence, leaves my national identity
and loyalty in question no matter which version I claim.

"Antoine's disappearance causes additional confusion.
Although the U.S. government has ruled that he died by
drowning, his missing body leaves that verdict in doubt.
Southern courts will not accept unsubstantiated Northern
proof of death, so the legal status of his will remains in question. No disposition of his company holdings can proceed
until seven years have passed without further evidence of his
fate. And that throws a cloud of uncertainty over any business dealings I might attempt. What can I do, Robert? What
are my options, or don't I have any?"

"Are you in a position to buy and sell cotton despite the
Northern blockade?"

"Well, if you are asking whether I have enough money to
continue to purchase raw cotton from our growers, the
answer is a tentative yes, depending on their willingness to

accept U.S. currency. If you're asking about the supply of cotton available in our warehouse, the answer is also yes. Our shelves are full, and our supplies are more than adequate if we can find a blockade runner to carry the bales to safety overseas." She hesitated, frowning. "That one little word—if —is the problem, isn't it?"

"Yes, it is. Here. The problem requires further sustenance." Bunch lifted a tiered platter from the sideboard and placed it between them on the table. "That's a fine English Stilton on the top, with an assortment of double-cream soft cheeses from Normandy surrounding it. The toasts come from baguettes freshly baked in our own kitchen, and on the bottom tray you'll find an assortment of Persian dates, Moroccan dried apricots, English walnuts, and Georgian pecans. You see in front of you a strong argument for cooperation rather than conflict between nations."

Henrietta caught her breath. "I haven't tasted a good Stilton since I left Oxford. How do you stock your larder with such international delicacies?"

He grinned. "That roomy diplomatic pouch sometimes carries an odd assortment of purchases. Help yourself as you mull over my profound statement of its symbolism."

"I didn't miss your message, and I agree with the sentiment. It is the implementation I find difficult. I would stop this silly war in an instant if it were possible, but we both know American pig-headedness will not allow that. I ask you again. What can I do?"

"You can create your own bastion of international cooperation that functions despite the war."

"I don't understand."

"You identify like-minded people who conduct their affairs according to a broad world view and cast your lot with them. And you keep your options open until the conflicts around you resolve themselves."

"Are there such people—and options—in Charleston?"

"You know more of them than you realize. The most important is George Trenholm."

"Trenholm? I don't know him all that well, but Antoine always dismissed him as a lightweight—a dabbler in the cotton trade, not a serious rival."

"His short-sighted mistake. George Trenholm is an international powerhouse, and part of his mystique is his ability to disguise his financial dealings by appearing to be unaware of the broad picture. But make no mistake. He dips his fingers into every pot of gold that passes."

"Such as—?"

"Where does the Beauchene Company keep its accounts?"

"It splits them between the Bank of South Carolina and the Bank of Charleston."

"George Trenholm is the major stockholder in both. If you want a loan, he has final approval. If you dealt in low-grade cotton, how would you get those bales from upstate areas to Charleston?"

"I don't know. I've never considered it. But I suppose, if there weren't a war going on, we'd use the railways."

"Trenholm has major interests in several South Carolina railroads. He would help determine your freight charges, which could make or break you."

Henrietta was shaking her head. "I did not understand his business dealings. And you said he was an international figure, too. The Trenholm Brothers Trading Company does not appear to have any influence outside of Charleston."

"He is an international figure. He began his career in the accounting department of Fraser and Company, a South Carolina shipping company. As the company grew, so did his involvement. Within a few years, he and his brother Charles seized control, and the company became Fraser, Trenholm, and Company. At their suggestion, the company moved their operations to New York City to have better access to world traders. From there, they expanded to England, where they established a major ship-building yard in Liverpool. They have now added a branch in Bermuda to position themselves on the Atlantic trade routes. In Liverpool, Charles K. Prioleau manages the company of Fraser, Trenholm, and Company. He is a Charlestonian by birth and a hand-picked lackey of the Trenholm family. Prioleau has contacts with the major textile manufacturers in England. So, George Trenholm and his brother Charles have their fingers in all the business matters that might affect you."

"I knew nothing of this."

"Which is as they want it. You regard George as just another cotton factor, running a small family firm. He is that. And he's much more."

"Was Antoine aware of his business connections?"

"I think not, which made your brother-in-law vulnerable in any deal between your two companies. That's why I want you to understand Trenholm's power. With charm and a little luck, you may put all that power to work on your behalf."

"And just how do I go about managing that outcome?"

"You came for help. My best advice is that you ask George Trenholm to step in and guide you.

"You're serious?"

"Dead serious. Your company can't challenge him, but he holds the ability to destroy you at will. But there is something seductive about—"

"Seductive? Oh, no, I draw the line at—"

"No! Henrietta! I should have said there is something appealing about a damsel in distress. When you ask him for help, you will remind him he is a Southern gentleman, and he'll respond by doing everything he can to help you. He holds the keys to several of the situations you see as problematic. You worry about currencies and exchange rates. He has banking interests in the Confederacy, in the United States, and in England. You've lost your only blockade running vessel. His Liverpool firm is working night and day to turn out new blockade runners. He's planning to mount an all-out effort to keep the Atlantic shipping routes open. You have problems, and he's the man with the solutions."

"I understand what you're saying about his businesses, but I doubt sheer philanthropy will move him. He has much to offer, but what can I provide in exchange? I've already told you, I can't offer to sell him our company."

"No, but you have two things he needs—a warehouse full of top-grade cotton and a stock of fine luxury goods, and a base of operations in Nassau, where he does not have a foothold. And besides, he's feeling guilty about roping Antoine into the adventure that took his life. He'll be open to your proposal."

"And just what is that proposal?"

"That your two companies work together to form a temporary consortium devoted to preserving the cotton trade during this unfortunate war. Once the government settles the questions of secession and independence, you can reconsider the future of that consortium."

Henrietta stared at Robert for a moment and then stood. She walked to the window and looked out over scenery she loved. Was Charleston, and all it stood for, worth the fight that awaited her? As she contemplated her decision, Robert approached her from behind and placed his hands on her shoulders. The gesture was comforting, and for a moment, she wanted to lean back into his proffered embrace—to give in to the pull of the bonds that connected them. Then she straightened and pulled away.

Robert responded to her gentle rebuff by dropping his hands and stepping to her side. "You don't have to make a snap decision, my dear. Today is only Tuesday. George Tren-holm is away and won't return to Charleston until Sunday at the earliest."

"Engaged in some international skullduggery, I presume."

He refused to rise to her bait. "No, I believe he is in Columbia to consult with the governor and legislators about the best way to respond to the blockade. Even high-powered politicians recognize his diplomatic skills, you see."

"Politicians are not the most honest of men, are they?"

"Henrietta, you face many problems. Go home. Sleep on this decision. Talk to your daughters—and to your visiting cousin. Consider the advantages of such a consortium, and the dangers you will face by going it alone. Don't decide until next week."

THE GREAT CHARLESTON FIRE
OF 1861

December 11, 1861
Charleston, South Carolina

*T*he next morning, Henrietta headed for the office to distract herself with some account books. As she entered the front door, angry voices greeted her. She had hoped for solitude. Irritated, she peered into her daughter's reception area office.

"Elise? Who's in the warehouse? And what on earth is going on back there?"

"It's Cousin Richard and Joshua. But I don't know what they're arguing about. I was just about to go back and see if I could calm them down."

"Richard? What's he doing here? Did you invite him?"

"No. He strolled in a few minutes ago and asked to look around. He said he was taking over some of Uncle Antoine's responsibilities. Should I have refused?"

"Oh, no, my dear. He's family. But I'm not pleased to find him nosing around on his own. It's true he has offered his help with the business, but I've been holding off about taking him up on the offer. Don't worry about it. I'll handle him from here."

Henrietta stopped by her own office to drop off her reticule and cloak. Then she took a few deep breaths and headed to the warehouse. As she entered, Joshua's eyes widened and then crinkled as he realized she was glaring at the visitor, not him.

"Richard? What are you doing back here? And why are you shouting at our faithful office manager? In all the years I've known Joshua, I have never found it necessary to speak to him with such an insulting tone."

"He's a slave, Henrietta, and an impudent one at that. I asked him to make basic changes back here, and he refused. Said he didn't know me and wouldn't do anything without your approval. If I was his owner, I'd have him whipped to teach him his place."

"As far as Joshua knew, you were a stranger, with no authority to be back here at all. It sounds as if he was doing an admirable job of protecting our property. Now, I can correct part of this problem. Joshua, this is Richard West-haven, Master Pierre's cousin. You remember Aunt Maggie, I assume? Richard is her son. He is now living in Aunt Maggie's old East Wing apartment after being driven off his Edisto cotton plantation by the Yankee invasion. From now on, if your paths cross, please treat him as a member of the family."

"Yes, ma'am. Sorry, ma'am."

"As for you, Richard, while I am grateful for your offer of help with the family business, I don't recall having accepted it."

Richard stared at her with a startled expression on his face. He opened his mouth but found no words.

Henrietta wanted to laugh but didn't. The man could not have been more shocked if the cat had spoken to him, she realized.

"I thought I made my offer clear. I'm prepared to step in and take over Antoine's responsibilities."

"Well, that will not happen—at least not for a while. I am engaged in some delicate business negotiations, the nature of which I am not at liberty to discuss. When I have a clearer idea of the direction in which I intend to take this company, I will be happy to revisit your offer.

"In the near term, I must ask you to limit your help to matters at the house. You may stay for an indefinite period, and there may be changes you and Suzanne will want to make. No one has occupied those rooms in the East Wing since your mother died. They are sorely in need of refurbishing, and you may exercise your organizational skills toward making yourselves comfortable. However, if you intend to remain in Charleston, you need to understand that here we treat our black servants with respect. They are not the field hands you berated on the plantation. The house servants will be happy to do your bidding if you treat them with the respect they deserve."

"You pamper them, too, I take it."

"I believe all persons deserve simple courtesies, such as 'please,' and 'thank you.' It may surprise you to find that kindness accomplishes more than threats of punishment. Now, if you are on your way, we'll all get back to work."

Richard gave her one last incredulous look before whirling and stomping out the door. Joshua covered his mouth to contain his chortles. "Oh, Miss Henrietta, you set that man back on his heels."

"Before you get too cocky, you might tell me why he was so upset."

"He said the warehouse was a firetrap—he wanted to move that rum and gunpowder away from the cotton. But there's no place else to put it."

"All cotton storage is dangerous if a spark sets off a fire, but that will not happen here. Our brick walls and metal roof protect us well. You might sweep, however—at least make the place a little neater."

"Yes, ma'am."

LINGERING TENSIONS KEPT DINNER CONVERSATIONS LIMITED TO polite requests and safer topics such as the unusually warm weather. Richard made a show of thanking the servants each time one passed him a dish. The girls, still missing their Uncle Antoine, reported on their day's activities without their usual enthusiasm. Only Suzanne chattered on about the difficulties of finding suitable new furnishings for the East Wing. All the best furniture makers and upholsterers had gone off to war, she complained.

A sudden clanging of church bells startled everyone. Richard and Suzanne, conditioned to react to the dangers of invasion, looked toward the door as if expecting someone to burst into the room. Henrietta and her daughters recognized the sound—a call to the city's volunteer fire crews.

Elise glanced at her mother. "Speaking of men going off to war, I wonder how many volunteer firemen we have left."

"The older men are still here," she said, "They are the ones with experience, although they don't move as fast as they used to."

"I know our German Fire Company has closed its doors for the duration of the war," Rachel said. "You'll remember that at our Bastille Day party, they wore their new Army reserves uniforms. The Army called them up in July to work on the fortifications at Bay Point, near Hilton Head. No one at the church has heard from them since they left."

Richard and Suzanne exchanged knowing glances at the mention of Bay Point, but neither wanted to speak about the obvious conclusion. Their neighbors at Bay Point had found few if any survivors after the Battle of Port Royal. Henrietta, too, wanted to avoid upsetting Rachel again by commenting. Instead, she turned to Mrs. Jernigan, who had been waiting to clear the table. "Would you ask two men from the yard to find out where the fire is, please?"

"Better, yet, I'll go with them. Let me make myself useful, Henrietta." Richard pushed his chair back and stood, heading for the stables.

"Wait, please, let the younger men go on ahead." Suzanne caught at his sleeve to hold him back. "I'm frightened. Don't leave us women alone."

Irritated, he shook off her clutching fingers. "It's not another invasion, my dear. But I'll see if I can spot the trouble from the piazza. I suspect the fire is nowhere near us."

HE WAS WRONG. HE COULD SMELL THE SMOKE THE MINUTE HE stepped outside. And as he looked to his right, he saw the fire's glow over the docks, just two blocks away. He hesitated and then hurried out to the sidewalk where neighbors were already gathering. They were eager to report every rumor. Some said the Yankees had set the city on fire. Others had heard there was a slave rebellion. And a third view blamed the blaze on vagrants. All shared one common thread—the fire had consumed the market area and was spreading to the waterfront.

"They're summoning firemen from all over the city, but the pumpers will not keep up with the flames if this wind kicks up," someone observed.

"It's blowing from the northeast now. That usually means a storm's coming, so it could be a blessing to us. At least it will blow the hot embers away from our houses."

"But the wind will drive the flames toward Meeting Street and the whole city center."

As the crowd milled about, Richard looked up to see Joshua running full tilt toward the house. He broke away from a garrulous old man who was making dire predictions of doom and pushed the gate open to admit the warehouse manager.

"Don't tell me the warehouse is on fire. I knew it! I had a strong premonition this morning that disaster was about to fall."

"No, sir, it's not our warehouse." Joshua gasped and bent over to clutch at the stitch in his side. "At least not yet. They're hoping to stop the spread before it reaches Queen Street. But I thought Miz Beauchene would want to know what's happening."

"Yes. Come up and catch your breath on the piazza while I get Henrietta."

He didn't need to go inside. Henrietta was already at the door. "I'll talk to Joshua, Richard. I need you to tell Nate to bring the gig around to the front entrance at once."

"The gig? Why? Surely you're not thinking of going anywhere in the middle of all this turmoil?"

"Don't argue with me, Richard. I don't have to explain myself to you. Just do as I ask. Now, Joshua, fill me in. Where is the fire and where is it headed?"

"From what folks are saying, the fire broke out behind Russell's Sash and Door Company on Hassell Street. Russell has lots of scrap lumber back there, and vagrants use it as an overnight shelter. One of their fires got out of hand, and they didn't know how to put it out. The wind was still out of the west, and it blew the flames across the street to Cameron's Foundry and then the munitions dump. Those first explosions you heard came from there. Once the first embers touched those shells, it was all over. There was red-hot metal flying and setting fire to everything it touched. And from there the fires spread up Hassell Street and down East Bay, setting the first row of warehouses ablaze and headed right for us."[1]

Richard turned back at the mention of munitions. "See, Henrietta? That's what I was trying to tell you about your warehouse this morning. Put a spark to gunpowder and you can kiss any nearby buildings goodbye."

"Richard, please! Don't chortle over being right while lives and property are at risk. Besides, we have nowhere near as much ammunition as the munitions dump held, and the fire is not threatening our warehouse. Go find Nate! Now!"

She took Joshua's arm and turned him away from the rest of the listening family. "Tell me quickly. How dangerous is it, Joshua?"

"I had my doubts for a while, Miz Beauchene. I closed our metal doors to protect the cotton. But then the wind shifted around out of the nor'east, and that sent the flames in another direction. Right now, it looks like the fire won't spread south of Cumberland, which means you're safe here, and St. Philip's and the new hotel are in no danger. But the fire is burning all those flimsy wood structures on Market Street and heading right toward Meeting Street."

"Are the fire companies working yet?"

"No, ma'am. Most of them went off to war, and the old fellows aren't much good on those heavy pumpers. From what I hear, they're calling out the Army engineers to blow up buildings along the north side of Queen Street. They hope to create a firebreak so the flames won't be able to jump the street. If the fire gets there first, they'll move the barrier to Broad, trying to protect everything south of Broad at all costs to the rest of the city."

"I'm still anxious. There's so much smoke and such a wide swath of destruction it's hard to imagine anything will survive. I must get to the warehouse to protect the company records—and the cat. Was Calico shut up in the warehouse when you closed the fire doors, Joshua?"

"I'm not sure, ma'am. Animals can take care of themselves in times of danger, can't they?"

"Not always. I must go."

"Mother! You can't risk going in there alone." Elise grasped her arm, but Henrietta shook her off.

"Elise. Stay here and keep watch to make sure the house is not in danger. As you know, all the important business records are in one spot at the warehouse. I'll gather them up in this net shopping bag, get the cat, and come right back home." She stepped up into the gig and nodded to the driver. "Nate, let's move quickly."

By the time Nate and Henrietta reached the warehouse, both were coughing from the smoke. Henrietta jumped down and ran to the front entrance. When Nate tried to follow her inside, she shook her head. "No, you stay out here and make sure the door doesn't blow shut and trap me inside. And if the cat comes running out, you catch her and hold her for me."

Nate watched from the doorway as Henrietta made her way across the reception area and then disappeared amid the swirls of smoke. Shaking his head over her folly, he moved back from the door to find some clearer air. He patted the horse who was shaking her mane and flicking her tail as if the smoke irritated her, too. Or perhaps it was the unfamiliar noise that bothered her.

The air echoed with explosions coming from somewhere along Queen Street. The fire bells were still ringing, and from all over the city, the church bells joined the chorus. As whole buildings succumbed to the fires, windows shattered, roofs collapsed, and the walls sighed as they gave way. Even the stone and brick structures added to the racket. The flames were hot enough to melt the mortar that held their building blocks together. As the stones shifted and pulled apart, they sent up an eerie moan before they crashed down.

Time passed. Nate had no way of estimating how long Henrietta had been inside. Then a movement near the doorway attracted his attention. He approached, only to find a dirty and panting calico cat staggering over the threshold. When he picked her up, her little body felt almost lifeless. He carried her back to the gig and laid her carefully on the lap blanket. "You rest there. You're safe now," he promised her. "Wish I could say the same for your owner."

PICKING UP THE PIECES

December 12, 1861
Charleston, South Carolina

*N*ight fell, but instead of a horizon disappearing into darkness, the world glowed red and orange. Shadows moved of their own accord as the flames flickered in the wind. Around midnight, a gentle rain fell, and Nate awoke from his drowsing state to lift his face toward the life-saving water. Hope made him smile, and the moisture woke the cat and made her stretch. But it was not to last. The heat of the fires turned the small drops to steam, and they evaporated before they could reach the ground.

A shape materialized through the smoke to reveal a gentleman Nate recognized from his visits to the house. "Massa Bunch?"

"Yes. Oh, it's you, Nate. What are you doing out here on the street before dawn?"

"I'm waiting for Miz Beauchene."

"Henrietta? Where is she? She didn't go into the warehouse, did she?"

"Sure enough. She wanted to find the cat. The cat came out, but she didn't."

"Oh, God, no! How long has she been in there?"

"I don't know. Long time, it seems. She told me to wait, and that's what I've been doing."

Robert Bunch unwrapped his neck scarf and covered his mouth and nose before he dashed into the smoky warehouse. Nate waited by the gig until he heard a long, anguished "No-o-o-o!" coming from inside. Struck with fear, he took several hesitant steps toward the door, but he stopped when Mr. Bunch reappeared. He was pale and wracked with coughs, tears streaming down his cheeks.

"She's gone, Nate. Dead."

"No, that can't be. The building is not even on fire."

"It's not burning, but it's filled with smoke from the fires. There's not enough air to breathe. I found your mistress on the floor where she collapsed. She's blue and cold to the touch."

"We've got to get her out of there."

"No. We must notify the constabulary and let them send the coroner to make the final pronouncement before she's moved. It's much too late to help her now. She's been dead for hours. Come. I'll ride back to the house with you and take responsibility for telling the family. Then we will notify the proper authorities."

IT WAS AN UNENVIABLE TASK. THE THREE BEAUCHENE GIRLS had spent the night huddled together in the ladies' parlor, hoping that Henrietta's absence only meant that the firemen were keeping her from reaching the warehouse. Cousin Richard and his wife had gone to bed although neither slept much. Now, as the sun rose and pushed its rays through the pall of smoke that overhung the city, Richard was out on the street again hoping someone would bring news of survivors. He was the first to spot the returning horse and its open carriage, but he did not recognize the man who swung down from the seat and approached the house.

"Sir?"

"Are you Richard Westhaven, Henrietta's cousin?"

"Yes, yes, where is she?"

"I have some terrible news. Can we go inside so I only have to tell the story once?"

"Wait! Who are you? What authority do you have?"

Robert Bunch struggled to contain his grief and his anger that this fellow was standing in his way. He pulled a *carte de visite* from his pocket and passed it over. "My authority comes from the British Consulate. I am Her Majesty's official spokesman in the City of Charleston. Now, either come inside with me, or get out of my way."

Elise met them at the door. One look at Bunch's sooty and tear-streaked face was enough to confirm her worst fears. "She's gone."

"Yes, my dear, I can only wish I could bring you a better report. Your mother entered the Beauchene warehouse sometime last night. It was never in danger of burning, but the smoke from nearby blazes must have filled the building through its ventilation shafts. She was gathering up the company ledgers when she collapsed. I found her body this morning when I came to check on the warehouse. She was on the floor near an open wall safe, with various papers and record books strewn around her. The smoke was still too thick to allow me to breathe, but I lingered long enough to determine that her body was cold and blue—suggesting her air supply had run out."

Elise was not listening to the details. She swayed on her feet for a moment and then turned to the parlor doorway where her sisters were staring, wide-eyed with fear. She stretched her arms out to them and all three wailed. Robert Bunch stood by, helpless and wishing he could indulge his own grief instead of hiding it.

As she so often did, Mrs. Jernigan, the housekeeper, took charge. She turned first to the gaggle of wide-eyed slave girls who had gathered at the end of the hall to see what was happening.

"Why are you hanging about? There has been a death in the family. Who and how need not concern you. Your job is to prepare the house for proper mourning. Stop all clocks and set their time to midnight. Cover every mirror. Find black crepe material in the attic and drape the windows and doorways. Clear the parlor of decoration and make room for a bier to hold a coffin. Arrange a reception table in the front hall with a tray for calling cards, and line up extra tables in the dining room to hold the food offerings that the neighbors will bring in. And above all, don't gossip or make guesses about what has happened. The rule for this week will be silence."

"Now," she added, turning toward Elise, "your first order of business must be to eat breakfast."

"Eat? No, we couldn't."

"You must keep up your strength and to set an example for your sisters. I'll have the cook prepare something that goes down easy—and coffee—lots of coffee. Mr. Bunch, you are welcome to join the family."

"Thank you, but there is much to do. Elise, if I can trouble you for a few more minutes—"

"Please. I do not understand what to do."

"Well, first, is there someone—a family friend, perhaps, who could step in and take the pressure off your shoulders?"

"Oh, yes, Aunt Elizabeth—that's Mrs. Elizabeth Dubois, who lives on Legare Street. I'm sure the fire didn't reach that far. She's mother's best friend, and godmother to all three of us. She will want to be here."

Mrs. Jernigan stepped in once more. "I can take care of that, sir. I'll send one of our drivers to break the news and bring her back to the house."

"Do that, Mrs. Jernigan. Now, who else? You'll need the family lawyer and your parish clergyman."

"The lawyer would be Arthur Middleton, but I don't want him here, at least not yet. But the clergyman might be of help. That's Reverend Howard at the Huguenot church. He's also Rachel's employer, so he needs to know."

"If one of your men can deliver those messages, too, it will be helpful." Mr. Bunch hesitated and then plunged ahead. "The police and the coroner will identify the body and examine it in place before anyone can move her. I'll handle those details, but first—"

"What?"

"Elise, my dear, may we speak in private?"

"Can it wait?"

"No. Mrs. Jernigan, please take the rest of the family to the dining room and close this door behind you."

"You're scaring me."

"I don't mean to do that, but this can't wait. When I found your mother, she was lying on the floor as if she had just collapsed. The office safe was open but empty, and papers and notebooks cluttered the surrounding floor. Did you know about that hidden safe and its contents?"

"Yes, mother showed me how to find it. She worried if something happened to her, no one would ever know it was there. She showed me the combination, but with strict instructions never to look inside unless she was . . . dead." Her voice cracked with emotion.

"I assume that the contents were important enough for her to risk her life retrieving them. I think it unwise to let the

"I must. Nate can drive us there since he already knows
what happened."

"Let's do this and get it over with. Will you summon him?"

On the way to the warehouse, another thought occurred
to Elise. "Nate, whatever happened to mother's cat?"

"Oh, ma'am, I brought her back to the house. She was
dirty and hacking a little, but I gave her to the cook. When I
left them, the cook was making soothing sounds at her and
feeding her scraps of something."

Elise smiled despite her grief. "Mother would like that.
Thank you."

AT THE WAREHOUSE, A PALL OF SMOKE STILL HUNG IN THE AIR,
but it was clearing out. Robert Bunch led Elise to her mother's office and held her elbow for support when she saw the
body. He guided her to the chair behind a desk which
blocked her view.

"Sit here, and I'll bring the documents to you. You can
decide what to do with them one at a time, and I'll either put
them in the safe or scatter them on the floor again."

He started with a roll of currency. "Money's not incriminating, but these are U.S. Treasury bills. The Confederacy
might want to confiscate them."

"Mother told me about the money. It was Grandfather
Beauchene's nest egg, saved in case the family was in dire

straits. Awful though her death is, it doesn't qualify as that. Put the money back in the safe. Mother had never counted it, and neither will I."

"Done. Now these ledgers. The heading claims these are unsecured loans, made under the counter, and most of them never repaid. I'm not sure what anyone would want with the records now. Blackmail, perhaps, but that seems out of character for the Beauchenes."

"I know nothing about those. However, they support mother's statement she wanted to rescue the company records. Maybe they are best left on the floor."

"This is a strange document to find in a cotton warehouse. It appears to be a scientific study about phosphate deposits along the Ashley River."

"I can't explain that, either. It may have something to do with the property my grandfather passed to my mother. Perhaps it would be best to put it back in the safe."

"Next, something I recognize. This envelope, labeled 'My Life as a Spy,' contains copies of letters I asked Henrietta to write for me earlier this year."

"Did you say, 'as a spy?' That's ridiculous. Mother would never have spied on her own country."

"I'm sure she meant it as a joke. Your mother sometimes had a quirky sense of humor. I wouldn't call her a spy. She helped me send important information about secession and the forming of the Confederacy to friends in England. I told her what to write, and she disguised the messages as casual chatter to a non-existent friend. The letters went to a sham drop box where a go-between intercepted them and delivered them to people with influence in the Admiralty Office. We hoped to influence the English government's decision to side with the South and fight a blockade of our ports."

Elise stared at him, struggling to comprehend the impossible. "But, why—why would she keep copies of the letters? Was what she was doing illegal? Treason? What?"

"In times of war, it's hard to know what's dangerous and what's not. I think she was trying to protect us both. But it doesn't matter now. These must not fall into the wrong hands. I'm the only other person involved in these letters, so, with your permission, I will assume responsibility for them. I'll take them with me and burn them at the first opportunity this evening."

"All right. Anything else?"

"This bundle of notebooks." He handed her a stack of seven leather-bound journals, tied together by a deep blue velvet ribbon. "Have you seen them before?"

"No." She untied the bow and opened the top volume. "It appears to be her personal journal. The inside cover has her name and the date—1832. That's the year she married my father. Each one seems to be a different year—and they end in 1838, the year after my father died."

"Her personal diary and an important family keepsake."

"One I can't bear to read right now. Just the sight of her signature has started me crying again. Put them away, please."

"The obvious conclusion is that she was trying to rescue her personal papers, but we must make her appear to be protecting the company. Are there some other business papers we can scatter around? And shall I attempt to close the safe?"

"No. I'll do it. You should not see its hiding place. Why don't you send Nate for a constable while I close it? I'll also scatter a few ledgers from her office files to make it look like she was collecting company records." With one deep breath to regain her composure, Elise stood and took charge of her new responsibilities.

RESURRECTION

Late December 1861
Charleston, South Carolina

*T*he best thing about a funeral is that the human mind refuses to remember much of it. Investigations of the local police and the coroner's office took two days. On Friday, the undertaker had delivered Henrietta's body for a wake, and for the following two days, the house filled with people. Flowers and candles served as decorations and odor disguisers. Neighbors brought casseroles and pies while casual business acquaintances dropped in to leave their regrets and a calling card. The family, dressed in full mourning, took turns accepting the polite sympathies of strangers and listening to friends reminisce. Meals were casual and late at night after the last visitors went home. Official word of Henrietta's death did not appear in the *Mercury* until Sunday, December 15, and burial took place in the cemetery of St. Philip's Church on Monday, December 16. Only then did the family relax, look to one another, and realize how much their world had changed.

Grief had given way to a deeper sadness that made the sisters reluctant to retire for the night where dreams would disrupt their rest. The three young women were still lingering around the parlor fire Thursday evening when a loud pounding on the front door disturbed their comfort. Mrs. Jernigan, always the last to retire and the first to awaken, hurried to answer the door, but a sudden fear made her open it only a crack to learn who was there. She screamed, clutched at her throat, and tried to push the door closed again. "No! Go away! You're dead, and we've had enough of dead people this week. Go away, I say!"

The door slammed open. "Stop it, woman! I'm no ghost. I'm very much alive—always have been, and this is my house."

"Antoine." Rachel shrieked and hurled herself into the arms of her uncle.

He laughed and pushed her away. "Well, thank goodness someone in this household has not taken leave of her senses."

Elise and Juliette were also on their feet, staring in disbelief at the figure who now filled their doorway. Rachel patted his sleeve as if feeling to see if he was still wet. "You didn't drown. Even Elise said you were too good a swimmer to let that happen."

"No, dear heart. I didn't drown when I jumped overboard. I dived and swam underwater to the far side of a nearby ship before coming up for air. Is that what they told you—that I drowned?"

"The letter from the U.S. Navy said they had searched the harbor for your body and found no trace. They presumed you were dead." Elise spoke as if arguing with the fact of his presence.

"Sorry to disappoint. Mind if I sit down? It's been a long day."

Antoine had a story to tell. He had gone into hiding with

some of his old privateering friends in Nassau. Losing his *Slippery Eel* was bad enough. He had no intention of also ending up in a Northern jail. After the authorities abandoned their search for him, he had made inquiries and looked for deals, selling off some of his warehouse stock to support himself while he searched for a new way to challenge the blockaders and make a quick profit.

Ships arriving in Nassau after December 11 carried the news of the Great Charleston Fire. At first, he had listened with concern but saw no reason to return. Then a passenger ship brought copies of the Sunday *Mercury,* and he read his sister-in-law's obituary.

"I couldn't believe it! The front-page article said it was a miracle that only two people died—an old slave woman, who went back inside her owner's house to retrieve some forgotten articles, and the widowed owner of one of the city's most prominent cotton factoring companies. There was only one person who fit that description, and a tribute to Henrietta confirmed her death. I realized then you girls needed me more than I needed to make a quick profit. I booked passage on the first ship headed to Charleston. But I gather I have missed the funeral."

"It was Monday afternoon. We had no way of knowing you were on your way, but even if we had known, we couldn't have waited any longer."

"Her body didn't burn?"

"No. She died from smoke inhalation. The fire did not reach the warehouse."

"What about the cotton?"

"Ever the entrepreneur, aren't you?" Elise felt a sudden surge of anger and resentment, but she struggled not to show it. "No, the cotton has only minimal staining, and your precious rum and cigars escaped damage. Joshua made sure all the heavy fire doors leading to the warehouse were closed, but the heavy smoke came into the office area through the ventilation shafts when mother propped the front door open."

"A tragic accident, then. But at least the business survived."

"What business there may be." Juliette spoke up to support her sister.

"Still, you will need me to take over."

"Well, Richard is already here."

"Richard?"

"Your cousin, Richard Westhaven. Oh, that's right. He arrived after you went off to play at being a pirate. The invading Yankees forced him and his wife from their Edisto plantation, so they have moved back into our East Wing."

"I see. We still make a good-sized family unit, then. That would please father. Once we get Henrietta's affairs settled, I'll work at turning my smuggled imports into ready cash to support us."

"And what do you mean by 'Henrietta's affairs?'"

"Reading her will. That hasn't yet taken place, I assume."

"No, nor will it until after the New Year. Remember, Christmas is just five days away, even if none of us will be up to celebrating it."

To her sisters' surprise, it was Rachel who eased the growing tensions. "Forgive us if we're all short with you, Uncle Antoine. It has been quite a difficult time for us, and your sudden resurrection will take getting used to. But we welcome you home, I promise. Your rooms in the West Wing should be just as you left them. Now, I suggest we all try to sleep."

THE NEXT MORNING, ANTOINE WAS THE FIRST TO ARRIVE FOR

breakfast. He took his seat at the head of the table to empha-size his role as the new patriarch of the family. He greeted Richard and Suzanne as if he had always known of their arrival and waited for the girls to assemble before he gave the signal for the slaves to bring in the serving dishes.

"It must be a strange feeling for you to return home to find your beautiful city in such a state of destruction," Richard said. "You'll discover that Institute Hall burned, along with the Circular Church and the Cathedral of St. John and St. Finbar. The flames obliterated Market and Meeting Street west of the Mills House. Today's paper says 540 acres of the city are in ruins. Six hundred buildings burned, along with five churches."

"Ah, Charleston will recover, I know. We are a resilient bunch, and with the holidays so close, our citizens will rally around to celebrate as usual. And that reminds me, Cousin Richard, please join me at the warehouse this morning. I want to assess the goods we have there. Some of them may be in demand from the military."

Richard frowned at Antoine's disregard for the calamity. He had been about to offer a little good news by providing a list of the landmarks that had survived. Now he decided not to bother. "I assume you are referring to the munitions stored there. I worried about the dangers of having such explosives near other combustible materials. Henrietta did, too. In fact, I suspect that was in part what led her to go to the warehouse the night of the fire."

Antoine was quick to anger. "Are you implying, sir, that my goods were to blame for her death?"

"Not at all. But the sooner we can move them out of the cotton storage area, the happier I will be."

"Good. Then let us take a quick inventory and be off to negotiate with the Confederate commander. From what I heard upon my arrival yesterday, General Lee has moved out of the Mills House and is now staying at the Edmondston-Alston House right down the street on East Bay."

Antoine's assessment of the military's current shortage of munitions was accurate. General Robert E. Lee, appointed to defend the coastal waters of South Carolina and Georgia, leaped at the chance to replace the explosives destroyed during the great fire. He agreed to come to the warehouse that same afternoon with a pair of wagons to transport his purchases.

"It's all about predicting what your customer may need or want," Antoine explained to Richard as they returned to the warehouse. "We'll bring the general back here to inspect our military offerings, but we'll also have a case of rum and a case of cigars on display—just by accident—so he cannot miss them. If he's the officer and gentleman I think he is, he'll see them as a Christmas bonus for his men."

Once again, Antoine was correct. Lee welcomed a good supply of rifles and ammunition at the warehouse, but his eyes lit up at the sight of the other luxuries on view.

"Add two cases of rum and a case of cigars to my tally," he ordered. "My officers have had a hard time for the past few weeks. They deserve a Christmas celebration."

"Thank you, sir. Before hostilities broke out, I had started an import business to bring such luxuries to Charleston, but once we were at war, I channeled my efforts to smuggle shipments of more useful goods for our military. I haven't had the heart to advertise luxuries when our soldiers have been in need. But if a good cigar and a sip of something heartening can brighten their holidays, I can supply them."

"We must never forget about the finer things of life," Lee agreed. "I'll pass the word to my unit commanders, and to the fellow who manages the gentlemen's saloon at the Mills House. Will there be someone here if they come by?"

"Yes, sir. We'll be open every day except Christmas itself."

"I must give you credit," Richard slapped Antoine on the back as the general left. "You are a good salesman."

"It's only a matter of being smarter than your customer."

"Or more arrogant," Richard muttered to himself.

This time, Antoine's optimism failed him. General Lee had no time to send them new customers because the latest threat against the city demanded his attention. On Thursday night the Union Navy had sailed its stone fleet into Charleston Harbor. The old whalers that made up the fleet contained blocks of granite designed to sink the old ships to the bottom, thus blocking the channels used by smugglers to enter and leave the port. Once in position, skeleton crews opened a few plugs to let water flow in and then abandoned ship. By the end of the day on Friday, sixteen derelict hulls blocked the main shipping channel. Confederate frustration soared as Lee realized there was no way to stop a fleet bent upon self-destruction. And by Monday morning, December 23, frustrated officers and barkeepers lined up to claim their share of Antoine's choice offerings.

At dinner that evening, Richard congratulated Antoine again. "You may have set a holiday sales record today. Have you anything left to sell?"

"Nary a leaf nor a drop! But that is not good news—not when I have no means of replenishing my stock. A reputation as a supplier of luxury goods depends upon a steady supply. And until I can find another way to beat the blockade, I am out of business."

Elise stared at him while chewing her lip. Then she ventured into the discussion. "When we thought you were dead, Mother struggled with that same problem. I don't know you would approve of the solution she was considering, but—"

"Well, out with it, girl! What did she have up that sneaky sleeve of hers?"

"She was considering joining George Trenholm to form a consortium of cotton dealers for the duration of the war."

"Hah! With George?"

"Yes. She heard his ship-manufacturing company in Liverpool is building several sleek new blockade-runners, and the Trenholm brothers intend to keep the trans-Atlantic cotton trade alive. I don't know all the details, but she was considering joining their effort by supplying our long-staple cotton and offering the use of our—your—warehouse in Nassau as an alternative transfer point. Do you think a similar arrangement might help your own supply problems?"

"It's an interesting proposition, one perhaps more suited to a weak woman than to a strong rival such as I. But there might be a way. I shall take it into consideration once our lives have settled onto a more even keel."

A THIRD CHALLENGE

Tuesday, January 7, 1862
Charleston, South Carolina

$\mathcal{A}$fter the holidays, the Middleton Law Firm was ready to get down to business. Williams Middleton, who had served the Beauchene family for thirty years, arrived at Oak Hall to read Henrietta's will. The girls had expected his arrival, but he asked that the other members of the household join them. "Better that the family hears the reading in person to eliminate future misunderstandings," he said.

When everyone settled in the front parlor, he began with an explanation. "Henrietta came to our office the day after she heard of Antoine Beauchene's disappearance. She feared that if something happened to her, there would be no family member available to provide guidance to her daughters. She repudiated her previous will written while her husband was still alive and dictated the following document to my clerk. After reading the draft and correcting a few legal niceties, she signed the new will on that same day in our presence. It reads as follows."

I, Henrietta Ainesworth Beauchene, of the City of Charleston and State of South Carolina being of sound body, mind, and memory declare this to be my last Will and Testament in manner and form following,

I give my soul into the hands of Almighty God my Creator and my body for burial in a decent and Christian-like manner in the cemetery of St. Philip's Church in Charleston at the left hand of the body of my beloved husband, Julien Roget Beauchene.

I declare the following disposal of my worldly goods and responsibilities:

To my daughters, to wit: Elise Antoinette Beauchene, Juliette Louise Beauchene, and Rachel Marie Beauchene, I leave my share of the family home, Oak Hall, on Chalmers Street, this city, as specified in the will of my father-in-law, Pierre Lefebvre Beauchene, in joint possession with his heirs. While the said inheritors may have full use of the property to whatever purposes they so choose, they may not sell said property or any portion thereof. At the death of one inheritor, the surviving inheritors may continue to hold the property. When all inheritors have passed, the property will devolve to their descendants in joint possession, share and share alike, until all agree upon its sale.

Regarding our family business, The Beauchene Company, Factors of Fine Cotton, I reaffirm my joint ownership of the company, because of my holding of sixty percent of the stock, with Antoine Georg Beauchene, who, at the time of his disappearance in 1861, held forty percent of the stock. However, by the terms of my husband's will, my shares in the company must pass to my daughters, to wit: Elise Antoinette Beauchene, Juliette Louise Beauchene, and Rachel Marie Beauchene, share and share alike.[1] There being no further entail upon these shares, my daughters may do with them as they will, with this one proviso, that if one daughter wishes to sell her shares, she must give her sisters the first chance to purchase them.

Antoine pushed his chair backward with a crash as he rose to his feet. "Stop right there. I wish to serve notice I challenge the legality of this will."

Everyone in the room gasped, and Mr. Middleton slammed his palm down on the small table in front of him. "Mr. Beauchene, sit down. Although this is not a court of law, you are out of order. You may challenge a will, but not until someone has read it in its entirety. I will tolerate no further interruptions until I have finished the reading. Now then. The document goes on."

To my eldest daughter, Elise Antoinette Beauchene, I bequeath all monies left in my public accounts after all my just debts, funeral expenses and charges of this my Testament have been in the first place paid and discharged. I also bequeath to Elise Antoinette my personal effects, including the contents of my jewel case.

To my middle daughter, Juliette Louise Beauchene, I provide the attached key which will unlock the contents of my safe box in the library on Chalmers Street. I bequeath to the said Juliette Louise the entire contents of that box, including the monies, property deeds, and stock holdings in it. Although I cannot control what she may do with the proceeds from the eventual sale of these items, I encourage her to use them to finance the school she has long desired to establish.

To my youngest daughter, Rachel Marie Beauchene, I leave this attached envelope containing the combination to the safe in my office at the company warehouse. In the contents of that safe, she will find my journals and the answers to her several questions, along with a sum of money large enough to allow her to do as she will with the information she gains thereby.

I now nominate and appoint Williams Middleton of the City of Charleston Executor of this my last Will and Testament. I now revoke and make void all former wills by me made and declare this only to be my last Will and Testament, In Witness of which, I the said Testator, have set my hand and seal this fourteenth day of November AD one thousand eight hundred and sixty-one.

[signed] Henrietta Ainesworth Beauchene. [seal]

For a few moments the room seemed suspended in time. No one moved. No one spoke. Then Rachel drew a shaky and audible breath to break the spell. Antoine was already rising from his chair. He sneered at the solicitor, gave an exaggerated bow, and spoke again. "May I assume it is now permissible for me to speak?"

"If there are questions or objections to the contents of this will, I will hear them now."

"Then I am serving notice upon everyone in attendance

here. I challenge the validity of this will because it contains erroneous identifications."

"And what might those be?"

"Julien's will did not mention his daughters by name; only Henrietta's will does so. However, I can provide proof that Miss Rachel Marie Beauchene is not a legal heir of Julien and Henrietta Ainesworth Beauchene."

Rachel gasped and shook her head in disbelief. "Uncle Antoine! What are you saying?"

Antoine ignored her plea and spoke to the lawyer. "I can prove that Rachel is not Henrietta's daughter, nor is she the daughter of my late brother, Julien Beauchene."

"If you have such proof, please produce it."

"The proof, which I know to exist, is available only in England. I intend to ask a probate judge for a continuance of six months, which will allow me the time to travel abroad and return with documentation and sworn statements."

Now everyone was standing and speaking at once, and Williams Middleton pounded on his small table again to demand order. As the family members settled into their chairs, Elise raised her hand. "May I address a question to Antoine?" she asked the lawyer.

"You may do so."

"Uncle Antoine. You and I heard Mr. Middleton read Grandfather Beauchene's will—in this room—just a little over a year ago. His will also named the three of us as the daughters of Julien and Henrietta Beauchene. Why did you not raise any objection to that will if what you now say is true?"

"Two reasons. The first was that I was a named beneficiary in father's will, whereas, I am not named in Henrietta's will except for being presumed dead. To have questioned father's will would have seemed greedy and self-serving. And second, I had only suspicions a year ago, and I do not base my actions on guesswork. Since then, I have made numerous inquiries and have located individuals able to speak to the validity of my claim. But to get their sworn statements, I must appear before a British magistrate. Therefore, I am requesting a legal continuance that will allow me to do so."

For several minutes, silence filled the room, broken only by the sound of a young woman weeping. Then Mr. Middleton spoke again. "This accusation horrifies me, but I have no choice except to grant such a continuance. If I did not do so, this matter would become public knowledge and would then damage the reputations of this entire family even if the accusations are not true. So, Mr. Beauchene, I grant your request. No further action or implementation of this will may take place until July 7, 1862. But please be clear. If you have not produced your 'proof positive' by that date, the courts will allow no further discussion of this matter. If you violate that ruling, I will charge you with impeding the course of justice."

"Thank you. Now, if you will excuse me, I shall pack a small bag and be on my way."

ANTOINE LEFT THE PARLOR, HEAD HELD HIGH. NO ONE watched him go. Richard nudged his wife, and the two of them slipped out of the room, heading toward their own quarters to leave the immediate family in privacy. Mr. Middleton, shaking his head in dismay, offered one bit of advice. "Six months is a long time. Many things can happen. Try not to give your imaginations free rein. Life goes on, even when the world seems to collapse beneath your feet."

Elise and Juliette were too busy comforting Rachel to heed that good advice. After the lawyer left, the three young women huddled on a sofa. They held hands as if the world might sweep them apart forever.

At last, Rachel controlled her tears and straightened her spine. "I swear to God! If another person tries to tell me how I should feel or how I should handle my grief, I shall not be able to control my actions."

"Most people mean well," Juliette said, "but they don't know what to say. When you listen, you realize they are all mouthing the same set of platitudes."

"I know they are, and I have to hold my breath to keep from snapping back at them."

"Everything happens for the best." Juliette mimicked an old lady shaking her finger at the mourner.

"Oh? How should you know?" Rachel put on her best sneer as she responded.

"Someday you'll look back on these events with gratitude for the good result."

"Do you think I'll ever be able to say I'm glad my mother died in a fire?"

"I'll be praying for you."

"Do you think God needs you to remind him to be nice?"

"This too will pass."

"Oh, that's the worst one. It always makes me think of grandfather's bout with his kidney stones."

Elise allowed herself to smile as she listened to her younger sisters' banter, but as the eldest, she needed to caution them. "I agree with everything you say, but you need to control your impulses this afternoon. Aunt Elizabeth has sent word she will drop by around two o'clock and hopes to see all three of us."

"We haven't talked to her since the funeral. I'm sure she's just checking in to be sure we're all right."

"I will be on my best behavior, I promise. But if I get snippy, you have my permission to step on my toe."

ELIZABETH DUBOIS ARRIVED ON SCHEDULE, CARRYING A SMALL basket. "I've brought your favorite shortbread cakes, and I also have a small jade plant for each of you. I grew them from cuttings taken from a plant I've had for years. They have several advantages, the best being a reputation for bringing the owner good luck. It is also impossible to kill them. If you love them and talk to them, they'll reward you by growing in all directions. And if you neglect them, they settle down, determined to remain green until you remember to water them. I hope they will remind you of my undying love, even when I'm no longer around."

"What? What do you mean by that? Why wouldn't you be around?"

"Because I'm moving away, dear heart."

"No! Why?"

"The past few months have devastated me, and I have reached the end of my tether. Oh, I know. You've had your heartbreaks, but so have I. My eldest granddaughter, Charlotte, lost her husband in the Battle of Port Royal, which left her eight months pregnant with twins. The invading Yankees overran our Edisto Island plantation, just as they did your cousin Richard's home. Then came the great fire, and my daughter Susan's house burned to the ground. She and Jonathan were lucky to escape, but they brought their whole family—seven children, plus the infant twins, and a yard full of slaves—to my house on Legare Street. Now my quiet refuge is more like a madhouse, and—worst of all—I no longer have my best friend to listen to my complaints."[2]

"But where will you go?"

"Two lovely maiden cousins occupy my family home in Flat Rock, North Carolina. It's a huge house in a quiet mountain setting, and they have invited me to share it with them.

Susan's husband is traveling with me on Thursday's train to do the heavy lifting. I've already packed the few things I cannot live without in a peaceful old age. Flat Rock is close enough for visits but removed from the daily drama. I will, however, miss you girls, and I hope we can remain in touch."

"We will. And if life in Charleston get too hard to bear, we may even come to visit you."

"Speaking of the hard things in life, did you read your mother's will this morning? I'm sure it was difficult for you."

"Oh, you will not believe it!" Rachel shuddered and then nodded at her sister. "Go ahead, Elise. Tell her about Antoine's latest disruption."

As Elise described the scene, Elizabeth's face grew grim. "I know some of what happened, Rachel dear, but it was not —and still isn't—my story to tell. Your mother kept a diary, and I warned her about keeping it hidden lest Antoine put his hands on it."

Elise shook her head. "I've seen it, Aunt Elizabeth, and I know where it is now. It's safe. I don't believe he has read it although I could be wrong. But we don't know what he intends to find in England."

"No, neither do I. But whatever he's after, I have a strong recommendation for you. Henrietta left her journals to Rachel because she wanted her to read them. You need to make that happen before Antoine can produce his evidence, whatever it is. Talk to Williams Middleton and explain the situation to him. Get permission for Rachel to view the journals—maybe not right away, but in two or three months, when emotions have run their course. It will be easy for you to see this as a family matter, but there are serious legal consequences involved. You need to approach the journals from that understanding."

WHERE DO WE GO FROM HERE?

January–March 1862
Charleston, South Carolina

*A*fter Elizabeth embraced her goddaughters and took her leave, the sisters lingered in the parlor to discuss her advice. Rachel paced the floor as she wrestled with the problem. "I've asked these questions again and again—who am I? Why don't I have a birth certificate? What is the stain on my pedigree? I should have expected a response like Antoine's."

"I've heard mother talk about your birth a dozen times. If what Antoine says is true, she lied to us all for over twenty years. How is it even possible to think about that?"

"It comes down to a question of whom you can believe, doesn't it? Do you listen to a hard-drinking, irresponsible gambler—a womanizer, a ne'er-do-well, an impractical fellow who often finds himself too deep in debt to dig himself out? Or do you listen to the devoted mother who has taught us all to be honest in everything we do?"

Elise shook her head. "How could she keep such a secret for her entire lifetime?"

"I don't know. Perhaps she could if she were trying to protect me. The same questions keep coming up—first the ladies of the St. Cecilia Society, then the formidable Madame St. Croix, and now my uncle—assuming he even is my uncle."

"I don't think we should pay much attention to the fact that the accusations have come up more than once," Juliette said. "It's only human nature that once a possibility arises, others will latch onto it. And let's not forget that last bequest in mother's will. She herself says the answers to Rachel's questions are available in her office safe. Rachel can discover the truth for herself."

"I can't do anything of the sort. Antoine got his continuance. That means they will not allow me to get into the safe for six months."

"Yes, you can, even if Mr. Middleton is of no help." Elise smiled for the first time. "Mother showed me the safe at the warehouse and gave me the combination. That was several days after she wrote this will. I know the combination works because on the day we found her body, Mr. Bunch and I used it to put away the papers we didn't think the police would need to see."

"You know what's there?"

"I do. The safe now contains only a large amount of U.S. Treasury notes, an odd scientific article about phosphate, and a stack of mother's journals, dating back to the day she met our father. I didn't think I could bear to read them that day, but I know they cover the years between 1832 and 1838— which will include your birth, Rachel."

"But you shouldn't open the safe again."

"Nonsense. Our lawyer may say I shouldn't, but my heart says I need to do this. Let's set a date, say March fifteenth—a deadline of sorts. If we don't have legal permission by that time, we will go to the warehouse, lock ourselves into mother's office, and remove the journals. You can read them to see what they say, and then we'll put them back."

"On the Ides of March? A fateful anniversary. Who will get stabbed in the back?"

"No one, I hope, but if there must be violence, I'd rather be the stabber than the victim. If the date bothers you, we can start on the fourteenth. That's a Friday, and I can give the warehouse crew the day off. Then we'll have the whole weekend to work our way through the journals."

"And what if the journals confirm what Antoine says, which I fear they may? What then?"

"Then at least you will know the truth and be ready for whatever follows."

"But that's two months from now. What do we do in the meantime?"

"Simple. We go back to work. All three of us have jobs and people who depend upon us."

"We're still in mourning."

"We're through the worst of it—the smelly crepe-wearing stage is behind us, and the slaves have restored the house to normalcy. Now we're only required to look serious and to refrain from any frivolous activity. No dinner parties, shopping trips, or social visits. We go to work and we take care of business. I have a huge pile of correspondence to get through at the warehouse. Juliette's little scholars are in danger of forgetting their ABC's and 123's, and Reverend Howard is floundering again as he tries to keep his schedule straight without Rachel's steady hand."

"I'm not sure I can concentrate on work yet."

"You will. Habit will kick in. Besides, work is a way to handle overwhelming grief. Most of us do not have minds that can do two things at once. When you sit and do nothing, grief pushes its way to the forefront of your attention. When you let your work absorb you, grief retires to a corner. It's always there, but it doesn't have to preoccupy your every thought."

❧

THE SISTERS NEED NOT HAVE WORRIED THAT TIME WOULD SIT heavy on their hands for the next two months. There was a war going on and a major cleanup effort as the city of Charleston struggled to cope with the after-effects of the Great Fire.

Elise returned to the Beauchene cotton warehouse to discover a heavy backlog of correspondence from clients and customers. Cotton planters who had picked an early crop and shipped their bales to Charleston worried about the effects of the fire. Had the bales burned? Was there smoke damage? And would the new shortage of cotton raise their prices or dampen the amount of business from buyers on the continent? Elise copied a form letter, providing what answers she could. The cotton survived. Smoke had damaged few bales, and those only on the edges, not the interiors of the bales. And shortages always resulted in higher prices.

She was less optimistic about the prospects for overseas shipments. Despite the efforts of blockade runners, Confederates were no match for the power of the U.S. Navy. More and more ships were arriving to help with the blockading effort. On January 26, for example, a second "Stone Fleet" blocked Maffitt's Channel, leaving only one narrow passageway for smugglers to break out of Charleston Harbor. The North posted three ships just beyond the mouth of the little Swash Channel and picked off unwary smugglers with ease. The best of the blockade runners still managed to move supplies in and out of the harbor, but they represented only a trickle compared to the flood of shipments that had made

Charleston the center of the world's cotton trade before the war.

As for the future of cotton, the Beauchene Company had no easy answers. The occupation of the Sea Islands by Yankee troops drove most planters out of business. Lincoln's government had sent a cadre of cotton agents to gather what cotton they could and ship it North to aid in the war effort. Sometimes there came a report that a grower had burned his crop rather than let the cotton agents confiscate it. But there was no profit in such a move, only a vindictive satisfaction that came from defiance.

Of more serious concern was the loss of valuable long-staple cotton seed. William J. Reynolds, Lincoln's man in charge of cotton, was a dedicated bureaucrat with no under-standing of the nuances of cotton raising. Unaware of the years it had taken planters to develop a seed that grew only in the salt marshes of the Low Country and produced a fine fiber, Reynolds shipped out any cotton he confiscated without ginning it first. The special seeds traveled North in their cotton wrappings, passed through a rough cotton gin, and ended up as cattle feed. Sea Island cotton teetered on the edge of extinction. Elise had no answers for her clients.

Meanwhile, Juliette was following reports of another Northern agent. Edward L. Pierce visited the Sea Islands in January and went home to recruit a team of teachers to help educate the abandoned slaves of the Sea Islands. Juliette followed newspaper stories coming out of New York and Boston as volunteers signed up to join the effort. She wasn't sure how her own small efforts could contribute, but she recognized that the plans of these missionaries were much like her own. She hoped they might join forces to help freed slaves become full, literate citizens instead of property. In the meantime, she poured all her energy into her own small classroom.

Rachel received a warm welcome when she returned to her post at the Huguenot church. Reverend Howard refused her apologies for missing the Christmas activities. "The devastation of the fire muted our celebrations," he explained. "We skipped the hot chocolate and cookies and concentrated on the real meaning of the Christmas story. But I know our parishioners will enjoy seeing what delights you come up with in this new year. You'll also find the calendar weighted down with requests for weddings and baptisms. There's a fear associated with the war that spurs people to speed up their family plans."

"The calendar won't be a problem, but I have no ideas for providing what you referred to as 'delights.' There will be no Bastille Day fireworks this year. No Fourth of July celebration, either. We can't celebrate our enemy's success, can we?"

"No, but there's always Easter. It falls late this year—on April 20—so the weather should be suitable for an Easter egg hunt for the children."

"I can handle that, but it wouldn't do to start Lent with a Mardi Gras party, would it?"

"Ah, yes, Lent. It will be difficult for our parishioners to find things to give up this year. The war effort and the destruction in the heart of our city have already deprived them of so much."

"That's fine. I've never liked the idea of giving something up, anyhow. Too many people cheat by giving up lima beans or Brussels sprouts—things they already hate. Almost nobody gives up chocolate, I've noticed."

Rachel had jotted the words "GIVING UP" on her notepad. Now she crossed them out, only to hesitate and then encircle the first word. "That's it! Can we spend Lent giving rather than giving up?"

"A fund-raiser? Bad timing on that, I fear."

"No, I'm not talking about money. I mean looking at what

we have in terms of talents—things we can share with others. Giving our time to play catch with a little boy whose father is off fighting in the war. Taking a plant to a shut-in. Reading a book to someone who has gone blind. Tearing our old bedding into bandages for wounded soldiers. Teaching an expectant mother how to knit warm booties. Carrying a heavy bundle or chopping a load of firewood. Just GIVING, not GIVING UP."

"Oh, my dear child. Your Christian spirit of love puts my own to shame. It's a beautiful idea, and I'm off to re-write my homily for this week. This may be the best Lent any of us have spent."

Thus the days and weeks passed. The Beauchene sisters learned that Elise had been right in her analysis of the value of work. As they concentrated on the needs of others—whether cotton planters or church goers or small black children—their own grief became more manageable.

As for Elise herself, she was finding a new strength and confidence in her abilities. As the Ides of March came closer, she announced, "I've changed my mind. I will not ask Mr. Middleton's permission to look at Henrietta's journals. Antoine used to quote an old saying that it is easier to ask forgiveness than to ask permission. This is our decision. We will read the journals because it is our right to do so. And no one needs to know about it—either before or afterward."

FAMILY HISTORY

Friday, March 14, 1862
Charleston, South Carolina

On their chosen morning, the three sisters made their way to the warehouse on foot, not wishing to explain their plans to one of their drivers. They had little to say along the way. Elise was practicing what she would tell Joshua about their need for privacy. She also worried that David Manwaring might have returned from a sales trip with questions waiting for her. Rachel was afraid to think about what she might discover about her identity, and Juliette was having second thoughts about the wisdom of this whole venture.

Joshua was there, opening the front door for them and offering to take their cloaks. "You want to go through your mother's things, I suspect. If there's anything I can do to help, I'll be in the warehouse, cleaning up a mess of old pallets and crates. None of the other workers are coming in. I've told them to take the weekend off, and Massa David is using this lull in our workload to escort his wife to visit friends who live upstate. I'll put the closed sign on the door, and no one will bother you."

"Thank you, Joshua. We'll be fine."

"He's a real gem, isn't he?" Juliette said. "He seemed to know what we were thinking."

"He's been with the Beauchene Company all his life. Grandfather once told me that Joshua has worked here since he was five, using a small broom to sweep up cotton lint. I'm convinced he thinks he's a member of the family, and I know he's grieving over mother's death almost as much as we are."

"So, where's this safe?" Juliette asked. "I don't see it."

"That's the way it's supposed to be, my dear." Elise hesitated before going on. "Please don't misunderstand what I'm about to say. I love and trust you both, but I think it would be best if you don't see the exact location of the safe right now. That way, if anyone should later question our actions, you can both claim innocence."

"Where do you want us to go? Joshua will come running if he sees us leave the office."

"I know it sounds silly, but close your eyes. Turn your backs. Go over there and study that picture on the wall. Just give me a few minutes to get the journals."

She opened the secret panel, twisted the dial on the safe, and removed the stack of leather-bound notebooks. Her shaking hand hesitated a moment over the money roll, then pushed it aside and re-locked the safe. With the false shelf of books firmly in place, she walked to her mother's desk before speaking.

"Here they are—all seven volumes—one for each year of her marriage."

Rachel hesitated, her fingers trailing gently over the blue velvet ribbon that held the stack together. "I don't know how I feel. I'm curious but also afraid to look inside. It feels like a violation, somehow—as if I'm about to see into my mother's soul and learn her innermost secrets."

"I understand how you feel, but remember the will. Those were her words—no one else's. She willed these journals to you. She wanted you to read them—to understand why she did whatever she did. You will honor her memory by doing as she asked."

"That makes them mine, now, doesn't it? I can do with them as I wish?"

"Yes, at least, within reason."

"Well, I want to share them with both of you. I want us to read them together—to get everything out in the open, so there are no more secrets within the family. It has always been the secretiveness of this whole question that bothered me—more than the possible answers. If I'm not your real sister, that's fine. I'll love you both just the same. But I want us all to understand what happened."

"It's a wise decision, Rachel. Why don't we do this? She wrote the first three books before any of us were born—except for my birth at the end of 1833. Why don't we each read one of them this morning, and then we can share anything we think is important? After that, we can do as we see fit with the other four volumes. Perhaps we can start a habit of gathering in grandfather's library after dinner and reading aloud from them. The crucial details will come at the end, to be sure, but I suspect that there is much background information we need to know first."

For the next hour, the sisters read Henrietta's journals. Pages turned softly, and occasionally a chuckle or sigh interrupted the silence, but each daughter found herself transported to another time and place as she followed her mother's adventures. Rachel was the first to finish reading. She had chosen the volume from 1832, not just because it was short but because she hoped it would introduce her to a side of her mother she had never known.

While her sisters finished their reading, Rachel moved quietly around the office, touching her mother's possessions as if they could tell her more about this woman she had never fully understood. When at last Elise and Juliette closed their volumes, Rachel was the first to break the silence.

"I feel like she's here—as though I could turn around and she'd be sitting right over there at her desk, smiling at us."

"I know. I kept hearing her voice as I read her words. Is this what people mean when they say the dead are never far from us?"

"Maybe so, Juliette. I agree with both of you. But let's share what we've learned. You first, Rachel, since you had the earliest book. But before you start, I have one suggestion for us. When we're talking about what happens in these journals, let's refer to everyone by their first names. It may keep our comments more impersonal and maybe less emotional."

"Yes, definitely. Mine's a love story, obviously, and it will be easier to talk about Henrietta, rather than mother, which always sounds intimidating."

"Did she intimidate you, Rachel?"

"Oh, she did. And that seems strange now. I learned Henrietta and her mother did not get along, either. She thought her mother was much too domineering, and there were few signs of any real affection between them."[1]

"Yes, I noticed that in my book, too," Juliette said, "although she sees things a little differently once she becomes a mother herself."

"That's interesting. And she decided things quickly, didn't she? She did so when she met Julien. Henrietta loved him from the moment she met him, although looking at their relationship from the outside, it's obvious that neither of them knew what they were getting into. They're from two entirely different worlds, and they don't take time to question what that might mean to their marriage. The question of slavery comes up once or twice, but they both avoid the issue by changing the subject.[2]

"They have a whirlwind courtship, an idyllic English wedding, and a honeymoon aboard ship, and then suddenly they are in South Carolina, surrounded by slaves, and they face a full-blown moral crisis. The slaves are not only a shock to Henrietta; Julien and his father interpret her horrified reaction as a personal insult. She has no choice but to accept the slaves into her life. And it's not only the slavery issue. Julien informs her that in South Carolina law, she has no rights at all—that she is his property. There's a telling scene in which her father-in-law announces that he expects her to throw a formal reception for all their business clients. She tries to tell Julien she can't do that, but he ignores her protest. As I read it, the scene seemed prophetic. I suspect much of her life was a replay of that moment."[3]

"Thus, one of her favorite words became 'compromise.' How often was that her answer when one of us didn't want to do something? We had to compromise, which in her mind meant we had to give in."

"Yes, and she did it quite well. Within weeks of her arrival in the South, she was managing a house full of slaves and sashaying around in hoop skirts. But that didn't mean she was happy about it. Nor was she happy about meeting Antoine. From the first day, she called him a fast-talking con artist, and a few days later she referred to him as a spoiled and lecherous playboy. My volume was short and only covered a few months, but I recognized the picture it gave me of Henrietta. How was her next year, Juliette?"

"IT WAS MORE OF THE SAME THINGS YOU SAW. SHE WAS learning to deal with life in South Carolina, although by her second year here she had made friends with Elizabeth Dubois. That friendship helped her learn not to take Southern attitudes personally. Aunt Elizabeth, as we all know, has always been the practical one. She was quick to share what she knew about the South—and about Southern men—with Henrietta. It was thanks to her that Henrietta came to understand her own power over her husband."[4]

"The focus of 1833 was Henrietta's pregnancy, and I found those pages rather boring because she was so wrapped up in herself. But then came the birth of Elise, and I must admit, dear sister, I am jealous. How many babies have their births marked by a gigantic meteor shower?"

"That happened, Elise? No one ever told me. I thought lines in Shakespeare about the heavens themselves blazing forth announcements of great events was just so much poetry."

"You're both being silly. The only astounding part was that Henrietta wished upon a falling star her baby would be born soon, and then immediately felt her first birth spasm."[5]

"Yes, that's in the journal. Then Henrietta learned another lesson as grandfather told her he had named her baby after his beloved wife. But for me, the most interesting part of the journal was a conversation Henrietta had with Antoine right after she told the family she was expecting. He comes across as supportive and kind although Elizabeth warns her the kindness won't last. Still, he gave Henrietta some good advice about living in Charleston. He also revealed another family secret—that our Beauchene grandmother was also an immigrant instead of a member of a fine old Charleston family."

"No!"

"According to Antoine, the first Elise was a French orphan from Barbados who came to Charleston with her guardian one day and caught the lecherous eye of our grandfather, who married her despite all the family objections.[6] That made me fonder of both Antoine and our grandfather."

Rachel grinned as she considered this discovery. "So much for stuffy old Charleston blue bloods who demand proof that your family has been in the city for ages. So, Elise, did you live up to your famous birth announcement?"

"Live up to it? I doubt it, but I admit, the journal for 1834 makes me sound adorable. Both Henrietta and Julien doted on this new little creature in their lives, but then, that's typical of most first-time parents. As far as what the next journal tells us, however, I am not the star. Oh, I'm featured at the beginning because of my baptism and at the end with my first birthday. But the real message has to do with a raging fight between Henrietta and her father-in-law."

"More disagreements over slavery?"

"Only peripherally. In March, grandfather called Julien and Henrietta into his office and informed them he was reorganizing the company. He was planning to step down into an advisory role and turn the day-to-day operation over to Julien. He gave Julien fifty-one percent of the company's stock, with the other forty-nine percent going to Antoine. But he also had a role for Henrietta to play. He wanted her to work in the warehouse, learning the business and acting as his personal secretary.[7]

"She protested she had a new baby to raise, but he shrugged that off and told her it was time to wean the baby and turn her over to a nursemaid. Henrietta declared that she would not allow a slave to raise her child, and he informed her that in his house, people did whatever he told them to do. She accused him of treating her like one of his slaves, Julien didn't correct her, and grandfather threw both of them out of his office. Julien was furious with Henrietta for defying his father, and she ran off in tears to the nursery, where she hid out for the rest of the day and into the next morning."

"What a scene that must have been!"

"Yes, I could imagine that all the frustrations Henrietta had been bottling up burst out at once. Anyhow, around mid-morning the family lawyer showed up asking to see her, and she was sure he would tell her she was being sent back to England. Instead, he was there to deliver a lesson in humility.

"Grandfather had asked him to explain South Carolina law to Henrietta, including the legal provision that a woman's family could grant her *feme sole* status. That allowed her to be an independent woman, to earn wages, own property, and control her own affairs. He wanted that designation for Henrietta so that in the event of Julien's death, she could inherit his entire estate, including ownership of the company —thus keeping control out of Antoine's untrustworthy hands."

"It must have stunned her."

"It did, and embarrassed her, too. They gave her three days to absorb the lesson. Then grandfather sent her a note telling her a trusted slave from the yard would be a new member of the household staff in charge of Baby Elise. Henrietta herself was to appear at the warehouse that after-noon ready to start work."

"And she did so?"

"She did. She put a little twist into the agreement, however. While she was touring the warehouse, she noticed a beautiful orange cat prowling around. She stopped to make friends with it and then informed her father-in-law she would accept his offer—if she could keep the cat as her office pet.[8] They sealed their bargain, both thinking they had won."

Rachel stood and stretched, releasing the tensions that

had been building in her all morning. "So it's a happy ending for all, including the cat. But it answers nothing for me."

"You weren't born for another several years, dear. This is all background."

"I understand that. And I think we've chosen a good way of getting through these journals. May I make another suggestion?"

"Go ahead."

"Let's take the next three volumes and handle them the same way tomorrow morning. That will get the preliminaries out of the way. We can take that last volume, which, if I remember correctly, covers only the first half of 1838, and read it out loud on Friday. That will give us the weekend to absorb whatever we find."

AN INTIMATE GLANCE

Saturday, March 15, 1862
Charleston, South Carolina

*A*fter a night of restless sleep, Henrietta's daughters
gathered again to explore the diaries their mother
had left behind. Their dreams had been full of half-remem-
bered images, voices they did not recognize, fears without
focus. Joshua had once again admitted them to the warehouse, but this time without comment. He locked the door
behind them and moved away to give them their privacy. Did
he suspect what was going on? Elise pondered the question
and then dismissed it. They had a task to complete. Best to
move through it at once.

"Let's keep the same order as yesterday, all right?" She
handed Rachel the volume for 1865, passed Juliette the one
for 1866, and then took 1867 for herself. They settled down to
read without conversation. During the next hour, few giggles
punctuated the silence, unlike yesterday's readings. One of
them gasped as she absorbed disturbing content. And as they

finished their assigned readings, they hesitated to discuss them.

Rachel grimaced as she tried to find a place to start. "I could tell you that nothing happened until the last two months of the year, but that's not true. There's a lot going on here, most of it the everyday things you would expect to find in a diary, but I suspect Henrietta herself remembered two occasions.

"The first was a fire that burned within two blocks of Chalmers Street and destroyed St. Philip's Church where the Beauchenes had worshiped for years. The threat was so close that Julien and Henrietta took the baby and walked to the corner to get a better view of what was happening. They were in a good position to see the landmark steeple catch fire and burn through the roof of the church, setting the whole structure ablaze and causing the front portico to collapse into Church Street.[1] It must have been terrifying, and the experience left a permanent mark on Henrietta.

"In the next few months, two more fires spread through the city, and Henrietta worried and raged about the dangers. In her logical mind, she could not understand why the city fathers did not make the city less vulnerable to accidental fires. As she often did, it was Aunt Elizabeth who explained the Charlestonian attitude toward the inevitability of fire. It started when the fine old families moved their home kitchens to separate buildings behind the main dwelling so that when a cooking fire started it wouldn't burn down the whole house. No one seemed to worry about damage to slave quarters. Then it was a short leap to ignoring damage to neighborhoods occupied by the dregs of society. People shrugged off damage to areas used by freed slaves or poor transients. Let fire destroy the favorite church of the wealthy, however, and there was a great hue and cry."

Rachel stopped to catch her breath and then laughed at

herself. "Goodness! I sound like Henrietta. Who would have thought it!"

"What did she want them to do?"

"Well, she didn't have an answer for that, but she knew what they shouldn't do. Aunt Elizabeth had explained that city officials viewed fires in poor neighborhoods as an efficient way of getting rid of local eyesores. They let the fire burn itself out, then purchased the land at a cheap rate, cleared out the debris, and erected lovely classical buildings that would bring in new money. Better a fancy new hotel than a brothel or a saloon or a flophouse. Investing money in the new fire-fighting equipment was not popular.[2]

"Anyhow, much of Henrietta's journal for the first half of 1835 deals with her fear of fire. And given what has now happened, I found it disturbing. It's almost as if she has a premonition she will face great danger from fire. And from what she described, the practices have changed little since 1835. There was no effort to stop the spread of this year's fire through the market and the docks. But when homes south of Broad lay in the path of the flames, they blew up buildings to create a firewall to protect the wealthy."

"What was the other issue?"

"An even more disturbing one, at least for me. In late summer, Henrietta learned that she was pregnant again, and, like the first time, she delayed telling the family. She chose the evening after Elise's second birthday party. It was a happy occasion. The news of a new baby delighted everyone. They drank a celebratory glass of wine, and then Henrietta went out onto the piazza to have a private moment and get a breath of air. She was not aware Antoine was already there. He had been drinking, and he made suggestive remarks about her pregnancy. Then he tried to force his attentions on her, and she realized she was afraid of him. When she tried to go back inside, he grabbed her wrist and hauled her back. They struggled, and by the time she could break his hold, he had bruised her wrist.[3] She tried to hide the marks from Julien, but he saw them and demanded to know what had happened.

"She begged him not to make a fuss, but the next morning, when Antoine arrived at the warehouse, nonchalant about what had happened, Julien threw a coffee cup at him. The two ended up on the floor of the reception area beating each other to a pulp, with grandfather standing over them and threatening to use his cane on both.

"Once the fight broke up, grandfather sent Julien to his office to clean up the spilled coffee and the broken cup. He banished Antoine from the warehouse and the family dining table until further notice. Then he apologized to Henrietta for his sons' behavior, but he took no real action. I remembered Antoine's earlier behavior toward Henrietta. When she first arrived, he was only suggestive in his remarks. But this time, he assaulted her, and I couldn't forgive him as his father seemed able to do.

"I had another image in mind as I read. I remembered how I railed at Henrietta the night she told us that Uncle Antoine had drowned in Nassau Harbor. I accused her of hating him and demanded to know why. She refused to answer, and now I understand. She did not want this ugly story to overshadow our good memories of him. I feel terrible."

"You can't blame yourself for things you could not know."

"Maybe not, but I'm angry at myself about how I treated her."

"If it upsets you, Rachel, turn your anger onto those who let Antoine act that way. I don't understand why our father and our grandfather didn't punish him for his actions."

"He got away with it?" Juliette shook her head in disbelief.

"Yes—and in spectacular fashion. After a week, he

showed up at Sunday breakfast, asking about church services. He was 'in need of prayer,' so he said. He sat in the family pew while the minister delivered a convenient homily on the Prodigal Son—a topic not lost on Julien, who resented it. But that was grandfather's solution. He had decided that Antoine needed more love and responsibility. He gave him a new position in the family business and announced that Antoine would travel to the Caribbean after the holidays to see about opening a new branch of the company.

"And that's how my year ended. The church teaches us to forgive those who sin against us, but I can't forgive Antoine. The man was a lecher, a drunk, a wastrel, while Julien worked hard and Henrietta put the family's interests above her own. It was not fair."

"My dear little sister, when have you ever felt that life was fair?" Elise accompanied her remark with an indulgent smile to lessen the sting.

Juliette sprang to Rachel's defense. "This time, Elise, she's right. When I read the first entries for 1836, I couldn't understand why Antoine was such a changed character. But now I can see he didn't change at all—it was his father's acceptance of him that had changed. And he had done nothing to deserve it."

"Maybe not. Tell us about the next year, Juliette."

"It will prove I'm correct."

"FIRST, IT FELT STRANGE TO READ ABOUT MY BIRTH THAT YEAR. I may have found Henrietta's account of her first pregnancy boring, but this one was downright irritating. Unlike Elise, who arrived early, I was late, and Henrietta grew angry and impatient. At one point she threatened to give birth in the street.[4] And when I arrived, there was no shower of stars. I got an eclipse of the sun and a midwife mumbling about what bad luck that was."

Elise was laughing again. "You don't believe slave superstitions, do you?"

"Well, it was not the welcome one would expect."

"Did she name the person for whom it would be 'bad luck'? Was it you, or your parents, or maybe the whole family?"

"I don't know. I've had a lucky life so far, but this makes me worry about the future. Anyhow, let's get back to Antoine. That spring, everyone was happier because Antoine was away somewhere in the mid-Atlantic. So maybe that part of grandfather's solution made sense. But when Antoine wrote home, he irritated everyone even from that great distance."

"How so?"

"Grandfather sent him to work for the benefit of the company, but his letters were full of good times. He watched street entertainments, danced, ate strange food, drank too much, slept through hot afternoons, and stayed until dawn at the gambling tables."

"Sounds like a typical day for Antoine."

"Grandfather was furious. And when Antoine made recommendations about doing business in the Caribbean, his advice was to ignore racial differences and make friends with would-be pirates."[5]

"Pirates?"

Juliette rolled her eyes. "I know, it sounds silly, but Antoine loved pirate stories, and he seems unable to distinguish between a romantic seventeenth-century legend and a bunch of petty crooks. Grandfather hated his suggestions, and the whole family agreed with him.

"Meanwhile, there were other interesting developments going on in South Carolina. Grandfather reacted to my birth the same way he had to yours, Elise. He wanted Henrietta to turn me over to a slave and get back to work in the warehouse. Here, however, Julien stepped up and proved that he was changing for the better. This time he defended Henrietta and informed his father he would not allow her to return to the docks area until after the threat of summer fevers had passed. During the summer, he and Henrietta came up with a new solution to their problems with child care. They invited Henrietta's young cousin to come to America and live with them as an *au pair*. They expected her to teach Elise her first numbers and letters while Mrs. Brown took care of me full time.

"The beautiful Abigail Ainesworth arrived in August, but she was unprepared for what she found here. She opposed slavery in all its forms, and she blamed Henrietta for adapting to Southern customs. The two of them clashed. Then Antoine returned home, bringing a whole new set of problems into the mix."

"Such as?"

"Henrietta knew he would find a beautiful young woman under his roof irresistible, but Abigail refused to believe her warnings against him. She believed nothing Henrietta told her. It didn't take long for the lecherous Antoine to move in on the beautiful Abigail. There was another family argument when Henrietta discovered that the two were meeting every day in the nursery at lunchtime."

"I remember Miss Abby, and I remember playing with Uncle Antoine, too, but nothing concerning the two of them together. A child would not notice flirting, I suppose—not at that young age."

"Whatever was going on, it worried Henrietta enough for her to consider sending Abigail back to England. But she didn't do it. My year ended at that point, leaving me to wonder if she would regret that decision."

Juliette closed her volume with a snap and then hesitated

as she placed it on the desk. "Wait. There's one other item. It's a short scene, unrelated to anything else that had been going on, but I had a sense of impending doom. In late November, a young black child died. Someone had left the back gate open. A dog ran through it, the child chased the dog and ran straight onto Broad Street where a delivery wagon hit him and ran over his body. Henrietta was home that morning. She heard the commotion, came out onto the back porch with me in her arms, and witnessed the young mother collapsed in the dust over her dead child. Maybe it was her first experience with death up close, but she didn't seem to know what to do. The faithful Mrs. Jernigan took over, telling Henrietta that she should leave well enough alone. The slaves had their own ways of dealing with death and would handle the situation. But then she made a dire prediction about such deaths coming in threes, and it felt—ominous."[6]

Elise chewed her bottom lip for a few minutes as if she could not decide what to say. Then, shaking her head, she stood and moved toward the office safe. "I've read the volume for 1837, but there's so much going on there that I'm not ready to talk about it. Your discoveries this morning have made puzzling comments clearer, but I need time to sort out the events that occurred. Forgive me, but I'm calling a halt to today's discussions."

Rachel offered a suggestion. "If we delay for another day, may I read the final journal this afternoon? It's bound to contain the secrets Henrietta wanted me to discover, and I, too, may need time to ponder them before I discuss them with you."

"I'm not sure that's a good idea. You first need to learn details from 1837 that will influence your understanding of the final events in 1838. Let's try a solution that works for both volumes."

"One of Henrietta's famous compromises, I presume?"

"Yes. I need at least two hours to organize my thoughts, so let's take a break now. I'll have a cup of tea in my office here, while the two of you go out for a lovely luncheon, perhaps at the new hotel that survived the fire. Nate can return to the house to fetch me a snack if I decide I'm hungry. We'll come back together around two o'clock, and I'll fill you in on the details of 1837. Then Rachel can take the final volume home with her to ponder at her leisure, and we'll deal with her conclusions tomorrow morning when we are all fresh and rested."

A WRONGFUL DEATH

Saturday–Sunday, March 15–16, 1862
Charleston, South Carolina

The afternoon's bright sunshine and warm temperatures lifted everyone's spirits as the three sisters gathered once again in Henrietta's office to listen to her words. Juliette was smiling and even Rachel seemed more relaxed than she had been for several days. Elise watched them as they settled into their favorite chairs. Much as she might wish not to spoil the mood of the moment, she knew the news she was about to share would break their hearts.

"Let's start with that throwaway event Juliette told us about just before we broke for lunch. Mrs. Jernigan had warned Henrietta that an accidental death such as the one that had befallen the small slave child often appeared in a group of three. You might dismiss it as a silly superstition. Henrietta did so as she treated the new year with renewed optimism. Buyers paid high prices for fine cotton. The children were healthy and learning new skills at a prodigious rate. Abigail and Antoine had given up their noontime dalliances, and even the news from England was encouraging as the country waited for little Princess Victoria to assume her rightful place on the throne.

"Family members accepted Aunt Maggie's decision to travel to Edisto Island when her son and his family returned there in February. Maggie had been a virtual recluse in the East Wing of Oak Hall for over fifty years; now she wanted to relive some of her fondest childhood memories. She had even made a list. She wished to eat seafood fresh from the ocean and cooked on the beach, smell pure pluff mud, watch wild ponies grazing on sea oats, and see new cotton plants break through the rich island soil. If behind those wishes there lay a veiled criticism of life in Charleston, no one commented on it. Instead, they saw each scenario she painted as a comment on how good life was in South Carolina.

"When a black-bordered letter announcing her death arrived in April, the Beauchenes took comfort from the realization she had orchestrated her own peaceful last days. Only Henrietta connected her passing to the death of a toddler. 'Deaths like these come in threes,' Mrs. Jernigan had warned. If so, this was number two. Whose was yet to come?"

"And now, thanks to Henrietta's journal, that's what we're all thinking," Juliette said.

"And even I, who was not yet born, can guess what's coming next," Rachel added. "1837 is the date on our father's tombstone, isn't it? I noticed the date when we went to the cemetery to take care of the family plot because it meant he died before I was born."

"Yes, he died on the Fourth of July that year, and the journal devotes several pages to what was going on that day. The dramatic events started when Henrietta found Abigail out on the piazza during a downpour of rain. She was bent over the side railing, throwing up her breakfast in a pose reminiscent of Henrietta's behavior the day Elizabeth Dubois discovered she was pregnant with me. Abigail admitted her pregnancy and added that the father of the child was Antoine."[1]

"Wait. I wasn't expecting that. I thought we were talking about Julien's death."

"It's all connected. Henrietta had feared this might happen. Now, she insisted that Abigail tell the family. They came together in the front parlor later that afternoon to discuss the problem. The accusation brought out the worst in Antoine. He denied he had any responsibility for Abigail or her child, and when his father and brother pressed him to do what was right, he turned his accusations on everyone but himself. He jeered at Julien, reminding him that no man could ever be sure that a child born to his wife was his own. At that insinuation, Julien flew into a rage and attacked his younger brother."

"Another re-play, wasn't it? It sounds just like their earlier fight over what Antoine had done to Henrietta."

"Except that this time Julien choked Antoine. And to break his grip, Antoine plunged his arms upward and pushed Julien to one side. He fell, hitting his head on the corner of that marble-topped table next to the sofa. The journal breaks off with Julien lying in a puddle of blood, Henrietta kneeling at his side, and me standing in the doorway watching the whole thing and clutching my old rag doll."[2]

"You saw it, Elise?"

"Henrietta says I did, but I remember nothing. And I give thanks for that. It was horrible enough having to read about it." For a few minutes Elise lost her usual composure, and her sisters rushed to comfort her, each one holding one of her hands and trying to wipe away the tears as they fell.

Once she was calmer, Juliette had more questions. "You said the narrative breaks off at that point. Does that mean we know nothing of what happened next?"

"That's the strange part. There are no entries for six or seven weeks, and then Henrietta wakes up in bed, with no one around but the slaves and no memory of what has been happening. She had suffered an emotional or mental break-down that no one understood. She had been semi-conscious for weeks. The slaves had fed her and cared for her but they couldn't explain things to her. Then Aunt Elizabeth came to visit and told her what had happened.

"Julien was dead, killed by that blow to the head. Old Mr. Beauchene purchased two ship's passes—one to carry Abigail to England and one to take Antoine to the Caribbean. Then he shut himself up in his office, refusing to see anyone except the slave who brought him his meals. Mrs. Brown had been caring for the two children. In fact, everyone had been waiting for Henrietta to wake up and tell them what to do."

"In September, both Henrietta and grandfather pulled themselves together to save the business and the remains of the family, although the adjustments were hard. When the coroner announced that he would hold an inquest into the cause of Julien's death, grandfather agreed to testify, but he told the court Julien fell without warning—that no one was touching him. The court found the death accidental and exonerated Antoine of all responsibility. Henrietta was furious, but when she tried to confront her father-in-law, his answer was, 'They are both my sons.'[3]

"At that point, Henrietta decided she needed to get away for a while and asked permission to take the children to England for the holidays. Grandfather worried she wouldn't return, but she promised that she would be back by spring. Then he showed a whole new side of himself by offering to emancipate Mrs. Brown so she could travel with Henrietta to help with the children.

"The trip to England was not a complete success. Henrietta discovered that she and her mother still didn't get along.

Mrs. Ainesworth harbored such deep prejudices she even made Mrs. Brown use the back door because of her dark skin. Other family news about Abigail disturbed Henrietta. When she had arrived home, her parents disowned her because of her pregnancy, and Henrietta's parents refused to take her in because doing so would anger Mr. Ainsworth's brother. Abigail abandoned Oxfordshire for the anonymity of London. So, after Twelfth Night, Henrietta moved her entourage to London where she could look for Abigail while she contacted cotton buyers there.

"And that brings us to 1838. Did you still want to finish reading that volume tonight, Rachel?"

"Yes. If Henrietta meant what she said in her will, the answers to my questions must lie in London."

THE EAGER RACHEL WHO SCOOPED UP THE LAST JOURNAL AND tucked it away in her reticule was not the same person who joined her sisters the next morning. When she came to breakfast, her face was pale, her eyes swollen and red-rimmed, curly tendrils of hair around her face escaping from her messy bun.

"The eggs are cold by now, Rachel. Let me send Mrs. Jernigan for a fresh plate."

"Don't bother. I only want coffee."

"Darling girl, you look terrible. You need to eat something."

"I can't eat, Elise. Can we move on to the warehouse and get this over with?"

When they had reassembled in their mother's office, the door locked again, Rachel plunged into her story. "The first part of this volume is a sweet little travelogue, listing all the sights and experiences Henrietta and you girls shared in

London. It's the source of that famous story about you singing to London Bridge, Elise."

"Please. Spare me. That's all anyone remembers about my childhood."

"Well, count yourself lucky. The tales of my early life aren't so attractive." For a moment, Rachel appeared ready to burst into tears. She shook her head, took a deep breath, and started her story again.

"The touristy visits were nothing more than a distraction. Everywhere Henrietta went, whether it was to visit the Queen's stables or the offices of an important cotton dealer, she was searching for Abigail. She seems to have had this fantasy they would meet on a busy London thoroughfare and rush into each other's arms in delight. But it didn't happen that way.

"She gave up and hired a private investigator, Solomon Preis, who needed only a few details about the pregnancy to get to work. He soon found a birth record at a maternity house run by the Sisters of Mercy, and there it was—all laid out for me—everything I ever wanted to know about my birth."[4]

"You're Abigail's child?" Juliette blurted out the question without thinking.

"Abigail's and Antoine's—born in November." Rachel's voice was hoarse, and the hand she used to cover her mouth shook with uncontrollable emotion. "At least my name is correct. I've always been Rachel Marie Beauchene. You know —the one with the stain on her pedigree?" Then sobs erupted from all three sisters.

Rachel was the first to recover, perhaps because she had already shed so many tears over this story. "It gets sadder from here on, my dears, so blow your fancy little noses and let me finish the story.

"The private investigator took Henrietta to an address on

Pickle Herring Street in Southwark—the stews of London, where Abigail worked as a charwoman in a decrepit apartment building. The landlady confirmed Abigail lived there—and she had a baby the landlady took care of while Abigail worked a second job at night. But when Henrietta knocked on her door, Abigail took one look at her and slammed the door in her face. That's when Henrietta herself collapsed and gave in to the grief she had been swallowing for so long. The landlady took her in, gave her a cup of tea, and then told her the rest of the story which was even worse. Abigail was working as a prostitute on the weekends when men had money in their pockets. She did her business down the street at a gambling house and opium den."[5]

"Oh, Lord, save us all. What a comedown for the poor child."

"I think the landlady felt sorry for her, too. She insisted Abigail was trying her best to support herself and the child and didn't need help even from a well-meaning family member. Henrietta seems to agree—or maybe she gave up. She left her address in case Abigail changed her mind."

"Two weeks later, that cry for help arrived. Because Henrietta was meeting with cotton buyers, Mrs. Brown left you two girls with the elderly couple who owned the house where you were staying and hurried off to Pickle Herring Street to help. The landlady had found Abigail unconscious on the floor of her room and flew into action. She had sent for both Henrietta and a doctor. The doctor had discovered an opium pipe under the bed and recognized a severe overdose. By the time Henrietta arrived, the doctor and Mrs. Brown had Abigail on her feet and were forcing her to walk off her stupor. Although the doctor assured them Abigail would survive, he warned that a second overdose would kill her. That was when Henrietta took charge of the baby until Abigail recovered."

"You keep referring to 'the baby.' You're talking about yourself, aren't you?"

"Yes. But it's easier to think about these events in a more impersonal way. I prefer to talk about neglecting a baby rather than about neglecting me. And that was Henrietta's fear. For an opium addict, nothing is more important than the next dose, not even her own child.

"To Henrietta, claiming the baby as her own was a way to protect her, to assure her safety and welfare. But once she went back to their lodging, there didn't seem to be any way to let go. The doctor had predicted that Abigail would die of her next overdose, and that would mean that her child would end up in an orphanage. Taking the baby from Abigail was Henrietta's way to prevent that outcome."

"So she intended to keep the child from the start?"

Rachel nodded. "That same night, she told Mrs. Brown to pack, and the two of them stayed up most of the night arguing about it. When Mrs. Brown warned of kidnapping charges, Henrietta said she had already kidnapped the child. And when Mrs. Brown chided her about lying, Henrietta just made up more lies. There was no doubt about the outcome of the discussion. Mrs. Brown had been an obedient slave all her life. She would not disobey her mistress now.

"How to get the child back to America was a real problem because she would need milk for the four- or five-week voyage. Henrietta's solution was to buy a cow and take it with them on the ship. I had to smile when I read that because I knew where the idea originated. I didn't mention this story to you when we started the reading because it didn't seem important. But in that first year's journal, Henrietta learned that many immigrants to America brought their farm animals with them—so many that Julien had referred to their ship as a Noah's Ark. Now that lesson came in handy.[6]

"The other problem was one of timing—how to explain a

pregnancy that didn't show before she left Charleston in November, nor at Christmastime in Oxford, but resulted in a full-term baby who was several months old by May. Part of the elaborate lie they made up blamed the lack of a midwife's birth record on a blizzard that forced an at-home delivery. But the only heavy snowfall that winter happened on the first of February, so that had to be the birthdate, even though the child had been born almost three months earlier."[7]

"What a complicated fabric of falsehoods!"

"Yes, and one that almost undid her. When they returned to Charleston, her father-in-law saw through the subterfuge at once and demanded the truth. Henrietta feared what he might do to the child, but he adored the baby at first sight. And as he pointed out she was, in fact, his granddaughter. The two of them teamed up to carry off this elaborate deception, with promises to each other never to reveal the truth."

"Which is why Henrietta couldn't answer your questions."

"Until she could pass along the journals. Can we stop now? Please? I don't want to think about this or talk about it. Take me home and give me a good book about somebody else's problems."

"That's your privilege. We started this quest to prepare you for whatever Antoine discovered on his trip to England. But he won't be home for weeks or months. There will be plenty of time for all three of us to sort out our thoughts and feelings. Give me a few moments to put these journals back in the safe. We'll lock them up and not discuss them again until you are ready."

Elise stacked the journals in order, tied their blue ribbon around them and waited for her sisters to leave the office before opening the safe and locking everything away—everything except the words seared into their memories.

MORE BAD NEWS

Monday, March 31, 1862
Charleston, South Carolina

*M*ondays are seldom popular, but when this Monday fell upon the eve of April Fool's Day, Elise found her friends' antics even more irritating. The French seemed to think they could take credit for creating the April Fool—a story that dated back to the European world's adoption of the Gregorian calendar. Whatever the origin, the French took great delight in playing elaborate pranks on their unsuspecting neighbors and colleagues, and preparations started days in advance. When the telegraphed letter from Scotland Yard landed upon her desk Monday afternoon, Elise almost tossed it away. Then she inspected the date stamps and realized it did not contain a joke.

To Whom It May Concern:
On March 15, 1862, in the borough of Southwark, London, the constable on patrol discovered a body

lying in the middle of Pickle Herring Street outside a local inn. The time was 2:35 GMT. Papers on the body identified the deceased as one Antoine Georg Beauchene of Charleston, South Carolina. His employment information included the ABC Company and the Beauchene Company of the same city.

It was the middle of the night and the street was dark; the coroner called for the morgue wagon and postponed his post mortem examination until morning. Cause of death was one of twenty-three stab wounds. The murder weapon was an unidentified long and narrow blade, wielded with some force. Because examiners found a large sum of money on his person, along with a gold pocket watch and a signet ring of some value, the coroner has ruled out robbery as a motive. He presumes a sudden quarrel or an act of passion precipitated the death. The constable found no weapon at the scene, and no witnesses have come forward.

Because we have no facilities to hold the dead during warm weather, and because no one claimed the body, we have provided burial in a plot set aside for indigent deaths outside the city walls. If at some later date the family should so desire, they may disinter and re-bury the body in a more prestigious setting provided they pay all associated costs. We can use the extra space. However, the family should also realize that reburial is difficult to arrange unless they have reserved a plot before the time of death.

We cannot issue a formal certificate of death until someone with proper credentials confirms the identity of the victim by viewing the pictures taken in the morgue and the contents of the victims' pockets. We will assist in this process if the family's agent reports to the coroner's office here at Police Headquarters, London. If no one comes forward within a year, we will seal the death records and sell the victim's possessions to recover our costs.

I remain at your service,

Inspector Rupert Z. Waggoner

Police Headquarters, 4 Whitehall Place

London, England

For some time, Elise sat at her desk, staring at the sheet of flimsy that changed everything. She tried once again to convince herself that this was a distasteful April Fool's prank, but the details and the wording were too British to be a joke. Memories of a previous announcement of Antoine's death followed by his miraculous resurrection flashed through her mind. Maybe this was another of his devious schemes. Was he still alive somewhere, waiting to see how his nieces would react to this news? Did he not find his evidence? Was he now avoiding having to come home and withdraw his objections to Henrietta's will? Could it have been a case of mistaken identity? Might he have killed someone and then changed clothes with his victim to conceal a greater crime?

No explanation made sense, but one thing was clear. Like it or not, Elise would have to be the bearer of the news. She closed her office for the day, telling Joshua she was feeling ill and was going home. She hoped to have the house to herself for a few hours, but her luck did not hold. For various reasons, both Juliette and Rachel were home this afternoon. When they asked why she looked so serious, she summoned them to their grandfather's old office.

"I hate this room," Rachel complained. "It still smells of whiskey and cigars, and something else—maybe fear."

"An unpleasant setting for some unpleasant news," Elise

said. "I don't know how to explain this, except to read it to you and let it hit you as it has hit me."

Juliette and Rachel sat, frozen in place, as she read the impersonal report.

"Do you believe it's true?"

"I don't know. I've been asking myself that question ever since the telegram arrived."

"It's happened before."

"I know, but it feels different somehow. The report of his drowning only presumed his death. These twenty-three stab wounds seem rather conclusive."

"But how ironic. You remember your Shakespeare, don't you? And it happened on the Ides of March. I wonder if the murderer made that connection?"

"Antoine was no Julius Caesar, much as he might have wanted to be."

"No, he wasn't, poor man. He never had that greatness in him."

"What do we do, Elise?"

"I don't know. I wish I did. Maybe our best move is to contact the Middleton Law Firm and see what they say. What do you think? Should we send Nate to their office to see if Mr. Middleton can come here to talk to us?"

"I think it's a good idea. If we don't like his advice, we don't have to follow it, but we need a disinterested person's reaction."

Rachel was wandering around the room. "Why don't I feel anything?" she asked. "Just two weeks ago, I learned I had a real father, someone I knew and could throw my arms around if I wanted to. But I took no pleasure from that discovery. And now I know he's dead, and I still feel nothing. Shouldn't I weep at this point? Is there something missing inside me?"

"No, dear heart, there was something missing in him."

"Do you think he knew I was his daughter?"

"I don't know—and neither do you. Don't pursue that question. And remember, we can't tell Mr. Middleton anything about your relationship—at least not yet."

IT WAS ALMOST DINNERTIME BEFORE MRS. JERNIGAN OPENED the front door to admit Williams Middleton. He bustled into the parlor with an aggrieved expression. "You young ladies need to learn that a law firm cannot dance attendance upon your every minor crisis. We lawyers are busy people with many clients just as important as yourselves. Now what is so pressing it demands a personal visit at this late hour? If it's about the continuance, there's nothing I can do. Once we set the court date, it—"

"Please sit down, Mr. Middleton. I'm sorry we have inconvenienced you, but this notification demands your immediate attention." Elise could be as officious as he was. She handed him the telegram and moved to the nearby settee.

The silence lasted for some time. His irritated frown changed to a wide-eyed expression of shock. The sisters watched as he reached the end of the letter and returned to the first page to read it again. Then he shook his head and cleared his throat.

"This is an unexpected development. When and how did you receive this message?"

"The telegraph office delivered it to the warehouse this afternoon. We are as shocked as you are. But we need to know what will happen now, and what we need to do."

"Well, first, Mr. Beauchene's death will cancel his challenge to your mother's will, unless it turns out he had the proof of his accusation in his pocket at the time of his death. In which case, I suppose we should have to consider its validity, but that would be difficult without his spoken testimony to back it up. I think we can ask the court to void the challenge and let the will stand as written."

"How long will probate take, and will you require our presence again?"

"No, I should think not. My office clerks can pay out your mother's final expenses and issue a call for any debtors to inform us of her outstanding obligations. Probate should clear the court docket within two weeks after that, and I can then distribute the specific bequests to each of you. We should complete the process by, say, the first of May."

"And what of Uncle Antoine's affairs?"

"Ah, that involves several issues. Will you wish to have the body re-interred as this letter suggests?"

The sisters looked at one another, shrugged, and shook their heads. Elise spoke for all of them "No, I think not. We cannot bring him home at this late date. Even with embalming, the body of our Great Aunt Maggie became—uh, fragrant—by the time her family moved her from Edisto to Charleston. I cannot imagine how an ocean voyage—"

"No, no, but an indigent grave—meaning an unmarked one in unsanctified ground—may not be an appropriate final resting place for an upstanding citizen of Charleston."

Rachel snorted, drawing everyone's attention. "We're talking about Uncle Antoine here. Everyone knows he was a scoundrel and a gambler. Well, this was one gamble he lost, and the indigent lot sounds suited to his character."

"I might not put it quite that way, but I agree with my sister," Juliette added. "Antoine died as he lived. Besides, it is my understanding that English parish churches are chary about the persons with whom they share their already-over-crowded graveyards. I doubt any of them would welcome an unknown American murder victim."

"I assume none of you will care to visit his grave. Thus we

shall let him rest where he lies. I must warn you, however, that you can expect to receive at least one gravedigger's bill, and one from a coffin-maker, too. The city of London will not absorb those costs for someone who was just passing through."

"We'll forward any such charges to your office, and you may subtract them from his final estate. He can afford to pay for his own burial."

"Ah, but there lies another problem. Antoine was intestate."

"What does that mean?"

"He did not leave a will—at least, not that our office has seen. I know your mother urged him to arrange the disposal of his assets. In fact, they had quite an argument about it in my office one day. He maintained that his father's will, along with his brother Julien's testament, had so encumbered his possessions he could plead total poverty."

"Fine. The Beauchene Company will pay his gravediggers. But what will become of his things? The notification letter mentions the valuables they found on his body, and I know his rooms here are full of his personal belongings. He had at least one bank account and a warehouse full of trade goods in Nassau."

"The courts will declare their disposition. Unless someone turns up claiming to be his child born on the wrong side of the blanket—which is unlikely—"

Rachel coughed.

Mr. Middleton looked at her for a moment and then apologized. "I'm sorry, Miss Beauchene, for offending you by mentioning such matters in polite company. We must be sure we cover all eventualities."

"I'm not offended by such matters. You caught me by surprise because I had never considered such a possibility."

Nice save, Elise thought to herself. "You were saying?"

"As I was about to say, the three of you are his closest living relatives and will share the final settlement of his estate."

Juliette moved to change the subject. "One further matter, Mr. Middleton. The letter suggests that we need to send someone as the family agent to identify the remains before the police can issue a proper death certificate. Does that mean an English lawyer, or can we handle the matter ourselves?"

"That's a formality. We can hire someone to drop in and—"

"It doesn't sound like a formality. They want someone to look at the pictures taken by the coroner and to examine the items he had on his person. I'm not comfortable handing such a responsibility over to a stranger."

"I agree," Rachel said. "and I'm willing to go and identify the body."

"Oh, child, you're too young to—"

"I'm not a child, Mr. Middleton. I'm over twenty-one, and this affair involves me on a personal level. Uncle Antoine was in England to disprove my identity. If he found any such evidence, it might well have been among his possessions. The estate doesn't matter, but I am as interested as anyone else in learning whatever facts he sought."

"But it could be dangerous. Let us not forget. Someone committed a serious crime, and the police have not apprehended a murderer. A young woman wandering around a strange town unaccompanied might be an irresistible target."

"Then I shall go with her," Elise volunteered. "Juliette is busy with her classes, but Rachel and I have little to do with our time. A trip will comfort us, I think."

"Well. Since your purpose will be to get a valid death certificate which we will need to handle Antoine's affairs, the Middleton firm will arrange for—and pay for—your ship passages. We will also provide you with identification and authorization to act on behalf of the family. That should let the police business proceed. I assume you are ready to travel?"

"As soon as possible."

"Then I shall let you know when I have arranged your passages."

NUMBER 4, WHITEHALL PLACE

*T*raveling to England in wartime took several weeks but was not impossible. Elise and Rachel took a train to Wilmington, North Carolina, where a small steamer operating out of Cape Fear carried them through the blockade and delivered them to Nassau. There they had a layover of several days, during which they sought and met the manager Antoine had hired to run his smuggling warehouse. Gerald Trevelyan proved to be an honest and affable gentleman. He was at first shocked by the news of Antoine's death but accepted Elise as his new employer.

"Good for you, Miss. If you have inherited the Beauchene Company, I am sure it will be in capable hands—maybe not so flamboyant as Master Antoine's efforts but steadier and less risky." He showed them around the warehouse and gave them a rundown of the inventory stored there.

"There's nothing here that will deteriorate during several months of storage. Rum and cigars both age well. You can wait until you get home to decide whether to continue this operation."

"Thank you, Mr. Trevelyan. I hope you will stay on in our service. I will trust your judgment on business matters here. If you can sell some of these goods, please do so. And if a bargain comes your way, you may make reasonable purchases. We'll see how our inventories look in a year. If you prove to be the astute businessman I sense you are, you may find a permanent place in our operation."

From Nassau, the sisters took a well-equipped passenger ship with French registry, the *Normandie*, through the Azores and disembarked at Portsmouth. A short coach ride delivered them to London, where they found comfortable travelers' lodgings in the home of Mrs. Perkins, a widow who welcomed their company. She and her housekeeper, Mrs. Higgens, loved to cook, and the sisters enjoyed tasting English dishes they had only read about in their mother's diary. The enforced leisure of the voyage had relaxed both young women, and they felt well-prepared to face whatever challenges they might find at Police Headquarters.

It was not as easy as it sounded.

NUMBER 4 WHITEHALL PLACE PROVED TO BE A CONVERTED residence whose lot backed up to Scotland Yard, the site of a medieval palace once used by Scottish royalty. The old building still showed its bones, but its amenities had disappeared. No carpets now cushioned the scarred wooden planks of the floor. Few books filled the library, but the shelves overflowed with stacks of paperwork. Bare window panes filmed by coal dust looked out over the yard, but iron grates to keep vandals out of the offices and prevent evil-doers from making a break to freedom marred the view. Red-

glowing coal fires sputtered to warm the drafty rooms, but they succeeded only in spreading a sulfurous odor.

The Beauchene sisters approached what appeared to be a front desk where a clerk with bad teeth was shuffling papers. "Excuse me. We are looking for Inspector Waggoner?" Elise used her best business voice, although she realized her Southern accent marked her as a foreigner.

"And what is it you want with the Inspector? He's a busy man."

"We are here at his invitation and direction." She was holding the flimsy telegraph but did not offer to turn it over.

"And your business might be?" The clerk would not knuckle over to any vague request.

"We are here to identify the remains in a murder investigation. If you would summon him, we'll leave you to your paper-shuffling."

With a sigh meant to convey the full extent of his irritation, the clerk reached for a series of call bell ribbons behind him. "If he is available, he will come for you. If not, come back another time."

Elise and Rachel exchanged an irritated look of their own, but in just a few minutes, a rear door opened and a small but dapper fellow appeared. "Crenshaw? What do you need now?"

"People to see you, sir. Don't know what their business is. They said you invited them. Thought you should take a gander at them." He nodded, pointing at them with his chin.

"Mesdemoiselles, I am Rupert Z. Waggoner. You were inquiring for me?"

This time Elise handed over the telegram rather than trying to explain.

"Ah, yes! I remember now. Our mysterious Julius Caesar imposter."

Elise and Rachel exchanged another glance and then

looked away, afraid one of them might giggle. At least they knew they were dealing with an educated man.

"And what, may I ask, is your relationship to our victim?"

"I am Elise Beauchene, and this is my sister, Rachel Beauchene. The deceased is our uncle, younger brother of our late father. We are his closest family members."

"Identifying a body from the morgue photos can be a disturbing experience. Are you sure you would not prefer to have a male relative handle this matter?"

"Yes, we are sure." Elise hoped her glare conveyed her disdain.

"In that case, if you will please follow me, we will get on with it." Inspector Waggoner led the way through the door he had entered and down a long, covered passageway to another building resembling a workshop or carriage house. He pointed to two chairs facing an empty desk. "Please have a seat. I shall return."

"I'm glad I do not have to work in this institution," Rachel whispered. "Everything has a peculiar odor. Have you noticed?"

"I smell bleach in here, but I don't want to know why."

When the inspector returned, he placed a small cardboard box on the desk, turning it so they could see the name Antoine Beauchene hand-printed on the label. He removed the lid and handed Elise several daguerreotypes, each showing a sheet-covered body from various angles. "Is one of these your uncle?" Elise fought not to grimace as she pointed to Antoine's image, then passed the pictures to Rachel, who nodded and returned the stack to the inspector.

"Yes, I recognize Antoine Beauchene. His is the picture on top." Elise noticed that Rachel did not use the family title. She hoped the inspector would not ask why.

"Good. Then as to his possessions. We did not preserve his garments. After the twenty-three knife cuts had shredded them and the wounds had bled, we needed to dispose of them. We removed from his body a gold pocket timepiece and a signet ring. Can you describe them?"

"I've never seen his pocket watch, but his ring bears the family crest. It boasts a garnet stone with an inset of a golden oak tree. The tree represents our name, you see—a beautiful oak."

"Yes, yes. In his pockets, we discovered a large amount of cash—American currency in bills of high denominations. Can you explain that?"

"He had traveled for several months, so neither of us is familiar with his recent business dealings. However, he traded in high-end luxury goods—items he sometimes transported in his own ships and sold to individuals interested in avoiding tariffs. I assume he completed such a business dealing. But, no, I don't know for sure where the money came from."

"There was just one other item—a *carte de visite* bearing on its back the signature of one Solomon Preis, a gentleman who conducts private investigations for people who do not want their affairs to become public knowledge."

"All the more reason I would not understand who that is or why Uncle Antoine was carrying his card."

"Then I have nothing more to tell you. We have finished."

"No, wait," Rachel interrupted. "We have several questions for you."

"Such as?"

"About the evidence at the scene of the murder. Were there no footprints or trails of blood to reveal where the murderer went?"

"You, my dear young woman, have been reading too many stories by Edgar Allan Poe. Detective C. Auguste Dupin's bloodstains and footprints make delightful clues in a storybook. But one does not leave footprints on a cobblestone street."

"All right, then. What about the murder weapon?"

"The wounds suggest a sharp and narrow blade, about four inches long, a weapon the murderer might have concealed on his person. But there was no such weapon found at the scene."

"And the location where the murder occurred?"

"As I have informed you, they found the body in the street outside the Cozy Den Inn on Pickle Herring Street in Southwark. At one time that was a very dangerous neighborhood, but it now houses more genteel residents. The inn itself was once a notorious gambling den, but after the owner, Sam Yonkers, married, his wife put an end to the goings on there. She ran off the prostitutes that hung around the bar, padlocked and then set fire to the opium den, threw the wooden dice onto the fire, and cooked the fighting cocks for Sunday dinner."

"What a wonderful story!"

"I can't swear to it, but the establishment is now a safe lodging for weary travelers and a favorite dining place for neighborhood families. They still have a bar, but the wife keeps close tabs on it to make sure no one overindulges."

"And no one there saw anything?"

"Not a thing. Two customers thought the victim might have been at the bar earlier in the evening. A man was asking for someone, but no one recognized the name. When their denials irritated him, the woman behind the bar asked him to leave, and he did so, escorted by Mr. Yonkers himself. The business closed at its regular 'last call' time—around eleven, and the owners went home. They live in a small cottage across the street. Neither of them noticed anything amiss and heard nothing of the incident until morning. The constable on patrol passed down the street at midnight. He checked the locked doors of the inn, and he walked right over the spot where he later found the body. That tells us the murder took place well after midnight. But that's all we found, and all we are likely ever to find. I suggest you let the story rest there."

"One more matter, however. We need the official death certificate so that the lawyers can settle Uncle Antoine's estate."

"There is that, but I cannot accommodate you today."

"Why not? Is there another problem you haven't shared?"

"Not one that impinges on your particular circumstance. Mr. Willoughsby, a fellow with excellent penmanship, hand-letters our certificates. But, his daughter got herself married on the weekend, and Willoughsby spent just a touch too much time sampling the bubbly. His hands shook so much this morning, we had to send him home. If you could stop by later in the week—say, Friday—Crenshaw will have your certificate at the front desk."

"So much for British efficiency," Rachel grumbled as the sisters retraced their steps to the main entrance.

"But it gives us more time to investigate. We can pump Crenshaw for information, starting right now." Elise approached the front desk with her most ingratiating smile.

"I apologize for disturbing you again, Mr. Crenshaw, but the inspector suggested we come back on Friday to pick up the death certificate for our late uncle. I wondered if you could suggest the best time for our arrival on that day. We do not want to interrupt your schedule."

Crenshaw smiled at such consideration. "How thoughtful of you. Nobody ever minds disturbing me around here. On Friday—Let me think—Late afternoon might be best. Old Willoughsby will have a pile of work to do when he sobers up, but he will finish before the weekend."

"I shall look forward to seeing you then." Elise cocked her head in a pose she hoped would make her more appealing.

"Oh, while we're chatting, have you ever heard of a private investigator by the name of Solomon Preis?"

"Price, like the cost of your cuppa, or the one with the funny spelling?"

"Yes, it's P-r-e-i-s, I believe."

"Him, eh? Yes. Everybody around here knows him. He's forever nosing around in our business. What would you want with him?"

"He's the friend of a friend back home. We promised to look him up, but I don't have the faintest idea how to find him."

"In that case, I can give you his address. We keep it around in case anyone needs to hire him."

Crenshaw shuffled more papers and uncovered a box full of bits of paper. "Let's see here—Smithers, no, Robinson, no. Ah, here he is—Solomon Preis. He lives and works in the East End. You'll find his office above a haberdashery shop on the Wapping High Street. That's near The Tower, if you're into touristy sights."

"Is there a number?"

"Doesn't seem to be, but ask anyone on the street. Chances are they'll know him. He's been around for years."

"Thank you. You've been most helpful."

"Always happy to serve a lovely lady." The fussy little clerk gave Elise a broad, almost leering grin that exposed his crooked and blackened teeth.

"What on earth were you saying to that horrid little man," Rachel asked.

"Flattery sometimes wins the day. I now can find Mr. Solomon Preis."

MORE PIECES OF THE PUZZLE

Tuesday, June 9, 1862
London, England

*T*he next morning, Elise and Rachel made their way to the East End and found the Wapping High Street with little trouble. It ran along the banks of the River Thames, and by looking across the water, one could see the bustling neighborhoods of Southwark. "I know I'm letting my imagination overrun my good sense, but after reading Henrietta's journals, all these names sound like home," Rachel said. "When the detective mentioned Pickle Herring Street, I had to struggle to keep from admitting I already recognized it."

"It's a natural reaction because we're retracing Henrietta's adventures. And look here. This is a haberdashery, and it has a side entrance with a nameplate on the door. Yes, it lists a Mr. S.L. Preis on the second floor. Ready to meet your first private detective?"

"Lead upward." As the sisters climbed the grubby staircase, both remembered Henrietta's first visit to this same spot. Not much had changed.[1]

The man who met them at the door was twenty-five years older than he had been when Henrietta hired him, but, except for his gray hair, he hadn't changed either—still overweight and grubby. His expression, however, suggested extreme shock. He took a step backward, shaking his head and lifting his hands as if to ward off a blow. "Who are you? What do you want with me?"

The sisters stared back at him, wondering if he suffered from some age-related confusion. "We didn't mean to startle you. I'm Elise Beauchene, and this is my sister Rachel. We're from South Carolina, but we're in London to deal with the death of a family member. We were hoping you might have time to answer a few brief questions."

"Beauchene? Beauchene? That's why I thought I recognized you. Are you by any chance related to a Henrietta Beauchene?"

"She was my mother."

"Was?"

"Yes, she died several months ago in a fire." Then, seeing the pain in his eyes, she hastened to add, "She died of smoke inhalation."

"You look so much like her—as she was when I knew her many years ago. But your sister looks more like—never mind."

"Mr. Preis. we can see you are trying not to say the wrong thing, so let us start again. I am Elise Beauchene, Henrietta's oldest daughter. You knew her when she visited London back in 1838."

"And I am Rachel Marie Beauchene. You may recognize that name, too. It belonged to the baby Henrietta hired you to find back then. Abigail Ainesworth was my mother. You are looking at the child Henrietta kidnapped and took back to America. Her family raised me to believe Henrietta was my mother. I only learned the truth a few weeks ago when I read Henrietta's diary."

"The two of you have given me a shock. You, Rachel, look like your mother, too. I recognize the black curls and brilliant blue eyes. For a moment, I feared I was seeing ghosts."

"We're hoping to find Rachel's birth certificate and learn the details in that story—things we didn't read about."

MR. PREIS BUSTLED ABOUT, FETCHING ANOTHER CHAIR AND settling them in front of his desk. After a hesitant offer of tea, which they refused, he steepled his fingers in front of his nose and made a small humming noise. "There's not a lot I can tell you. I assume you know Henrietta hired me to find Abigail, and I did so through the local Sisters of Mercy."

"Yes, her journal gave us the details of your discovery, including the wording on my certificate of birth."

"You also know I accompanied Henrietta when she paid her first visit to Abigail's building. That was my only active participation in the matter. I learned about Henrietta's second visit and about the kidnapping when Abigail's landlady told me about them much later. If I had known what Henrietta was planning, I would have advised against it."

"We're not here to blame you for anything, Mr. Preis. We're only trying to understand what took place. For instance, how did you happen to be back in touch with Mrs. Merriwether?"

"Well, there's a time gap. In August 1838—several months after my last meeting with your mother—I received a letter from Mr. Pierre Beauchene, who claimed to be Henrietta's father-in-law. From him I learned Henrietta had taken the baby to America. Abigail's well-being concerned him, and he wanted to hire me to check on her. He sent along a retainer for my time, plus a generous bank draft for a year's support if I could find an organization that would take Abigail in and wean her off her opium addiction."

Rachel and Elise were staring at one another in surprise. "Grandfather did that? I don't think Henrietta ever knew it."

"Perhaps not. Those who give the most in philanthropic endeavors do not wish others to hear of their largess. I went back to the Pickle Herring address to see if I could find Abigail, and that's when I learned that she had not wanted to give her daughter to Henrietta. Mrs. Merriwether had kept that secret for months and took delight in talking about it.

"Next, I talked to Abigail. She was distraught at that point. Sometimes she wept as she talked about how much she missed her baby. At other times she seemed relieved to no longer have the responsibility for another person. And she was ashamed of her addiction. She couldn't handle her life.

"With her permission, I went back to the Sisters of Mercy at whose lying-in facility Abigail had given birth. They cared about her welfare and were more than willing to take her in if she came with a payment for her room and board. I did not share with them the full extent of my new knowledge about the kidnapping. I only told them that the child was now in the care of a family member, which was true, if not quite the whole truth.

"Abigail thrived in her new setting. The Sisters are non-judgmental. They love everyone who comes into their care, no matter how unlovable they may be. They nursed Abigail through the worst days of her cravings. Then, when she seemed free of her demons, they put her to work within the Sisters' quarters. She did chores, learned to cook, took up knitting—anything to keep her mind and her fingers busy. I checked on her now and then and sent regular reports to Mr. Beauchene. After she had been there a while, they let her talk with the new mothers, and she was skillful at reassuring the unwed girls. The only area to which she did not have access was the nursery because the sisters did not want to remind her too soon of her own loss."

"She was there for a year. Then what became of her?"

"I don't know. I can't help you with the birth certificate, either. I don't have it and never had it. The Sisters of Mercy allowed me to copy its information, but my transcription wouldn't stand up in court. You must ask them for a certified copy. Here. I'll show you where to find them." He reached for a used envelope and sketched out the route on the back. "They may give you more details on Abigail."

"Thank you for your help, Mr. Preis."

BACK ON THE STREET, ELISE LINKED ARMS WITH HER SISTER AND pulled her close. "That was valuable information, but the Sisters of Mercy may have more current knowledge. Let's not stop now. Let's talk to them."

"I agree, but I'm not concerned about getting the birth certificate. Why would I need it?"

"To press your claim as Antoine's legal heir, my dear. You may have forgotten about that unfortunate remark of Mr. Middleton's—when he mentioned the possibility of Antoine having a child born on the wrong side of the blanket—although he couldn't have known he was talking about you."

"And I still think it's an ugly phrase. But it doesn't matter. I will not claim his estate, Elise."

"You deserve to inherit Antoine's estate. Don't be silly."

"I meant what I said, Elise. I have no intention of pressing a claim to Antoine's money."

"But it is yours. He gave you nothing while he was alive. You at least deserve to profit from his passing."

"And why would I want to? Do you think I'm proud that

my real father was a drunkard, a lecher, a smuggler, a rapist, and a murderer? What kind of legacy is that to leave a child? I would rather be an orphan with no known family."

"We don't get to choose our families, dear heart."

"Don't we? Am I not free to recognize all that Henrietta did for me and because of that to call her 'Mother?' I had a real grandfather. And for twenty-four years I have had two sisters who loved me and teased me and taught me what family means. Should I now reject all of you and cling to the memory of a scoundrel who fathered me but never wanted me?"

"No one's asking that of you, dearest. But I think it would be a good step in this investigation of ours to keep a complete paper trail unless you are ready to let the whole matter drop. We can do that. We've given the police everything they have asked. By Friday we'll have the death certificate that the Middleton firm needs. We can go home and forget about this whole sordid tale if that's what you prefer. No one beyond the three of us need ever know more."

"No. I'm not rejecting the story—and for your informa-tion, I don't regard it as sordid, either. I don't want to profit from the mistakes my parents made."

"Then we're off to talk to the Sisters of Mercy in the morning?"

"We are."

THE REST OF THE STORY

Wednesday, June 10, 1862
London, England

Following the hand-drawn map, Elise located the two-story hospital that would serve as their landmark. "This is the corner of City Road and Old Street, and there it is—The London Lying-In Hospital."

"But read the rest of that sign." Rachel had stopped in the walkway to stare at it. "It's a hospital for poor married women —married women, Elise. Not for any poor woman who needs them. What was someone like Abigail to do? Did they expect her to drop her baby on the street?"

"I suspect they didn't care, so long as they did not have to spend city money on women with low morals."

"But—"

"I know, dear, but the hospital originated in the last century, and it takes time to change attitudes. That's why there's still a need for groups like the Sisters of Mercy. And that should be their house, just across the street."

A young woman in a plain gray dress and white apron

responded to their knock. "May I help you find the address you're seeking?"

"Is this the Sisters of Mercy residence?"

She studied them in some confusion. "I don't mean to question you. The sisters would never allow that. But you don't look like the kind of women who seek our help."

Elise smiled. "Neither of us is expecting, if that's what you mean, but we are looking for information about a woman who gave birth here twenty-four years ago."

"Oh, my! I wasn't even born then! You must talk to one of our older sisters. I'd suggest Sister Veritas. She loves to solve puzzles. If you'll wait here in the vestibule, I'll see if I can locate her."

As they waited, Elise surveyed their surroundings. The furniture was sparse and plain, but everything appeared to be clean. A long hallway led past a series of closed doors. From somewhere in the distance they could hear faint cries of pain and a baby's softer cries.

"That might have been me," Rachel whispered as Elise squeezed her hand in understanding.

The door to their left opened, and a small woman in a grey gown and a full wimple smiled at them. "Our Sister Beatrice tells me you ladies are looking for information about a former guest. I am Sister Veritas, and I've worked here ever since 1810. Perhaps I can help. Won't you come in?" She stepped back and ushered them into a small parlor where a fireplace offered more light than heat to the simple room.

They took seats on unpadded, straight-backed chairs, mimicking the upright posture of the older woman. Elise introduced herself and Rachel without identifying Rachel as the one whose birth they were investigating. She noticed, however, that Sister Veritas was studying Rachel with more than normal curiosity.

"We are trying to locate a woman named Abigail

Ainesworth, who gave birth here in 1837 or 1838. I wonder if you might recall the name, or perhaps you could find a record for her?"

"Abigail! Oh, who could forget one of our greatest success stories? And that's who you remind me of, Miss Beauchene—the same bright blue eyes, the same black curls. You're how old? Twenty-two? Twenty-three? Is it possible that—?" She let the obvious question dangle in the air.

Rachel drew a shaky breath. "Yes. I am the daughter of Abigail Ainesworth and Antoine Beauchene. That's why we are trying to find her."

"How did you know to come here?"

Elise stepped in to explain their connection to Solomon Preis and his suggestion they consult the Sisters. "He confirmed the baby had been born here but couldn't tell us anything after the following year. We're hoping someone here remained in contact with her."

Sister Veritas was still staring at Rachel, and a mixture of emotions played across her face as she spoke. "I can take Abigail's story further for you, and it's a happy one." She smiled and then bit her lip. "I have now lost contact with her, but perhaps what I know will help you. The year Abigail spent with us changed her life. Her addiction no longer had a hold on her, and she had put on enough weight to be healthy. She had no more nightmares about her former life, and she was ready to face the future with optimism and energy. I can't say she had become a convert to our religion, but she had absorbed a desire to be of service to others.

"She returned to life on the outside and planned to ask a former acquaintance, Sam Yonkers, for a job at his tavern. The other sisters and I argued against that, fearing it would pull her back into the ranks of prostitutes and addicts. But she insisted she could be a good influence in leading others away from those temptations. We had to admit she was a free adult and could do as she liked."

"She went back to the Cozy Den, and Sam Yonkers hired her as a barmaid. Within two years, we learned that she and Sam planned to marry. She brought Sam with her one day to introduce him to us. This houseful of women intimidated him, but we could tell that he adored Abigail and wanted what was best for her. We offered them our blessing, and they invited us to their wedding.

"It was a simple affair at the Cozy Den. We all attended, dressed in our finest habits, complete with the conical head-dresses, the distinguishing mark of our original order. Abigail made gentle fun of us. She said it looked like a flock of gray chickens had invaded the wedding. We had a wonderful time. Although we could not take part in the dancing, we clapped and kept time to the music. It was a fairytale conclusion to what had started out as a tragic situation.

"And then came another magical transformation. Abigail insisted that Sam become a legitimate business owner instead of running a gambling and bawdy house. He wasn't sure how to do that, so he let Abigail take over. She drove the drunkards and gamblers, the petty crooks, the addicts, and the prostitutes out of the establishment. Within weeks they reopened as a neighborhood gathering place and as a haven for travelers passing through the city."

"This must be same story we heard at Police Headquarters. They told us that Mr. Yonkers' new wife closed down the games, set fire to the opium den, threw the wooden dice into the fire, and cooked the fighting cocks for Sunday dinner."

"I can't testify as to the fate of the roosters. I would imagine they were too old and tough to eat. The rest of that description is accurate. Under Abigail's stern eye, the tavern became a family-style restaurant with a tiny bar in one corner, and the rooms upstairs, once rented by the hour, now received a complete make-over to become comfortable overnight lodgings for affluent travelers. I like to think the Sisters of Mercy changed Abigail, and then Abigail brought those changes to a whole neighborhood.

"But tell me, what were you two young ladies doing at Police Headquarters? And why were you talking to them about the Yonkers?"

"We are in London to deal with the death of a family member. Someone murdered Antoine Beauchene, our uncle —or rather, my uncle and Rachel's father—outside the Cozy Den Inn on March 15. We came here to identify his body from the morgue pictures, collect his belongings, and get his death certificate."

"Murdered? Antoine Beauchene? By whom?"

"No clues. But while we are here, we thought we'd try to find out more about Rachel's mother and get a copy of Rachel's birth certificate. She'll need that to press her claim to be Antoine's legal heir."

Rachel threw her sister a look meant to keep her from saying anything else. "Let's get back to Abigail. You said you'd lost track of her, Sister Veritas. When did she stop contacting you?"

"Oh, years ago. Once they had the business running, I suspect she got busy with those details. We heard several years ago that Sam Yonkers was ill. The Sisters sent her a note asking about his health, but she never answered."

"You know nothing further? Not even whether she's alive?"

"Oh, I'm sure we would have heard if she had died."

"But the police detective said the wife of the owner of the Cozy Den is a woman named Mary Yonkers, not Abigail."

"What was Abigail's full name?"

"Abigail Marie Ainesworth."

"Marie and Mary are the same name, are they not? Except

that Marie doesn't sound English. And it doesn't fit well with the last name of Yonkers."

"Why would she change her name?"

"She changed her life. I suspect she erased anything that might remind her of those bad years."

"But you've never checked on her."

"No, we assumed she wanted to start a new life, and we honored that decision by not pursuing her."

"Well, I guess there's nothing more to learn, except by knocking on her door and asking my questions."

"Oh, my stars, no. Please don't do that."

"Why not? If she's my mother, I have a right to know why she never attempted to find me."

"Have you thought about this? From what I can tell, you have had a comfortable life in a family that loves you and supports you. You're well-dressed, well-fed, well-traveled, and you speak of inheritances as if they are commonplace. Let me assure you that if your mother had not gotten help from your American family, she would not have lived another year. You would have grown up in an orphanage with none of the advantages you seem to ignore."

"Perhaps so, but if she's my mother, I can't go home without attempting to see her, put my arms around her, and get to know something of her life."

"You imagine a tearful but joyful reunion. The reality could be different. And even if she should welcome you, what then? You spend a few days hugging and talking? And then you board your ship and sail back to South Carolina, leaving her alone again, to feel the same loss she felt in 1838? How cruel that would be."

"You've said your piece, Sister Veritas, although you have made an unwarranted assumption. You can't understand what I feel in my heart, but I promise you I won't hurt my mother. Thank you for seeing us." Rachel gathered her shawl and reticule as she stood up. "We can find our way out."

ELISE FOLLOWED HER YOUNGER SISTER OUTSIDE AND THEN whirled on her. "How could you reject her advice out of hand? She was trying to be helpful. You're plunging ahead into the unknown, while I agree with Sister Veritas's advice to move with caution."

"I don't care. I'm not ready to give up."

"You didn't even ask about your birth certificate."

"As I told you, I'm not trying to claim an estate, Elise. I want to learn what happened to my mother. And if she's still alive, I want to meet her."

"I will not tell you what to do, but I think you must make a choice between your birth family and your adopted one. You don't get to claim both, and Sister Veritas was warning you not to make that choice in haste."

"Will you come with me to Southwark?"

"Not today. I want you to do a little more thinking before you act. There's an old saying about being careful what you wish for because you might get it. I think it applies in this case."

"Meaning you think I won't like the answers I find?"

"Yes. Mary Yonkers is likely to be Abigail, but if you force her to admit it, you may not approve of her reasons for changing her name."

"And if I should discover what happened to Antoine?"

"That's unlikely. If the police can't find his killer, you can't do more than they can."

"Except they don't know the whole story. They don't know who he is. And they know nothing about the connections between Antoine and the Cozy Den—connections that would lead straight to Abigail, who has now changed her name, for who knows what reason."

"Stop it, Rachel. Stop it right now. You're letting your imagination run wild, and that's dangerous when you're talking about matters of life and death."

ABIGAIL IS NOT HERE

Wednesday–Thursday, June 10–11, 1862
London, England

*T*hat evening, Rachel paced around their small bedroom until Elise could no longer stand it. "Sit down, dear. You're making me nervous."

"I can't sit still. I have too many questions rolling around in my head."

"Then let's talk them out."

"Only if you promise to listen and not launch into your big-sister-knows-best routine."

"Do I do that? Yes, I suppose I do. I'll try to be quiet while you lay out the problems so we can study them."

"Fine. One at a time, then. We have traced Abigail's movements through 1842 or thereabouts. Then she disappeared. The Sisters of Mercy attempted to contact her, but when they did not receive a response, they left her in peace. That was twenty years ago! Just think how much could have happened to her."

"I agree. It's worrisome, and you are right to be

concerned. But I don't see how you can probe those twenty years now."

"There is one clue. We know that Abigail married Sam Yonkers. The Sisters of Mercy witnessed the wedding, and that description—when Abigail said they looked like a flock of gray chickens—is too precise to be a lie. Abigail became Mrs. Sam Yonkers, or Abigail Marie Ainesworth Yonkers, as any official record would list her.

"The people we have talked to, including the police, now refer to Sam Yonkers' wife as Mary Yonkers. There are only two possible explanations. Sam may have married for a second time, which would suggest that Abigail died. Or, as Sister Veritas suggested, Abigail may have simplified her name to Mary Yonkers. I prefer that explanation, which, I admit, may be nothing more than wishful thinking. The only way I can see to determine the truth is to ask Mary Yonkers herself."

"If she changed her name to distance herself from a life that embarrassed her, what makes you think she won't lie about it? Oh, I know. People call her a virtuous woman. But changing one's name is, in fact, a lie, so why would she hesitate to lie again to hide the deception?"

"That's what troubles me. What gives me hope is our obvious physical resemblance. People who knew her in the 1840s now look at me and see her. She, who has looked at herself in mirrors all her life, would be the first to recognize my black curls and blue eyes. That's why I must confront her, face to face."

"Fair enough. I agree. But what then?"

"Again, there are two possible outcomes. If she recognizes me and confesses that she is Abigail, we will both have to deal with the implications of our relationship. And no— before you ask—I'm not sure how I will react. Do I throw myself into her arms? Do I offer to shake hands? I won't be able to walk away. A positive response will demand much of me, and I don't know how I will feel. I must go with my first impulses there.

"If she denies she is Abigail, I will have to seek another way. I'm thinking my first step should be to talk to the neighbors and the inn's employees—anyone who might be likely to enjoy gossip. If no one can answer my questions, I'll seek the London newspapers. An obituary or a divorce decree might turn up to reveal the truth. As a last resort, I could hire Mr. Preis, or someone like him, to track her down."

"We don't have that much time, dear. I need to get back to company business before it collapses."

"Which is why I'm pushing to see Mary Yonkers—first thing tomorrow morning."

"Then we'd better go to sleep."

"Not yet. There's another issue—one that troubles me. What if it was Abigail—or Mary—who killed Antoine?"

"You cannot think it—not for a moment."

"Why not? I've never believed in coincidences. Events happen for a reason. They are never random. We may not see every connection, but the links are always there if someone looks hard enough. And the coincidences in this case are too involved to have occurred by accident. From the moment the telegram arrived, giving the address where they found Antoine's body, I have wondered about it. I mean, how many streets do you think there are in all of London? There must be thousands. And Antoine just happened to die in the street outside the establishment where Abigail once worked as a prostitute? No. I don't believe it's a simple coincidence."

"What would he have been doing there? How could he have known to go into that bar and ask for her?"

"I wondered that, too, at first, but the answer is obvious. He must have read it in Henrietta's diary."

"Impossible. She kept those journals locked away, first in

the attic, then in the safe in grandfather's office, and then in the warehouse safe. He couldn't get to them."

"No. But he could have read them when she was writing them—or when she first returned from England and he wanted to know where the new baby came from. Antoine was a sneaky bastard."

"Rachel!"

"Well, he was. I have this picture in my mind. Grandfather and Henrietta are playing with me in the office, and upstairs, Antoine is sneaking into Henrietta's bedroom to read her diary. That would not be a coincidence. It is a distinct possibility."

"All right. I'll give you that one. But how do you get from that to Abigail as a murderer?"

"Antoine shows up at the Cozy Den asking for Abigail. Mary hears the question and recognizes him. She stays out of sight and asks Sam to send him packing. Mary fears Antoine will destroy her life, and Sam dislikes her emotional reaction to this man. Husband and wife both have a motive for killing him. Antoine comes back after closing to snoop around, they hear him, and one or both kill him. It makes much more sense than assuming a random killer happened to be walking by."

"Where does the knife come from?"

"The bar serves meals. That means they have a kitchen, and kitchens have knives."

"It wasn't an accident, then. They prepared. And if that proves to be the case, what will you do? Do you turn them in or hide the truth and risk becoming an accessory after the fact?"

"I don't know!"

"A happy mother-daughter reunion in a jail cell." Elise's voice was bitter. "Oh, Rachel, what are you risking?"

"I'm hoping it doesn't come down to that. The police consider the case closed. Perhaps it will stay that way."

"Even knowing where this could lead, you still want to know if Mary is your mother?"

"I have to know."

"Then I will go with you tomorrow morning. Maybe I can protect you from yourself."

THE SISTERS STOOD SHOULDER TO SHOULDER ON THE LITTLE stoop outside the cottage door. For a long moment, both forgot to breathe. Then Elise stepped backward, gesturing toward the door knocker. "This is your show. Let's get on with it."

The woman who answered the door was plainer than either Elise or Rachel had imagined. She had oiled her iron-gray hair to lie close to her scalp and then pulled it into a tight bun at the base of her skull. Only a few short strands at her temples had escaped to reveal that her hair had once been a mass of curls. Bright blue eyes looked dull behind greasy wire-framed glasses. Wrinkles had replaced dimples in her cheeks, and harsh lines ran from her nose to upper lip and from the corners of her mouth to either side of her chin. To complete a picture of total anonymity, her dress was a grubby brown and several sizes too large, and her high-top shoes bore scuff marks.

Swallowing hard, Rachel launched into a well-rehearsed speech. "Good morning, Mrs. Yonkers. I'm sorry to disturb you so early, but I wanted to make sure I caught you before you went across the street to the inn. I'm trying to locate someone important to me—Miss Abigail Marie Ainesworth. Someone told me she once worked at the Cozy Den, and I'm hoping you know where I might find her now."

Mrs. Yonkers stared at her. She squinted her eyes and then touched her own hair as if remembering a time when it had been as black as this young woman's curls. Then her fingers curled into a fist, the nails digging into her palm. "Who are you? Who sent you here?"

"My name is Rachel Marie Beauchene, and I'm from Charleston, South Carolina."

The woman's head jerked back. Then she grimaced as she spoke. "Abigail is dead—has been dead for a long time."

"Are you sure?"

"You're wasting your efforts. Go home." She moved to shut the door at the same moment that Rachel reached out to keep it from slamming.

"I know she once married a man by the name of Sam Yonkers. Is that your—" But it was too late. The door crashed into its frame, and Rachel heard the click as the lock slid into place. Tears flowed down Rachel's cheeks as she turned away.

Elise put an arm around her shoulders and pulled her close. "I think a strong cup of tea is in order." She led her across the street and into the dining room of the Cozy Inn.

THE LAST BREAKFAST CUSTOMERS WERE JUST LEAVING. AS SOON as she had dealt with their bill, the waitress hurried to their table. "Good morning. I'm Maisie, the only help you're likely to get around here this early in the day. Breakfast is pretty much over but I can get you some tea and toasted crumpets if you like."

"That would be lovely," Elise replied. "And then, could we trouble you to answer a few questions about this neighborhood?"

"Sure. I'll be right back."

"I don't want to eat, Elise."

"You're in a tough fight. You need to keep up your strength."

"Crumpets will be a few minutes. In the meantime, what can I help you with? Didn't I see you over there at the Yonkers' door a few minutes ago? Not that I was spying, mind, just happened to look out the window."

"We were trying to talk to Mrs. Yonkers, but she wasn't willing to let us in."

"She's not the sociable type, she isn't. Don't like folks prying into her business."

"That's her right, I suppose. Is she, perhaps, a second wife? Was Mr. Yonkers married before her?"

"Oh, heavens, no. He was a real bachelor till she came along, so I hear. But he went tail over teacups for her. Don't let her appearance fool you. In her day she was a real looker. But she's let herself go now she's caught her man."

"That happens. What about someone who used to work here? Did you ever know a girl named Abigail?"

"No, and I'd remember that, if I had, because Abigail was my grandmother's name. I always thought I'd name a daughter after her."

"Have you worked here long, Maisie?"

"Ever since Mrs. Yonkers kicked the gamblers out and turned this place into a restaurant. She wanted all new help. Hired new cooks, too. Didn't seem to want anyone around who knew her. I always thought it was funny."

"Are you here every day?"

"Except Sundays. That's my day off. Otherwise I come in for the breakfast rush and stay through dinner although Mrs. Yonkers will take over if we have a small crowd. Happens sometimes. Most days, it's just the neighbors, and they come as much to see each other as to eat the food."

"Would you remember if a newcomer showed up?"

"Probably."

"What about the fellow who got himself killed outside in March? We heard about that. Sounded gruesome."

"Oh, yes, but wait. Cook's signaling your crumpets are ready. Be right back."

"Elise, you are amazing. You're talking to her in her own lingo, aren't you?"

"Makes her feel more comfortable. Oh, my, Maisie, those look fantastic."

"Try them with some of that there honey."

"We were talking about bloody awful things—that stabbing victim. Do murders like that happen often around here?"

"Hardly ever. The only person I know who carries a knife is Mrs. Yonkers, and hers is just for keeping the drunks in line."

"She carries a knife? Really? She doesn't look like the type."

"Well, you don't want to mess with her. She has this neat little shiv, all pointy and sharp. Carries it in a skirt pocket, she does, and can whip it out before you see it coming."

Rachel choked and dropped her crumpet, then tried to pretend she needed a sip of tea.

"Did they ever find out who did it? The stabbing, I mean."

"Not that I ever heard. Some folks said the bloke was in here earlier that evening, asking about a girl he knew, but nobody had ever heard of her. Wait! Come to think of it, her name was Abigail, too. That's a coincidence, eh? Well, I'd best get back to work. Here comes the boss." She nodded at the window as Mrs. Yonkers crossed the street.

"Caught!" Rachel murmured, but Mrs. Yonkers did not even glance their way as she headed for the kitchen.

DISCLOSURES

Thursday Morning, June 11, 1862
London, England

*M*ary Yonkers approached the table as Elise and Rachel gathered their things and prepared to leave. "Sit down, ladies. I owe you an apology, and I don't want to deliver it to your backs. Maisie, heat this teapot with a fresh brew, please. I suspect we will be here for a while." Instructions given, Mrs. Yonkers pulled out a chair, sat down, and steepled her hands in front of her face.

Elise sat, while Rachel hesitated, looking at the door as if she might make a run for it. Then she, too, settled into her chair across the table. She searched Elise's expression for guidance about how to handle this new development. Her eyes darted around the empty restaurant as if searching for help.

Mary looked from one young woman to the other, shaking her head. At last, she spoke. "My husband tells me I should not have slammed the door in your faces. He's right, but he could not understand the shock I felt at that moment.

I looked at you, my dear, and had the odd sensation I was looking into a mirror. Your face, your coloring, your expressions are amazing duplicates of how I looked twenty-four years ago. I've never forgotten that I once had a daughter, but I never thought you would be so like me."

"You are Abigail?"

"Correction. I used to be Abigail."

"You are my mother?"

"I may be the woman who gave birth to you. I can't claim to have been much of a mother."

"But you said Abigail was dead—that she died a long time ago." Rachel buried her face in her hands. "You're talking in riddles and I don't understand what you're saying."

"I'm sorry. But before we go any further, help me identify your companion. I recognize you, too," she said, turning to Elise. "Or at least I think I do. You resemble my cousin, Henrietta Ainesworth, who married into the American Beauchene family. You must be one of her daughters."

"I'm Elise Beauchene, and if you are Abigail, you will remember me as the four-year-old for whom you served as a governess in Charleston."

"Yes, although there were two children, were there not?"

"My younger sister Juliette has remained in Charleston, keeping the house and business on an even keel while Rachel and I . . . but never mind why we are here. For the moment, all that matters is that you and Rachel establish your connections. Ignore me."

"All right then. Let me restate my identity. I was born Abigail Marie Ainesworth, and I grew up believing I should have only one purpose in life—to seduce a rich man, get him to marry me, and let him take care of me for the rest of my days. What an empty goal that was, and what a foolish, simpering child I was to believe in it. It didn't take long for me to discover that real life doesn't work that way.

"By the time I was twenty, I was alone, uneducated, and penniless, with a fatherless child growing in my belly. In a struggle to survive, I became a cleaning woman, a prostitute, and an opium addict. And then, I lost my child to someone I once trusted. My cousin stole my four-month-old baby and carried her halfway around the world to keep her out of my reach. If it had not been for the Sisters of Mercy, I would have died in a gutter somewhere. And if it had not been for my cousin, the baby would have died along with me.

"When the good Sisters saved my life, cured me of my addiction, and set me on a better path, I knew I could never go back to being that Abigail again. I chose a new name— Mary—plain Mary. And I let Abigail Ainesworth die. My family had already disowned me, and I owned nothing but the clothes on my back and a few shillings the Sisters of Mercy provided. It was easy to choose a common name and forget everything that had happened before that moment."

"Including me?" Rachel asked through her tears.

"Including you. If I had tried to keep your memory alive, I might have shriveled up in grief. As it was, I returned to my familiar haunts and begged the owner of the Cozy Den for a job as a barmaid. He recognized me and called me Abigail. I told him that was only my prostitute name, a profession I had left behind. 'Just call me Mary,' I told him, and he did so. In time, we grew to be friends and then a wedded couple. I have been Mary to him ever since then, and if you ask him about a woman named Abigail, he will deny ever knowing her. Abigail is dead, and I had intended to keep her that way until you showed up this morning."

"What changed your mind?"

"Seeing you. Being unable to deny that you are a part of me. Realizing how many people I have affected by my actions. Recognizing how I have failed you. Pick one."

"What happens now?"

"That's the question, isn't it? Other people need never hear about this meeting or the questions it has raised for me. But I will always know, and I will have to live with my two identities. I can't deny Abigail any longer because she made you possible. And I can't give up Mary because her life is important to many others. Can I be both Mary and Abigail?" She chuckled to herself, making the girls smile, too. "Perhaps I'll set up a schedule. I'll be Mary on weekdays and Abigail on holidays and weekends."

She took a deep breath and stared out the window at the cottage across the street. Another breath, and she let her eyes roam over these two new acquaintances who represented a long-lost life. "How odd! I feel more alive—and larger—as if something fragmented me years ago, and now I'm whole again."

"Excuse me. This room is suffocating me. I need fresh air. Now!" Rachel pushed herself upright and without waiting for a reaction hurried to the door, yanking it open as if she could not wait to escape. Elise moved to follow her, but Mary put out a hand to stop her.

"She needs to be alone for a few minutes. I understand that feeling all too well. Perhaps it's a family weakness."

"She looks ill," Elise protested.

"It's not a physical illness. She's being bombarded by new emotions. I'm betting she never expected to find her mother. She believed in the search but never thought she would find me. I've overwhelmed her."

"She's vulnerable right now. We've had such an emotional year, not just because our country has gone to war with itself but because we've lost so many members of our family."

"I didn't realize that. Who?"

"First our Grandfather Beauchene died of a stroke right after Lincoln's election. Antoine—who we now know was Rachel's father—became involved in a smuggling operation, lost his ship, and pretended he had drowned, although the police couldn't find a body. Then the Northern invasion of our Sea Islands trapped friends and family, and many of the people we knew, including our cousins, lost homes and livelihoods. A fire destroyed half our city, and our mother died of smoke inhalation as she tried to save our warehouse. Uncle Antoine turned up alive, only to cause more problems for members of our family. He left Charleston in anger and sailed for England. And then we received word of his murder near your inn. We're raw and on edge. If there's a limit to how much emotion a person can experience, we must be close to the danger level. I fear Rachel has crossed that line."

"I'm so sorry. You may not know this, but I enjoyed the time I spent with your family, and despite the rift that occurred between us, I loved Henrietta. She was my only girl cousin, and we grew up together. I once tried to tell her how I felt about the Beauchenes, but I'm not sure she understood how badly I needed that kind of love and forgiveness.[1] I sometimes hated her for stealing my baby, but at other times I gave thanks for her intervention. And Mr. Beauchene treated me well when I struggled to adjust to life in America. It's true he sent me away when he learned I was pregnant, but that announcement shattered his dreams as well as mine. He did what he thought was best."

Elise listened with sympathy and wondered if Henrietta had ever realized that Rachel had inherited the same neediness. "Did you know it was Grandfather Beauchene who arranged and financed your year-long stay with the Sisters of Mercy?"

"No, I didn't. What a tangled web binds us together. Whatever made me think I could just ignore our relationships?"

"I'm not sure I will ever understand how families can be

so fragile and yet have unbreakable bonds. But speaking of being unbreakable, here comes Rachel."

"Forgive me for being so melodramatic. I needed time to let my mind catch up with my feelings."

"We understand, dear. And you've given Elise and me time to share old memories."

"I don't suppose she asked you the other burning question that's been haunting us."

"What question is that?"

"What happened to Antoine? I learned that he was my father at the same time I identified you as my mother, except that I could never discuss it with him before he died. I feel lost when I think of him. It would help if I knew what he was doing outside your inn and who killed him. Is that asking too much?"

"You sound as if you already have well-honed suspicions."

"Perhaps so. I don't believe in coincidences, so I assume his presence—and his death—had something to do with you."

"Yes, he was here, and he was looking for me. I didn't know why. He came into the bar that evening and asked for Abigail. When no one recognized the name, he refused to accept their denials. I never talked with him, but I saw him from the kitchen doorway and recognized him. Sam sent him away while I stayed out of sight. But that was all I knew until the police came to talk to us the next day."

"So they told us. But it looks suspicious. What you've just said gives you a motive for killing him. And we've learned that you carry a knife, one whose blade matches the nature of his wounds."

"Yes, I carry a knife. This is still a dangerous neighborhood at night. Do you want to see it? Here." Mary dropped her hand to her lap and then tossed the dagger onto the table. "There it is. Check it for yourself. Although, I will assure you I would have cleaned any incriminating blood from the blade."

"Can you look me straight in the eye and tell me you are innocent?"

"I didn't kill him, Rachel. I feared him, and sometimes I wished him dead, but I had nothing to do with his murder."

"Can you say the same for your husband? You asked Mr. Yonkers to get rid of him, didn't you?"

"I asked Sam to send him out of the bar, not to kill him. Besides, Sam was with me the whole night. We went home and went straight to sleep. Sam never left the bed. I would have heard him because I'm a light sleeper and I worry about his health as he gets older."

"I want to believe you. But Antoine was a threat to you, and it makes little sense that a stranger would protect your secret by stabbing him twenty-three times."

"No, you're right. It makes little sense, and I have my suspicions. I have no evidence, mind you. This is only a hunch, and you must promise not to go to the police with the story."

"I'm not trying to solve the case. I only want to put my mind at rest."

"Well, when I insisted that Sam close down his gambling activities and remove all the crooks and ne'er-do-wells from the premises, there were two blokes he refused to dislodge. Bill Henessey, Pete Wilson, and Sam were tent mates in India during the Burmese War in 1825. They had several harrowing experiences and came out of them determined to have one another's backs for the rest of their lives. Henessey still spends every evening in the bar and acts as our unofficial bouncer. Wilson is the neighborhood handyman, so he's often underfoot. When he's down on his luck and can't pay his rooming house rent, he sleeps in our toolshed. We don't pay either of them, but they hit the beer taps often enough to cover their duties.

"They're good fellows and devoted to Sam, but they can get a little over-excited sometimes when they've had a sip too many. Henessey helped Sam escort Antoine out of the bar that night, so he would have understood Antoine meant trouble for the Yonkers. And the two fellows were likely to jump on any stranger who came snooping around after closing. What good would it do to blame them for removing a troublemaker like Antoine from an otherwise peaceful scene?

"There it is. I'm not a murderer. Neither is my husband. And if we have our suspicions, we would never act on them. Case closed. Antoine's dead, and although he was your father, the world is a better place without him. And that, I think wraps up our business, at least for today. You'll both be welcome here anytime, and I will guarantee your safety." With that statement, Mary picked up her dagger from the center of the table, dropped it between the folds of her skirt, and marched off to the kitchen.

HENRIETTA'S LEGACY

Thursday, June 11, 1862
London, England

*E*lise and Rachel returned to their rooming house without conversation. Rachel appeared deep in thought, and Elise respected her need for privacy. Mrs. Perkins met them at the door with a cheery smile. "I suspected you'd be home by lunchtime, so I've had Mrs. Higgens lay out a Ploughman's Lunch on the sideboard.[1] Sometimes a crust of bread and a hunk of cheese can hit the spot. There's cider, too, and some hard-boiled eggs. Just help yourselves whenever you're ready. Be sure to try the pickle. I made it myself."

She started back to the kitchen, only to meet the cook in the doorway. "Did you need something, Mrs. Higgins?"

"I'm adding these fresh onions and radishes to the Ploughman's. And I was wondering what you want me to do for supper."

"I suspect one of our guests has had a difficult morning. Perhaps a warm bowl of soup would comfort her."

"Aye. There's an old rooster in the yard, just asking for plucking. He's been annoying the hens and waking the neighbors. He's too old to be chewable, but I imagine he'd boil up nice with some noodles. Will that do?"

"Yes, if you can catch him."

Rachel sent Elise a silent, imploring message by closing her eyes and turning away from the sight of food. "I can't eat," she whispered when Mrs. Perkins left them in the dining room. "I didn't sleep at all last night because of worrying. Now I'm about to collapse. If you don't mind, I'll head up to the room and take a nap. You have lunch."

"You look pale, love, but sleep may be your best cure. I'll have a bite and then curl up in the parlor with one of Mrs. Perkins's magazines for proper ladies. Come find me when you've rested." Elise watched her as she made her way up the curved staircase and then turned back to the ample spread on the sideboard. She smiled as she remembered a ploughman's lunch had been the first meal her parents had shared on the day they met. An appropriate way to remind me of how fortunate I was to be born into the Beauchene family, she thought.

Rachel did not emerge from her nap until late afternoon. She had more color in her cheeks, but her loose curls suggested her dreams had been restless. As if she had been watching the stairs, Mrs. Perkins followed her into the parlor. "Dinner will be at eight. We're waiting for some new guests to join us. In the meantime, Mrs. Higgens is on her way with a pot of tea and some cucumber sandwiches to tide you over."

Rachel reached for a tiny sandwich and bit into it. Then her head jerked up in surprise. "I'm starved, and these are superb. I expected nothing but a slice of cucumber. Instead, there's a thin layer of creamy cheese and fresh herbs, too. I hope you don't like them, sister dear, because I have a missed meal to catch up on."

"Oh, eat away. I will enjoy seeing your appetite has returned."

"I feel good after all my worrying and fussing. Meeting my mother at last has lifted a huge load from my shoulders. No more fears. No more shame. I know who I am now, and I can move forward with my life."

"What was it that so changed your outlook?"

"Well, the simplest matter turned out to be the responsibility for Antoine's death. I realized that I didn't much care who had removed him from our lives so long as the guilty party was not someone I cared about. Old Henessey and Wilson may have killed him. They may have not. I don't know them and have no reason to report them or see them punished. They can go back to their beers, and I can move on without Antoine lurking as a stumbling block in my life."

"He was still your father."

"No, he wasn't. He didn't earn that title in life. For twenty-four years, he could have claimed me as his child. He didn't, and that's all right. But he doesn't now deserve the respect one would give a father. End of story."

"Not quite. How are you feeling about Abigail?"

"A little ambivalent, maybe. She's not what I expected. She's a real person—vivid, self-assured, strong—not the made-up version I'd imagined. I've learned much about myself because of that. Can you stand to listen while I bare my soul, or should I leave it at ambivalence?"

"Oh, please, bare it all. You may have a few lessons to teach me along the way."

"I went into that meeting with a preconceived notion of what my mother would look like. Whenever Henrietta and I clashed over a detail of my life, I compensated by telling myself that she must have adopted me. I pretended that someday my real mother would appear and carry me off. She would be beautiful, loving, and understanding. And then I could pretend that Henrietta was the exact opposite of her, which let me resent her even more. I was horrid! I recognize that now, and I'm ashamed of myself."

"You figured that out just this morning?"

"That makes me sound stupid, but, yes, it's true. When I met Mary and learned she was my mother, all my fairytale princess dreams exploded. Mary is not young and beautiful. She's stern and reasonable, but she's also strong. Most of all, she's real, and if I claim her as my mother, I must accept her for what she is.

"To take this one step further, if I see Mary for what she is, I also have to see Henrietta for what she was. She was under terrible pressure. Even though she thought she was saving my life, in the eyes of the law she was a kidnapper. Anyone who knew the truth could have sent her to prison. Worse, she and grandfather had a solemn pact not to tell anyone about the kidnapping. And there I was, shouting at her that if she loved me, she'd tell me the truth. I will regret my behavior for the rest of my life, but I'm also grateful to Mary for helping me to understand what was going on.

"So, that puts an end to my searching for answers," Rachel declared. "I know who I am. I've met my real mother. I have seen the proof that declares me Antoine's daughter and therefore his heir. I have a new identity, and now I need to decide what I will do with it.

"You, Elise, have a family business to uphold and no further responsibilities here beyond picking up that death certificate on Friday. While I do penance for my failures, you can honor Henrietta's memory by using that business to help former slaves become cotton planters. It's time for you to go home."

"I agree that there's nothing more to do here. Poor Abigail —or Mary Yonkers, as she now calls herself—has suffered enough and now deserves to live out her life in peace." Elise frowned for a moment. "I wonder how long it will take us to book passage to Charleston. I'll look into both the southern and northern routes, taking whichever one gets us home sooner."

"Maybe you didn't hear me. I said it was time for you to go home. I'm staying here."

"What? What more do you hope to accomplish?"

"Let's start with building a new life for myself as an English citizen."

"Rachel! No! Your mother was English, but your father was an American. You already have the privileges of being both."

"Yes, so it would seem. But there's a record of my birth in London, which proves my identity. I'll find acceptance here, unlike the lip-curling glances I got in Charleston when I didn't have a birth certificate to prove I was a member of the local aristocracy."

"You're not still smarting over that slight by the St. Cecilia Society, are you?"

"It may sound trivial to you, but—" Rachel's eyes filled, as they had after her debutante bid failed in the face of Charlestonian snobbery.

"But what will you do? How will you support yourself? You know no one here. You have nowhere to live. No friends, no job, no money, and no support in case you fall ill. I won't let you stay here."

"I'm an adult, Elise, not your responsibility. All those difficulties have solutions."

"All right. Let's hear your plans."

"First, Mrs. Perkins has agreed to let me stay here at the rooming house until I settle into London life. And I have money. There's a sizable roll of banknotes in the warehouse safe that Henrietta left me, and she outlined what she wanted me to do with them. She would approve of my decision.

Further, I saved almost all my salary from working as parish secretary for the Huguenot church. Before we left home, I made arrangements with the bank to forward my savings account once I send them the details of my new account here."

"Before we left? You've been planning this all along?"

"I considered it as one of the possible outcomes. I also left arrangements with the Middleton Law Offices to transfer my twenty shares of company stock to you and Juliette when I send them word. The challenge to Henrietta's will is no longer an issue because Antoine is dead. But fair is fair. The wills are clear. Mother held sixty percent of the company stock, but upon her death, those shares were to go to the legitimate offspring of Henrietta and Julien Beauchene. We've now confirmed what Mother's journals revealed—that I am the cuckoo chick in the family nest."

"Stock holdings don't matter, Rachel. I care about your long-term support."

"I care, too, but I won't accept something I don't deserve. My first step will be to go back to the Sisters of Mercy. They have the records that prove my birth and parentage. And, yes, you were right. I need that copy. They can help me take care of the formal paperwork, and then, perhaps, they will know of an available job. I can also call upon Mr. Preis, the private investigator, and Inspector Waggoner at Police Headquarters for recommendations. England is more willing to hire women than South Carolina is."

"You have no friends here."

"My mother is here, and I want to get to know her better. She said I would be welcome at the inn and the cottage. Besides Mary and Sam, I have cousins somewhere. Henrietta and Abigail both had brothers, all of whom by now have families. I may have more relatives in England than we have in South Carolina."

"But you're talking of living alone. You'll be lonely."

"I'll get a cat."

"I'm serious, Rachel. Everyone needs friends, and a cat doesn't count."

"There are things much worse than loneliness, and, yes, a cat does help. Nothing could be lonelier than the complete social ostracism I suffered in Charleston. Sometimes, Henrietta's warehouse cat was the only one who purred when she saw me. So please stop throwing up roadblocks for me, Elise. I've decided. Henrietta's journals helped me grow up. Reliving her experience here in London taught me I share her courage. But it also showed me that reliance on compromise can lead to unforeseen consequences. That's her real legacy, and I will honor it by tempering any compromise I make with a good helping of strength, honesty, and independence. I'm counting on Mary to serve as my model.

"Now, tomorrow, you can take yourself off to the steamship ticket office and make your travel arrangements, leaving me to pick up the death certificate from Police Headquarters. It's time for both of us to face the future."

ALSO BY CAROLYN P. SCHRIBER

TITLES IN BOLD ARE CITED IN THE
FOLLOWING ENDNOTES.

CREATIVE BIOGRAPHY

The Dilemma of Arnulf of Lisieux (1990; reprint 2012)

A Scratch with the Rebels (2007; revised, 2015)

Beyond All Price (2009; 2nd ed., 2018)

Left by the Side of the Road (2nd ed., 2012)

The Road to Frogmore (November 2012)

HISTORICAL FICTION

Damned Yankee (2014)

Yankee Reconstructed (January 2016)

Yankee Daughters (December 2016)

Henrietta's Journal (2017)

THE ART AND CRAFT OF WRITING

The Second Mouse Gets the Cheese (2011)

The Second Mouse Goes Digital (2017)

NOTES

1. CONFRONTATION

1. *Henrietta's Journal*, 206:

I'm trying, but it's hard to know how people expect me to behave. The local society mavens promulgate and enforce the rules for a new widow: eighteen months of mourning for a husband, handled in six-month increments. A widow must wear a wardrobe that gradually changes from this horrid black crepe to regular black cloth to shades of dark gray or lavender. She must wear only severe hair styles, with no jewelry or other decoration. And she may attend no parties, public appearances, entertaining, or visiting. But friends and family members urged me to cheer up, get over it, enjoy life, or keep busy.

Today I went to church for the first time in full, heavily-draped widow's weeds. People avoided me as if I were the carrier of some loathsome disease. The seats all around me were empty. Those who did greet me did so furtively, with a quick hand squeeze or shoulder pat before scurrying off without a comment lest they be bitten by the same disaster that has befallen me. And those who asked how I was disappeared before I could answer. I felt as if I were both deaf and dumb.

2. A FAVORITE CLIENT RETURNS

1. *Henrietta's Journal*, 94:

As if he understands every word I say, Marmelade now spends almost every afternoon with me. He has a basket under my desk, padded with one of Julien's old sweaters (although Julien doesn't realize that). I keep a bowl of fresh water for him (the cat, not Julien), and I often bring him little packets of meat scraps that Mrs. Thompson makes up for him when she scrapes our plates after dinner. Julien got upset with me once when he discovered that I was feeding the cat. He said I was ruining him as a rat catcher. My response was that cats are plentiful on the waterfront. There would always be another one willing to take Marmelade's place in the warehouse while he keeps me company in the office.

2. Pluff mud is a kind of unstable, quicksand-like soil unique to the

shores of the Low Country south of Charleston. One sailor described it in *Beyond All Price*, 143–44, this way:

"It's 'pluff mud,' which also defies description. That grass grows in a sticky, deep mixture of dirt, sand, ground up oyster shells, and rotting plant and animal matter, all diluted with sea water. When the tide comes in, you can paddle a small boat on it. When the tide goes out, it looks like dry land. Sometimes in the summer, it bakes in the heat until it is solid—at least for a few hours. And it gives off an awful stink, like a rotten egg or a powerful fart, begging your pardon, ma'am."

3. *Henrietta's Journal*, 135:

"Cubans are sitting on a gold mine. I know that the gentlemen of Charleston, Savannah, and coastal North Carolina would pay high premiums for real Cuban cigars and rum. Charleston's upper classes love luxury goods of all kinds, but they have little access to them. As far as I can determine, right now the Cubans are exporting almost none of their commodities because no one is offering to ship their products. If we had our little steam-powered ships, we could run back and forth between Charleston and Havana even during hurricane season, when English lines are not willing to risk crossing the Atlantic. We could purchase the native rum and cigars with our surplus cotton, and the Cubans could re-sell that cotton to British shippers when they come through here in calmer months. The bottom line? We'll get rich selling the 'expensive stuff' to Charleston's aristocracy."

5. A JOB OFFER

1. *Henrietta's Journal*, 87:

"Fine. Go ahead." I sat down, rather rudely, I suppose, and glared at him. I was not going to argue with him, but I didn't intend to make his task any easier, either.

He began by explaining the general law concerning married women—that all the wife's rights and property passed to her husband when she married. That much I knew. But, he went on, in exchange, the husband is required to provide for all of her needs and those of her children, to protect her, speak in her stead, and defend her in court. That's called "covering," and in legal terms, we refer to such a wife as a *feme covert*, a protected woman.

"And we are supposed to be grateful, are we?" I couldn't help but sneer at the male attitude behind that law.

"Wait. There's more. A strong woman can find a way around that provision with the cooperation of her husband. If she has come into the marriage with a great deal of personal property, perhaps inherited from her family, she can arrange a marriage settlement that puts her property into the hands of a third person, such as a solicitor, who will protect her property from her husband's possible mismanagement. I understand, however, that is not the case in your marriage."

"No, I held no personal property before we married." I was starting to realize the full weakness of my position.

"I thought not. So what Mr. Pierre Beauchene is envisioning for you is the application of another provision designed for a *feme sole* or independent businesswoman. All the woman needs is a letter of intent from her husband allowing her to conduct her affairs, open a business, or earn a salary. He simply promises not to interfere with her business or claim the profits from that business. Pierre Beauchene wants you to work in the family company, but as a business woman, not as the dependent of your husband—or of him."

7. A CHRISTMAS PAGEANT

1. *Henrietta's Journal*, 88:

"And there's one further provision that your father-in-law didn't get around to explaining. In his new will, Pierre Beauchene intends to entail Julien's shares of the company so that upon Julien's death the shares can only pass to you, or to your children if you predecease your husband."

"My God," I said. "He was prepared to give me control of the company, and I defied him."

10. DINNER TABLE DEBATES

1. A more detailed discussion about Baltimore appears in *Beyond All Price*, 2nd edition, 32–34:

"Men, we may face unpleasantness in Baltimore," he warned.

"You mean more trouble like what them Michiganders faced?" someone called out.

"Well, we hope it won't be quite so serious."

"What kind of trouble was that?" someone else asked.

Nellie listened with mounting horror as the story unfolded. "Here's what we know," Captain Leckey began. "Maryland is a border state. They have not seceded, but neither have they supported the Union cause. There are many slave owners in Baltimore, and they lean toward the side of the South. President Lincoln is worried those who support slavery might try to block the rail lines bringing troops to Washington."

"Well, why didn't we go another way?" asked a disembodied voice in the darkness.

"There isn't any other rail line. Worse, this track ends on one side of Baltimore, and the line that will take us to Washington is on the other side of town. There's nothing else for it. We will have to disembark and walk through the town."

"What happened to them boys from Michigan?"

"The incident that occurred back in April involved the Sixth Michigan Regiment. Renegade firefighter gangs control Baltimore, and one of those gangs, called the 'Plug-Uglies' for reasons you can figure out, objected when Lincoln sent troops to Baltimore to protect the soldiers who were passing through. Both sides fired shots. Before the violence was over, twelve citizens of Baltimore lay dead, along with four members of Michigan's regimental band."

"Damnation!" huffed John Nicklin, who had enlisted as the drum major of the Roundheads. "Why would anyone shoot a musician? Was their playing that bad?"

"It shouldn't happen again, but there is a rumor a hostile crowd has gathered around the station waiting for our arrival. The engineer is slowing the train, and we'll try to wait them out. We're hoping they'll get tired."

"What about how tired we are?"

The weakness of machinery helped to delay their arrival. At one point, a coupler broke, allowing several cars to come loose from the main train. Once the engineer realized his train was too light, he needed to back up and reattach the cars. More mumbling and grousing surged through the boxcars, and many soldiers got off the train to stretch their legs while they watched the repairs. Re-boarding extended the delay, and they did not arrive in Baltimore until 3 A.M., by which time even the most malicious of trouble-makers had given up and gone home.

The regiment marched across town without incident. Baltimore was a grubby city, its streets lined with ramshackle buildings and lean-tos, rubbish accumulating in gutters and vacant lots. The recent rain had done little to wash away the dirt; instead it had turned it into mud that made footing precarious. Staff officers surrounded Nellie, so she would not stand out as a target. Still, the fear was palpable until they made it to the safety of the relay house, where they were to pick up the Washington and Harper's Ferry Railroad. James Cline later described the scene in a letter to his wife:

"Streets lit up by the uncertain glare of the street lamps, with double police at every corner. It looked more like a funeral cortege of some departed spirits than the march of a regiment of soldiers."

14. A HOUSE DIVIDED

1. The difficulties and misunderstandings surrounding the freeing of a slave in the 1830s became obvious in this conversation between Mr. Beauchene and the slave Gladys Brown. *Henrietta's Journal*, 212–13:

"Well, it appears that it will be necessary for me to emancipate you so that you can travel as a free woman of color. Is that all right with you?"

"Emancipate me? Set me free? Send me away from here? But sir, I don't want to be free. What would I do? Where would I go?" Her eyes grew wide, and her voice had a tinge of hysteria.

"I thought all slaves wanted to be free."

"Maybe we do—someday. But I was born here, sir. My parents belonged to your father. My brother and my sister and I—we've lived here all our lives. The graves of our ancestors lie in your slave plot. The slave yard out back of here—that's my home. That's where my family and my friends all are. If you send me away, I'll have no place to go and no one to share my life. Making me a free woman may be a blessing in your eyes, but to me, it's a terrifying thought."

"I'm offering to make you free. I'm not driving you out into the cold."

"But . . ."

"Maybe you don't yet understand what freedom will mean to you. When you are free, you have choices. You get to decide where you go and what you do. So if you want to find a house of your own, apply for work in other places, create a whole new life for yourself, you can do that. But if you choose to live here in your accustomed slave community, to return to your old cabin, to share your life with your slave friends, that will be up to you."

"You'd allow me to do that?"

"Certainly. And as long as you keep working for Henrietta, she will pay you for your labor as well. In my business world, we'd call this a bargain. You agree to become Harriet's assistant and help her with whatever she needs. And she will pay you a salary and throw in some other benefits—like a free trip to England and a home to live in when you get back. What do you say?"

"How . . . How does it happen? What do I have to do?"

"I'll start the process by having my lawyer draw up the paperwork. Then we'll all have to appear before a civil judge. He'll ask me if I am willing to free you. He'll ask Henrietta if she can employ you and pay you a salary. And he will ask you if you accept our offer. We'll be nodding and saying 'Yes, sir.' Then we'll all sign the papers, and you'll be a free woman. By the way, can you sign your name?"

She almost smiled through her fears. "Yes, sir, I learned to read and write a long time ago. I just never told you."

17. HIDDEN TREASURE

1. The first such clash between Henrietta and her father-in-law occurred when Father Beauchene informed Henrietta that he expected her to turn Baby Elise over to the care of a slave and come to work with him in the company office. *Henrietta's Journal*, 85–86:

"You must know that I still hold many reservations about the whole institution of slavery, and I . . ." My voice trailed off as I realized he was not taking my protests seriously.

"First of all, in my house, slaves do what I tell them. A slave woman will care for your child because that is the assignment I give her."

Before I could stop myself, I spit out the angry thought that arose. "And I will go to work for you as well because that is the assignment you give me? Then I am no better than a slave."

Julien reached for my hand to quell my outburst. His father reacted even more furiously, pushing his chair back standing, and looming over me. "You do not give me much credit, daughter-in-law, but I cannot control your thoughts. If you want to consider yourself my slave, so be it. Now I think we have had quite enough of this discussion for the moment. We shall continue it when tempers have cooled. You may go, both of you."

2. The last entry in the journal explained her decision to save her journals. *Henrietta's Journal*, 207:

I've been keeping this journal ever since the day I first met Julien Beauchene. Its entries chronicle a marriage with all its high points and frightening valleys. I once worried about other people reading it but gave up on the idea of hiding it or writing in code to keep my secrets intact. I have taken pride in the fact that whatever I have written here is the absolute truth. I may lie to other people if I have good reason to, but I do not lie to myself. That is still the case. But this is my last entry. After tonight, I will close the book. I intend to stack all the small notebooks together (they average one a year) and tie them up with a wide ribbon and bow. And then I will hide them safely away, keeping them under lock and key in case someone should locate their general hiding spot.

What has changed? Not the journalling. Not my determination to be honest. Not the circumstances or people that surround me. Rather, life events changed my world. In these pages, there are happy moments. But there are also terrifying events, and—sadly—criminal ones. The facts discussed here could offer vital evidence about rape and murder involving members of my family as both perpetrators and victims. The question of my involvement in a kidnapping also hangs over these pages like a cloud.

In each of those cases, I have come to believe that it would be wrong to convict the guilty at the expense of doing irreparable harm to the innocent. And so I compromise and hide the evidence away. But I do not destroy it. I leave it to the judgments of the future.

19. FIRST SHOTS

1. Antoine explained more of his views on the future of the family business in a second letter. *Henrietta's Journal*, 142–43:

"You would find it easy to set up a business here in Nassau.

The outlying areas, of course, are populated by former slaves, especially those freed during the effort to eliminate the British slave trade. In some areas, too, there are pockets of refugees from Haiti who speak their own Creole French language. The downside for our business interests is that despite all the best efforts of the French, British, and American navies, equipped though they are with the latest steam power, privateers still range freely among the many small islands that make up the Bahamas.

The British proclaim that the Age of Piracy is over, and the Spanish take pride in their capture and execution of the Caribbean's last pirate, Roberto Cofresi in 1825. But like a bad weed, freebooters are notoriously hard to root out, particularly here. The small islands offer coves, inlets, hidden streams, even caves, where those who are avoiding capture can disappear—for a while.

Would pirates interfere with your business ventures? Maybe, maybe not. Some privateers still seek out letters of marque, permitting them to attack and capture enemy ships and cargo. Others, still following the example of Roberto Cofresi, act like today's version of Robin Hood They go after rich men's goods and redistribute them to the poor people who inhabit these islands. The cargo on cotton transports is too bulky to make pirating attacks worthwhile, but luxury goods are a different matter."

20. THE THREAT OF BLOCKADE

1. *Henrietta's Journal*, 10:

He heard one of the library clerks refer to my father as "Sir Ephraim," and he demanded to know if members of my family were titled nobility. I launched into an explanation of the baronet's title that

Father holds. A baronetcy ranks higher than a knight, but does not convey membership in the peerage, I told him. It does not entitle the holder to a seat in Parliament. The title of baronet may sometimes be inherited if it is tied to a particular bit of property, as is the case with the higher ranks of the titled nobility or peerage, but it is only an honorific. In Father's case, the title came to him along with his appointment as Keeper of Ancient Manuscripts at the Bodleian, so it is attached to his position, not to a piece of property. He is correctly referred to in correspondence as Sir Ephraim Ainesworth and addressed as Sir Ephraim. His wife has a courtesy title of Lady, used with her surname: "Lady Ainesworth." She is never addressed as "Lady Luella."

23. FALLOUT

1. *Henrietta's Journal*, 230–31:

I avoided the answers all week by shepherding my little brood around the sights of London. We finished by reporting, as the friendly Bobby had recommended, to the west portal of Westminster Abbey early on Sunday morning. We were not disappointed. Right on schedule, the troop of cavalry rode through the street clearing the way. We huddled closer to the walls of the Abbey, hoping we would not be asked to move. Then came the golden carriage in all its wondrous glory. As we watched, Queen Victoria appeared in the doorway of the carriage, reached down to take the hand of one of her faithful attendants, and stepped into full view. Gladys and I said the same thing at the same moment: "She's tiny!"

Slender and well under five feet tall, she almost disappeared in the drapery of her cloak. And yet there was no mistaking the power of her personality. She looked around at the gathering crowd, raised a delicately gloved hand in greeting, and then disappeared like smoke through the portal.

"If she can do her job," I whispered to myself, "I can do mine."

25. RUMORS ABOUND

1. This description of the departure of the Great Atlantic Expeditionary Force comes from *Beyond All Price*, 2nd edition, 105–06:

The fleet lifted anchors on Tuesday, October 29, 1861. The seas were still rough, but a warm breeze and a brilliant blue sky promised better weather ahead. For many of the Roundheads, this would be the first time they had sailed beyond land, and the experience was as exciting as it was terrifying. Most of the soldiers had learned Nellie's trick of watching the horizon rather than objects that lay close by, but when the horizon no longer revealed the promise of dry land, they became disoriented. The result was another bout of sea sickness so pervasive that later the *Camp Kettle* recaptured the experience:

"If any body wants to get to the depth of deepest misery, let him just go to sea, and encounter a small gale the first day out. At first it is all nice, and consummately funny. The ship rises and sinks, and rolls and pitches, and settles away and comes right up again to go through the same gyrations over and over again, and your gait becomes unsteady, and rocky, and your companions laugh at you, and then you laugh at them, and it is all delightful, but by and by, you begin to experience a sort of goneness all over, some thing not exactly desirable, until at last the vessel rears up at the bow and again goes down and you feel as if the bottom of the briny deep was rushing up through your epigastrium. And you make a rush for any convenient place, and aah! It's disgusting."

Nellie kept busy, offering advice, honey, ground ginger, and dry crackers to those most afflicted. When all else failed, she sent the sickest ones to the prow of the ship, telling them the captain had ordered them to keep a sharp lookout for Confederate pirates. It didn't matter that the captain had given no such order, or that there were no Confederate pirates. The subterfuge worked by forcing them to look out over the water and to shift their feet to keep their balance. Most handled their discomfort with a characteristic touch of humor. Private James C. Stevenson remarked, "I wouldn't care for throwing up the rice and beans, but I hate to lose the crackers after so much hard chewing to get them down."

By the second day, the seas had calmed, and the epidemic of seasickness passed. The fleet stretched out as far as the soldiers could see, the ordered sails and funnels of the ships providing an artificial reassurance that all was well. As the men lounged about the deck, the officers had time to catch up on paperwork and administrative duties.

27. THE FATE OF THE LOW COUNTRY

1. *Henrietta's Journal*, 203–04:

"I have just received the verdict from the Coroner's Office," he said. "I will read it aloud for you:

We, the duly assembled Board of Inquiry and the coroner, Mr. Samuel Briscoe, having heard all the evidence in the case of the death of Mr. Julien Beauchene, late of the City of Charleston, do unanimously affirm the following conclusions:

1. The death of Mr. Beauchene occurred on the afternoon of July 4, 1837, when the said Mr. Beauchene stumbled, fell, and struck his head on the sharp edge of a marble-topped table. The coroner states that the blow resulted in an open depressed fracture of the skull at the right temporal bone. Bone fragments driven into the brain by the force of the blow caused immediate death.

2. Seven persons witnessed the fall: to wit: Mr. Pierre Beauchene, father of the deceased; Mr. Antoine Beauchene, brother of the deceased; Mrs. Henrietta Beauchene, wife of the deceased; Miss Elise Antoinette Beauchene, daughter of the deceased; Miss Abigail Ainesworth, an English woman employed as an *au pair*; and two persons of unfree status, Ben Benjamin and Bessie Jernigan. All witnesses answered questions at the time of the incident, except for the minor child and the wife who was prostrate in her grief.

3. The board has heard additional testimony from Mr. Pierre Beauchene and the two unfree blacks at this inquest, all others being unavailable or exempt from testifying.

4. Although there was a verbal argument going on among family members at the time of the incident, no person was in physical contact with the victim when he lost his balance and fell into the table.

5. It is, therefore, our unequivocal finding that the death of the said Julien Beauchene was entirely accidental, and no blame or responsibility does now or shall in the future rest on any other person.

6. Therefore the reading of the Last Will and Testament of the deceased may proceed without prejudice, and its terms and provisions applied without further delay."

Those words, exonerating Antoine from all responsibility, shall be forever seared into my memory

2. *Beyond All Price,* 2nd edition, contains a description of the Battle of Port Royal Sound, 147 and 150:

DuPont led his fleet of fifteen ships into the harbor on the morning of November 7. Sailing west and staying on the starboard side of the channel, each ship fired upon Fort Beauregard as it passed Bay Point. Then the ships executed a wide turn to port that brought them to an eastern heading in front of Fort Walker. Again, each ship fired as she passed and continued toward the mouth of the harbor and another sweeping turn to port that brought her back onto the course, ready for a second pass at each fort. The gunners in Fort Walker had little hope of hitting the moving targets of the Union ships even if they had mounted their cannons on carriages that allowed rapid swings. The Union guns, however, could remain almost stationary. When one gunship sailed out of the range of the fort, the next ship took over.

"The battle is over," Mary shouted as she rushed into the sick bay.

"Shhhh." Nellie hushed her and then looked apologetic. "They've stopped shooting at each other?"

"Yes, about half an hour ago. The rebel fort quit returning fire, and Captain DuPont signaled his ships to do the same. Then he led one last foray past Fort Walker and sent out a landing vessel. We watched as the men disembarked and waded ashore. We were all holding our breath, waiting to see if someone would shoot at them. But there was no response at all. Our boys walked right into the fort through some big holes they had blasted in the wall, and then, after a few minutes, we saw the Confederate flag come down and the U.S. flag go up. We've won."

3. The slave woman Rina describes (in the Gullah language) how the slaves reacted to "The Big Shoot" in *The Road to Frogmore*, 2–3:

Massa Pope, he want fuh take Zannah an Ol Bess an me wit dem, cause we be house slave, an he need sumbody fuh take care uh de clothe an de cookin an de chillun, but we aint gwine go. He keep runnin intuh de slave house lookin fuh we, but when he come in de front door, we jumps out de back door or de window.

Poor Ol Bess, she hab dis big ol sore on she leg dat not healin, so she caint run fast nuf. An she hab de baby Leah, what jis be larnin fuh walk. So she take Leah an go out in de cornfield an lay down between de row fuh hide. Poor baby hab a cough, so Bess keep her han ober she mout fuh keep she quiet. Near strangle dat poor chile.

De young missus catch Zannah in de kitchen tryin fuh hide sum food so de Massa not take it all. De young missus be cryin an say, "Oh, Zannah, de Yankee gwine kill you! Ifn you see a Yankee, it drive you crazy."

"Why, Missus, aint dey natural folk?"

"Oh, no, Zannah, they don look like we!"

So when soljers come, Zannah run to she man Marcus an say, "Oh, de soljers, dey come fuh kill we."

Marcus say, "Don be silly. Dey be jis mens." Zannah soon find out de soljers be such purty men, an so respectful.

Most uh we slaves, we jis listens to what de buckra says an den do nuttin, cause we gots bedder sense. Massa tell we fuh burn de cotton in de field when dey gone, but we say, "Why fuh we burn de cotton? Where we get money den fuh buy clothe an shoe an salt?"

Massa say ifn we don go wit he, de Yankees gwine kill we or send we to Cuba. We says, "Dat not true, cause we jis poor black folk who duz no harm an we only be guide by white folk."

So by de nex day, de buckra all gone. An we look round an say,

"What now?"

Uncle Amos, Massa Pope driver, he call we all togedduh, an he say, "We be gwine keep doin zackly what we always duz. De Massa gwine come back, sho nuf, an ifn he don see work bin done, he gwine lick all uh we. Sides, we gotta chance fuh work de crops an git lots uh egg, an take what we needs fuh we."

So life go on, same as usual. Cept we hab mo time fuh visit wit udder black folk an hear what be gwine on udder places. We hear bout de mess sum black folk make in Bufor, when dey broke intuh house an stole de carpet an de curtain an de silverware. But dat dint happen here, less we was really needin sumptin.

We jis lives our lives an eats what we wants. An we be purty happy fuh a while, til food start runnin low. Den we worry, cause it be diffrunt. Nobody left who kin take care uh we.

Eberting change after de Big Shoot.

29. THE GREAT CHARLESTON FIRE OF 1861

1. Henrietta had always been aware of Charleston's vulnerability to fire; *Henrietta's Journal*, 104–05:

Charleston is uniquely vulnerable to such disasters. Because the city sits on a small peninsula, real estate is at a premium. Buildings are located close together, especially in areas where poorer shopkeepers and businesses cater to transients. Taverns, boarding houses, and brothels open for business among repair shops and warehouses. They share walls or lean against one another to keep themselves upright. Any one of them could trigger a fire that would engulf the whole neighborhood. Moreover, most of those same areas are on the eastern side of the peninsula, where the prevailing winds from the east can carry flying sparks and debris across the rest of the city.

Building materials are limited. Stone is generally unavailable, except for the cobblestones salvaged from ships' ballast and used to pave the streets. Masonry is expensive and requires skilled slave labor, both for the production of bricks and for completion of the construction. A few builders experiment with tabby—a concrete mixture of sand, lime, and crushed oyster shells, of which the city has a surplus except during the summer months. But the process is also expensive and time-consuming. Wealthy families and profitable businesses can afford to build fire-resistant structures. Ordinary people settle for highly flammable local wood.

Charleston, surprisingly, has always suffered from a lack of water. Yes, it sits on a peninsula surrounded by two rivers and a harbor bordering the Atlantic Ocean, but getting the water from where it flows to where a fire is burning is difficult. There are as yet no wells or holding ponds or lakes to store useful water. Most households rely on cisterns that collect rainwater for the family's use. The city's fire equipment consists of horse-driven wagons fitted with hand pumps. Volunteer fire crews must drive the wagons to the river, pump the water into a holding tank, and then drive to the site of a fire, where they must drain the water out of the tank and carry it to the fire. The only alternative for stopping a fire involves blowing up a line of buildings to cut off the flames from their fuel source. And that's a solution often more destructive than the blaze itself.

32. A THIRD CHALLENGE

1. *Henrietta's Journal*, 206:
   "To my wife, Henrietta Ainesworth Beauchene, I bequeath all my real properties and my stock holdings in the Beauchene Company with one restriction. While the said inheritor may have full use of all such properties and may collect and use all incomes from said shares to whatever purposes she so chooses, she may not sell said properties and shares or any portion thereof. At the death of the inheritor, the said properties and shares shall descend to the surviving children of Julien and Henrietta Beauchene and their heirs and assigns forever, share and share alike."

2. Elizabeth Dubois' move from Charleston to Flat Rock appears in more detail in *Damned Yankee*, 135. Elizabeth had notified her family of her plans to leave Charleston shortly before Thanksgiving.:
   "But I do have some plans you are not aware of. I have two lovely first cousins who have joined together in their widowhood to form a household in Flat Rock, North Carolina. They've invited me to join them, and I'm seriously considering doing so."
   "Flat Rock? I don't even know where that is."
   "It's a resort area in the hills of western North Carolina. The climate is moderate because of the altitude, and it is rather off the beaten track. Lots of Charleston families spend their holidays in the hills during our hot summers. The Middletons, I understand, spend a great deal of time there."
   "But you have your wonderful house here . . . and all your family . . . and . . ."
   "And a very lonely life. Oh, having Charlotte staying with me last fall helped some, but I miss your father, and I miss spending time with people my own age who share my interests."
   "If you're lonely, you could always move in here." Susan felt Jonathan kick at her under the table, but she ignored him.

"You're not hearing what I'm trying to say, Susan. I love your family, of course, but with all seven of my grandchildren in and out, and two more babies on the way, your house would wear me out! I love you, but I don't want to live with you. I want to spend my last years being me, doing as I like. What I want to do is sell that old house with all its furnishings in it, pack a few clothes, and go off on a new, grand adventure. And that's exactly what I intend to do."

34. FAMILY HISTORY

1. *Henrietta's Journal*, 89:

From the moment Julien met my family outside St. Michael's by the Gate, I felt myself losing control of our blossoming friendship—and of my life as well. He greeted my mother in the most polite fashion imaginable, and she returned his overtures with a raised eyebrow and sharp eyes that whipped back and forth between his face and mine. We both blushed a little under her penetrating stare. Then she turned to my father, and there transpired one of their long discussions carried out without speaking a word. She questioned, he answered with a nod, she cocked her head with other concerns, and he responded by smiling gently in my direction. Eventually, she nodded, and then took Mr. Beauchene's arm, saying, "Come, sir, and tell me about your parents."

To his credit, he handled her inquiries with grace. He spoke of his mother's untimely death with exactly the right mixture of sorrow and pathos. He praised his father's business acumen and described his younger brother's antics with loving amusement. He even told her of the hairy creature of a dog that had adopted the family and made the ledge in front of the parlor hearth his kingdom.

She loved it and him. How could I tell? At dinner she plied him with food, passing him all the most tender bits. When he responded with compliments, she positively beamed. And when he announced that he must leave to board the coach taking him back to London that afternoon, she was the one telling him that he must return soon. I could feel myself fading into the woodwork. In her mind, we were already a couple, and I was not the most impressive half of that relationship.

2. *Henrietta's Journal*, 11:

Julien listened to all of that and then shook his head in dismissal. "Ridiculous," he said. "It makes me proud to know that in America we did away with all titles along with our allegiance to the British monarchy. Our constitution holds that 'All men are created equal,' and for that belief, I am eternally grateful."

He sounded so pompous that for a moment I felt a flash of anger. "All men are created equal? What about women? And how do you justify the enslavement of those African natives who cultivate your cotton fields and do your other hard labor? You should remember that Parliament abolished slavery in England and all over the British Empire almost ten years ago. If Americans had not fomented their revolution. . ." But I hesitated, not being at all sure what the result would have been.

It was our first quarrel, and we both caught our breath, unwilling to venture deeper into a discussion of our cultural differences. "Let's not fight over something that neither of us is in a position to change," Julien suggested. And he turned his attention to the racers on the river. "Do all young Englishmen have to learn to row a boat?"

3. *Henrietta's Journal*, 45:

I'm terrified! Father Beauchene just announced at our usual Sunday dinner that he had invited all of the company clients to a Christmas reception here at the house on Sunday evening, December 23rd. I must have had a stricken look on my face because he reached across the table, patted my hand, and said, "I've told everyone I want them to meet my new daughter-in-law. I'm sure you'll make a delightful hostess. You'll just need to lay out an ample supper buffet so that people can help themselves, and then you'll be free to circulate and introduce yourself."

Easy enough for him to say. Impossible for me to imagine. I don't even know what would be an appropriate menu, and I'm terrible at introducing myself to strangers. And since I know that they will all be clients, that will put even more pressure on me. I can't! I can't! I can't! And all Julien has to say in response to my protests is that I must. I must. I must.

4. *Henrietta's Journal*, 68–69:

"Look, Henrietta. Despite all the things men think you can't do, you have enormous power on your side right now, because you can do the one thing that they can't ever do—create human life. And that scares them. Southern men are always terrified of a pregnant woman because she is about to learn how powerful she is. Once the child is born, however, a Charleston man takes full credit for producing his son or daughter, and he can conveniently forget about his wife's role in the process—until the next time."

"Is that why some women bear so many children—to regain that feeling of wielding power?"

"Perhaps so. In any event, you'll be happier if you try to see your family's behavior as a typical Southern response instead of a judgment on your worth."

5. *Henrietta's Journal*, 73–74:

"What is it, Julien? What's happening?"

"It's called the Leonid meteor shower. It happens every few years, but during most years we can't see it at all. I saw a note in today's paper that there would be good viewing tonight, but even I did not expect such a show as this."

"Are they truly falling stars?"

"If you want me to be boringly accurate about it, it's a field of debris from the tail of a comet. But yes, I think it is safe to call them falling stars."

"And if I wish upon them. . ."

"All your dreams will come true."

"All right. I hope with all my heart for a happy, healthy baby. And if you are listening, Stars, please make it soon."

And then, as if upon my wish, the first contraction hit me.

6. *Henrietta's Journal, 65:*

"She will be a welcome and valued commodity—the future wife of another aristocratic young man, helping to cement the ties between the great founding families."

"Commodity, indeed! Poor thing! Born only to be a bargaining chip!"

"No, she will be loved, I promise you, even if you call her Victoria —although I suspect Father would insist that you name her for his dear departed wife, Elise—who was, by the way, very much a late-comer to Charleston."

"Really?" I couldn't help but smile at the idea. I didn't know that I was not the first newcomer to the family.

"Yes, Mother was born in France, a penniless orphan—the only survivor of a tragic and fast-spreading epidemic—shipped off to the one living relative the French courts could identify. That cousin was a small planter from Martinique, who used the Beauchene Company as the factor for his cotton crop. The gentleman brought his foster child to the office with him one day. Our young Pierre took one look at her, fell hopelessly in love, and married her despite the disapproval of his family. He's forgotten those uncomfortable years now, but one day he'll remember. Give him time."

7. *Henrietta's Journal, 85:*

"Thank you, sir, but I'm still puzzled by your insistence that Henri-etta is here and by your comment about Elise earlier."

Father responded by addressing me directly. "That's because I also have an assignment for you, Henrietta. Now that you can be free to leave your child in the care of others, I am appointing you as my secre-tary to help me oversee the day-to-day operation of the firm. You will handle the personnel matters, greeting our clients, remembering their significant anniversaries, answering their inquiries, and offering our sympathies in cases of misfortune. And you will be paid out of my private investments."

8. *Henrietta's Journal*, 92-93:

"No, wait." I evidently hadn't learned my lesson about contradicting my betters. "A cat?" I turned to Julien. "You didn't tell me there were cats here. I'd have come much sooner if I had known."

"Well, of course, we have cats, Henrietta. Every waterfront has rats that arrive on the ships. So every warehouse keeps cats to fend them off."

The big orange tomcat, who had defied all who tried to catch him, now took up a position of domination on top of that newspaper-strewn table. He stared me in the eye, and I looked steadily back, blinking slowly. After a few seconds, he sneezed, daintily shaking his whiskers, and I felt sure he was mimicking me.

"What's his name?"

Joshua chortled. "Damn Cat, usually."

"Cats don't have names. They're not pets, Henrietta. They're mangy and wild. They come and go. We don't even feed them. They catch their dinners."

"Ewwww," I said, thinking of dead rat. "But this one's beautiful, not mangy. Look at that pattern of dark swirls on the animal's flanks. In England people who know cats would classify him as a classic British Shorthair Tabby. He must have deserted from an English ship, and I'm sure he once had a name."

"If so, he hasn't told us!"

"Well, then, I shall call him Marmalade. Does that suit you, my handsome fellow?"

Marmalade stood slowly, stretched front and back, and then walked deliberately to where I stood. With a loud purr, the cat rested his massive head on my arm. The men watching this little demonstration were speechless. Even my father-in-law had nothing to say.

Gently I scratched the cat behind his ears and then patted him in dismissal. "If I'm going to be working here, he must be allowed full access to my office. Having a cat seals our deal."

35. AN INTIMATE GLANCE

1. *Henrietta's Journal*, 105–106:

"Wait, Julien. I'm coming along with you." I covered a sleeping Elise with my shawl, and the three of us made our way to the corner of Chalmers and Church Streets, where we got our first glimpse of St. Philip's. It was one of those sights I didn't want to see; yet I couldn't tear my eyes away.

Tongues of fire were already licking at the dome in the middle of the white steeple that had served as a landmark since 1723. As we watched, the flames wrapped around the steeple and engulfed it, spreading at last to the base of the tower where it met the roof. And slowly, as if hesitant to move, the steeple sank from view, dropping through the ceiling into the center of the sanctuary. Another pause suggested the worst was over, but it wasn't. A sudden burst of flame shot back through the hole in the roof, and the entire building succumbed. We were cold and hot at the same time. We stood for almost an hour, chilled by the wind but feeling the heat from the burning building. At last the fire seemed to exhaust itself as it ran out of fuel.

The sun was coming up as we finally turned away. Our steps dragged as we headed back down Chalmers Street. As if it intended to follow us, a new sound penetrated our benumbed minds. The crash echoed up and down the street. The front portico of St. Philip's, still standing when we started home, now wavered, shook, and fell into Church Street. Julien stopped again and turned his face toward the ruined building. His words, when they came, carried a hint of ironic laughter. "They thought St. Philip's hindered the free flow of traffic on Church Street. Wait till they see what it has done now!

2. *Henrietta's Journal*, 110–111:

"I know the city council has been working hard to repair the damage and make repairs to the Market Street area, but that's a matter of locking the proverbial barn door after the horse has escaped." I shook my head. "Why aren't they spending their time figuring out how to prevent these fires in the first place? Or thinking about improving their fire-fighting capabilities?"

"You're thinking logically, my dear. You forget that this is Charleston." Elizabeth smiled indulgently.

"What does that have to do with it?"

Although they might never admit it, she explained, the city council and the members of the city's old aristocracy were not devastated by any of these losses, with the exception, of course, of what had happened to St. Philip's. The dwellings that burned were mostly inexpensive wooden structures that failed to add anything of value to the city's appearance. The small businesses and shops catered to the lower classes—transients, poor whites, and freed slaves. If the owners of such establishments went out of business, they would leave the city, carrying with them the dregs of society. And their disappearance would allow for the construction of much finer establishments, like the new Charleston Hotel on Meeting Street.

"So the aristocracy see the fires as ultimately beneficial because they help clean up and transform the city into a place for rich people?" The very thought made me angry.

"Charleston has always aspired to be a golden city, Henrietta. Wealthy planters who fancied themselves the natural inheritors of the world's great cultures built the first public buildings on classical models. Our citizens still emulate the ancient Greeks and Romans. They send their children to schools to learn Greek and Latin; they read the classic works written by philosophers and historians; they copy Greek architecture and the Roman government. And they are well aware that they have the time and leisure to do so because they have slaves to do all the manual labor for them. Shake up any element in that model, and you threaten the traditions and beliefs of a lifetime. That's the Charleston you will have to learn to accept if you are ever to feel comfortable here."

3. *Henrietta's Journal*, 114–15:

It had been a pleasant day, but after the Dubois family had departed, I found that the wine had made me a little woozy. I wandered out onto the piazza for a breath of air and a few moments alone. Then a voice from the corner interrupted my thoughts.

"So we meet again, Little Mama."

"Antoine! What are you doing out here in the dark?"

"Waiting for a beautiful lady."

"You're drunk!"

"No law against that. Just been celebrating your good news. Blooming again, aren't you? I should have noticed a pair of hints."

I was beginning to be nervous. Antoine's voice had taken on a sinister tone, and, if I was not mistaken, he had just made a deliberately suggestive remark. "It's colder out here than I realized. I'm going back in."

This time he stepped directly in front of me, swaying a little but still looming over me. "What's your hurry, darling?"

"I told you. I'm cold."

"No, no, no. You're anything but cold. You're having a baby, aren't you? You don't get one of those by being cold."

"Stop it, Antoine. You're boorish."

"No, I think you like it. You like being with me out here in the dark, hearing what I think about you. You do want to know that, don't you?"

"No. Now get out of my way."

I tried to move around him, but he reached out and grabbed my wrist. "Not so fast, little lady. I want to find out what my stuffy old brother sees in you. I can't imagine him being much of a lover, so you must be a hell of a lot sexier than you pretend to be."

I twisted away from him, putting downward pressure on his thumb joint to force him to loosen his grip. As my hand came free, I sprinted for the French doors and slammed them behind me. Then I bent over, nursing my wrist. I could see that it was already red and promised a nasty bruise by morning.

"Henrietta? Are you all right?" At the sound of Julien's voice, I hid my arm at my side and forced a smile. "The wind's come up. It seemed to pull that door right out of my hand."

4. *Henrietta's Journal*, 137:

I am gigantic and uncomfortable! Since at this stage of my pregnancy I am willing to believe every old wives' tale I have ever heard, I decided to walk over to Legare Street to visit with Elizabeth. Vigorous exercise is reported to bring on early labor, and I am more than ready to meet this new child in person. It was a lovely spring morning, with the temperature just on the warm side, but by the time I reached my destination, I was sweating.

"Whatever were you thinking?" Elizabeth scolded me as she led me into the coolness of their front parlor. "Nine blocks is too far for you to be walking by yourself at this late date. What if you had gone into labor halfway here?"

"I'd have dropped the child right there in the middle of Broad Street if I had to. I'm that tired of being pregnant!"

5. *Henrietta's Journal*, 142–43:

Personally, I am fascinated by this whole pirate culture. I have found a couple of gentlemen who are familiar with the Bahamian pirates, and they have promised to take me out to meet some of them in person. I know they won't be the colorful, peg-legged, swaggering heroes of the Blackbeard legends. They won't have bandanas tied around their heads, or eye-patches, or viciously long swords, but I am hoping for a parrot or two, and maybe a cask of rum.

I am thinking a decade or more into the future when I say I hope the pirates will keep hanging around here. If, as some pundits predict, the South eventually has to go to war with the U.S. Government to protect our political independence and our right to hold slaves, a cadre of pirates would be very useful in keeping us supplied with needed goods. And in that eventuality, it might also be wise for us to have an official business presence here in Nassau. I intend to look into these matters further.

6. *Henrietta's Journal*, 171:

I shook myself into action at last. I passed Juliette off to Abby and walked out to the laundry to consult with Persephone. "What do I need to do?" I asked. She reacted kindly but with firmness. "You white folk need to let the black mourners have their time. We have our customs. There will be a funeral procession tonight with torches to light our way to the black burial ground on Calhoun Street. Our mourners will follow the coffin to the grave site and help to cover the grave. We will leave some tokens for little Marcus to take with him on his next journey. We will mark the grave with a conch shell, so he can sail back over the water to where we started. None of that needs to bother you white folk. You just give us the time to take care of him, and we'll do it our way."

Mrs. Jernigan had come into the laundry house while Persephone was setting out the rules. She gently led me back to the house, fixed me a cup of her ever-present sassafras tea, and offered what comfort she could. "I know you wish you could do something to make this better, but you can't do anything but keep your family inside tonight. Let our people do what they must. And pray for strength for all of us. We may need it in the months to come. Deaths like this come in threes."

36. A WRONGFUL DEATH

1. *Henrietta's Journal*, 192–93:

"I don't believe you for a moment. Are you pregnant?" I didn't see that there was anything to be gained by mincing words.

"No! I mean . . . I don't think so. I can't be. He said I wouldn't get in trouble because it was my first time. And I felt fine until last week when I started getting sick every morning. And then it goes away—"

"Antoine?"

"Yes, but—"

"Abby, I want you to start from the beginning and tell me exactly what happened."

Her story was an all too familiar one. It started the night of Aunt Maggie's funeral. She hadn't been able to sleep, so she came downstairs and noticed that the piazza door was open. Then she heard someone sniffling outside and discovered Antoine in the dark.

"He was crying, Henrietta. He loved that old lady—lots more than the rest of you did. I didn't know what to say, so I put my hand on his back, like you just did for me, and tried to comfort him. He turned to put his arms around me, and we hugged for a while. And then—then it changed, somehow, and he was pushing me back onto the chaise and fumbling with my skirt, and . . ." She stopped and pressed her lips together in denial of what had followed.

I didn't force her to continue. There had already been enough forcing going on in her life. "Have you told him?"

"No, not yet, but maybe he'll be pleased. He's always talking about your girls and how he misses not having children of his own. So I hope . . ."

"I wouldn't count on him if I were you, but you have to tell him,

Abby, and right away. Should the two of you decide to get married, it will need to happen immediately, so the gossips can at least speculate about whether the baby is going to come early."

"I'm waiting for the right moment."

"No. Do it now. Today." She glared at me, but I took that as a good sign. At least now she was angry and not feeling sorry for herself. "Oh! And Abby, I will have to tell Julien. I can't keep this from him. If he learns by accident, he's going to react before he has a chance to think. Better that he has some time to prepare himself for the inevitable face-down with his brother."

She started to walk away from me and then turned back. Despair lined her face as she sank into a chair. "Whatever will I do if Antoine won't marry me? Help me, Henrietta. Tell me what to do."

2. *Henrietta's Journal*, 198–99:

"It was that rainy Fourth of July. Father had summoned us all to the parlor for a family conference. There was Father Beauchene, Julien, Antoine, of course, and Abigail, and me. Julien informed Father of Abigail's pregnancy, and they asked Antoine what he intended to do about it. Antoine shrugged his shoulders and said 'Me? Not my problem. I'm not going to do anything.' That's the last thing I remember."

"All right. As I understand it, your father-in-law and Antoine had a screaming argument about responsibility. Julien was concerned that his father was getting too angry and tried to step in. That's when Antoine turned on him. Julien said that everyone ought to be thinking about the unborn child, not themselves. Antoine suggested that if Julien was so worried about it, he could adopt the little bastard himself. Julien said something to the effect that the baby would be Antoine's, not his. And Antoine responded that people could say the same thing about your two daughters."

"What? That doesn't make sense."

"This is hard for you to hear, I know. Antoine was suggesting that you and he had been lovers. Everyone knows that is ridiculous, of course, but Julien flew into a rage and tried to choke his brother. They wrestled, and then . . ."

"Go on. Say it. I need to hear you say it."

"Antoine thrust his arms up to break Julien's grip. Then he grabbed him by the lapels and pushed him violently to one side. Julien fell, hitting the side of his head on the corner of that marble-topped table at the end of the settee. It killed him instantly."

"The puddle I kept seeing in my dreams. It was blood."

"Yes."

As the clouds of fog lifted, I saw the scene vividly, laid out in front of me like a tableau. There was Father Beauchene—once the proud father of two handsome sons, now one dead and the other standing guilty of murder. I knelt on the floor beside the body, once a happy wife, now a widow. Abigail, blossoming in the promise of motherhood, was now wretched with guilt. Antoine, still breathing hard from the fight, looked defiant in the face of having just destroyed his family. And in the doorway, a scared little girl, her eyes almost black in their fright, clutched a bedraggled rag doll in her arms to serve as her only shield against the horror that had unfolded in front of her.

"Death comes in threes."

3. *Henrietta's Journal*, 202:

"And then he's going to put me under oath and ask me what happened." Father looked stricken.

"Will they want me to talk to them, too?"

"No, as the widow, you are exempt from testifying. But you may attend if you wish."

"To hear the whole episode hashed over again? When I relive it in my dreams every night? No, thank you. But you? Will you be able to—?"

He gave a bitter laugh. "Will I ever be able to forget? Of course not, but it is something I must do."

"And what will you say—under oath?"

"An oath is a serious matter, and I have always taken pride in my veracity. The coroner will give me a Bible—the sacred Word of God—and ask me to swear to tell the truth. But while I have great loyalty to my country and state, and although my faith in God is strong, my love for both my sons dominates my heart. I shall tell him that my sons were both honorable men with deep measures of brotherly love for one another. They sometimes argued and jostled but never with malice or hatred for one another. I shall swear it was an accident—only a tragic, unforeseeable accident."

4. *Henrietta's Journal*, 236:

"Found her!" he announced. "Wasn't hard, neither, although I had to go back further than we thought in the midwife's records."

"How far back?" I asked, my dread mounting.

"Well, a Miss Abigail Ainesworth gave birth on the morning of Thursday, November 30, 1837. Here, see for yourself." He showed me a folded piece of paper onto which he had copied the information. The child was a girl, weight about six pounds, apparently full-term and healthy. She was named Rachel Marie Beauchene, and her father was listed: Antoine Beauchene of Charleston, South Carolina, America. "Not much room for doubt that this is our girl is there?"

5. *Henrietta's Journal*, 239–40:

"Ah! Probably too late for that, isn't it? As I said, she's a hard worker, and she's supporting herself and her child."

"Doing what? Where does she work?"

"So you don't . . . uh, Miss Ainesworth is a lady of the night."

"She's a prostitute?" I was horrified.

"A street-walker, a lady of pleasure . . . Call it what you will. She usually just works weekends when gentlemen are most likely to have money in their pockets."

"But where . . . I mean, how. . .?"

"You want the details? All right. She works out of a tavern a couple of blocks from here—The Cozy Den, it's called. Sam Yonkers—he's the owner—has all sorts of enterprises going there: rooster-fighting in the back yard, dice games in the basement, card games in the back room. Anything you can gamble on, he has it available. Of course, there's a barroom and empty rooms upstairs that he will rent by the day or by the hour, depending on your needs. He supports a stable of girls, too, just in case one of his customers is in the market. And if the rooms aren't full, he lets the girls use them for their business. Rumor has it he keeps his girls happy by supplying them with opium, but I don't know that for a fact. I do know, however, that he has a separate building in the back that houses an opium den, where real addicts can light up their pipes in comfort and drift far away on clouds of shared oblivion."

"Opium!" I thought I had heard horrors enough, but this was taking me to places I could not have imagined. "Surely Abigail is not involved in using drugs!"

"I would hope not, for the infant's sake. But I worry about it, never-theless."

"I must see her and persuade her to give up this life before it's too late."

"Oh, my dear, innocent lady. It's already too late for Abigail, don't you see? She's chosen her path, and you must now let her walk on down it to wherever it leads."

6. *Henrietta's Journal*, 246–47:

"Listen to me, Gladys. I know how to do this. When Julien and I got married, our honeymoon was a trip across the Atlantic from England to South Carolina. We traveled in first class accommodations and took our meals with the captain, but we were in a tiny group of passengers who could afford to do that. Most of the hundred or so other people aboard were steerage passengers, immigrants who were going to settle new homes wherever they could find vacant land. They were expected to bring their food with them, but they also brought seeds, equipment, and children—lots and lots of children. And to feed those children? Many of them had animals along. They brought chickens to provide eggs, lambs for meat, and cows and goats for milk. They had pigs, too, along with sheep, mules, and even the occasional horse."

"All traveling together?" Gladys still thought I was suffering from some mental failing.

"The animals went to the hold, where they had their stalls. The farmers provided fodder and feed for them along the way, too. It was an amazing sight to see them all being boarded on the day before we sailed. There was a separate gangplank that led directly into the hold, and you would have thought our captain was Noah himself, loading the animals, two by two, into the ark."

Gladys grinned in spite of her worries. "So you're going to buy a cow, and we're going to take it to Charleston with us? But on board the ship? How does that help?"

"I'll go down to the hold every morning before breakfast and milk our cow. Then Rachel—and our girls, too—can have fresh milk every day."

"You're going to milk the cow? Miss Henrietta, have you ever in your entire life milked a cow?"

"Well, no, but I can learn."

"While the ship is bouncing up and down? That would be something to watch. No, Miss Henrietta, better leave the milking to me. I've had lots of practice."

And just that easily, Gladys seemed to fall in with my plans.

7. *Henrietta's Journal*, 249:

Here's the plan I've devised. I could have been about six weeks along when Julien died, without yet realizing it. Then I suffered that two-month gap of mental breakdown, which left me weak, severely underweight, and distracted from the normal processes of life. Even when I started to gain weight with the pregnancy, I could claim it was just the usual process of regaining the weight I had lost. I didn't feel quickening until November, by which time I was boarding the ship for England. So I went ahead with my travel plans and hid my expanding waistline under those ugly widow's weeds. It isn't a flawless plan, but it sounds workable.

When little Rachel woke for a feeding in the middle of the night, both Gladys and I stayed in the kitchen, sitting awake long after the baby had dropped off to sleep again. I tried my explanation out on Gladys, and she hit back with that irritating moral simplicity and purity that dominated her thinking. "But they're all lies, Miss Henrietta. You can't tell lies."

"Of course I can. I have to."

"Do I have to believe you?"

"It would be helpful."

"But then I'd be lying, too."

"Sometimes lies are necessary."

"But they're never good."

I moved on, trying to ignore her inescapable logic. "Now, then, if I had been pregnant at the end of May, the baby would have been due around the end of February, but she could have been born two or three weeks early. So let's give her a birthdate—say, February 2nd."

"Didn't that Mr. Preis who found Abigail for you—didn't he find her from a record of her child's birth?"

"Yes."

"But there won't be a record of this February date. What if somebody tries to find it?"

"Ah, that's easy to explain. There was a heavy snowfall, and it was bitter cold in London that day, remember? The midwife couldn't come, and I couldn't get to a maternity hospital. So you and Mrs. Carruthers helped me with her birth at home. We never registered it because we were headed back to America for the baby's baptism."

"That's another lie."

"Yes, it is. So?"

Gladys threw up her hands in surrender.

39. MORE PIECES OF THE PUZZLE

1. *Henrietta's Journal*, 235:

In my more realistic moments, I knew I needed help, so I arranged an appointment for this morning with a private investigator.

Solomon Preis's office sat at the edge of the business district. The building was a bit shabby, the stairs creaked, the gas lights were dim, and the furniture showed scratches. Mr. Preis was somewhat shopworn, too. He was in his late forties or fifties. His greased hair hid a growing bald spot, and his vest bore testimony of several hastily eaten meals. His eyes, however, were kind, and he ushered me to a chair with perfect gentlemanly manners

42. DISCLOSURES

1. *Henrietta's Journal*, 187–88:

"The Beauchene family is unusual, you know."

"How so?" I was a little surprised at her reaction to them.

"They love one another. Surely you've noticed that."

"Yes, of course. I just never thought much about it."

"Compare them to our family, Henrietta. Not that I'm actively unhappy with my parentage, but I never saw this same degree of warmth and love in my household—nor in yours. My father hides it well, but he resents the fact that Uncle Ephraim has a title and he doesn't. My mother feels left out of English society, so she is usually busy defending her Irish ancestry even when no one mentions it. Your father hides out in the Bodleian to avoid other people, as he was teaching you to do until Julien rescued you. And Aunt Luella is so addicted to controlling everything and everyone around her that I often picture her as a border collie or old English sheepdog."

I laughed out loud at her imagery, mostly because she was right.

"You may laugh, but it's true. The Beauchenes know how to love, and that's a rare trait. The family even forgives those who don't quite live up to the mark."

43. HENRIETTA'S LEGACY

1. *Henrietta's Journal*, 4–5:

"Well, Toad in the Hole is a Yorkshire pudding with a whole meal stuffed inside it. The concoction we call Bubble and Squeak is our traditional way of using leftovers from the Sunday roast. One smashes them all together—potatoes, cabbage, carrots, onions, pot scrapings, bits of meat—and fries them into a patty. And Bangers and Mash is nothing more than link sausages and mashed potatoes."

"Interesting, but a bit heavy for lunch, no?"

"Not if you've been thatching a roof all morning," I teased, "but you might be happier with a Ploughman's Lunch."

"Which is . . . what?"

"A hunk of bread, a wedge of local cheese, an apple, and, if you're lucky, some pickle and a hard-boiled egg."

"Sounds perfect."

It was perfect, too, once we overcame the hurdle of the pickle. Apparently, Julien was expecting tiny cold cucumbers in a salty brine. He got our usual bowl of sticky brown vegetables chopped and cooked beyond recognition in a mixture of brown sugar, spices, and malt vinegar. "What's in this?" he asked, poking it doubtfully with the tip of his knife.

I shrugged. "Hard to tell. Usually onions, apples, rutabagas, plums, dates, raisins. Whatever's handy."

"And what does one do with it?"

"Spread it on the bread, pile it on the cheese—it goes with everything."

I also recommended a glass of cider rather than a pint of beer. It was just relaxing enough to let us feel like old acquaintances without sloshing into maudlin promises of undying friendship. We sipped, and nibbled, and talked for a couple of hours before I reluctantly urged him back to the library. As it was, Father gave me a quirked eyebrow when we arrived, but much to my surprise he didn't ask where we had been all that time.

www.ingramcontent.com/pod-product-compliance
Lightning Source LLC
Chambersburg PA
CBHW022240020726
47496CB00004B/998